SEVEN TO DIE

An absolutely gripping crime thriller with a massive twist

MICHELLE KIDD

DI Jack MacIntosh Mysteries Book 1

Originally published as *Seven Days*

Revised edition 2023
Joffe Books, London
www.joffebooks.com

First published in Great Britain in 2020
as *Seven Days*

This paperback edition was first published
in Great Britain in 2023

Cover art by Nick Castle

ISBN: 978-1-80405-585-4

CHAPTER ONE

Time: 7.35 a.m.
Date: Friday 20 July 2012
Location: Southeast corner of Hyde Park, London

Had the grass been any longer, he might not have seen it.

And had the diamante buckle not caught the early morning sun, glinting lazily through the light summer dew, he might have carried on walking and missed it altogether. DI Jack MacIntosh knelt down in the ankle-deep grass at the edge of the park and parted the fronds with a gloved hand.

"Over here." Careful not to disturb the scene, Jack straightened up and took a step backwards. The crime scene manager was already making a beeline for him, closely followed by two suited-and-booted scene-of-crime investigators. The shoe was gently lifted from its resting place on the bed of grass, and slipped into a waiting evidence bag.

"Wait." Jack motioned for the bag to be passed to him. Taking it in his still-gloved hand, he cast his eyes down on the newly found shoe. "Shit," he muttered, the beginnings of a frown appearing on his forehead. "Shit."

Jack returned the evidence bag and carefully retreated, allowing the scene to be secured and processed. He knew the drill — he'd been through it often enough. Making his way back across the grassy wasteland, he headed towards the small white tent which was already buzzing with white-suited bodies.

As was true of most murder scenes, the atmosphere was heavy and somewhat subdued. There was a calm, respectful silence as people quietly went about their work; whether it was out of respect for the dead or for the living, Jack was never quite sure.

"DI MacIntosh." A tall man with a wiry frame stepped out of the tent and nodded his balding head at Jack. He unzipped his white protective suit to reveal a well-tailored light grey suit beneath, complete with waistcoat and bow tie in an oddly contrasting burnt orange. "You know how to keep a man busy on his day off."

Jack offered a brief smile. "Can't have you taking it easy with a boiled egg and the *Daily Telegraph*, can we, Doc?"

Dr Philip Matthews, the Metropolitan Police's senior pathologist, returned the smile, his light blue eyes twinkling. "Indeed we cannot, Detective Inspector, indeed we cannot."

Jack self-consciously rubbed a hand over his chin's three-day stubble, trying not to notice the immaculately shaved features of the police pathologist. He gestured towards the white tent. "Anything?"

Ducking beneath both inner and outer cordon tapes, Dr Matthews headed away from the scene. Jack followed, watching the pathologist shed his protective suit as he reached his aged Volvo, parked illegally by the side of the road. At just after seven thirty on a Friday, the area was already building up with traffic; bad-tempered drivers leaning on their horns as they negotiated around the well-polished Volvo that was impeding their crawl to work.

"Just the preliminaries. You'll get my full report tomorrow, after I've had a chance to look at her properly. But for the moment — white female, approximately twenty to twenty-five years of age, slim build. Well nourished. Obvious ligature marks to the neck, but I'll need a closer look before committing myself to the cause of death." Dr Matthews paused by the side of the Volvo, catching Jack's gaze. "And yes, before you ask, just the one shoe on the victim."

"Like the other one." Jack felt the all-too-familiar clenching in the far reaches of his stomach.

"Indeed," concurred Dr Matthews. "Just like the other one."

With a curt nod, the pathologist slipped into the driver's seat, no doubt heading home to Mrs Matthews to explain, once again, how his leisurely day off was to be disrupted with another urgent post-mortem.

Jack sighed and made his way back towards the tent and the surrounding hive of activity. He could do with a strong coffee . . . and, right now, a cigarette.

"Boss?" A ginger-haired officer broke away from the crowd and headed in Jack's direction. "The crime scene manager says you found the shoe?" DS Chris Cooper raised his eyebrows expectantly at Jack.

"I found *a* shoe, Cooper, *a* shoe. But not *the* shoe." Jack motioned for DS Cooper to follow him back to their car, stripping off his white protective suit as he walked. "A black stiletto type shoe. A good four-inch heel. Velvet, I think, with a diamante-style buckle."

"But they say the victim was wearing flat shoes, boss — not heels." DS Cooper walked round to the passenger side. "And white ones, too."

"Indeed she was, Cooper. Indeed, she was."

"So, if it wasn't the victim's shoe that you found, whose was it?"

Jack let the question hang in the air, unanswered. Slipping into the driver's seat, he waited for Cooper to join him. Starting the engine and pulling out into the ever-building traffic, Jack wound down the window to let in some cool morning air. "That's the million-dollar question, Cooper. Before we try to answer it, let's go and get a coffee. I think we'll need it."

* * *

Time: 8.15 a.m.
Date: Friday 20 July 2012
Location: Isabel's Café, Horseferry Road, London

The Ascaso coffee machine gave out a forceful yet satisfying rush of hot steam, causing Isabel Faraday to take a hurried step back.

"Whoa!" she exclaimed, wafting her hands vigorously through the thick curtain of vapour that enveloped her. "That's more like it!" Reaching for her cloth, Isabel began wiping down the stainless steel casing to the coffee machine, deftly securing the steam wands back in place. She slotted the drip trays into the recesses until they gave a satisfying click, and wiped her forehead with the back of her hand. Taking a step back, the vapour having now dissolved into a light mist, she gave her handiwork the once-over. The machine was her pride and joy; the single most expensive investment she'd made, and she couldn't afford for it to be out of action for long.

Wiping the last of the damp vapour from around the workspace, Isabel tossed the cloth into the bucket by her side and tilted her head back towards the rear of the coffee shop.

"Dom, I think I've fixed it!"

Moments later a tall, somewhat gangly-looking figure popped his head through the archway that separated the coffee shop from the rest of the building at the rear.

"That's good news," he remarked, nudging the thin wire-framed glasses higher up onto the bridge of his nose. "Can't run a coffee shop without coffee."

"Indeed we can't, Dom," smiled Isabel, reaching down, picking up the bucket of soapy water and heading towards him. "How did you get on with the ordering?"

Dominic pulled a notepad from the rear pocket of his faded jeans and flicked the pages with a long, delicate finger. Pianist fingers, his mother had always called them. "Order complete. 7.52 a.m. Delivery scheduled 6–7 a.m. tomorrow, Saturday 21 July 2012. Order reference TXT52017."

"Perfect. I knew I could rely on you." Isabel put the bucket of soapy water down and slipped behind the front serving counter, resting on one of the tartan-covered stools. "Thanks for coming in this morning. I really do appreciate it."

Dominic lowered his eyes, his pale cheeks beginning to flush pink. "It was no trouble. Mum said you needed my help."

"All the same, I do appreciate it. I know it's not your day to work."

Dominic nodded but continued looking at his feet, shifting the weight from one foot to the other in a regular rhythm, counting to three on each foot.

"What have you got planned for the rest of the day?" Isabel pulled a plate of homemade chocolate brownies towards her. She'd missed breakfast, what with the malfunctioning coffee machine emergency, and her stomach was growling.

"Planned?" Dominic raised his head and frowned for a second. He slowly rubbed a well-manicured finger over the beginnings of a neat goatee that hugged his chin. "Well, it's Friday. I walk the dog at 12.30 p.m., help Mum with the cooking at 4 p.m. — we have fish on a Friday — and then load the dishwasher at 7 p.m."

"Wow, that sounds like a busy day." Isabel smiled and pulled the cling film from the plate of brownies. "You'd better pop off home then."

Dominic nodded and, opening his notebook again, he retrieved the pen from his back pocket. Leaning on the counter, he methodically began to write in his neat, carefully constructed handwriting. Isabel strained her eyes to decipher the printed lettering. "Friday 20 July 2012 — Isabel's coffee shop. Time of departure 8.21 a.m."

Placing the lid back on his pen, Dominic slipped both pen and notepad into his back pocket. Without a further word, he collected his jacket from the coat stand by the front window and left, the bell jangling as he closed the door behind him.

Isabel took a large bite from one of the chocolate brownies, and chuckled. Insanely clever, with an almost photographic memory, Dominic Greene was a sweetheart — the twenty-one-year-old son of a friend of a friend, brought in for a milkshake by his older sister not long after Isabel had opened her coffee shop. The rapport she'd felt with him was instant. His mother, Sacha, popped in not long afterwards, filling Isabel in on the background to her son's engaging behaviour and idiosyncrasies. *"Somewhere on the spectrum"* had been her explanation, giving Isabel a smile and a shrug, folding her hands around her cinnamon-flavoured latte. That had been as far as they'd managed to get towards a "diagnosis". Sacha later explained that Dominic's almost obsessional desire for routine, the repetitive rituals — such as the hopping from foot to foot and note-taking — was his way of coping with the world. Merely placed "on the spectrum" by his GP, essentially that had been that. Whereabouts on the spectrum was either a very closely guarded secret or no one quite knew.

But Dominic didn't let that stop him. With a naturally helpful nature and a surprisingly sarcastic sense of humour, he soon slipped into the role of part-time coffee shop assistant. A few hours here and there to begin with, more to keep him occupied than anything else, had led to a more permanent three-days-a-week job offer — plus more when Isabel was busy.

Like this morning.

And now Isabel couldn't do without him. Although not entirely comfortable serving behind the front counter, Dom was a whizz behind the scenes. He ordered all the stock for the kitchen, made sure the cleaning rotas were planned to within an inch of their lives, and kept the art studio well stocked and organised.

In short, Dominic Greene was her saviour — and Isabel thanked the Lord that his sister had chosen her coffee shop for that milkshake.

And it wasn't just Dominic to whom Isabel was grateful. Sacha — the best baker this side of the river — started supplying homemade cakes and biscuits and Isabel's café soon started to get a well-deserved reputation for quality.

And that wasn't all that made Isabel's café stand out from the rest — for Isabel's Café wasn't your regular run-of-the-mill coffee shop. Yes, it sold coffee, and pretty good coffee by all accounts, but it offered a whole lot more than that. The café itself housed several comfortable leather sofas, a collection of well-loved armchairs, plus a scattering of bean-bags and bar stools. In addition, there was a large bookcase covering the far wall, rammed full of books and magazines. Customers were encouraged to relax, put their feet up, and immerse themselves in a novel while sipping their cappuccinos. Books could be borrowed and returned at a later date if wished, and donations of other unwanted books were gratefully received, adding to the already groaning bookshelves.

What made Isabel's unique, however, lay through a low archway adjacent to the serving counter, where the café turned into a small art studio. A surprisingly large room tucked away to the side of the kitchen housed a large drawing table and several free-standing easels which could be rented by the hour. The art studio was flooded with natural light from two large floor-to-ceiling windows, and a concertina-style patio door that, when fully open, led out to a small courtyard at the rear. Customers were encouraged to view the artworks that adorned the walls, some of which were available to purchase.

Isabel wrapped the plate of brownies back up and pushed herself off the stool, wiping the chocolate from her lips. Although she usually opened the café seven days a week, the malfunctioning coffee machine had forced her to keep the "CLOSED" sign hanging in the window while she dealt with the emergency. Picking up the bucket of soapy water, she disappeared behind the counter into the small kitchen space, tipping the water into the sink while contemplating opening the café for the final push of the working week.

As she did so, she heard the bell jangling from the front door.

"Just a minute." Isabel sloshed the rest of the water down the plughole and stowed the bucket beneath the sink. "Sorry, we're closed at the moment. Had a bit of an emergency."

Wiping her hands on a tea towel, Isabel emerged from the kitchen to find out which of her customers couldn't quite read the closed sign.

* * *

Time: 8.30 a.m.
Date: Friday 20 July 2012
Location: Horseferry Road, London

Traffic on Horseferry Road could be heavy at the best of times, especially so at this time on a Friday, but Jack groaned when he saw the tailback ahead. Cars were moving, albeit slowly, but it would be a frustrating journey. He contemplated turning around, but the lure of a good coffee kept him going. He ran a hand through his hair as they passed a well-known hair salon, unable to remember the last time he'd had a haircut.

"What do you think about the discovery this morning, boss?" DS Chris Cooper gazed out of the side window, charting their tortoise-like progress. "Another body — it must be linked, right?"

Jack returned his hands to the wheel and nodded. It was at times like these — sitting in more-or-less stationary traffic — when he felt the all-too-familiar cravings begin to resurface. It would be easy enough to wind the window down and reach for a cigarette. Instead, he strummed his fingers on the steering wheel and felt for the packet of nicotine gum he kept in the side door. Shoving a stick into his mouth, he winced as he chewed. He wasn't a fan of gum — nicotine or otherwise — so the whole process added another layer of torture to his thirty-nine days of abstinence.

"Has to be, Cooper," Jack eventually replied, pulling the sun visor down to shield his eyes from the glare of the morning sun streaming in through the windscreen. "Too many similarities for it to be unconnected."

Jack glanced across at his detective sergeant, a smile teasing his lips. Cooper was dressed smartly enough in a pale grey suit, but his tie looked as though it'd either been knotted in a great hurry, or in the dark — possibly both. The red-haired detective caught Jack's gaze and started to adjust it.

Jack's grin widened. "Take it off, Cooper. Today's going to be a scorcher. The last thing you need is a tie."

Just as DS Cooper began to pull the offending article from around his neck, the traffic in front started to move. At last, thought Jack, managing to slip the ageing Mondeo into second gear as they passed the White Horse and Bower pub. But no sooner had they made a few metres' progress than there was an almighty bang from somewhere up ahead and the traffic ground to another halt.

A succession of horns honked from behind, but Jack ignored them. As they inched forwards, Jack saw a motorcycle rider dressed in black leathers crawling towards the kerbside, the remains of his motorbike lying in the gutter.

More horns honked, but Jack dismissed them with a wave of his hand as he exited the Mondeo, flashing his warrant card in the vague direction of the noise.

DS Cooper hesitated before following suit, joining Jack at the side of the road.

"That was quick." Isabel Faraday was already kneeling at the motorcycle rider's side, a concerned hand on the man's shoulder. She looked up at Jack as he arrived. "I haven't had the chance to ring it in yet." She held her mobile phone loosely in her other hand.

Jack shook his head. "We were just passing. What happened?"

Isabel shrugged. "I've no idea. I was inside the café and heard this godawful noise from out here. Then I saw the bike and this poor guy sprawled over the tarmac."

Jack looked behind, noting the smashed bollard in the middle of the road which looked to have taken the full impact of the bike. "He hurt?" Jack nodded towards the dazed motorbike rider.

The leather-clad rider shook his head, starting to pull off his helmet.

"I'm not sure you should . . ." Isabel tried to stop the man from removing his helmet, but her attempts were waved away.

"I'm all right — no need for a fuss."

As Jack stepped closer towards the kerb, the bike rider angled his face towards him.

"Hello, Jack." The motorbike rider's voice was steady but guarded. "Fancy seeing you here."

CHAPTER TWO

Time: 8.35 a.m.
Date: Friday 20 July 2012
Location: A cellar in London

Using his shoulder against the ageing wood, he pushed open the heavy oak door. Peering into the inky blackness that infiltrated the musty cellar, he paused to let his eyes adjust to the dark. The thin, fluid-stained mattress in the furthest corner lay empty. The blanket, riddled with holes and frayed around the edges, so rough it would surely merely scratch and scathe the skin, lay crumpled on the ground. A solitary wooden chair in the opposite corner hosted a plastic tumbler of stale water and the remnants of last night's supper; thin crusts of bread, now curled and stiff.

Where was she? A momentary flicker of panic welled up inside him, his heart beginning to race at the thought that he may have lost her already. Although he knew there was no way out of this dank, dark place other than the stairs he'd descended, the feeling that she'd managed to escape filled his veins with ice-cold fear.

But then he saw her.

The outline of a huddled figure, almost hidden behind the heavy oak door, appeared through the blackness. He turned towards her, and even though the darkness sucked out any source of light and seemed to squeeze the very oxygen out of the air, he could clearly see her quivering form. Clutching her knees up to her chest, she hugged her arms tightly around herself.

"Now now," he murmured, a broad, reassuring smile crossing his tight lips. "Let's get you back over to the bed, shall we?" He stepped forwards, silently amused at how his mere presence caused her to shrink further back into the cobweb-filled corner. His hand grasped her firmly around the wrist. The coolness of her skin beneath his fingers sent familiar jolts of electricity through his body. "Sssshhhh now . . . I'm not going to hurt you."

Two wide, doleful eyes peered up out of the dimness, a look that he recognised. Wariness, trepidation and fear, tinged with just a tiny flicker of hope.

"That's better," he murmured, coaxing the quivering girl out from the shadows and across the rough concrete floor towards the makeshift bed. The sound of the weighty metal chain clunking against the floor filled the silence. He checked that the clasp on the metal cuff that attached the chain to her ankle was still secure. It was. The other end of the chain wound its way through the dust and dirt to a lone radiator fixed to the opposite wall; a radiator that'd long since ceased to emit any form of heat or comfort.

Satisfied his captive was secure, he bent down to stroke her hair, gently brushing the strawberry blonde wisps away from her beautiful yet tear-stained face. He felt her flinch beneath his touch, a faint whimpering escaping her lips. "There, there," he breathed, letting the once soft and silky strands caress his fingers. "You get yourself some rest."

His soothing tones seemed to do nothing to quell the girl's simmering fear — he watched her narrow shoulders shudder with each sob. He let a small chuckle tease his lips.

"I'll be back soon, my sweet," he murmured, picking up the plate of stale bread crusts from the wooden chair and replacing it with a bowl of cereal. He smiled at the tinny sound of pops and crackles filling the dank air. "Have your breakfast, Jess — there's a good girl. It's your favourite."

* * *

Time: 8.40 a.m.
Date: Friday 20 July 2012
Location: Isabel's Café, Horseferry Road, London

Isabel placed two cups of steaming coffee down onto the low table, her face etched with concern. Under one arm she carried a small first aid kit.

"I really do think we should call an ambulance."

"No ambulance, I'm fine."

"You could be concussed. Anything."

"I didn't hit my head — like I said, I'm fine."

Isabel glanced towards Jack and DS Cooper sitting on one of the sofas opposite. She gave a faint shrug. "At least let me dress that scrape on the back of your hand." She nodded at the painful-looking red wound spotted with blood and grit.

"Just do as you're told, Stu." Jack reached for his coffee mug. He'd dispensed with the chewing gum outside, needing a caffeine hit more than he needed nicotine right now. "For once in your life."

The frown forming on Isabel's brow was matched by that on Cooper's. Jack saw the looks they exchanged and took a sip of his coffee before replying. "Isabel. Cooper. This is my brother — Stuart."

"Your brother?" Cooper's hand hovered in front of his mouth, a chocolate chip cookie only millimetres from his lips. "I never knew you had a brother."

Jack eyed the leather-clad biker over the rim of his mug. "I haven't seen him in a while. He normally only pops up when he wants something."

Stuart MacIntosh's eyes widened. "That's not fair, Jack. It wasn't all down to me that we lost touch. And call me Mac — everyone else does."

Jack wasn't prepared to argue the point. "Just let Isabel patch you up, will you? Otherwise I'll drop you at A&E myself."

Jack saw his brother's jaw tighten before he eventually nodded. "OK. Do your worst."

A few moments of relative peace fell over the café. Isabel had kept the sign in the window and, for now, they were alone.

"It's good to see you, Jack." Isabel carefully dabbed an antiseptic wipe over Stuart Macintosh's raw wound, feeling the biker's body tense as she did so. It looked like there were a few pieces of grit from the road embedded in the cuts, but nothing more sinister. "You've not been in for a while."

Jack placed his coffee mug back down on the table. "You know how it is — work's a nightmare right now. We're on our way back to the station — thought I'd introduce Cooper to your coffee and cookies as we were passing. We can't stay long."

Jack had stumbled across Isabel's café earlier in the year, and although he wasn't an expert on coffee, he knew a good cup when he drank one — streets better than the muck from the station vending machine, anyway.

"These are amazing," mumbled Cooper, his mouth full of cookie crumbs. "How come I never knew about this place?" With one cookie already eaten, he reached for another. Seeing Jack's expression, he added, "I missed my breakfast this morning, didn't I? What with our early morning wake-up call."

"Fill your boots, Cooper," replied Jack, glancing at his watch. "We've a long day ahead of us." Turning his attention back to his brother, Jack saw Isabel applying a thin layer of antiseptic healing cream before covering the wound in a large adhesive plaster. "So, what happened out there?"

"Some dickhead just ran out right in front of me." Stuart MacIntosh winced as he flexed his wrist. "Nothing I could do. Luckily I wasn't going very fast, due to the traffic. Couldn't avoid that bloody bollard, though."

"So you're a courier these days?" Jack had noted the logo on the back of his brother's leather jacket.

"Yep — nine months now."

"And you're living locally?"

Another nod. "Well, up in Islington, if you call that local. Just a small place. Nothing grand. It's just me, so suits me fine."

Jack reached for the last of his coffee, regarding the brother he'd only seen sporadically for the best part of twenty years. Placed into foster care when they were small, after the death of their mother, they'd been separated not long afterwards, each following a distinctly different path.

"What about you?"

The question made Jack hesitate. Finishing his coffee, he wiped his mouth with the back of his hand. "I've a place not too far from the station. Like yourself — nothing grand. It's just me."

"Eternal bachelor," cut in Cooper, finishing the rest of his second cookie and washing it down with the dregs from his coffee mug. "We can't live without him, but it seems nobody is quite brave enough to live with him, either." He began to chuckle at his own joke, brushing stray cookie crumbs from the front of his shirt. "Isn't that right, boss?"

"So some would say, Cooper," conceded Jack, feeling a twitch at the corners of his mouth. "No one quite brave enough to take me on." He turned his attention back to his empty mug, wishing he still had some coffee left to hide behind.

"Well, that's a shame." Isabel snapped the lid back on the first aid box and got to her feet. "You need a good woman in your life, Jack. Someone to look after you. Everyone deserves some happiness."

Jack gave a conciliatory nod in Isabel's direction, eager to change the direction of the conversation. His eternal bachelorhood wasn't something he felt comfortable explaining over coffee, especially not in front of his brother. Although more than content with it himself, for some reason others

— usually women, it had to be said, and well-meaning women at that — seemed to beg to differ. He deserved happiness, apparently. And happiness, it would seem, could only be achieved with the company of another.

Jack didn't necessarily see the connection.

I'm more than capable of ironing my own clothes and doing my own housework. He glanced down at the more-than-slightly crumpled suit trousers that he'd pulled on that morning, together with the barely matching socks — then the images of the pile of dirty dishes in his kitchen sink flashed through his mind. Getting to his feet, Jack hastily pushed the thoughts away and turned his attention back to Cooper.

"Well, Cooper's tasting the single life once again, too — aren't you, Cooper?" He nodded at his partner, hoping that at least one of them would take the hint and leave Jack's personal life out of the discussion. "He's the one you really need to watch."

"Oh, really," enquired Isabel, turning her attention towards the ginger detective whose cheeks were now starting to take on the same colour as his hair.

Cooper nodded. "Well, the divorce is underway and I've moved out of my parents' house now — into my own place. It's only temporary — still need somewhere bigger so the kids can come to stay."

Isabel began clearing away the empty coffee cups, noticing two potential customers hovering outside, perusing the menu in the window. "That's nice. How many kids do you have?"

"Two. Thomas and Chloe. They're nine and seven now. Growing up fast."

Isabel went to turn the door sign to "Open" and slipped back behind the serving counter. "Are you going to be taking them to any of the Olympic events? Or are they too young?"

"Oh, don't get me started on the Olympics! They're obsessed." Cooper followed Jack's lead and pushed himself off the sofa. "I blame the schools. It's all they ever talk about now. Thomas is really into cycling, so hopefully we'll get to go and watch something at the velodrome. And Chloe loves her swimming — so I'm hoping to buy a few tickets for that, too."

The bell above the door jangled noisily, as the hovering customers stepped inside, clearly enticed by what they'd seen on the menus outside.

"We'll leave you to it," said Jack, nodding towards the couple making themselves at home on one of the sofas. "We need to get back to the station. What about you, Stu? You need a lift anywhere?"

Jack's brother shook his head. "I'll ring the company. They'll get someone to come and recover the bike and give me a lift back to my flat."

"Well, you take it easy for the rest of the day, Stuart." Isabel wagged her finger. "Doctor's orders."

"Call me Mac." He glanced over at Jack. "No one calls me Stuart anymore."

"Well, I think Mac suits you." Isabel gathered up some laminated menus ready for her new customers. "You don't look like a Stuart."

"Let's go, Cooper." Before heading towards the door, Jack pulled out a business card and scribbled his mobile and home address on the reverse. He passed it to his brother as they left. "Just in case, Stu."

Although it was still early, they could both feel the heat rising from the pavement once they stepped outside the café, the sun steadily rising into the cloudless sky — any early-morning clouds having been scorched into oblivion as the temperatures began to soar. The heatwave that'd begun some two months ago showed no signs of abating.

"Come on, Cooper." Jack began to stride quickly in the direction of his car, parked on a double yellow line outside the café. "We need to get back. We've a killer to catch. He's killed twice now. And unless I'm very much mistaken, this one won't be his last."

CHAPTER THREE

Time: 10.30 a.m.
Date: Friday 20 July 2012
Location: A cellar in London

With her throat feeling dry and scratchy from breathing in the musty cellar air, she thirstily gulped down the tepid, stale water. She eyed the bowl of now-soggy cereal, but not even the painful hunger pangs that clenched her stomach could force her to eat the mushy brown lumps that had settled in the bowl. No longer snapping, crackling or popping — the sight made her feel nauseous.

Returning to the threadbare mattress, dragging the metal chain attached to her ankle in her wake, she resumed her position, hugging her knees tightly to her chest. Her body trembled.

Was anybody looking for her?

Had anybody even realised she was missing?

Surely they had to.

Surely someone would've realised something was wrong when she didn't turn up to collect Hope from her day nursery.

Hope.

Fresh tears brimmed as she thought about her daughter's wide, innocent eyes — that toothy grin and tiny button nose.

Painful memories flooded her head — hearing Hope's happy gurgles as she smiled; the sweet smell of baby shampoo in her hair.

Not that it would've been the first time she hadn't shown up at nursery.

Maybe no one was looking for her after all. Maybe they all thought that she'd just done a runner.

Like the last time.

And the time before that.

She'd had her final warning from Social Services — they'd told her in no uncertain terms. *No more mistakes, Hannah. You have to put Hope first. Her welfare must be your one and only priority. This is your last chance.*

Your *very* last chance.

Even if she managed to get out of this godforsaken cellar, she was unlikely to see Hope again — she knew that. As the memory of her daughter's face filled her head, Hannah sank down beneath the stained blanket and sobbed.

* * *

Time: 10.30 a.m.
Date: Friday 20 July 2012
Location: Metropolitan Police HQ, London

Jack placed the plastic evidence bag containing the black stiletto shoe onto the table in the centre of the incident room. DS Cooper and DC Cassidy both stood facing the largest of the whiteboards that adorned the main wall.

"Patricia Gordon." Jack touched the whiteboard screen and a small photograph of an attractive brunette appeared in the top left-hand side. Another touch and this was followed by a series of known facts. "Age forty-five. Lived alone. Occupation, housekeeper. Smoker. No tattoos or body piercings. Birthplace, Worcester. Height, 1.70m. Weight, seventy-five kilos. Hair, brunette. Skin, fair. Distinguishing features, none. Date of death, twelfth July 2012. Location of body, thirteenth July at St James's Park. Cause of death, strangulation."

Jack paused and looked at the series of bullet points that had materialised on the screen.

"Getting used to our new toy?" DS Cooper turned towards one of the desks behind him which temporarily housed an array of assorted mugs, mostly chipped and unwashed, plus a hot water urn. He selected the cleanest of the mugs he could find, deposited a few teaspoons of ground coffee into each and filled them with hot water from the urn. With a greasy film on its surface, the resulting murky liquid looked unappetising — Isabel's hazelnut latte it was not.

Cooper placed the coffee mugs on the centre table, and nodded towards the screen. "Good, isn't it? The way you can pull up all sorts of information from your computer, send it to the screen and add all sorts of other stuff, pictures and the like — and you can still write over the top of it with a marker pen. It's amazing."

Jack grunted and reached for one of the mugs. Amazing was not a word he would use for this new piece of high-tech equipment the Metropolitan Police had invested in. His eyes strayed towards the far end of the incident room, his gaze falling on the now forgotten — and apparently old-fashioned — cork pinboard. The board was now gathering dust among a collection of boxes and broken chairs. He didn't share Cooper's enthusiasm for this latest piece of technical kit foisted on them by the chief superintendent. An interactive whiteboard? What was the world coming to? He longed to reach for a drawing pin and stab it into the centre of the new whiteboard in sheer defiance.

"So, Patricia Gordon." DS Cooper sniffed his coffee before taking a tentative mouthful. "Definitely linked to the one found this morning?"

"Without a doubt." Jack tore his eyes away from his beloved pinboard, and touched the screen once more. The right-hand side was now populated with another series of bullet points. "A second body was discovered earlier this

morning, and as yet we don't have a positive identification."
Few details had made it onto the screen, other than the time
of discovery and location. Hair colour was documented as
blonde. Age was estimated at twenty to twenty-five. The only
photograph available was a head shot — a hasty Polaroid
taken in the white tent earlier that morning. Not a particularly pretty sight.

"How can we be sure they're linked, guv?" DC Amanda
Cassidy had been watching the screen intently, ignoring
the mug of coffee Cooper had nudged in her direction. DC
Cassidy had only joined the team a few months ago, and she
was brimming with enthusiasm and vigour. Her jet-black
hair was scraped into a loose ponytail, her eyes peering out
from beneath a pair of long eyelashes. "There's quite an age
gap between them. And we don't yet know the cause of death
of the woman found today. I know they've both been found
in parks, and the parks are quite close to each other — but
the word on the grapevine is that the shoe found at today's
scene didn't belong to either of them."

Jack turned his attention to the slightly built DC perch-
ing herself on the corner of one of the desks. DC Cassidy was
a useful addition to his team, someone he knew he could rely
on to accurately assimilate the evidence and come up with
credible arguments and theories. She was smart. And Jack
liked smart. "That's entirely correct, Amanda. We don't have
much to go on yet from this morning. But the crimes are
definitely linked."

"How so?" persevered Cassidy.

"The shoe," replied Jack, simply.

"But we've just established the shoe found today didn't
belong to either victim." DC Cassidy reached for the plastic
evidence bag containing the black stiletto with its diamante
buckle.

"I don't mean *that* shoe." Jack selected a thin manila
folder from the desk closest to him, sliding out an 8 cm x 5
cm photograph. "I mean *this* shoe." He held the photograph up. "This shoe was found twenty-five metres away

from our first victim's body — Patricia Gordon — in St James's Park. Initial DNA samples don't link the shoe with her. Also it wasn't her size." Jack paused while DS Cooper and DC Cassidy both took in the photograph of a white, imitation-leather, slip-on shoe. "This morning's victim in Hyde Park was wearing a shoe identical to this. DNA tests will obviously be carried out, but I'm confident it belongs to our victim number two." He paused, casting a glance over at Cooper and Cassidy. "So, what does that tell us?"

"That the killer left the shoe of his *next* victim at Patricia Gordon's body site?" Frowning, Cooper sipped his unappetising coffee.

"And?" prodded Jack. "What else does it tell us?"

"It tells us whoever killed Patricia Gordon also killed our Jane Doe from this morning." Cassidy's eyes remained fixed on the photograph of the white leather shoe.

"Indeed it does. Which also means we have ourselves a serial killer." Jack plucked the evidence bag out of Cassidy's hands.

"A serial killer?" Cassidy's frown matched Cooper's.

"Yes, a serial killer." Jack turned the evidence bag over in his hands. "Because this shoe here belongs to his as-yet-unknown *third* victim." Jack let the words hover in the air for a moment before continuing. "And we need to find them – before it's too late."

* * *

Time: 11.30 a.m.
Date: Friday 20 July 2012
Location: A cellar in London

Hannah heard his footsteps descending the damp, stone cellar steps before the grating sound of the key turning in the lock, and then the heavy oak door opened. A thin chink of bright light invaded the inky blackness, but she turned her head to the side. She didn't want to see his face.

Or his eyes.

She especially didn't want to see his eyes.

She heard the sound of his boots scraping over the rough cellar floor as he made his way towards her. Shrinking further back into the corner, she crouched in a huddled ball on the thin mattress, hugging her knees to her chest as tightly as she could. His knees creaked as he bent down by her side, and she heard the soft rasping of his breath as he edged closer. She stiffened.

She knew what was coming next.

His touch sent rivers of ice coursing through her veins, her limbs trembling uncontrollably as she felt his fingers dance slowly along her forearms and up towards her shoulder. Fingers that were so light they barely touched her, but so terrifying they made her skin feel scorched. She could already taste the bile rising up into her throat.

"No need to be frightened, Jess." His fingers continued to stroke her shoulder, then moved up to smooth her hair and lightly caress her tear-stained cheek.

More uncontrollable shaking and retching made her shrink back even further into the dusty corner of the cellar, cobwebs clinging to her hands as she scraped fruitlessly at the walls. She would dig her way out if she had to — through stone, through concrete, through anything — anything to get away.

"Ssshhh now, Jess." His voice was barely more than a whisper. "Don't be scared. I've brought you something to eat as you didn't eat your breakfast. Can't have you going hungry now, can we?"

With a rush of relief, she felt his fingers leave her skin. The sound of rustling paper and something being placed on the mattress beside her made her turn her head slightly and cautiously open one eye. He was already walking away, back towards the cellar door, leaving a sandwich in a paper bag and a bottle of water by her side.

After a few soft murmurings that Hannah couldn't quite hear, he disappeared back up the stone steps, pulling the heavy cellar door closed behind him, the sound of the key scraping in the lock.

Hannah reached for the water bottle and drank, thirstily, not caring that water dribbled down her chin and onto her knees. She eyed the sandwich wrapper, but her stomach turned nauseously at the sight. She had no idea what time of day it was — or was it night? Time meant nothing anymore.

After draining the bottle dry, she dropped it back down onto the dusty floor, and thought — not for the first time — who was Jess?

* * *

Time: 12.45 p.m.
Date: Friday 20 July 2012
Location: Metropolitan Police HQ, London

"Coffee?"

"No thanks, sir."

Chief Superintendent Douglas "Dougie" King nodded towards the vacant chair opposite his desk. Jack took the seat as instructed. The chief superintendent's six-foot-four-inch frame lowered itself into a generously-sized leather swivel chair, the leather sighing as it took ownership of its new inhabitant. He reached behind to pour himself a mug of coffee from the sleek-looking percolator gently humming on the sideboard. Jack mentally compared the shiny, state-of-the-art coffee machine and its accompanying row of gleaming white coffee mugs to the aged and spluttering hot water urn and collection of chipped mugs with dubious hygiene that could be found two floors below in his own department.

Bringing the mug back to his desk, Chief Superintendent King methodically stirred in two sweeteners and a dash of low fat milk. "Do we know who this morning's unfortunate victim is yet?" he asked, taking a sip of the coffee and wincing as the scalding liquid hit his lips.

Jack shook his head. "Not yet, sir. No apparent identification on the body — forensics will swab for DNA and suchlike."

Chief Superintendent King nodded, bringing his fingers together to prop up his chin. "This needs to be wrapped up in record time, Jack, you know that."

Jack nodded. "Sir."

"In seven days' time, the world and his wife will be descending on London for the Olympics. We'll have the eyes of the world upon us, watching our every move. We can't be seen to have a serial killer on the loose in the city." The chief superintendent paused, and locked his gaze on Jack. "And you *are* sure we have a serial? No question?"

Jack shook his head once again. "No question in my mind, sir. Both women are the victim of the same killer. Or killers. And we've another potential victim out there. We just need to find them."

"Shit." The chief superintendent leaned back in his chair and rubbed his eyes. "Shit. Shit. Shit."

Jack let a small smile cross his lips. He liked the new chief superintendent. Dougie King was a man of the people. He was a copper's copper. He hadn't had anything handed to him on a plate, or received promotion just because he went to the right school, wore the right tie, knew the right people or could perfect the correct handshake. He'd earned his rise through the ranks by sheer hard work and being a damned fine police officer. The first black chief superintendent the force had ever seen. It was a well-deserved accolade, and most people were congratulatory. Most . . . but maybe not all. There was always someone intent on raining on your parade.

"I need you to put your best officers on this one, Jack. Your best team. No holds barred. No expense spared. Whatever resources you need, you have them."

"What about the cutbacks, sir?" The Metropolitan Police had been hit hard by austerity measures just like every other force in the country. "The ban on overtime?"

"Sod the cutbacks, Jack. You have my word." Chief Superintendent King took another sip of his coffee and gave a half-hearted smile across the desk. "Find me the killer, Jack. Preferably before the Opening Ceremony."

Jack nodded and pushed himself up out of his chair. He had a feeling the meeting was at an end. As he turned to leave, the chief superintendent caught his eye. "One more thing, Jack. I've drafted in another pair of hands to assist. Tomorrow you'll be joined by DS Carmichael from Sussex Police."

"Sir?" Jack hesitated as his hand reached for the door handle. He turned and faced his senior officer, eyebrows raised. "My team is more than capable . . ."

"I know, I know. It's just an extra pair of hands. An extra brain cell or two. Orders from above." The chief superintendent let his eyes drift skywards.

Jack nodded. "Sir." As he turned to leave and give the good news to his team, the chief superintendent's departing words followed him out into the corridor.

"You've got seven days to find me a killer, Jack. Whatever it takes. Seven days."

CHAPTER FOUR

Time: 1.45 p.m.
Date: Friday 20 July 2012
Location: Isabel's Café, Horseferry Road, London

As the bell above the door jangled with the last departing customer, Isabel sighed and flopped down into one of the armchairs. It'd been an extremely busy lunchtime, and she secretly wished she'd asked Dominic to stay on. Her last customers had brought a smile to her face, however — Don and Jean from Illinois. The two Americans had breezed in, dressed in their matching *I love London* T-shirts and Bermuda shorts, baseball caps pulled down firmly over their heads, and cameras swinging from their necks.

Isabel had served them her best cappuccinos, with a large slab of Sacha's homemade chocolate fudge cake — which, judging by the expressions on her new customers' faces, had gone down a treat. Having only just arrived in London the previous evening, Don and Jean immediately started asking Isabel about where they should visit during their three-week stay. Isabel had trotted out the usual suggestions — the London Eye, Trafalgar Square, Big Ben, Buckingham Palace, London Zoo, the Changing of the

Guard. Although here primarily for the Olympics, Don and Jean quickly began to pore over their *London A–Z* tourist guide in between polishing off another serving of fudge cake.

As they got up from the sofa, leaving a hefty tip under one of their napkins, they asked Isabel if they would get to see the Queen if they visited Buckingham Palace. Isabel smiled as she took away their empty coffee cups and plates, assuring them that if the flag was flying at the Palace, then the Queen was at home — and who knows what they might see? Don and Jean quickly gathered up their belongings and bade Isabel a cheery goodbye, chattering constantly about their chances of seeing the real Queen of England as they stepped out into the heat of the early-afternoon sun.

Sighing once more, Isabel pushed herself up onto her feet, knowing that she only had a brief lull before the café would be filling up again. Somehow she'd managed to cope alone with the steady stream of customers wanting their mid-morning and lunchtime caffeine hit, and the empty display cases on the counter proved just how popular her cakes and pastries were becoming.

Taking a dustpan and brush, she quickly swept the crumbs out of the display cases, ready for the fresh batch that she was about to place in the oven. If Dominic were here, the ovens would already be humming, she mused, smiling to herself as she worked. With the counter now crumb-free, Isabel stepped back into the kitchen and selected some fresh trays of sausage rolls, Danish pastries and cookies, and pushed them into the waiting ovens. Setting the timer so she didn't forget about them, she returned to the café and began straightening the tables and plumping the cushions.

Stepping briefly outside, she straightened the menu board on the pavement, shielding her eyes from the glaring sun as she did so. It was another scorching day, with not a cloud to be seen. She could almost feel the heat radiating from the ground through the soles of her shoes.

Jack's brother's motorbike had been collected and the traffic on the street was flowing gently. All that remained from that morning's incident was the crushed bollard and some fragments of the motorbike's smashed wing mirrors.

Despite the heat of the day, Isabel felt herself shiver when she thought about the morning's accident. She'd been so sure she'd heard the bell in the café, but when she'd gone to look there'd been nobody there. Convinced she'd heard the door open, she'd stood at the window and searched the road outside.

Then she'd seen him.

But surely it couldn't have been him, could it? Not after all these years?

Isabel steadied herself with a hand on the door frame, feeling the chocolate brownies from earlier still churning uncomfortably in her stomach.

She was so sure she'd seen him — a fleeting figure heading across the road just as Mac's motorbike careered into the bollard.

But it couldn't be.

It had to be a mistake.

With another shiver, Isabel headed back inside the café. With another hot day underway, she anticipated a run on cold drinks and would need to make sure the milkshake and frappé glasses were lined up in readiness, and the freezer was well stocked with ice.

And she needed to forget about *him*.

As she closed the door to block out the heat of the day, she felt something brush past her legs. Smiling, she looked down to see Livi, her beloved tabby cat, winding herself around her ankles and brushing her head against her skin.

"Come on, Livi," she smiled. "Let's get you some fresh water. It's too hot for you outside today. Let's get you upstairs before the afternoon rush starts."

* * *

Time: 3.15 p.m.
Date: Friday 20 July 2012
Location: Metropolitan Police HQ, London

With the incident room now set up as he wanted, interactive whiteboard notwithstanding, Jack eased himself back into his chair. DC Cassidy had managed to commandeer two floor fans from somewhere, and both were now whirring away on their highest setting — but, despite this, the room still felt warm and stuffy. Two more computers had been brought in, plus a printer — they were ready to go.

"I've linked through everything from the Patricia Gordon investigation, boss." DS Cooper clicked the mouse and brought up a series of files onto the interactive whiteboard screen. "Everything recorded so far, plus the post-mortem report."

"Good work, Cooper," replied Jack. "Both investigations are now going to be run from this room. The previous team handling the Patricia Gordon murder are more than happy for us to take over, bearing in mind the similarities to our case in Hyde Park. We'll need to look at everything in the Patricia Gordon case with a fresh set of eyes."

Cassidy sat down next to Jack and opened up her notebook. "What's first up then, guv?"

"Priority needs to be analysing any phone records. I'm sure this will have already been done for Patricia Gordon, but we should double-check. Once we have an ID for the body found this morning, we'll need to access any phone records for her, too. Focus on the weeks leading up to both their disappearances." Jack paused, mentally going through the checklist he'd constructed in his head. "Then we need to access any CCTV. Check what CCTV has been gone through already for Patricia Gordon. And then go through it again. And fixed cameras, too. We need images around both St James's Park and Hyde Park."

Cassidy nodded as she made bullet point entries in her notebook.

"And check for any recently released prisoners that flag up as a cause for concern. It's a long shot, but it's worth checking out." Jack got to his feet. "I'm going to see if I can get hold of Dr Matthews — see when he's likely to get the post-mortem done for the body found this morning. For the rest of the afternoon, I want both of you to familiarise yourselves with the Patricia Gordon case — you need to know it inside out. We'll meet bright and early at seven tomorrow — with a full briefing at ten."

"Boss." DS Cooper immediately began pulling up the files relating to Patricia Gordon.

Jack stepped out into the corridor and immediately felt the temperature rise several degrees. Heading back to his office with the sole intention of ignoring the ever-growing pile of paperwork that he knew would be there, his thoughts turned to Dr Matthews. Entering the office, he headed across to his desk and picked up the telephone receiver, which was miraculously still visible in among the towering files and folders. As he dialled the mortuary number, he couldn't help but think about the new DS arriving tomorrow. An extra pair of hands was always welcome, but Jack couldn't quell the sense of disquiet that was settling in his stomach.

He just hoped this new DS Carmichael was going to be an asset rather than a liability.

* * *

Time: 5 p.m.
Date: Friday 20 July 2012
Location: A cellar in London

He took the bread knife and carved himself a thick slice from the fresh loaf. He'd toyed with the idea of taking some down to Jess, but knew she'd just push it away and it would go to waste.

And he hated waste.

Spreading the bread with a thick covering of butter, he settled down at the kitchen table to eat. Despite the heat outside, he was ravenous. He couldn't remember the last time he'd eaten, and very quickly demolished the bread in just a few mouthfuls.

He poured himself a mug of tea from the pot and stirred in three teaspoons of sugar.

Carol always tried to stop him having sugar in his tea, telling him how bad it was for him — and trying to get him to use sweeteners instead.

Eyeing the sugar pot, he scooped up another teaspoon and deposited it in the mug.

Carol.

Why did you have to do what you did?

Can't you see what's happened now?

Everything is because of you, Carol.

Everything.

* * *

Time: 3.10 p.m.
Date: Friday 15 May 1998
Location: Arundel, West Sussex

He'd parked on the opposite side of the road, fifty metres away from the main entrance. She wouldn't be expecting him to be there, so he was quite sure she wouldn't spot him.

He glanced at his watch.

She was late.

Drumming his fingers against the steering wheel, he kept his eyes trained on the building's front door.

Come on, Carol. You finished work ten minutes ago. What are you doing?

Yes, Carol. What *are you doing?*

He could feel the anger welling up inside him already, like a carefully stoked fire, blazing away in the depths of his stomach. It was becoming a very familiar feeling, this anger; this fire. He steadied his breathing in an effort to quell the flames.

Stay calm, he muttered to himself. *Stay calm for Jess.*

He glanced at his watch again and grimaced. He needed to leave soon if he was going to get across town in time to pick up Jess from school.

Five more minutes.

He would give Carol five more minutes, that was all.

He tapped the steering wheel, counting down the seconds one by one. With hardly any through traffic, the street was quiet — so he had an uninterrupted view of the main entrance.

The entrance Carol should've walked through fifteen minutes ago.

He felt the anger building once again.

He needed to go.

Jess would be waiting.

Eventually, he turned the key in the ignition, the roar of the engine matching the anger growing inside him.

And then he saw her.

Carol.

And Brian.

Carol and Brian, leaving work together with smiles on their faces; their shoulders touching briefly as they both squeezed through the door at the same time.

He thrust the car into first gear and stepped heavily on the accelerator.

He'd seen all he needed to see.

CHAPTER FIVE

Time: 7.30 p.m.
Date: Friday 20 July 2012
Location: Kettle's Yard Mews, London

With rush hour over, not that it was ever truly over in London, the traffic was moving more steadily and it wasn't long before Jack pulled up outside his small flat. Kettle's Yard Mews was a narrow, cobbled street with a line of whitewashed mews-style properties nestled snugly together on both sides of the road. Jack's flat was at the very end of the street, and he skilfully managed to reverse park into a tight space outside.

With his keys in hand, Jack opened the communal front door and bent down to pick up the post from the doormat. After quickly seeing nothing was for him, he placed the letters on the wooden cabinet at the side of the hall and made his way up the winding stairs to the second floor. The flat was perfect for Jack. It was small and compact, with not a lot of room for furniture — but Jack didn't need much. He'd acquired few belongings in his forty-five years, preferring the simple life without many trappings. The others at the station often wondered how he could afford to live in such a select and central part of the city, even on a detective inspector's salary. Speculation was rife, many favouring the idea of a rich widow who was keeping Jack in the luxury he could ill afford to keep himself. Such speculation made him smile, but Jack remained tight-lipped.

Opening the door to his flat on the second floor, Jack snapped on the lights and sighed when he saw yesterday's washing-up still piled up on the draining board by the sink, and the washing draped over the radiators. There was a faint mustiness in the air, a mixture of damp clothes and last night's takeaway — a rich widow there was not.

As far as bachelor pads went, it wasn't the most enticing place to attract female company, but Jack didn't mind. Loosening his tie, he shrugged off his jacket and threw it onto the sagging sofa that sometimes doubled as his bed. He immediately spied the bottle of Glenfiddich sitting on the low-rise coffee table, remnants from the night before, and slowly poured another few inches into the glass tumbler by its side.

He'd managed to speak to Dr Matthews and the post-mortem had taken place that afternoon — a draft report would be on his desk first thing in the morning. For the rest of the afternoon, Jack had immersed himself in the Patricia Gordon case.

It made for grim reading.

Knowing there was precious little he could do until the first forensic reports came through, Jack had eventually headed home.

As he sank a mouthful of whisky, he thought back to Isabel's insistence that he find himself a good woman. He almost laughed out loud at the thought of a wife. At forty-five, he had yet to come close to attracting a lifetime partner — or, indeed, anyone who wanted more than a passing acquaintance. He rubbed his hand over his coarse chin. It wasn't that he was a bad catch — he had a good job, a nice flat in a wealthy area of London, no kids, no baggage. And he wasn't all that bad-looking — in a rugged, well-worn kind of way.

Well, maybe no baggage wasn't entirely true, but on the face of it Detective Inspector Jack MacIntosh was pretty good marriage material — or at least half-decent cohabiting material. But Jack remained alone — and if he was being honest, he preferred it that way. He couldn't visualise sharing his life with anyone — the mere thought made him feel claustrophobic.

And being a confirmed bachelor meant that the fridge was usually well stocked with beer and convenience food.

The thought of food made Jack's stomach growl. Rummaging in the back of the fridge, he was pleased to find the remains of an Indian takeaway he'd had a couple of nights ago, and decided that was enough for dinner tonight. Grabbing a couple of bottles of chilled Budweiser, he zapped the leftovers in the microwave before taking everything over to the sofa to eat.

It didn't take long before the plate, and both bottles, were empty.

Leaning back against the cushions, Jack ran a hand through his hair and across his chin. He would shower and shave before bed tonight. History told him, and everyone around him, that Jack was not a morning person. Leaving such ritualistic tasks to the morning, following yet another fitful night's sleep, would be a fool's errand.

His last therapist had told him about the importance of routines. To get into the habit of the early morning shower, the early morning shave, the early morning jog before work. Jack lasted just the one session, and never went back. That'd been three years ago. He didn't need lectures on routines and timekeeping. He could tell the time. He could plan his day. He wasn't a child.

But what he couldn't plan for were the nights spent searching for elusive sleep. Sleep that teased him, pretending to be within reach, within his grasp, only to slip mischievously out of reach. Night after night.

After night.

Alcohol was another thing his last therapist had advised against. Probably another reason Jack didn't go back.

Sometimes alcohol, rightly or wrongly, was his only saviour in the midst of another sleep-deprived night.

At least he was trying to stay away from the hard stuff these days.

Jack glanced at the half-empty bottle of Glenfiddich standing, forlornly, on the coffee table. Before he could decide whether another glass was a good idea or not, a sharp beep cut through the silence. He reached for his jacket, which he'd slung across the back of the sofa on arriving home, and fished out his mobile phone.

A reminder from his appointment calendar.

8.30 a.m. Saturday 21 July.
Dr Evelyn Riches.
Psychotherapist.

Jack grimaced and headed to the fridge for another beer. He knew it was a bad idea, but right now he had precious few others to take its place.

Snapping the lid off the bottle, he returned to the sofa and thought about Stuart.

Jack hadn't seen his brother properly for years. Sent to an approved school when he was thirteen for his part in a violent robbery, the younger MacIntosh brother quickly progressed to youth detention for the rest of his teenage years, followed by an adult prison not long after. Jack barely saw him after that.

They'd not had the best start in life, that was evident, but Jack knew it was no excuse. Discovering his mother's body hanging from a light fitting when he was just four years old, Jack had struggled to rid himself of the memory. Stuart had been two, and Jack was unsure just how much his brother remembered. For his sake, Jack hoped it was very little. Never having known their father, the boys were immediately taken into emergency foster care and soon afterwards into a loving foster family home. Jack had flourished, Stuart not so much. The younger MacIntosh struggled with the change of routine and eventually the system separated them — sending young Stuart to a local authority children's home. When the care system eventually spat the brothers out at the other end, one had a solid career ahead of him in the police force, the other was already on a downward spiral into crime.

After prison, Jack hadn't been entirely sure where his brother had ended up.

Until today.

Seeing him like that, so unexpectedly, had transported Jack back to his youth. He found it odd hearing his brother's childhood nickname again.

Mac.

It'd been such a long time since he'd heard it spoken out loud.

To Jack he would always be Stuart.

Stu.

His baby brother.

But Mac?

Mac had been the nickname given to him in the children's home, Jack always assuming it was some kind of gang tag. When the welfare system had let him down, the street gangs were there to pick up the pieces and take young Stuart under their wing.

Mac survived fine on the streets. He was tough. He'd had to be. But Stu?

Jack wasn't so sure.

Taking a long mouthful of beer, Jack glanced at his watch. He knew he'd have to make at least a vain attempt at sleeping sometime soon. Draining the bottle, he placed it down on the coffee table next to his phone — the screen still showing his appointment reminder for the morning.

Dr Riches.

Apparently this one was different. Jack remained sceptical. Shrinks were shrinks, no matter how you dressed them up.

But he'd promised the chief superintendent that he'd try.

Again.

Rubbing methodically at his temples, he wondered if Dr Riches knew exactly what she was taking on. This would be his third, maybe fourth, therapist in as many years; he'd lost count. He rarely made it past the first session, but Dougie King had been persuasive enough to talk him into trying again.

One last time.

Jack picked up the business card that'd been sitting on the coffee table. It'd been over six months since the chief superintendent had pressed the card into his hand and given him that knowing look.

Just try it, Jack. For your own sake.

Jack had dutifully nodded and pocketed the business card — but, in true Jack MacIntosh style, he'd done nothing about it.

For a while.

But the nightmares continued — if anything, they intensified.

And even Jack knew the time was approaching when he needed to make them stop.

* * *

Time: 10 p.m.
Date: Friday 20 July 2012
Location: A cellar in London

Hannah stirred at the sound of scraping. Her eyes flickered open, struggling to focus in the dark. Her heart thumped.

Was he here?

Had he come back while she'd been sleeping?

Hannah's stomach tightened in fear, her skin cold and clammy underneath the scratchy blanket. She squinted again through the darkness, but couldn't find any shapes to focus on. She felt tired and groggy, her eyelids heavy, as though made of lead.

Maybe it was rats.

She shivered beneath the blanket at the thought.

Rats.

Suddenly, all she could think about were rats scurrying across the stone floor, nibbling and biting at everything in their path, their claws scraping over the concrete.

Hannah drew her legs up towards her chest at the thought of rats nibbling at her exposed toes.

And then she heard it again.

Scraping.

As the fog in her mind began to lift a little, she realised what it must be. It was just the chain attached to her ankle scraping across the floor as she moved. She reached down and ran a quivering finger around the cold metal clasp, her skin chafed and sore beneath. Pulling at the chain only made it feel tighter.

A tear trickled down her cheek as she closed her eyes and thought of Hope.

CHAPTER SIX

Time: 10.15 p.m.
Date: Friday 20 July 2012
Location: Isabel's Café, Horseferry Road, London

Isabel woke with a start. The small clock on the bookcase opposite showed exactly 10.15 p.m. She must've dropped off. Her mug of cold tea sat on the floor next to her, untouched.

Picking up the forgotten cup of tea, she yawned and made her way through to the small, galley-style kitchen. Turning on the tap, she let the water run cold for a moment before filling a pint glass with the chilled water. She hadn't eaten anything since locking up the café, falling asleep on the sofa not long after making it up the stairs to the flat. But she wasn't hungry — thirsty, but not hungry.

It'd been such a strange day. She thought back to the accident earlier that morning, hoping Mac was all right. He'd taken quite a knock but vehemently refused to go anywhere near a doctor.

Mac.

Isabel thought he looked like a Mac — more than he did a Stuart, anyway. She didn't know Jack all that well — he popped in now and again for a coffee, and they'd pass the time of day

41

for the length of time it took to fill his takeaway cup. But she'd never known he had a brother.

And she didn't need to be a detective to sense there was more than a little history between the two MacIntoshes.

Growing up, she'd often wondered what it would've been like to have a brother or a sister. After losing her parents when she was six, Isabel had grown up alone. Her aunt had done her best, raising her in her childhood home in Surrey, and giving her everything she needed — but there was always that gap that could never be filled.

Families.

Thinking about her parents inevitably led to the familiar pang of guilt resurfacing — the bunches of flowers on their graves must look so dead and withered by now, lost and forgotten among all the other headstones. People must look at them and wonder who'd forgotten the poor souls who lay beneath the earth. Isabel made a mental reminder to make the journey one day soon. A pot of petunias would be nice. She'd pick out Mum's favourite colours. And, later in the year, she'd think about planting some snowdrop and crocus bulbs to bring some winter cheer. Dad would like those.

And then there'd been the figure she'd seen through the café window — or *thought* she'd seen. Maybe it wasn't him after all and her mind had just been playing tricks on her. The more she thought about it, the more she convinced herself it couldn't be him. It just couldn't.

Taking a long drink of chilled water, she headed towards the bedroom. She needed to at least try and sleep. She just prayed he didn't visit her in her dreams as well.

* * *

Time: 10.30 p.m.
Date: Friday 20 July 2012
Location: A cellar in London

He was concerned that Jess wasn't eating. He'd taken her one of those supermarket sandwiches earlier, but it remained untouched.

And that wasn't like Jess. Jess usually loved her food and would never leave a scrap of food on her plate. Especially if it was one of her favourites — like spaghetti bolognese. Or the homemade chicken casserole Carol often made.

Carol.

There she was again, infiltrating his thoughts at any given moment.

Every time he thought of Jess, he ended up thinking about Carol.

It was as if you couldn't have one without the other.

He could pinpoint the exact time when it all went wrong.

* * *

Time: 8 p.m.
Date: Friday 15 May 1998
Location: Arundel, West Sussex

Jess had been waiting for him outside the school gates. He'd mustered a smile for her, pushing the anger he really felt beneath the surface as he listened to her chattering about her day and what homework she needed to do that night.

The evening at home had been tense. Carol had acted as though nothing was wrong. Cooking their dinner as usual, quietly humming to herself as she stirred the bolognese on the hob. It took all of his restraint and resolve not to confront her there and then. But he had to think of Jess.

Jess mustn't see.

Jess must never see.

But now Jess was up in her bedroom, no doubt oblivious to the world around her with her headphones clamped to her ears, listening to some rock group or other.

Now it was just them.

Now it was just the two of them — alone.

And Carol had some questions to answer.

The evening progressed in silence. Carol had taken a shower and washed her hair, then caught up with one of her favourite soaps on the TV. He'd sat in the corner of the front room watching her towel-dry her hair, noticing how she occasionally looked at her phone as she did so. Although she'd put her phone on silent, he could see the screen light up from time to time with what looked like an incoming message.

And not just one message.

There seemed to be several, one after the other.

Brian.

It had to be.

Carol was flaunting it right in front of his eyes, and the expression on her face proved that she didn't even seem to care.

They were now standing together in the kitchen. Carol had begun the washing up, sliding the pile of plates splattered with remnants of bolognese sauce into the bowl of hot, soapy water. He watched from the doorway as she began squeezing and wiping the sponge over the dishes, her hands dipping underneath the foaming bubbles.

Her hands.

He'd always loved her hands.

"You could come and help rather than just standing there staring at me — it's creepy." Carol flashed him a look as she stacked a plate onto the draining board. "Here, start drying." She picked up a tea towel and threw it across the kitchen.

He caught the tea towel with a snatch of his hand, but remained motionless in the doorway. He continued to watch as she dropped a saucepan into the water and began to scrub the sides. He glanced at the pile of crockery at the side of the sink, still waiting to be washed. One more dinner plate, a chopping board, and Jess's glass with remnants of her strawberry milkshake still in the bottom. Two wine glasses rested by the side — glasses that he and Carol had sipped from, the alcohol having done nothing to thaw the chilled air between them.

His gaze then came to rest on a large bread knife Carol had used to slice up the fresh French baguette that had accompanied their spaghetti bolognese. He'd sharpened it especially beforehand, honing the blade so it glided effortlessly through the crispy crust.

He liked the feel of it in his hand; the way it made him feel centred and in control. Not taking his eyes from the knife, he took a step towards the sink, feeling the invisible pull of the blade. Twisting the tea towel in his hands, he silently crossed the kitchen floor until he was standing close to Carol's shoulder. He noticed she was wearing a thin-strapped vest top, which exposed the pale skin of her delicate neck.

Such an exquisite neck, he mused. Like a swan — a very elegant swan.

Carol had picked up the bread knife and was carefully washing it free of breadcrumbs, leaving it on the draining board when she was done. The metal gleamed in the low-level lighting of the kitchen. Unconsciously, he felt his hand reaching out towards the knife, eager to feel its power within his grasp.

Images of his wife and Brian danced at the edges of his vision. It made his fingers twitch.

It would be so easy.

So easy to bring it all to an end.

His fingers stretched towards the blade, drawn to it like a magnet.

It would be very quick — one slice and it could all be over.

So very, very quick, and so very, very easy.

Suddenly, a figure appeared behind him in the kitchen doorway.

"Have we got any lemonade?"

Jess.

His hand recoiled from the knife and he plastered a smile on his face as he turned towards her. "Of course — in the fridge." He glanced towards Carol who was rinsing a selection of spoons. "I'm just helping your mother with the washing-up."

With one last look at the bread knife, he reached for a plate and began to wipe the tea towel over its surface, sighing as the opportunity disappeared along with the soap suds.

* * *

Time: 10.01 p.m.
Date: 5 April 1971
Location: Old Mill Road, Christchurch

The kitchen window was cracked in several places, and the hinges didn't quite fit — so the howling wind outside was able to rush inside, unguarded and unchallenged. Angry raindrops pelted against the glass, accompanied by the occasional flash of lightning and deep rumble of thunder.

Whether it was the surge of wind that flooded through the chilled air of the kitchen, or some other unseen force, four-year-old Jack MacIntosh looked up from where he'd been crouching and watched his mother's body swing to and fro above him. Her arms hung limply by her sides, brushing against her nightdress as it billowed in the arctic breeze.

The creaking of the light fixing, as it took the strain of her thin frame, echoed eerily in time with the rhythm of the wailing wind outside. Creaking backwards and forwards. Backwards and forwards.

Creaking.

Creaking.

Creaking.

Jack reached out and touched his mother's foot.

So cold.

So very, very cold.

* * *

Time: 10.35 p.m.
Date: Friday 20 July 2012
Location: Kettle's Yard Mews, London

Jack woke with a start. The light summer breeze outside had strengthened a little, enough to cause the blinds across the small window in the kitchen to rustle and creak.

Creak.

Jack shuddered, instantly feeling a chill despite the clammy heat of the day still clinging to the air. He was drenched in sweat. A quick glance at the window confirmed it was getting dark outside. He must've fallen asleep on the sofa — again. As he sat there, blinking rapidly to clear his head, the blinds began creaking once more.

Creaking.

Creaking.

Creaking.

He got to his feet, collecting the three empty beer bottles from the coffee table on the way, and went to snap the kitchen window shut.

He could do without the creaking tonight.

Tossing the empty bottles into the sink to join the remnants of yesterday's unwashed dishes, Jack returned to the sofa, sweeping up his phone as he passed.

He looked again at his calendar.

8.30 a.m.
Dr Evelyn Riches.

CHAPTER SEVEN

Time: 6.30 a.m.
Date: Saturday 21 July 2012
Location: Metropolitan Police HQ, London

Jack picked up the envelope that only minutes before had landed on his desk. Dr Philip Matthews had been true to his word and produced his post-mortem report in his trusted expedient fashion, couriering the final version over to Jack's office not long after daybreak. Although the same copy would've been sent by email, Dr Matthews was a traditionalist.

Jack sliced the envelope open with his finger, full of admiration for the dry-witted pathologist who must've spent much of his Friday evening dictating and then typing his own report, and then ensuring it was biked over in time for Jack's early morning arrival.

He quickly skimmed through the preliminaries, briefly acknowledging DS Cooper as he entered the office bearing two mugs of coffee and what appeared to be a paper bag with something greasy inside.

"Is that the post-mortem report on our Jane Doe from yesterday?" Cooper nudged aside the scattered paperwork that littered Jack's desk to find a suitable space to deposit his coffee mug. "Anything useful?"

Jack silently nodded, flicking the report over to scan down to the conclusions at the very end. He reached for his coffee mug and took a long sip before replying. "Cause of death, strangulation. As we suspected." He paused and took another sip of coffee. "Superficial injuries to the left ankle, suggestive of some sort of restraint."

"Tied up?"

"Looks that way."

Cooper perched himself on the side of Jack's desk, leaning over to take a look at the report. He waved the greasy paper bag in Jack's direction. "Fancy half of my bacon sarnie?"

Jack held up a hand. "I think I'll pass, thanks." Instead, he turned his attention back to the report, rereading the conclusions in the final paragraph. Although his stomach was growling at him, reminding him that he'd yet to eat anything this morning, reading these "death reports", as they were sometimes colloquially known among the team, always managed to dampen his appetite. Food could wait. He wrinkled his nose as the aroma of bacon reached his nostrils. *No signs of sexual assault.*

DS Cooper took a large bite out of his sandwich, a thick globule of tomato sauce dripping from between the thickly cut bread slices and landing on Jack's desk. Or more precisely, on the envelope that had housed the post-mortem report.

Jack flapped his hands in Cooper's direction. "Go and make a mess of your own desk. We've a visitor coming this morning."

"Ah yes, the infamous DS Carmichael." Cooper hopped off Jack's desk and returned to his own chair, resuming the devouring of his breakfast. "Remind me why we're being landed with him again?"

Jack shrugged. "Who knows? Officially, it's to give us extra support with the investigation — orders from on high."

He raised his eyes to the heavens, and the offices above them. "But who knows what the real reason is. All I've been told is that we have to play nicely." Jack paused and watched DS Cooper push the final wedge of sandwich into his mouth. "And you shouldn't speak with your mouth full."

* * *

Time: 6.40 a.m.
Date: Saturday 21 July 2012
Location: Isabel's Café, Horseferry Road, London

Open.

Isabel smiled as she flipped the sign over. She loved this time of day. The city was starting to come to life, and already the sky was bright and clear. One of the reasons she'd decided to open her café this early was to catch the early risers, stopping off for their double espresso, skinny latte or flavoursome cappuccino with extra chocolate on their way to start their day.

The tantalising smell of freshly baked croissants, pastries and breads filled her nostrils as she turned towards the kitchen. Although it meant getting up while it was still dark to put the ovens on, Isabel wouldn't change her life for the world. With her small flat upstairs, she felt settled for the first time in a long while.

Just as she reached the kitchen, she heard the familiar tinkle of the bell over the door announcing her first visitor of the day.

And she knew exactly who it would be.

"Morning, Dominic," she greeted him, without turning round. "The pastries are just about ready to come out the oven."

Dominic, smartly dressed in dark-blue jeans and a white polo shirt, headed straight through to the kitchen, picking up his apron and deftly tying the strings around his small waist. Stopping by the sink, he deposited exactly three squirts of antibacterial handwash into the palm of each hand and began to rub vigorously. Switching on the hot tap, he continued to scrub his hands and nails for exactly sixty seconds. Isabel smiled in his direction before turning her attention to the front counter, placing a fresh supply of paper napkins, knives, forks and spoons within her customers' reach.

With the morning ritual complete, Dominic dried his hands on a disposable piece of kitchen towel, before turning his attention to the two ovens. Expertly donning a pair of freshly laundered oven gloves, he opened the oven doors and began extracting the appetising delicacies that had been browning inside.

Just then, the bell over the door tinkled once again.

"Morning, Isabel," said Angus, Isabel's regular 6.45 a.m. customer. Every morning, without fail, except for Sundays and bank holidays, Angus McBride would stop by for his regular white coffee with two sugars and a sausage roll. His deep, gravelly, coarse-sounding Glaswegian accent masked a gentle soul beneath. A broad smile split the greying beard that hugged his chin, and deep, cavernous laughter lines caressed the edges of his twinkling grey eyes. "It's a lovely day." He swung the heavy Royal Mail postbag from his shoulder, letting it drop by his feet while he reached into his pocket for some change.

"Morning, Angus," replied Isabel, slipping the freshly baked sausage roll into a greaseproof paper bag. "All ready to go."

"Ach, you're a sweet girl, Isabel." Angus dropped his change onto the counter and took a quick sip of the coffee. "Hits the spot every time, hen. Best coffee in toon." Although Isabel's coffee menu listed all manner of exotic choices, from lattes to espressos, cappuccinos to mochas, Angus's choice was always, "Just a coffee, hen. Nothing fancy." Turning his nose up at all the fanciful syrups on offer — and frowning at the "sheer nonsense, hen, it's just coffee" — Isabel would have his ordinary white coffee and two sugars — "white sugar, hen, none of that brown nonsense" — ready for his 6.45 a.m. call.

"See you Monday, Angus," smiled Isabel, scooping up the change. "Have a good day."

"Aye, you too, hen." With that, Angus hauled the Royal Mail postbag high up onto his shoulder and, grabbing the greaseproof bag housing his sausage roll, he disappeared out into the street with a wink.

The departure of Angus heralded the start of the breakfast rush. For the next two hours the coffee machine would be humming and spouting steam as a variety of tourists, weekend workers and taxi drivers stopped by for their caffeine fix. With a lucrative spot in the middle of Horseferry Road, Isabel benefited from being in the heart of wealthy Westminster, and close enough to attractions like Buckingham Palace and Tate Britain.

At just after nine, Isabel slipped herself onto one of the bar stools by the counter and let herself inhale the aroma from the mug of steaming Americano coffee she'd poured for herself.

The lull.

For the next hour, the steady stream of customers would reduce to a mere trickle, and Isabel could afford to take the luxury of a quick break before the mid-morning tea break brigade would descend.

"Dom?" Isabel sipped her coffee and eyed a buttery croissant in the display case in front of her. "Come and get yourself a drink and take a break."

Dominic's head dutifully popped through the archway that led to the small kitchen area behind the counter. "In a minute. I'm just finishing up."

Isabel's resolve finally faltered as she reached into the display case and extracted the still-warm pastry, breaking off a section and popping it into her mouth. She knew Dominic would be recounting his morning activities in his notebook, recording exactly how many croissants, pain au chocolat, Danish pastries and sausage rolls he'd supplied to the front counter. Isabel slipped another morsel of fresh croissant into her mouth and smiled. Better than any accountant, Dominic was the most wonderful addition to her enterprise.

"Eighteen sausage rolls, twenty-five croissants, nineteen pain au chocolat, but only eleven Danish pastries so far." Dominic appeared behind the serving counter, replacing his notebook in his back pocket. "Last Saturday we'd done eighteen Danish pastries by now. But not as many sausage rolls."

Isabel pulled off another tantalising corner of croissant. "Well I'm not sure I'd want a Danish pastry for my breakfast either . . . more of a mid-afternoon treat, that one."

Just then the bell tinkled over the door, announcing another customer arrival. Isabel swivelled on the bar stool, ready to greet her visitor. But when her gaze registered the slightly built figure backing in through the doorway, struggling with two oversized canvases, one under each arm, she beamed.

"Patrick, let me help you!" Jumping off the stool, she strode over to the front door, holding it open with one hand and taking one of the awkward canvases with the other.

"Thanks, Isabel. Much appreciated." Patrick Mansfield stepped through the doorway and into the café, slightly out of breath from his exertions. He leaned the remaining canvas up against one of the sofas, and from his shoulder he let a large rucksack swing to the floor. "I'd forgotten quite how far it was on the Tube." Still panting a little, he brushed away the fringe that'd flopped across his forehead, his green eyes twinkling as he smiled.

"You took these on the Tube?!" Isabel raised her eyebrows at the enormous canvases. "Are you mad? I bet you were popular."

Patrick grinned, and gave a small shrug. "What can I say? Mad artist, guilty as charged. I didn't think it would be that busy, not this time of the morning on a Saturday."

Isabel chuckled and made her way towards the back of the café and into the artist's studio. "Patrick, this is London. It's always busy!"

Following on behind with the other canvas and ruck-sack, Patrick grunted. "Next time I'll get a taxi. Honestly, you should've seen some of the looks people gave me when I tried getting into a carriage with this lot."

"And what is 'this lot', exactly?" Isabel leaned her canvas up against the art table in the centre of the studio. "What are you up to?"

"It's a commission." Patrick deposited the rucksack at his feet and leaned the second canvas up against the first. "Local advertising agency liked my work, and they've asked me to design them something for their brand-new offices, something for their front reception area. Big, they said." Patrick nodded at the canvases. "So, I've gone big."

As the resident artist at the café, Patrick Mansfield paid Isabel a weekly sum to rent the studio space at the rear. Some of his paintings adorned the walls of the café and were up for sale, others he exhibited at local independent art galleries to eke out a living. Arriving on Isabel's doorstep three months ago, dressed in cut-off denim shorts and sandy espadrilles despite it being a chilly April, Isabel immediately warmed to the softly spoken, unassuming artistic character who later introduced himself to her as Patrick Mansfield, travelling artisan. In his late forties, Isabel guessed — although he was always vague about his actual birth date — "age is just a number, my dear" — he had the longest fingers Isabel had ever seen, with perfectly manicured fin-gernails. Originally only calling in for a cup of Earl Grey to take away, once Patrick had seen the studio at the rear of the café he'd immediately offered to rent the space. And needing every penny for her new venture, Isabel had imme-diately accepted.

And so, along with Dominic, Patrick had become one of the family.

"What's the theme?" Isabel nodded once again at the canvases. "For the commission."

"Apparently I have full artistic licence." Patrick raised his fair eyebrows.

"How dangerous! They obviously don't know you very well!"

"Indeed. All I have to do is make sure it reflects their company ideology — *Innovation. Inspiration. Ideation.*"

"Well, good luck with that one! I'm just having a coffee before the mid-morning rush. Tea?"

Patrick flashed Isabel a warming smile. "An Earl Grey would be most perfect." Shrugging off a light jacket, he sat at the artist's table and reached for a sketchpad. "I guess I'd better start getting some inspiration while I have an hour or so to spare."

* * *

Time: 8.35 a.m.
Date: Saturday 21 July 2012
Location: St James's University, London

"Now, Jack, before we start I'll just ask you a few questions about yourself, so I can get a feel as to the best approach to your first session."

Dr Evelyn Riches, consultant psychotherapist, sat back in her leather chair and studied Jack with a pleasant, relaxed smile. "It's nothing to be worried about." Her voice was calming and reassuring. "Tell me what you like to do; what makes you feel happy?"

Jack looked up and stared blankly back at Dr Riches. *What makes me happy?* Jack tried to think back to the last time he'd felt happy. When had that been exactly? Could he remember? His mind whirred, searching and searching for even the faintest indication of a time when he'd felt happiness, true happiness, but it failed to connect to anything.

Have I really never been happy?

Jack fidgeted in his seat.

"Don't worry," smiled Dr Riches. "Everyone finds that question hard to answer. Try thinking about something you enjoy doing."

Again Jack felt his brain whirring, the cogs turning faster and faster as they searched for another elusive answer.

What do I enjoy doing?

Jack felt a frown darken his brow. *Do I actually enjoy anything?*

"Work," Jack heard himself say, his voice sounding disconnected. "I enjoy my work." He looked up and met Dr Riches' gaze, allowing himself a sheepish smile. "I guess that sounds very sad."

"Not at all, Jack." She rewarded him with another smile. "Not at all. If your work wasn't important to you then you wouldn't be here. Let's try and focus on a place that makes you feel safe. Can you close your eyes for me and think about where you feel your safest? Somewhere nothing can hurt you. Where do you feel safe, Jack? Think back to happy times — holidays, time spent with family and friends."

Jack closed his eyes, and sank back into the soft armchair.

Where do I feel safe?

Jack let his mind wander.

But he felt the same void building inside his head as before.

Where do I feel safe?

Dr Riches' words echoed inside his head. *"Think back to happy times — holidays, time spent with family and friends."*

Jack didn't go on holiday.

He didn't like beaches.

He didn't like the sand.

And wasn't keen on lakes, forests or the outdoors either. He couldn't swim.

And he didn't have anyone special in his life.

No wonder.

There was only one place where he'd truly felt safe.

"Old Mill Road in Christchurch." The words escaped Jack's mouth before they'd registered in his brain. "When I was four."

"OK, Jack. This place will be your safe place. Is there a particular room there where you felt happiest?"

Jack's mind transported him back in time — back to Old Mill Road where they'd lived as a family. He'd shared a bedroom with Stuart, and their mother had had her own room, next to the bathroom. There'd been a large living room plus a smaller box-like room filled with junk.

But there was really only one room that he truly remembered.

The room he would never be able to forget.

The kitchen.

The kitchen where he'd found his mother's lifeless body.

"The kitchen," Jack heard himself say, his voice sounding small. Quite why he'd said it, he wasn't sure, but the words had escaped his lips before his brain had a chance to catch up. Before he could give it any more thought, Dr Riches moved on.

"OK, so that will be your safe place, Jack. A place where nothing can ever hurt you." Dr Riches consulted the brief notes in front of her and continued, her voice taking on a measured and lyrical tone. "I want you to relax now, relax every bone and every muscle in your body. Starting at the top, from your head and neck, down through your shoulders, across each arm and down to your hands and fingers. Feel your muscles relax, feel how weightless you are."

Jack allowed himself to sink further backwards into the armchair, feeling it pulling him in, inviting him to sink further and further. He felt his neck and shoulders relieve their pent-up tension, felt his arms sag as their weight evaporated.

"Good. Feel the muscles in your chest and abdomen relax, spreading out down each thigh, across each knee and down towards your feet and toes. You feel so relaxed now, Jack. Every muscle in your body is slack."

At Dr Riches' suggestion, Jack felt all tension in his body subsiding. His body felt instantly lighter, as if he were weightless and floating in the breeze. He couldn't hear anything. There was no sound at all. Nothing except the rhythmical, soothing tones of Dr Riches, floating in nothingness.

"Now, Jack, I want you to imagine you're descending a staircase. There are ten steps. There is a rail on one side to hold onto. You're descending slowly, slowly, slowly — taking one step at a time. With each step you take, your body feels even more relaxed. And every step brings you closer to your safe place."

Jack found he could see a staircase in his mind. He moved instinctively towards it, gliding weightlessly through the air.

"You're at the top of the stairs now, Jack. Take your first step. Down you go. Nine. Your body is feeling lighter already, Jack. Your safe place is getting closer. Eight. Slowly, down you go. Control your breathing with every step — breathe in, and then breathe out. Feel your lungs inflate with every breath. Seven. One more step — further towards your safe place. You feel even more relaxed, now, Jack. Six. Keep breathing. In and then out. In and then out. Five. Halfway there, Jack. Keep going. One more step. Four."

Jack's chest rose and fell steadily. With each breath he felt lighter, with each breath his muscles felt as though they were no longer attached to his body. His body had no weight at all; he was floating gently within his own mind.

"That's it, Jack. One more step. Three. Nearly there now. Keep breathing, in and then out. In and then out. One more step. Two. You're so relaxed now, Jack. Nothing can hurt you. You are nearly at your safe place. Just one more step to go. Take that one final step."

Jack felt himself take the last step. He was surrounded by nothing, yet he could feel everything. He felt lighter than the air itself.

"You're nearly at your safe place now, Jack. Can you see it? Nothing can hurt you. You're completely safe. You're in control at all times. No one can make you do anything you don't want to do when you're in your safe place."

Jack reached out into nothingness. His safe place. A place where nothing could hurt him.

Apart from what was behind the door.

CHAPTER EIGHT

Time: 9.45 a.m.
Date: Saturday 21 July 2012
Location: Metropolitan Police HQ, London

Jack glanced at his watch as he jogged up the stairs to the second floor, heading towards the incident room. Running a finger along the inside of his shirt collar and loosening his tie, he could feel the temperature already creeping up, heralding yet another baking hot day on the horizon.

Very few offices at HQ had the benefit and luxury of air conditioning, that particular invention of the twentieth century having yet to make an impression on the Metropolitan Police budget, so Jack could foresee another uncomfortable day ahead.

Arriving on the second floor, Jack pushed the door to the incident room open with his shoulder, grunting at the wall of heat and stagnant air that greeted him. And the three pairs of eyes that looked up, expectantly, in his direction.

Three pairs of eyes.

Two pairs he recognised.

One unfamiliar.

"Glad you could join us." The voice had a clipped tone. "Tut, tut. Timekeeping not one of your fortes, Jack?" The man's bird-like eyes darted up to the clock on the wall and back again.

Jack paused in the doorway, holding the stranger's stare in his own. He noticed DS Cooper and DC Cassidy were both seated on the far side of the room, closest to the open window that was barely affording any benefit of cooler, fresher air; the air outside already humid and breathless. Cooper momentarily caught Jack's gaze and offered a slight raise of his tufty, ginger eyebrows. Next to him, DC Amanda Cassidy merely sat silently, wide-eyed, a small smile catching on her lips as she watched the theatrical display play out before her.

"I had a meeting." Jack's reply was equally clipped. "And it's *Detective Inspector MacIntosh*."

Letting the door swing shut behind him, Jack headed towards the nearest free desk. As he lowered himself into the vacant chair, he again fixed his gaze on the man leaning up against the far wall.

"You must be DS Carmichael."

Jack took in the thin face; the smooth, almost translucent pale skin; the beak-like hooked nose and beady, bird-like dark eyes that were fixing him with a humourless stare. Jack wondered, if he put bird seed out on the table, would the man start pecking?

"Indeed, I am." DS Carmichael pushed himself away from the wall and stepped forwards, hand outstretched. Jack hesitated for a moment — maybe a moment too long — before briefly shaking the proffered hand, wincing slightly at the dampness of Carmichael's palm. "Been to see the shrink?"

Jack dropped the handshake like a deadweight, feeling his initial tentative dislike morphing into something stronger.

"It was a psychotherapist. And also none of your business."

Despite the rising heat from the blazing sun outside, the temperature inside the incident room dropped several degrees. Silence descended like a musty, suffocating curtain.

DS Cooper rose quickly to his feet, his chair scraping noisily on the cheap linoleum flooring. Clearing his dry throat, he sought to dispel the creeping sense of hostility that was filling the room.

"Boss, I've printed out everything on the Patricia Gordon case, including her post-mortem report." Cooper pointed at the bundle of papers sitting in the centre of one of the desks. "And here's everything we have so far on yesterday's victim." His hand shifted to a much smaller pile. "And we now have a name for her."

Jack jerked his head away from DS Carmichael's stony stare. "We do?"

"Yes." Cooper reached for the remote control to activate the whiteboard. After a few clicks, the whiteboard was illuminated with a passport-style photograph of an attractive young woman with blonde hair.

"Georgina Dale, or Georgie as she was known to her friends and family. Aged twenty-one. Lived alone in the halls of residence at St James's University. We've got officers going round there today to see what other information they can gather, and forensics will process her room."

"How come we got her identified so quickly? She didn't have any ID on her. Did Missing Persons come up with something?" Jack's eyes scanned the scanty details on the screen.

DS Cooper shook his head. "No, it was DNA and fingerprints. The lab managed to rush through the DNA samples yesterday and the fingerprints flagged up this morning, just after you left for your . . . for your appointment." Cooper flashed a wary glance in the direction of DS Carmichael, but the new addition to the team remained silent. "She was on the system after a minor drugs offence two years ago."

Jack nodded, appreciatively. "Good work, Cooper. So what do we have for both of them? Any similarities?"

It was DC Cassidy's turn to get up out of her chair this time. As she rose, she noticed DS Carmichael remained on the far side of the room, leaning against the wall, watching

61

proceedings with a haughty expression. She didn't particularly like the way his gaze dropped to the curve of her skirt around her thighs as she stood.

"I've compiled a comparison list, guv. With all the facts we know about both victims so far." She took the remote control from DS Cooper and after a few clicks the whiteboard was filled with a table. "The left side is victim number one, Patricia Gordon. The right side is our latest victim, Georgina Dale."

Jack's eyes scanned the details on the screen, frowning slightly against the glare. He afforded himself a quick glance to the back of the room, where next to DS Carmichael rested his beloved cork pinboard. Dragging his gaze back to the screen, Jack read through the list of comparisons. Height, weight, hair colour, age, home address, ethnicity, employment status, marital status, distinguishing features.

Nothing seemed to match.

Not one single thing.

Other than the fact they were both female.

And both dead.

"Damn." Jack rubbed his eyes and refocused again on the screen. "So, apart from the fact that they were both strangled, we don't have any similarities."

DC Cassidy shook her head and clicked a button on the remote control to turn off the whiteboard. "It doesn't seem so, boss. Not yet." Reaching forwards, she took a couple of sheets of paper from the desk and handed one across to Jack. "I've put it all down on paper for you, too. Victim number one — Patricia Gordon — was aged forty-five years. Five foot seven. Weight eleven stones. Short dark brown hair with green eyes. Divorced. A smoker, living alone in St John's Wood. Worked as a housekeeper in a care home. Cause of death — strangulation." She paused, before continuing. "Victim number two — Georgina Dale. Aged twenty-one. Five foot three. Weight seven stones. Long blonde hair with blue eyes. Single. A non-smoker, living alone in the St James's University halls of residence. Full-time student, no part-time jobs we're aware of as yet. Cause of death — strangulation."

Jack scanned the comparison of their two victims. Nobody spoke.

"I'd say that's not much to go on." DS Carmichael's nasal tones cut through the silence. The other three pairs of eyes in the room flickered towards him, causing a crude smile to cross his thin lips and his beady eyes to glisten. "Apart from the cause of death, you've no credible connection."

"There's always a connection." Jack spoke quietly, casting his eyes back to the paper in front of him.

"Looks pretty random to me." There was a challenging edge to DS Carmichael's tone.

Jack let it go.

"Murders are never random. There's always a reason." Jack looked up and held Carmichael's stony gaze in his. "And it's our job to find it."

* * *

Time: 12.15 p.m.
Date: Saturday 21 July 2012
Location: The Shard, London Bridge Street, London

Craning his neck skywards, he shielded his eyes from the scorching rays that bounced off the mirrored glass. The building was magnificent; like nothing he'd ever seen before. So sleek. So clean. So elegant.

And so tall.

The Shard, as it was tentatively being called in the media, towered some three hundred metres above him. A master of design. A thing of true beauty; if indeed a building could be described as beautiful.

He felt a stirring inside, a quickening of his heart.

This was the place.

It just had to be.

He knew it the moment he saw it.

This was where he would find Carol.

CHAPTER NINE

Time: 12.30 p.m.
Date: Saturday 21 July 2012
Location: Metropolitan Police HQ, London

Jack sat alone in the incident room and ran a hot hand through his hair. The two fans were working at maximum capacity, but merely seemed to be circulating the already sticky, sultry air. He'd switched off the whiteboard monitor, the constant humming it gave off already getting underneath his skin. He'd also switched off some of the computers, convinced they were contributing to the uncomfortable heat of the room. Without the artificial glare from the monitors, and with the blinds shut, the room sat in semi-darkness.

A quick glance towards the pinboard at the back of the room caused a small smile to flicker. Pinboards don't hum, he thought. Pinboards don't need plugging in and rebooting. And pinboards definitely don't get overheated.

Jack sighed and turned back towards the stack of paperwork on the desk in front of him. DS Cooper had done a good job of printing everything off for the Patricia Gordon case, plus everything they had on Georgina Dale. It wasn't much. The plastic evidence bag containing the black stiletto shoe was still sitting on the side — its mere presence reminding Jack there could be another victim already.

Only minutes before, he'd put the phone down after a brief conversation with Dr Matthews — and it had done little to lighten his mood. The pathologist had no doubt that the same person was responsible for both killings — despite the lack of trace evidence.

He'd used the words "cold" and "clinical", quickly followed by "clean" and "forensically sterile" — words that no detective wanted to hear. They had to find a way to connect the victims to the killer somehow — but, right now, the trail was ice cold. With no foreign DNA or fibres recovered from either body, the investigation was no further forward than it had been before the post-mortem.

Jack sighed and turned his attention back to Patricia Gordon. DC Cassidy and DS Cooper were both off chasing phone records and CCTV footage, leaving him alone to collect his thoughts. DS Carmichael was nowhere to be seen. To begin with, Jack was relieved by his absence, but then it began to grate on his nerves. The man had been in the building for barely an hour before making some excuse about needing to sort out his ID badge.

And then he was gone.

And Jack had no idea when he would be back.

Jack leafed through the Patricia Gordon paperwork. The new addition to the team wasn't making the greatest first impression.

Not a great impression at all.

* * *

Time: 12.35 p.m.
Date: Saturday 21 July 2012
Location: The Shard, London Bridge Street, London

Leaning against the corner of a brick wall that housed an organic vegetarian bistro, he nursed a takeaway pot of wholewheat noodles with quinoa. Stirring the contents absentmindedly with a biodegradable cardboard fork, he inhaled the vaguely unappetising aroma.

He hadn't wanted noodles.

He hadn't wanted quinoa.

He didn't even know what quinoa was.

Or how to pronounce it.

He'd merely stabbed his finger at the first entry on the takeaway menu, one eye still on the building under construction across the road. Would he like a cardboard fork with his noodles? *"We don't stock plastic due to its impact on the environment,"* he'd been informed when his eyebrows hitched in response.

He agreed to the noodles, and the cardboard fork.

And now he waited.

Pulling the brim of his cap further down across his brow, he shielded his face from any prying eyes. But no one was paying him, or his noodles, any attention. He was just another face in the crowd; just another customer eating his quinoa noodles with a cardboard fork.

The main door to the Shard was flanked by sturdy protective barriers, a large "No Entry" sign hanging at an angle. Although practically complete on the outside, inside there were still some finishing touches necessary before the first tenants could take up occupation. As he watched from the shade of the awning outside the bistro, he saw the main door open, sending a searing flash of reflected sunlight towards him. He held his breath as she exited the smoky mirrored front doors, heading purposefully towards London Bridge Tube station. She had some form of portfolio tucked underneath her arm, hurrying through the general melee of midday office workers escaping from their cages and wide-eyed tourists consulting Tube maps.

Dumping the unappetising and uneaten noodles in a nearby bin, he adjusted his cap and set off in a gentle jog across the street.

Carol.

* * *

Time: 2 p.m.
Date: Saturday 21 July 2012
Location: Metropolitan Police HQ, London

"A press conference, Jack. This afternoon." Chief Superintendent Dougie King eased his ample frame into his chair and nodded at Jack to sit opposite. "Liaise with Pippa in Public Relations — you know the score."

"This afternoon?" Jack dutifully took a seat, his eyebrows hitching. "Doesn't leave us much time to put something together, sir."

"Indeed, Jack. Time is definitely not on our side. With the Opening Ceremony in less than a week, millions of pounds of taxpayers' money is being spent here, there and everywhere. They're saying it's going to be a sight to behold — the best opening ceremony in the history of the Games. There's even talk of James Bond, the Queen and some corgis making an appearance. The mind truly boggles." Dougie King paused. "So, we can't afford for this to become a problem, Jack. For the killer to still be out there. You understand me?"

Jack nodded.

"Then it's a press conference at four o'clock." The chief superintendent inclined his head, indicating to Jack that he was free to go. He caught his DI's eye and gave him a small smile. "Maybe smarten yourself up a bit, though — get that DS of yours to lend you a tie."

Jack returned the half-smile and rose from his chair. He left the chief superintendent's office and made his way downstairs. A press conference. Jack inwardly groaned as he jogged down the steps, two at a time. He hated press conferences with a passion. Detested them. Although acknowledging they were a necessary evil in today's modern world, where social media infiltrated every corner of every person's life, the public ever hungry for the twenty-four-hour hamster wheel of non-stop news, Jack found them nothing more than a gargantuan waste of time. You could never say what you truly wanted to say at a press conference — salient points of the investigation had to be withheld from the public to prevent scores of time-wasters who enjoyed nothing better than clogging up the phone lines.

So what was the point?

Send out a press statement, by all means. But a live press conference on national TV? Jack gave an involuntary shudder as he reached the bottom of the stairs. He ran a finger around the inside of his shirt collar, already feeling the sweat prickling at his skin in anticipation. He'd need to get that tie. And he probably could've done with a shave this morning, he thought, running the same finger over the short, sharp prickles hugging his chin.

Too late now.

He had two hours to come up with a suitably short and uninspiring press release. Plus, he needed to check one of the evidence rooms was ready for the defence lawyers coming to view the unused evidence in the Hansen case; an organised crime and people-trafficking case which was due to start at the Old Bailey in September.

Lost in his own thoughts, Jack rounded the corner and almost collided with DC Amanda Cassidy walking in the opposite direction, carrying a takeaway deli sandwich bag.

"Sorry, guv," she smiled, sidestepping out of his way just in time.

"Amanda, just the person." Jack came to a halt in the corridor and motioned for her to follow him. "Can I borrow you for a minute?"

DC Cassidy paused, eyeing the sandwich in her hand. She then spun round on her heels and followed Jack back the way she'd come. "Of course."

"I need you to help me set up one of the evidence rooms — we've got the defence team coming in later to look at the unused material for the Hansen case."

Cassidy nodded and quickened her step. "Will it be Anthony Saunders? Defence solicitor?" She followed Jack down a small corridor that led to three evidence rooms.

Unlocking the door to the first room, he pushed it open to reveal a tight space packed to the rafters with boxes.

"Saunders? I'm not sure. Probably." Jack stepped into the room and quickly surveyed the contents. There was a small, battered table that'd seen better days pushed up against the far wall. Surrounding it from floor to ceiling were cardboard boxes stacked one on top of the other, each marked with an identification tag and date, and, as far as Jack hoped, arranged in chronological order as set out in the schedule of unused material disclosed to the defence some weeks ago. A copy of the schedule sat on the battered desk. Jack gave it a cursory glance and nodded to himself. "Why?"

"Why?" DC Cassidy raised her eyebrows.

"Saunders. Why are you so interested in whether he's coming?"

Cassidy gave a small chuckle, her eyes sparkling as a broad grin crept across her face. "Anthony Saunders? You really have no idea, do you?" She shook her head, tucking a stray strand of her jet-black hair behind her ear. "He's only just about the hottest-looking defence solicitor there is. *And* I think he's single. You wait until Mary on the front desk clocks him." Cassidy giggled again, watching Jack's bemused expression. "Do you want me to hang on here and greet him? I don't mind." She lifted up her sandwich bag and waggled it in front of Jack. "I'm on my lunchbreak."

Jack felt his own smile twitch and slowly nodded. "OK, you greet our wonder boy when he gets here. But make sure everything's in order in here first. Put paper in the photocopier and suchlike. Check the boxes are all present and correct. They'll be here about half past four. I need to go and pen a press conference. But behave! I'll see you upstairs later."

With that, Jack pressed the key to the evidence room into Cassidy's hand and hurried back out into the corridor. He needed to start work on the damned press conference. Glancing at his watch, he sighed.

He needed to find Pippa.

* * *

Time: 3.45 p.m.
Date: Saturday 21 July 2012
Location: Metropolitan Police HQ, London

DS Carmichael pulled into the rear car park and instinctively checked his rear-view mirror. The place was deserted, save for a lone PC having a sneaky cigarette by the back entrance. Another glance in his mirrors reassured him that he hadn't been followed.

After the initial briefing with Jack and the rest of the team earlier that morning, he'd managed to slip away unseen on the pretext of needing to go and sort out his access badge with HR. Jack had looked mildly irritated, but nodded his acquiescence, having more than enough on his plate to keep him busy. He was unlikely to have noticed his newly acquired DS walking straight past HR and leaving the building.

Switching off the ignition, Carmichael replaced his ID access badge around his neck. It was the same one he'd had before — there never having been any problem with it in the first place. Just a convenient excuse to leave the station unchallenged. A glance at his watch confirmed he was in good time as he exited the car. He'd received a brusque message from Jack a short while ago, requesting his presence with regard to the press conference that was due to take place at four o'clock.

Carmichael smiled to himself. Although the message had been brief and to the point, he could sense the unspoken question that lurked beneath.

Where are you, DS Carmichael? That had been what Jack *really* wanted to say.

I'm right here, Jack.

I'm right here.

Jogging towards the rear entrance, Carmichael opened the door and used his fully functioning ID badge to swipe access to the building. He headed towards the stairs, noticing DC Cassidy leaning against the front reception desk, deep in conversation with another female officer. As he approached, Cassidy swung round and caught his eye.

"Jack wants you upstairs, right away. He's not happy." She nodded towards the ID badge hanging around his neck. "You manage to get your access sorted, then?"

Carmichael flashed her a smile and waggled the badge in front of her. "All sorted, thank you."

With another smile and a brief twinkle in his beady bird-like eyes, he pushed open the double doors and headed towards the stairs.

CHAPTER TEN

Time: 4.15 p.m.
Date: Saturday 21 July 2012
Location: Metropolitan Police HQ, London

Every chair in the conference room was taken. News about the hastily arranged press conference had spread far and wide, rippling through the journalistic community like a stone thrown into a stagnant pond, and it was standing room only. If that.

The air conditioning, if it was even working at all, was struggling to cope with the demand of over a hundred perspiring bodies jostling for position in the cramped media suite. Someone had opened the two side windows in the vain hope of locating some fresh air, but this only allowed more hot and humid air to seep into the already sauna-like conditions.

The main broadsheets and tabloids had secured the best seats towards the front — with sleeves rolled up and expensive digital recording equipment at the ready, they were good to go. The local newspapers and local radio reporters were relegated to the back benches, or standing propped up against the rear wall, most still relying on the trusty pen and paper.

A large TV camera was positioned to the left of the press conference table, which itself was on a slightly raised platform at the front of the room. Jack slid into the middle chair behind the table, flanked by DS Cooper to his left and DS Carmichael to his right. He could feel the hot, bright lights overhead, adding to the already sultry feel of the room. He took a sip of tepid water from the glass in front of him and nodded to Pippa Reynolds, head of PR.

Let's get this over with.

The TV camera began to whirr.

A tall, smartly dressed woman stepped forward. Despite the rising temperature, she was perfectly presented, her long, blonde hair pulled back into a no-nonsense bun. Light makeup dusted over a flawless complexion, and pale green eyes glinted from beneath luscious lengthy lashes. She addressed her waiting audience.

"Good afternoon, ladies and gentlemen. Detective Inspector Jack MacIntosh will now address you. Please keep any questions until the end." With a glance towards Jack, she smiled briefly from perfectly shaped lips, and mouthed the words "good luck" before retreating back into the corner and out of the spotlight.

Jack liked Pippa. They'd gone for a drink a couple of times, although nothing had ever come of it, as was usually the case when he went on a date these days. If it had even been a date. But he liked her company. And, looking out at the sea of expectant faces before him, feeling the palpable tension in the air that was always present at such gatherings, going for a drink with Pippa seemed like a much more attractive option right now.

All eyes now fell on Detective Inspector Jack MacIntosh. Clearing his throat, he ran a finger around the collar of yesterday's shirt and loosened the tie DS Cooper had produced from his desk drawer, then he picked up the single sheet of paper that hosted his hastily prepared notes.

"This is Operation Genevieve. As you will be aware, over the last week, the bodies of two women have been found in London. We are linking their deaths. Our first victim was Patricia Gordon, found on Friday thirteenth July in St James's Park." Jack paused while the large monitor behind him brought up a picture of the forty-five-year-old brunette. "Last seen on Friday sixth July as she left her job as housekeeper at The Briars Residential Care Home. The post-mortem estimates she was killed sometime between six p.m. and midnight on Thursday twelfth July, the day before she was found. Cause of death: strangulation. Yesterday, Friday twentieth July, our second victim, Georgina Dale, was discovered in a quiet corner of Hyde Park." The monitor behind Jack changed to show a photograph of the attractive blonde student. "Last seen at her halls of residence at St James's University, we believe she was killed on or around Thursday nineteenth July, again between six p.m. and midnight. Cause of death, once again, strangulation."

Jack paused again, letting his eyes scan the faces before him. He knew that much of what he was saying would be going out on TV and radio bulletins in time for the teatime news reports, his words appearing in print in newspaper articles hot off the press first thing in the morning. Maybe even front page. He glanced back down at his crib sheet, at the scanty details they had so far.

Just as he was about to continue, a voice cut through the stuffy, stagnant air.

"Are there any links between the two victims? Bearing in mind they were both found in London parks?"

Jack raised his gaze from his crib sheet, searching the many pairs of eyes trained on him, trying to identify the owner of the voice, and the question that he knew would be on everybody's lips. A question Jack knew he couldn't really answer.

"Jonathan," cut in Pippa, stepping forward from behind the TV camera. "All questions at the end, please."

Jack flashed a grateful smile in Pippa's direction, and then nodded at DS Cooper by his side. "Thank you, Jonathan," he replied, quickly catching the eye of the senior crime correspondent from the *Daily Courier*. "DS Cooper here will fill you in on the details we have so far."

Cooper quickly cleared his throat, his cheeks turning a stinging shade of pink as he gripped his own sheet of prepared notes.

"Yes, thank . . . thank you," he stuttered; public speaking was clearly not his thing. "At this present time there is no known link between the two victims, other than the cause of death. But enquiries are continuing."

"So why are the crimes being linked?" persisted the *Daily Courier* reporter, lifting his handheld recording device high above his head to ensure he caught everything that was being said.

Or not being said.

Other recording devices were raised high above heads and shoulders, causing the press conference to take on the look of a pop concert. *All we need now*, thought Jack, *is for them to all start swaying side to side in time with the beat of the air conditioning motor.*

Pippa went to step forward once again, but Jack caught her eye and raised a hand, giving her a quick nod.

"Due to operational constraints," he replied, directing his answer to the whole room but focusing his gaze on the *Daily Courier* reporter, "the reason for linking these two crimes cannot be divulged at this present time."

But the tenacious crime correspondent wasn't giving up that easily. "Is it DNA? Have you found the killer's DNA at both scenes?

Jonathan Spearing pushed his round-rimmed wire-framed spectacles further up onto the bridge of his nose and brushed away the unruly mop of fringe that dressed his forehead. Jack had had several run-ins with him in the past, unsure whether he admired the lean-framed reporter's dogged persistence or whether he found him irritating. He was one of the new breed of investigative reporters that fancied themselves as a detective, something that often made Jack's hackles rise.

"As I've already said, Jonathan, the reason we're linking these crimes cannot yet be divulged publicly." Jack held the reporter's gaze a second or two longer than necessary, affording him a stony stare that let him know to drop that line of questioning.

"So what lines of investigation *are* you pursuing?" This time it was a different journalist, seated towards the back of the room. Jack recognised him as a Sky News reporter.

"There are several active lines of enquiry ongoing at this time, Rob." Jack flashed an exasperated look at Pippa. The chief superintendent wouldn't be pleased at how the carefully constructed press conference had degraded so quickly into a free-for-all Q&A session. Thankfully Dougie King wasn't present, but he would no doubt catch the edited highlights soon enough.

"But you can't divulge what they are for 'operational reasons'?" Rob Haslet edged forwards in his seat, positioning his recording device so it was in Jack's eyeline. Jack afforded the Sky News reporter a strained smile.

"Correct. Although we believe the two women were not known to each other, we would welcome any information from the public as to their last known movements." Jack glanced down at the notes in front of him and tried to steer the conference back on track. "Patricia Gordon was last seen around four o'clock in the afternoon on Friday sixth July leaving work at The Briars Residential Care Home — did anyone see her after this time? Maybe later that evening? Did anyone see her in the company of anyone else?" Jack paused and allowed his eyes to scan the room, watching as reporters scribbled their notes into their notebooks or merely held their recording devices higher to catch Jack's words. Although he despised these rituals with a passion, he knew they could unearth the key to an investigation that would otherwise remain hidden. For that reason, and for that reason only, he continued. "Georgina Dale was last seen at her halls of residence on Thursday twelfth July. Did anyone see her leave? Was she with anyone? Even the smallest of details could be of crucial importance." Jack paused once again as the monitor behind him flashed up with images of both women, side by side. "Contact numbers for the investigation team here at the Metropolitan Police are on our website. Alternatively, information can be given anonymously through Crimestoppers."

Jack folded the piece of paper in front of him in half, and nodded at Pippa that the conference was finished.

"Are there any further questions?" As Pippa stepped forward, several hands shot up into the air.

Jack pointed at a young female reporter, sitting in the second row. "Yes?"

"Rachel Wiseman, the *Independent*." The young reporter's voice had a slight Scottish lilt. "With a serial killer on the loose, what advice are you giving to women who might be out late at night?"

Jack opened his mouth to reply, having anticipated this question would crop up at some point, but instead of his own voice he heard a voice to his right begin to speak.

"I think, Rachel, in the circumstances, women in the capital should be advised to remain vigilant at all times and not venture out alone at night until this murderer is found." DS Carmichael gave the young reporter a smile. "These are extremely dangerous times."

"Are you saying that women shouldn't go out after dark at all?" The reporter stared wide-eyed at Carmichael, thrusting her handheld recording device out in front of her.

Jack felt the hackles at the back of his neck begin to prickle. "I think what DS Carmichael is trying to say is for everyone, not just women, to be sensible and not take any unnecessary risks." He turned and glared at Carmichael. "But what we don't want to do is create any panic." Jack returned his gaze to the floor and pointed at another reporter he knew, standing at the back of the room. "Will?"

"William Goldmyer of the *Telegraph*. What implications does this have for the Olympics? The Opening Ceremony is only six days away."

Another question Jack had been anticipating, and one that the chief superintendent had already briefed him on as to his reply.

"No one is panicking, Will. This investigation is our topmost priority, and we'll be working around the clock until we catch the offender."

"Before the Opening Ceremony?"

"That is certainly our intention, yes."

"But you can't guarantee it?"

Jack paused, and held the reporter's gaze. "Nothing in life is guaranteed, Will, you know that. But what I can do is reassure everyone that we will not stop until the person responsible for these crimes is apprehended."

A reporter next to the *Telegraph*'s William Goldmyer now stepped in. A small, rotund man, dressed in a striped shirt and tie that would have looked more at home on the trading floor of one of the City's stockbroking firms, raised his hand. "With tens of millions of pounds of expected revenue to flood into the capital during the course of the Games, if the killer remains on the loose and people stay away, how will you explain that loss of revenue to the government and the taxpayers of the UK?"

Jack recognised him as an economics reporter for the BBC. He tried to keep the sarcasm from his tone. "My job is to detect crime and bring criminals to justice. I don't work for, or answer to, the Treasury." Several more hands shot into the air, but Jack waved them away and continued. "I think the people of the UK are more concerned about us removing a killer from the streets of London than whether there's an increase in the sale of floppy hats, cycling shorts or burrito wraps. In fact—"

"And on that note, I think we'll leave it there, ladies and gentlemen." Pippa stepped forward to bring the conference to a close, raising her arms to the side to usher the congregation out of the rear doors, something akin to herding cattle. "Full details of the press conference and the contact details for the investigation team will be live on our website shortly. Thank you very much for your time."

Jack remained seated at the table until the last of the reporters had vacated the room. Then he turned to Carmichael.

"What the hell was that all about? The last thing we need to do is create a wave of panic throughout London. What on earth were you thinking?"

Carmichael shrugged. "I just feel it's better to be honest. We've no idea what links these women, and we've no idea who else could be at risk. If any members of my family lived in London, I'd have no hesitation in telling them not to go out after dark."

"Well thankfully, you're not in charge of this investigation, and I . . ." Jack's voice began to rise several notches, but before he could continue his tirade the door to the conference room opened. Pippa popped her head back around the door frame.

"Jack?" She looked hesitantly across the room. "The chief super would like to see you before you clock off. I don't think he's very happy."

* * *

Time: 4.30 p.m.
Date: Saturday 21 July 2012
Location: Metropolitan Police HQ, London

"Hi, DC Amanda Cassidy." Amanda held out a hand towards her visitor, having stowed away her half-eaten roast beef and horseradish sauce deli sandwich under the counter at reception. She hoped the grease from the wrapper wasn't still clinging to her fingers.

"Pleased to meet you, Amanda," replied a deep, gravelly tone. A neatly trimmed white beard enveloped a full, round face with twinkling ice-blue eyes. A crop of equally ice-white hair covered the man's scalp. "John Fortmason."

Amanda felt her hand engulfed in a warm, two-handed handshake, and noticed the gleaming and very expensive-looking cufflinks glinting under the harsh overhead lighting. Sir John Fortmason was a well-known London-based QC, handling both prosecution and defence work, who had recently represented the Greater Manchester Police in a successful prosecution of twelve members of an organised crime gang operating across the North-West. The gang received a record total of 272 years in prison. This time, however, he was working for the defence.

"And this is my instructing solicitor, Anthony Saunders." The eminent QC stepped aside and nodded towards the figure languishing in his shadow.

Cassidy bit her lip as her eyes came to rest on Anthony Saunders.

"Hi, Amanda. Anthony." Anthony Saunders extended a hand which Cassidy grabbed, possibly a little too quickly, marvelling at the softness of his grip. She glanced down and noted the immaculately manicured nails — and absence of wedding ring. His grip was firm and strong, and somehow transmitted a weakness that reached her knees. "But you can call me Tony." Her eyes strayed from his handshake up to a ruggedly handsome face. With a clean-shaven square jaw, and closely cropped dark hair that matched the chocolate-brown eyes that sparkled, a lopsided smile crossed his lips. She could smell the faint aroma of his aftershave lingering in the air between them.

"Nice to meet you both," squeaked Amanda, letting the defence solicitor's hand drop to his side. *Get a grip, Cassidy*, she reminded herself. *Get a grip*. "If you'd like to follow me, I'll take you to the evidence room."

Cassidy turned on her heels and led the two lawyers through the building, turning sharply to the right to reach the corridor that led to the evidence rooms. Unlocking the first door with the key Jack had left her, she snapped on the overhead light and ushered them inside.

"Sorry, no windows, I'm afraid. So it's a bit stuffy. It was the only room available at short notice that was big enough for all the paperwork." She gestured towards the mountain of boxes surrounding them.

"Not a problem at all," replied Sir John, flashing Cassidy another warm smile. "I know things are a little busy around here at the moment." He cast a look towards the boxes and grimaced. "These trafficking cases — they certainly know how to generate the paperwork."

"I hear the press conference is in full swing." Anthony Saunders deposited his shoulder bag onto the floor. "I think you're best off out of it — a messy business by all accounts, those murders. And so close to the Olympics, too. I bet those upstairs are tearing their hair out." He grinned at Cassidy, a dimple forming in his cheek.

DC Cassidy was about to nod and make a comment, but thought better of it. With the press breathing down their necks, the last thing the department needed was a gossip. "There's a fan in the corner if it gets too hot — but it doesn't work all that well." She nodded at the free-standing fan plugged into the wall in the far corner. "Apart from that, it's all yours. The unused material schedule is on the desk, although I'm sure you already have a copy. The boxes should be stacked in order, with the reference numbers on the outside. If you need to make copies of anything, there's a photocopier over here." She pointed to the antiquated machine nestled behind the door. "Other than that, unless I can get you anything, I'll leave you to it."

Anthony Saunders nodded his thanks and strode over to the small table where he began unloading his laptop from his shoulder bag. "Thanks, Amanda," he smiled. "We'll be fine."

Sir John raised a hand to acknowledge his own thanks, while seating himself at the table and reaching for the unused material schedule. With one last look at the broad-shouldered, slim-waisted defence solicitor, Cassidy backed out of the room and closed the door behind her.

Anthony Saunders was in the house.

Tony.

You can call me Tony.

Grinning like a teenager, she started climbing the stairs in search of Jack.

CHAPTER ELEVEN

Time: 5.45 p.m.
Date: Saturday 21 July 2012
Location: Horseferry Road, London

Mac pulled off his motorcycle helmet and took in a gulp of air. Hot, humid, stale air — but it was, at least, air. His hair stuck to his scalp and, as he ran a finger around the inside collar of his leather jacket, he felt a layer of sweat clinging to his skin.

His hand still throbbed beneath his leather glove and the rest of his body felt battered and bruised. He could've taken a week's sick leave, but sick leave meant no pay. And no pay meant no money for the rent. London was an expensive place to live, even in the crappy part of Islington that he called home.

And he needed this job. There were plenty of people lining up to take his place — something his boss seemed to delight in reminding him. He'd been lucky to land the job in the first place, he knew that. His work history could be described as patchy at best — not too many employers looking past the "resident at HMP" section on the CV.

But it was his last delivery of the day.

Thankfully.

Swinging his leg over the back of the motorbike, he retrieved the final package of the day from the courier box on the back. Taking the helmet with him — you never could trust anyone these days, especially in London — he activated the bike alarm from his key fob and disappeared into the building at 111–113 Horseferry Road.

As soon as he stepped over the threshold, he was greeted by a bank of cool air, momentarily stopping him in his tracks.

Heaven.

Standing in the doorway with his eyes closed, he allowed the chill from the air conditioning to wash over his sweat-matted hair and soothe his burning cheeks.

"Can I help you?"

Mac's eyes sprung open at the sound of a pleasant female voice emanating from behind the sleek reception desk. Stepping forward, he brandished the thick, padded brown envelope in his hand.

"Sorry, just enjoying your air conditioning. It's been pretty hot out there today." Mac stepped towards the desk, and was greeted by an equally sleek receptionist. He placed his helmet at his feet and instinctively ran a sweaty hand over his rough, unshaven face. "Package for HLM Recruitment."

"Thank you," the receptionist smiled. "Have a good evening."

Dismissed, Mac left the cool interior of HLM Recruitment and stepped back out into the baptism of fire that was the Horseferry Road on a late Saturday afternoon. The atmosphere was thick and heavy, not a breath of wind to stir the already stagnant air. Traffic was crawling along the street, nose-to-tail, and the odd blast of a horn from a frustrated taxi echoed in the stillness. Weary cyclists weaved in and out of the near-stationary vehicles, some with face masks on to protect them from the hot dust and pollution. Everyone had their windows down, arms hanging out, faces turned to the outside air in the vain hope of catching even the smallest hint of a breeze.

Mac kicked his motorbike off its stand and pushed it towards a nearby zebra crossing. There was only one place he was heading to right now, and it wasn't going to be joining the monotonous stream of creeping traffic back to his flat. He gazed across the road and sniffed the air, the faint aroma of coffee and pastry greeting his nostrils.

* * *

Time: 5.45 p.m.
Date: Saturday 21 July 2012
Location: Metropolitan Police HQ, London

"So, Jack, what was that?" Chief Superintendent Dougie King nodded at Jack to take a seat, sighing as he lowered himself into his own swivel chair. "The press pack getting all hot under the collar — just what we didn't need. God knows what the headlines will be tomorrow."

Jack slipped into the vacant chair and shrugged. "You know what I think of press conferences, sir."

"A necessary evil, Jack, a necessary evil." Chief Superintendent King reached behind him to the sideboard that housed the coffee pot. "Coffee?" Jack shook his head. The chief superintendent put the coffee pot back down and reached for the drawer at the side of his desk, bringing out a half-empty bottle of what looked to Jack like a half-decent malt. "Something stronger?" Jack eyed the bottle but felt his head shake again.

"Best not, sir. Still some work to do this evening."

Chief Superintendent King nodded, and replaced the bottle in his desk drawer with a somewhat regretful look. "I guess you're right." He paused, leaning forward onto the desk and resting his chin on steepled fingers. "So?" Another weighted pause while he studied Jack's face. "Aside from the press conference, how are things shaping up?"

Jack knew the chief superintendent didn't have it easy. Being the first black policeman to rise to this level through

84

the ranks of the Metropolitan Police meant that it hadn't been a smooth ride. There'd been more than a few barricades along the way, and there were still some people intent on barring his progress any further.

But Jack liked him.

And respected him.

So Jack felt he couldn't lie to him.

"It's slow going, sir. There's not a lot to go on, if I'm honest. We've weeks of CCTV to trawl through, plus catching up with the FLOs, visiting the victim's homes. We'll just have to see what that brings."

"But at the moment?"

"It doesn't look good, I'll say that. It's early days but forensics are drawing a blank so far. The crime scenes are clean."

Chief Superintendent King nodded, Jack's answer clearly as he expected. "You're already aware of the added pressure we're under with this case — so I need you to bring in the forensic profiler, Jack."

"Sir, I . . ."

"No buts, Jack. Orders from above." The chief superintendent again raised his eyes heavenwards. "You know how it is. Send everything that you have on to the profiling team. And keep them up to date with any future developments."

"But profiling?" Jack sighed. Another bugbear. The force's profiler. It seemed to him that all police forces in the country were now employing criminal profilers, or criminal psychologists, to solve cases for them. Jack wasn't convinced, finding them more of a hindrance than anything else — their conclusions often being so vague that almost anyone, including half the police force themselves, could be highlighted as a potential suspect. But he wasn't such a dinosaur that he resisted all progress. Slowly, he nodded. "Sir."

"I know how you feel about profilers, Jack. But they can be useful. They've proved invaluable in several recent cases of ours." The chief superintendent paused and caught Jack's doubtful gaze. "At least hear them out. If you don't agree with what they say, then as the senior investigating officer you have the right to disregard it. But we need to be seen to tick that box."

Jack nodded.

He understood box-ticking.

He understood it all too well.

"And where are we on the Hansen case? I understand John Fortmason and the defence team were in today looking at the unused material?"

Jack nodded. "Yes. They might need to come back tomorrow — depends how they get on."

"We need that case to be perfect, Jack. No mistakes. There are some high-profile names on the indictment — it's our best chance at putting some well-known organised crime gang members away for a significant amount of time. I don't want to get to trial only for it all to collapse around our ears."

Jack understood the stakes only too well. One of the capital's biggest organised crime gangs had been infiltrated by an undercover officer, and now they stood a decent chance of putting a lot of the gang out of action for a considerable length of time. Maybe even life.

"I know. It's prepared as well as it can be. The CPS are happy there are no holes in our evidence."

"But we both know John Fortmason is ruthless when he puts on that wig and robe. We can't mess this one up." Chief Superintendent King picked up a paperweight, turning it over in his hands. "We might not have managed to get Joseph Geraghty — but if we can get his second-in-command and underlings off the streets then it'll be a job well done. What's the latest on him? Geraghty? Anyone know where he is?"

Jack shrugged. "Intelligence says he went abroad at the tail end of 2010 and he's not been seen since. Commands all his enterprises from some beach in Cuba, by all accounts. I'm sure he'll be happy enough to let his henchmen take the rap on this one — nothing ever sticks to him. He's not called the Teflon Man for nothing."

"Quite. Well, keep me up to speed. And what about DS Carmichael?" Chief Superintendent King settled the paperweight back down on his desk. "Is he settling in and helping out?"

Jack let out a breath. "I didn't like his input into the press conference, I will say that. The press will go to town over his comments that we advise all women in London not to go out alone. Talk about inciting panic. And he rushed off again straight after the conference — he's barely been here at all today."

The chief superintendent nodded. "I hear you, Jack. But let him settle in. Give him something constructive to do — keep him busy. Let him prove his worth." There was a pause before he continued. "But keep an eye on him."

Jack frowned. "You don't trust him?"

"It's not that." The chief superintendent shook his head. "I don't know the man, Jack. Orders came from above. But you know as well as I do — nobody trusts a cuckoo."

CHAPTER TWELVE

Time: 5.55 p.m.
Date: Saturday 21 July 2012
Location: Metropolitan Police HQ canteen, London.

"Good work at the press conference, boss." DS Cooper handed Jack a bottle of iced water from the fridge, and they both slipped into chairs close to one of the open windows at the back of the canteen. "What do you think tomorrow's headlines will be?"

Jack took the bottle, instantly ripping off the top and taking a long gulp. "Depends which news outlet you're talking about. The tabloids will probably lead with how we've no idea what we're doing, then they'll proceed to instil panic on the streets of London. The BBC will probably focus on how our inability to catch the killer will cost the UK taxpayer millions of pounds in lost revenue, and Sky will most likely claim we're keeping vital information from the public."

"Which we are." Cooper pushed a packet of crisps across the Formica table, remnants from its last occupants still visible on the sticky, plastic covering. Some random grains of salt. A blob of ketchup. A pile of stale crumbs.

Jack pulled a paper napkin from the metal box on the table and brushed the crumbs and salt away, smearing the ketchup stains. "Which we are indeed, Cooper. We are indeed." Jack took another swig of water and tossed the crumpled napkin onto a neighbouring table, already piled high with dirty plates and mugs. "The shoes are key evidence. We need to keep their existence away from the press for as long as possible. If anyone rings in with information about the shoes — we could have our killer."

"Something only the killer knows." Cooper nodded and twisted the cap off his bottle of cola. Bubbles instantly sprayed out of the top and then ran down the sides, covering his fingers, and spilling across the table.

"Exactly." Jack threw a couple of paper napkins in the direction of his DS. "Who've we got on liaison duty with the family of Georgina?"

DS Cooper wiped the stickiness from his fingers and reached into his jacket pocket for his notebook. He flipped over a few pages. "DC Rachel Baxter."

Jack nodded. "And for Patricia?"

"DC James Anderson."

"Good." Jack knew both DCs well, and knew they were highly experienced FLOs — family liaison officers — a vital source of information and support for the families concerned and an extremely important connection to the investigating team. "Let's catch up with them both first thing in the morning, see what they have. They'll need to work closely together on this one. Let's see if we can uncover anything that the two victims had in common."

DS Cooper pocketed his notebook. "I'll put in a call first thing. In the meantime, what should be top of our list? Amanda's already set up a trawl of the CCTV cameras around both locations where the bodies were found."

"Good. That's a top priority. Draft in some other bodies if we need the manpower. The Chief says there's no limit on resources. And get them to check CCTV from where the victims were last seen, too — in and around the care home and St James's University."

Cooper nodded. "Will do. Anything else?"

"Well, I think it's high time we caught up with our friend, DS Carmichael. Don't think I didn't notice him disappearing off site in the middle of the day — some ruse about his access badge. I don't buy it — I don't buy it for a second." Jack rose from his seat, picking up the water bottle and packet of crisps. "And then he did another disappearing act as soon as the press conference was over. Not great going on your first day in the job. I've got my eye on him. Let's see if he's made it back and put him to work. We've a potential victim number three out there somewhere, the owner of our black stiletto shoe. We need to find her — and fast."

* * *

Time: 5.55 p.m.
Date: Saturday 21 July 2012
Location: Isabel's Café, Horseferry Road, London

The enticing aroma of coffee and pastries outside was increased fourfold as soon as Mac stepped over the threshold into Isabel's café. He'd left his motorbike resting inside an alleyway several doors down, locking it to a drainpipe. Would it concern him if it got stolen? At this precise moment in time, the answer would be no. All he wanted to do was get these hot leathers off.

The café was empty and Mac headed for a battered-looking armchair by the window. He was still keeping an eye out for the idiot who'd knocked him off his bike yesterday — as unlikely as it was that he'd see him again.

"Hello again!" Mac turned towards the voice, finding Isabel heading his way. Her flushed face had a hot sheen to it, and she wiped her hands on a tea towel as she approached. "How's the hand?"

"It's good, thanks." Mac waved his gloved hand in the air. "Good as new. Thanks for scraping me off the tarmac like that."

"Oh, it's nothing," smiled Isabel, fanning her face with the tea towel. "All part of the service. It's a hot one today, isn't it?"

"It certainly is." Mac started to peel off his leather jacket. "Do you mind if I . . . ?" He gestured towards the rest of his leathers. "It's baking in all this stuff."

"Of course, of course. Feel free." Isabel's cheeks seemed to flush a deeper shade of pink as she backed away. "I'll get you a coffee in the meantime. Cappuccino with extra sugar, wasn't it?"

Mac nodded, impressed that Isabel had remembered his coffee order from yesterday. "That'd be great, thanks." Standing by the window, he began to shed his leathers.

"Stop gawping!" hissed Sacha, bustling out of the kitchen with a fresh tray of clean cutlery. "I can see you, you know!"

Isabel turned towards the coffee machine, her cheeks scarlet. "I don't know what you mean!"

"It's a pity he's got jeans on underneath," whispered Sacha, nudging Isabel's elbow as she passed. "It's a bit like that advert, isn't it? The one with that man in the launderette."

Isabel stifled a grin and set about making Mac's cappuccino. "Behave! The poor man's hot!"

"He is that," agreed Sacha, her eyes twinkling as she disappeared back inside the kitchen.

Drink ready, Isabel carried the mug across to Mac who was by now settled into the armchair, gazing through the window to the street outside. "Here you go — do you want anything to eat?" Isabel perched on the edge of a nearby sofa, and nodded towards the laminated menu on the table. "We've probably got some pastries that need eating up before we close — no charge."

Mac took hold of the mug but shook his head. "No, not right now, thanks. This'll do fine."

"You've been back working today, then?" Isabel nodded at the discarded bike leathers. "You sure you were up to it? That was some knock you took."

Mac took a grateful sip of his coffee, devouring the creamy taste. "I've had worse, believe me. Bit sore, but I need the work. Could do without this heat, though."

"They say it's here for a few more days yet — something to do with the jet stream."

"Great, that's all we need." Mac settled back in the armchair and sighed. "Jack was right — you really do make the best coffee for miles. And I should know — I cover most of London on my bike every day."

Isabel felt her cheeks warm once again. "Thank you — it's nice of you to say so. I put in a lot of research before I opened!"

"How long have you been here?" Mac looked around the café, taking in the bookcases stuffed full of books and other reading material. "It's a great idea — something a bit different to your usual coffee shop."

"I hope so — I got the idea from a café I found in Naples. I've not been open all that long — only since April. So I'm still learning!"

"It must cost a lot to run — the rents along here must be through the roof." Mac hesitated, his mug hovering in front of his face. "Sorry. I don't mean to pry."

"Oh, don't worry, I don't mind. And yes, the rent is high — extortionately high. I managed to strike a good deal but it's still a huge strain on the finances. Having the art studio at the back helps a lot." Isabel turned towards the archway that led towards the studio. "I don't think I'd manage if I didn't have the income from that. Patrick's my lifeline." She nodded towards the sandy-haired artist who was now making his way towards them.

"See you tomorrow, Isabel." Patrick tucked a sketchbook under his arm as he headed for the door. "I've got a long night ahead of me . . ."

"Good luck," smiled Isabel. "I was just telling Mac how you've really saved my life."

Patrick flapped a hand in the air. "Nonsense." He paused, and cocked his head to the side. "Mac, you say? You must be Scottish with a name like that."

Mac smothered a smile behind his mug. "Not that I know of. It's Mac, as in MacIntosh. Bit of a nickname."

"It's Jack's brother," explained Isabel. "The policeman who comes in from time to time."

"Ah," nodded Patrick, pulling open the door and making the bell jangle. "Well, I'll leave you both to it. I've a Tube to catch."

Once Patrick had departed, Mac turned towards Isabel. "I take it you've not always been a coffee shop owner, then?"

"Good God, no," laughed Isabel. "This is the first time I've ever done anything like this. I'm making it all up as I go along."

"So, what made you decide to do it?"

Isabel paused. "I'm not really sure," she eventually answered. "I went travelling across America, and then some of Europe — sampled an awful lot of coffee in that time. Some good, some bad. And then I just decided I needed to take a risk or two with my life, before I got too old. I sold my house — well, my family home down in Surrey — and poured all the cash into this place."

Mac sunk half of his coffee in one go. "Well, it's great. You should be proud."

"So, what about you? You always been a motorbike courier?"

Mac kept the mug in front of his face, lowering his eyes to the rim. Suddenly he started to feel warm and sticky once again. "Not exactly," he managed to reply.

Feeling the coffee swirling around in his stomach, Mac placed the half-drunk mug back down on the table.

And there it was.

Just when he felt he was starting to get on with things, live an ordinary life, his past came back to slap him round the face. As he desperately searched for some suitable half-truth to tell Isabel about what he'd been doing with his life up to now — anything to avoid having to tell her about his past — Sacha breezed across the café and turned the sign on the door to "Closed".

"Everything shipshape in the kitchen ready for tomorrow." She turned towards Isabel and gave her a wink. "Why don't you two disappear upstairs with your coffees and let me and Dom lock up?"

A fresh flush of colour flooded Isabel's cheeks.

"And there's a plate of pastries that need eating up — otherwise they'll just go to waste. Go on, shoo!" Sacha flicked a tea towel in Isabel's direction. "And you, young man. You make sure Isabel puts her feet up. She's been working solidly since five o'clock this morning. I'll fix you some fresh coffee to take up."

CHAPTER THIRTEEN

Time: 6.30 p.m.
Date: Saturday 21 July 2012
Location: Isabel's Café, Horseferry Road, London

Isabel's flat above the café might have been small, but it was light and airy. Mac sat himself by the open window and closed his eyes, feeling the welcome breeze from the full-size floor fan behind him. The sound of the busy street below filtered in like a gentle wave rippling on a sandy beach, and it was on the verge of lulling him into a light sleep when Isabel interrupted his meditative state, placing a tray of iced coffee and pastries down on the small wicker coffee table by his side.

"Nodding off?" She handed Mac a long, tall glass of iced heaven.

Mac prized his eyelids open and accepted the glass, gratefully. "Sorry, It's so nice up here."

"I hope you don't think I make a habit of this." Isabel sat herself next to Mac on the sofa, picking up her own glass of iced coffee. "Bringing strange men up to the flat."

Mac smiled, the skin around his eyes crinkling. It was then that Isabel saw it — the resemblance to Jack. When she'd seen them together yesterday, she'd never have put them down as being related, let alone brothers. But now, up close, she could see it. It was something in the eyes — that warm hazel hue — and the angle of the jaw and chin.

"I'm sure you don't," replied Mac, taking a sip of his drink.

They sat in comfortable silence for a few minutes, sipping their coffees and listening to the street outside winding down for the day. Mac glanced around the flat, noting yet another bookcase rammed with books — paperback, hardbacks and everything in between. His gaze came to rest on a silver-edged photo frame in the centre of the bookcase.

"Is that you?" Mac nodded towards the photograph.

Isabel's eyes flickered towards the picture, slowly nodding. "Yes, it was on my birthday — I was five."

"They must be really proud of you." Mac took another long sip of chilled coffee. "Your parents. I'm assuming that's them in the picture?"

Isabel felt her stomach momentarily clench. She nodded. "They died not long after that photo was taken."

What colour had been in Mac's face instantly drained. "Oh my God, I'm so sorry. I just didn't think. How crap of me."

Isabel's face softened. "It's OK. Really. It was a long time ago now."

"Maybe, but it never really leaves you, does it? And I *am* really sorry — putting my size nines in like that."

Isabel leaned forward, nudging the plates of pastries across the table. "Finish them off. Or take them home with you. They'll only go to waste."

Mac reached for a pain au chocolat but made no attempt to eat it. "I understand — about losing your parents. I know how it feels."

Isabel saw the muscles in his jaw tense. "You do?"

Mac nodded. "Well, maybe not quite the same. My mum died when I was two. Jack was four. We never knew our father, so she was all we had in the whole world." Mac continued staring at the pastry in his hands. "We went into care after that."

"I'm so sorry, I had no idea. Jack never said."

Mac wasn't sure how well Isabel knew his brother — but he wasn't surprised that Jack hadn't imparted something so personal. "He found her. She'd killed herself — Jack found her hanging from a light fitting in the kitchen of our old house."

Isabel's hand flew to her mouth. "Oh my goodness. That's awful. I truly had no idea."

"Well, I'm sure he doesn't go around talking about it." Mac picked off a section of pastry and popped it into his mouth. "Keeps his cards very close to his chest, does Jack."

"I hope I'm not speaking out of turn but, yesterday — I got the feeling you two hadn't seen each other in a while?"

Mac swallowed, the rich buttery taste of the pain au chocolat reminding him he hadn't eaten since early that morning — a hastily devoured toasted sandwich at a greasy spoon on the Old Kent Road. "It's been a while," he acknowledged, wiping his mouth with the back of his hand and draining the rest of his coffee. "We got separated in care — sent to different families. I eventually ended up in a children's home."

"That must've been tough." Concern edged Isabel's tone and she resisted the urge to reach out and offer Mac a hug. She had to remind herself she barely knew him — although she hadn't felt so comfortable in another person's presence in a long time. She was very quickly feeling like she could tell him anything.

"Maybe." Mac tugged at another piece of the pastry. "Although I'm sure I made life a lot tougher than it really needed to be. I have a special talent in that regard — making things worse." He tried to laugh but the sound that came out was hollow.

"I'm sure that's not true."

"Oh, believe me, it's true." Mac's eyes darkened. "Jack struggles, I know he does. We might not have spoken much over the years, but what happened that night has stayed with him. Changed him. And when I sit and think about things, I have this overwhelming feeling of guilt."

"Guilt?" Isabel frowned. "Why guilt?"

She saw again the haunted sadness behind Mac's eyes. "The fact that it wasn't me. That it wasn't me that found her."

"But you said you were only two?"

"I know it doesn't make any sense, but it doesn't stop me feeling guilty. Jack has had to deal with everything about that night on his own." Mac turned to look out of the window. "I don't remember anything — nothing from that night at all. Not really. Sometimes I don't think I even remember her — Mum."

"But you can't blame yourself, surely?"

Mac swallowed back the chuckle in his throat. "I blame myself for lots of things. I've had a long time to think about it. Sometimes I feel so useless — I can't share how he feels, because I don't feel it. I don't feel the same sense of loss that he does. Sometimes I just feel cheated — which seems so selfish. But I don't remember life with her — I just remember life without her. Being shunted from pillar to post, people shouting — usually at me — feeling like I was a burden that needed sorting. A problem that needed to be dealt with. I just ended up feeling angry the whole time."

"Angry at who?"

"Everyone. At Mum. At Jack. I blamed everyone for what happened to us. I needed it to be someone's fault that my life went down the toilet. Mum's fault for leaving us. Jack's fault for — I don't know, just being Jack. I was a mess."

"Shit happens, Mac. Sometimes you just need to accept it and move on. Tomorrow's always another day."

Mac turned his head away from the window and placed the half-eaten pastry back on the table. "Sorry. It's been a crap day — a long, hot crap day. I've been sweating buckets and feeling irritable all day. You don't need me whining on."

The smile returned to Isabel's face, and she resisted the urge to once again touch Mac's knee. "Don't worry about it. You're entitled to a crap day now and again. That's what my coffee and pastries are for. A well-known antidote for a crap day."

After a couple more minutes of comfortable silence, Mac got to his feet. "I think I'd better be on my way. The traffic back to Islington can be a nightmare some nights. And it looks like someone here needs feeding."

Livi jumped up on the sofa and began bobbing her head against Isabel's arm. "I think you might be right." Isabel began to scratch the tabby cat beneath her chin. "Drop by anytime. You'll always be welcome. And same goes for that brother of yours."

Mac managed a smile. "I'll let him know. In fact, I might head over to his now, see if he fancies a takeaway." He looked at his watch. He had no idea what hours a detective inspector worked, but guessed he'd soon find out. Talking to Isabel like this — opening up far more than any prison or probation counsellor had ever managed to get him to do — had made him think. Maybe reaching out and building a few bridges back into his brother's life wasn't a bad place to start.

Slipping back into his leather trousers, he grabbed his biker's jacket, helmet and gloves from the floor and headed for the stairs that led back down to the café. As he reached the door, he saw Isabel's laptop resting on a sideboard. "Hey. What's this?" He nodded at the open screen.

Isabel followed his gaze and gave an embarrassed chuckle. "Ah, that's nothing. Just a bit of fun to keep me amused in the evenings."

Mac studied the screen more closely, seeing it was open on a website called "London Life", the page displaying a number of passport-sized photographs of men. "Is this a *dating* website?" He looked at Isabel, unable to mask the smile playing on his lips. "Really?"

Isabel's cheeks tinged pink. "It's a *friendship* site. You don't have to meet anyone if you don't want to. You can just chat. Make new friends."

Mac placed his helmet at his feet and shrugged into his heavy leather jacket, feeling his skin start to overheat immediately. "Looks like a dating site to me. Surely you don't need something like that? You meet people all day long."

"I *see* people all day long. I don't actually *meet* them. I don't get to know anyone — short of how they take their coffee and whether they prefer white or brown sugar. Life can be a bit lonely at times." Isabel hovered in the doorway. "Anyway, I'm just chatting to people, nothing to get excited about. Doubt I'll even meet up with anyone. Now, come on, let's get you home and this cat fed."

* * *

Time: 6.50 p.m.
Date: Saturday 21 July 2012
Location: Metropolitan Police HQ, London

Jack pulled the blinds tightly closed, cutting out the last of the sinking sun's rays. He left the window open — for all the good it would do.

"So, where are we with the CCTV?" Jack directed his gaze at DC Cassidy. Looking cool and unflustered in the searing heat, sporting a short-sleeved tailored shirt over a lightweight summer skirt, she stood up from her chair and reached over to take the remote for the interactive whiteboard. Jack inwardly groaned, glancing briefly at the lost and forlorn pinboard still propped up at the back of the room.

The whiteboard hummed and sprang into life, showing a road map of London.

"We're running the CCTV tapes for this area here, around location number two — the south-east corner of Hyde Park." Cassidy clicked the remote and a large red circle appeared on the screen, encircling the location of the discovery of Georgina Dale's body and the surrounding streets. "We've taken a good number of streets in each direction, to see what we can find. I've got a team of three PCs looking at that right now."

"And location number one?" Jack perched himself on the edge of a desk.

Cassidy once again clicked the remote and a different road map appeared, with a different red circle. "The locations aren't that far apart — so some of the CCTV cameras will overlap. Patricia Gordon was found at the northern side of St James's Park, so we're checking all routes to the east and west. I've another team of three PCs on this one."

Jack nodded towards the maps. "Can we make sure they also check a good twenty-four to forty-eight hours before and after the finding of each of the bodies. Whoever this killer is, he must've been looking for a suitable dump site prior to disposing of the bodies. If nothing unusual shows up forty-eight hours before, increase the time frame. And we know some offenders revisit the scenes of their crimes — let's keep up an active log for the hours after the finding of the bodies, too. I'm guessing we're looking for a van, or a vehicle large enough to carry a body in the boot."

Cassidy nodded and made a quick note in her notebook.

"Anything more from the post-mortem on both victims?"

DS Cooper stood up this time and took hold of the remote control.

"Both victims were strangled with what looks like a ligature of some kind." Cooper clicked the remote and the screen was filled with the post-mortem pictures of both victims. The pictures looked almost identical. The delicate skin around the neck of each victim truncated by a thin, yet violent streak of dark purple and crimson bruising.

Jack studied both photographs. "Definitely a ligature? No chance of any finger marks?"

Cooper shook his head. "Dr Matthews was pretty conclusive in his report on both victims, boss. Definitely strangulation by ligature, not by hand."

Jack nodded, thoughtfully. "OK, any other similarities that we've missed?"

Cooper again clicked the remote control and two different photographs filled the screen. "No other similarities except that both seemed to have these abrasions around their ankles. Patricia Gordon's right ankle, the left ankle on Georgina Dale."

Jack remembered reading about this in both post-mortem reports. "Restraints, then. So he abducts them, keeps them restrained somewhere, before strangling and then dumping them." DS Cooper clicked off the whiteboard.

"Amanda, I'd like you to go and see both FLOs first thing tomorrow, spend some time with them. See what they've managed to come up with about both victims' lifestyles. See if they have anything even remotely in common, no matter how small." Jack paused and turned his head slightly towards DS Carmichael, who'd just breezed back into the building. "And take DS Carmichael with you. Unless he has something better to do."

"We'll get onto it first thing." Cassidy hid her expression behind her coffee cup.

"Are you involving the profiler?" DS Cooper glanced up at Jack. "I heard a rumour."

Jack grimaced. "Good news seems to travel fast, I see. And yes, it seems we have to. Orders from above. I'm sending everything across tonight."

"And what will you be doing, Detective Inspector?" Since arriving minutes before, DS Carmichael had been sitting quietly at the back of the room, coolly watching proceedings without comment. He looked down his beak-like nose at Jack, his beady eyes watching every move. "You seem to have allocated jobs to everyone else, I see."

Jack felt himself bristling as he clenched his teeth. He held Carmichael's gaze for several seconds before replying. "DS Cooper and I will be focusing on the shoe left at the second dumping site. Unless I'm mistaken, we've a potential victim number three out there. We need to find the owner of that shoe."

"I see." DS Carmichael rose from his chair and brushed non-existent specks of dust from the lapels of his expensively cut suit. "And after you've finished playing Cinderella?"

Jack felt his hackles rise even further, the heavy sultriness of the air in the room edging him closer to boiling point with every word escaping the detective sergeant's thin mouth. Clenching his fists behind his back, Jack addressed the newest member of the team. "We'll meet back here at four o'clock tomorrow afternoon. I want an update on the mobile phone records and the CCTV. Anything urgent, get me on my mobile beforehand."

Carmichael nodded slowly and then moved towards the door. "Well, if that's all, I'll make a move. The landlady of the hotel I'm staying in will be preparing dinner shortly." With that, he turned on his well-polished heels and left the room.

"Cooper?" Jack stared at the closed door behind the freshly departed detective sergeant.

"Yes, boss?"

"Find out all you can on why our friend DS Carmichael has been dumped on us."

"Will do."

"Discreetly, mind. See who's willing to talk back at his old station in Sussex. Coppers don't get farmed out to other areas for no reason. I want to know why they don't want him on their patch — and why he's turned up on ours."

CHAPTER FOURTEEN

Time: 7.10 p.m.
Date: Saturday 21 July 2012
Location: Metropolitan Police HQ, London

DS Carmichael swung out of the rear car park and headed out onto the almost deserted road. If anyone had been watching, they would've noted that his chosen route was in the opposite direction to his supposed hotel lodgings.

But nobody was watching.

Nobody was paying Detective Sergeant Robert Carmichael even the slightest attention.

He pulled the ID badge from around his neck and stowed it in the glove compartment. Where he was going, it wouldn't be wise to announce you were part of the Metropolitan Police Service.

No, that wouldn't do at all.

The traffic was light for a Saturday evening, and he made good progress.

Which was good — he had a busy night ahead of him.

* * *

Time: 7.15 p.m.
Date: Saturday 21 July 2012
Location: Horseferry Road, London

Leaning against the low-rising wall, he took a long drag on the hand-rolled cigarette dangling from the corner of his mouth. Cocking his head to one side, he stared across the road towards Isabel's café.

Yesterday had been close — he'd been on the verge of going into the café and finally seeing her in the flesh after all this time. But something had stopped him. Now wasn't the right time. He needed to be patient.

And then that stupid motorbike rider had got in his way. Before he knew what was happening, she'd rushed out of the café and headed in his direction. He'd had to be quick, slipping away and disappearing out of sight before she saw him.

But it'd been close.

Pushing himself off the wall, he watched as an elderly lady approached — out walking with her rat-like dog in the sultry evening air. The tiny, yapping bundle of energy strained on its leash, making a beeline for his feet — sniffing and snorting at his open-toed sandals. He fought back the urge to give the snapping dog a swift kick as he felt its drooling tongue lapping at his toes. Instead he maintained his plastic smile and inclined his head towards the elderly lady, who was trying her best to shoo the dog along, her arthritic limbs no doubt protesting wildly.

"Good evening," he greeted the woman through gritted teeth, as she tottered towards him. Her upper back was hunched forwards at such an angle that it made her appear a foot or so shorter than she actually was. He could smell her lavender scent already, and the hairspray that caked her blue-rinse hairstyle into its rock-hard shape. Two patches of inexpertly applied blusher and a smear of pink lipstick completed the look.

"Come on, Bertie," she croaked, the opening of her mouth causing crater-like wrinkles to appear either side.

"Leave that poor gentleman's feet alone. I'm very sorry." She looked up from her hunched frame, giving a smile through cracked lips.

"No problem," he replied, stepping to the side to escape the attention of the four-legged saliva machine below. "He's very sweet," he added, not meaning a word of it.

Bertie was eventually dragged away to continue his evening walk, leaving him to take one last look at the café before heading back towards the Underground station.

Another time, Isabel.

Another time.

* * *

Time: 8.30 p.m.
Date: Saturday 21 July 2012
Location: A cellar in London

Hannah watched, curiously, as the woman was dragged across the stone floor of the cellar to the bare mattress opposite, her body as limp as a child's ragdoll. She didn't make a sound, or even dare to breathe, watching him fasten the chain around the woman's ankle.

She tried to think back to when she herself had first arrived. How long ago was it now? One day? Two days? More? The eternal darkness and silence made each minute seem to last a lifetime. No day. No night. Minutes, hours, days just drifting in and out of her consciousness, merging into one.

But one thing she did remember was, when she arrived, she hadn't been alone.

There'd been someone else in the cellar as she took her own first drugged, stumbling steps across the cold, damp floor. She remembered squinting through the darkness to find a pair of wide, doleful eyes peering back out at her through the gloom. At first, Hannah wasn't sure who or what the eyes belonged to. Was it even human? Was it an animal?

The owner of the eyes didn't make a move or utter a sound, and Hannah began to wonder if she were hallucinating, seeing things that weren't really there. He'd drugged her; she knew that much. Her body felt strangely limp, her brain fogged and cluttered.

But then the eyes had spoken. Hesitant at first, and with a voice so quiet it was barely above a faint whisper. "Georgie," the voice had murmured. "My name is Georgie."

But then Georgie had gone.

Just like that, she'd been released from her chained restraints and taken from the room.

And Georgie hadn't returned.

Hannah continued to watch as he placed a fresh bottle of water by the woman's side. As he did so, he muttered something under his breath, in such a hushed tone Hannah couldn't make out the words. As he turned towards her, she averted her gaze, not wanting to look into those eyes.

Leaving the woman's limp form on the bare mattress, he padded silently across the stone floor towards Hannah. She shrank further underneath her blanket and closed her eyes, holding her breath and pretending to be asleep. It was always better if she pretended to be asleep.

"There, there," he whispered. "You sleep tight, Jess." Hannah heard the sound of water being trickled into the empty bottle by her mattress, but firmly kept her eyes clamped shut. After several seconds of keeping the air within her lungs, she heard the cellar door being pulled shut and the key turned in the lock. She exhaled gratefully, pulled the blanket further around her body and let a silent tear slide down her cheek.

CHAPTER FIFTEEN

Time: 9.30 p.m.
Date: Saturday 21 July 2012
Location: Kettle's Yard Mews, London

Jack left the living room curtains open to allow the faint evening breeze to waft through the open window. At least it was cooling down now that the roasting sun had slipped behind the horizon, turning the skies into a mesmerising streaked light show of vivid pinks, purples and dusky oranges. He'd left the window open all day; if a determined burglar really wanted to get inside, then he'd have to scale a two-storey building in full view of the whole street. Policeman or no policeman, Jack couldn't face another sticky, humid night.

"Coffee?" Mac snapped on the small recessed lights that shone above the kitchen sink. He placed the remains of the Chinese takeaway he'd picked up from around the corner onto the worktop while reaching for the kettle.

Jack nodded and collapsed into the comfort of the sofa. "You might need to check if there's milk in the fridge, though."

Mac pulled the door of the fridge open and rummaged inside. "Hmmm, no milk, brother."

"I had a feeling I might've used the last of it this morning." Jack loosened his tie and put his feet up on the small table. "Sorry. You'll have to take it black."

Mac grimaced. "Beer?" He raised a questioning eyebrow at Jack, while eyeing the row of beer bottles in among a solitary egg and slab of cheese.

"Beer," agreed Jack.

Mac pulled out two bottles of Budweiser from the fridge, snapping the lids off with the bottle opener he spied lying conveniently by the side of the kettle. He brought the bottles over to the table along with the cartons of Chinese takeaway. It'd been his idea to grab a takeaway after he'd left Isabel's earlier. Not fancying the journey back to Islington until the heat had died down, he took the plunge and messaged Jack — suggesting a Chinese on the way home. To his surprise, Jack had agreed, but made him wait while he finished whatever it was that kept a detective inspector so busy.

Passing Jack a beer, Mac sat down and took a long gulp from his own bottle, feeling the ice-cold liquid slip down his throat and quench the thirst that'd built up on the drive over. "How's it going?" He nodded at Evelyn Riches' business card, propped up against the half-empty bottle of Glenfiddich. "I take it you're in therapy again?"

Jack took a swig from his bottle. "Had a session this morning."

"You going back again?" Although Mac hadn't been in Jack's life for a while, he'd been well aware of his brother's stop-start reputation with therapists.

Jack gave a non-committal shrug. "I might. She was different. Not like the others."

"For what it's worth, I think you should. Go back, I mean. Give it another try."

Jack continued to sip his beer, his own mind still undecided.

"I went back to the café today — the one where I had my accident."

Jack's eyebrows hitched over the rim of the bottle. "Oh? Was Isabel there?"

Mac nodded. "I just wanted to say thank you for scraping me off the road. She told me about her parents."

"Her parents? What about them?"

"You don't know?"

"Stu — I pop in now and again for coffee. We might chat for a bit but we don't exchange in-depth discussions about our private lives. I've no idea what you're talking about."

"I just thought maybe, you and her — you know."

Jack's eyebrows raked even higher. "Me and Isabel?" He couldn't help the smile tugging at the corners of his mouth. "You *really* don't know me very well, do you, Stu?"

"Everyone needs someone in their life, Jack." Mac glanced around at the evidence of Jack's bachelor existence. "Even you."

Jack pushed the thought aside. "So, what about her parents? What did she tell you?"

"That they died — when she was little. I felt kind of, I don't know, connected to her after she said that. She knows what it feels like. She understands."

"She's a good person, Stu. There's not many of them about." Jack got to his feet. "You fancy a coffee before you head off?"

Mac shook his head and made a face. "Not without milk, no."

Jack took one look at the pile of paperwork sitting by the side of the coffee table and decided to go and fill the kettle. The Hansen case. He'd brought a few files home with him — if he was going to have another sleepless night he may as well make it a productive one.

"You working tonight?" Mac nodded at the paperwork as Jack came and sat back down.

"Just a bit. We've a big people-trafficking case going to trial in a few months — needs to be watertight. No room for errors." Jack could almost hear the chief superintendent's words echoing round his head. Picking up the files, he stacked them up on top of the table. As he did so, several sheets slipped out and fell to the floor.

Mac bent down to scoop them up, and as he went to place them back on the table, he caught sight of the topmost photograph. A frown instantly creased his brow. "Who's this?"

Jack gathered up the loose papers and slipped them back inside one of the files. "Sorry. You shouldn't have seen that."

"Yeah, but who is it?"

Jack hesitated, considering whether he was crossing any lines of privacy or confidentiality — but the guy's face was one of the most recognised in organised crime circles in the capital, if not further afield. It'd appeared in the newspaper more times than Jack wished to mention. "His name is Joseph Geraghty. He heads up one of the biggest organised crime gangs London has ever seen. Teflon Man, we call him."

"Teflon Man?"

"Nothing sticks. No matter what we do, no matter how much intel we have on him, we never get to the point of having enough evidence to charge him with anything. He lives a charmed life. Gets away with murder — literally." Jack heard the kettle switch off and went to pour himself a strong black coffee. "This trial starts in September — several members of his gang are facing charges of people-trafficking and drug running. We can't get anywhere near him, but at least some of his goons stand a chance of being hauled off the streets for a while. He'd be the icing on the cake, but we've no idea where he is."

"Well, I do."

Jack returned to the sofa with his coffee. "How can you possibly know where he is, Stu?"

"Because that nutter knocked me off my bike outside the café yesterday."

Jack almost dropped his coffee. "He did *what*?"

"Knocked me off my bike. Like I said. Came running out across the road, not looking where the hell he was going, and made me swerve into that bloody bollard. Then the tosser legged it."

CHAPTER SIXTEEN

Time: 10.15 p.m.
Date: Saturday 21 July 2012
Location: Kettle's Yard Mews, London

Jack leaned against the window frame and watched Mac pull away from the kerb. The throaty sound of the motorbike engine carried effortlessly through the still night air.

Joseph Geraghty.

The news hit Jack like a bolt from the blue. Was it just a coincidence that the head of the Hansen gang was back in the country just months before one of the biggest trials was due to start? A trial where several of his own were facing the prospect of lengthy jail terms?

Jack wasn't a fan of coincidences.

We need that case to be perfect, Jack. No mistakes.

I don't want to get to trial only for it all to collapse around our ears.

Jack could hear the chief superintendent's voice inside his head. Should he tell him? Should he go and tell Dougie King that the capital's most wanted man was walking the streets of London?

Jack pushed the thought from his mind. He knew he should tell the chief superintendent — but he also knew that he wouldn't. Not until he knew more. Was Joseph Geraghty here to disrupt the trial? Intimidate witnesses so his henchmen walked free?

As he watched his brother disappear out of sight on two wheels, Jack felt a familiar and unwelcome wrenching feeling in the pit of his stomach, taking him back thirty years.

* * *

Time: 1.35 p.m.
Date: 10 May 1982
Location: West Road Comprehensive School, Christchurch

"Don't be so stupid, Stu. Put that down and come back inside with me." Jack nodded towards the motorbike helmet in Stuart MacIntosh's hand. "Lunch break ended five minutes ago; we'll be late." Jack pushed himself off the low wall he'd been sitting on and headed back to the entrance of West Road Comprehensive School, swinging his rucksack high up onto his shoulder. "If we run down the side of the gym we might not be seen."

Jack paused just inside the school gates and turned to look back over his shoulder, noticing how his brother hadn't moved an inch. Stuart MacIntosh stood next to the bike, one hand resting on the worn leather seat, the other one swinging the battered helmet by his side. A smirk crossed his face, his hot eyes full of defiance.

"You can't make me, Jack." Stuart MacIntosh thrust his thirteen-year-old chin out and fixed his older brother with a hard stare. "You can't make me do anything." His tired-looking school jumper was tied around his waist, revealing a stained and creased once-white shirt beneath. His tie was undone and hanging, loosely, around his neck.

Jack sighed and looked at his watch. He'd get a detention for being late to Mr Buckley's chemistry lesson, his third this month already. And always because of Stu. They'd only recently been placed in the same school, Stuart having been kicked out of every one he'd attended before. This was his last chance; placing him with his older brother was seen as a last-ditch attempt to curb his unruly ways.

It wasn't working.

"Stu, come on. Don't be daft. Stop hanging around with that lot, they're bad news." Jack gave a discreet nod towards the gang of teenagers congregating at the side of the road, circling like vultures around three more motorbikes. Three broad-shouldered youths, dressed in a uniform of black jeans and hoodies, stared out at Jack with their hollow eyes. None of them were pupils at West Road Comprehensive School. Jack suspected they weren't pupils at any school — most likely suspended or expelled from any institution they'd been enrolled in, and then allowed to melt away from the education system into insignificance. They clustered together like wolves in a pack, passing skinny hand-rolled cigarettes around with dirty, nail-bitten fingers.

Jack didn't know where Stuart had met them, but anything was possible at the children's home he'd been placed with for the last five years. Living as he was on the other side of Christchurch, out in the rural stretches towards Hinton and the New Forest, Jack barely saw his brother, other than at school. When Stuart could be bothered to attend, that was. Separated when Jack was six, Jack had been lucky and taken in by a succession of loving foster families, eventually settling into a permanent placement when he was nine — somewhere he was allowed to settle and grow. Stuart hadn't been quite so lucky. A series of short-term foster placements followed, each family finding it harder and harder to manage his temper and wayward tendencies. So much so that for the last five years, Stuart had been living at the St Bartholomew's Home for Boys, an imposing building on the outskirts of Christchurch, housing a disturbingly growing number of boys that society had abandoned.

"They're my friends," retorted Stuart, his breath coming out hot and thick.

"They're not your friends, Stu," replied Jack, eyeing his watch again. "They're using you. They'll get you into all sorts of trouble — and you've been caught enough times by the police recently. You know the next time you get caught, they'll take you away. You'll end up in Borstal."

Stuart laughed and kicked the side of the kerb with a dirty boot. "I don't care, Jack. No one cares about me, so I don't care about them. Just go, Jack. Leave me alone." With that, Stuart MacIntosh crossed the road, pulling the motorbike helmet onto his head and swinging his leg up over the bike seat. Grabbing hold of the waist of the equally defiant teenager at the front, and before Jack could say anything more, Stuart sped off down the street, the high-pitched whining of the motorbike engine filling the air.

* * *

Time: 10.15 p.m.
Date: Saturday 21 July 2012
Location: Kettle's Yard Mews, London

Jack listened to the last echoes of the motorbike engine filtering through the sultry evening air, before pulling the curtains closed and collapsing onto the sofa. That ride on the motorbike had been Stuart's last, for a while at least. Later that day, he was arrested with the rest of the gang for a violent robbery at a local corner shop; the terrified shop owner subjected to the teenage mob brandishing baseball bats and knives — all for the sake of a few packets of cigarettes and cans of cheap lager. The father of five later died of a heart attack brought on by the ordeal. Stuart spent the next three years in an approved school, followed by several more in youth detention then adult prison, eventually disappearing from Jack's life.

Jack shuddered, even though the evening air was still sticky and warm.

Reaching for the bottle of Glenfiddich still sitting on the side of the coffee table, he sat and poured two inches of amber liquid into a glass, swirling it briefly before gulping the entire lot down in one. He grimaced at the fiery back burn in his throat, but welcomed the warmth as it slid down towards his stomach. Placing the empty glass back down on the coffee table, he sighed and closed his eyes, rubbing at the faint throbbing headache threatening his temples.

He leaned forward and picked up the bottle again, pouring another two inches into the bottom of the glass. As he replaced the bottle, his eyes came to rest on the leaflet sitting by the side of the pile of as-yet unopened post.

PTSD — The Facts.

Dr Riches had given it to him at the end of their session that morning. Jack swung the glass back up to his lips and drained the whisky in one again, wincing as the alcohol made his eyes water. As he replaced the glass, he picked up the leaflet and stared at it.

Post-Traumatic Stress Disorder.

This was what his new psychotherapist said he had.

Apparently.

It had a name.

Jack held the leaflet in his hand and continued to study the front cover. There was a picture of a brain in the centre — a normal-looking brain with various speech bubbles surrounding it, each containing the description of a particular trauma.

I bet they don't have "finding your mother's dead body hanging from a light fitting", mused Jack, the neat whisky now penetrating his bloodstream. He could feel the light-headedness beginning, his muscles starting to relax, his mind beginning to wander. He took a swig directly from the bottle, bypassing the glass this time.

Post-Traumatic Stress Disorder.

A label.

Not a label he particularly liked; but then again, Jack didn't particularly like any labels.

Flipping the leaflet over, he scanned the back where it gave a list of websites and telephone numbers for accessing emotional and wellbeing support. Turning the leaflet back to the front again, he tossed it back onto the coffee table.

Emotional and wellbeing support.

I'm forty-five years of age, thought Jack. I think that ship has well and truly sailed.

Knowing more whisky would be a bad idea, Jack left the bottle on the coffee table and went in search of sleep.

* * *

Time: 10.35 p.m.
Date: Saturday 21 July 2012
Location: A cellar in London

"He calls me Carol." The woman's voice shook, quivering at the edges just like the tremor she no doubt felt in her limbs. "He calls me Carol."

Hannah found herself nodding, even though the cellar was too dark to see. "I know. I heard him." She paused, searching through the gloom to try and make out the form of her new companion, but all she could see was a dark mound on the mattress opposite. "He calls me Jess."

Hannah saw the mound shifting in the murky shadows, and then the glimpse of white flesh as two legs appeared from underneath the blanket.

"I'm Zoe," the woman added, uncurling herself so that Hannah could see the rest of her.

Hannah pushed herself off her mattress and shuffled tentatively across the stone floor, the sound of the cumbersome metal chain being dragged in her wake scraping over the concrete. She stopped by the side of Zoe's mattress, the chain now taut and preventing her from moving any closer. She could now see Zoe much more clearly, dressed in a close-fitting business suit with her dark hair scraped back off her face and tied into a loose plait behind her. Loose wisps of hair had worked themselves free and framed her pale face. Her skin was wan and blotchy, her eyes red and raw with painfully shed tears. Her smooth, slim legs were tucked at her side, encased in thin, sheer tights that now sported gaping holes ripped through them.

117

And she only wore one shoe.

As did Hannah.

Hannah looked down at her feet, and the solitary black stiletto she still wore. Somehow she hadn't wanted to take it off.

"I'm Hannah." She introduced herself, giving the closest thing to a warm and welcoming smile that she could muster.

"How . . . how long?" Zoe's voice cracked, her head dropping down so her chin rested on her chest. Her shoulders heaved in time with the rhythm of the tears cascading down her cheeks.

"I'm not sure," replied Hannah, truthfully. "A day? A couple of days? Longer? It's impossible to tell in the darkness."

"How . . . how do we . . . ?" Again Zoe's voice broke off as she rocked slowly from side to side. Hannah noticed the dark, wet stain underneath Zoe's skirt, spreading out onto the mattress beneath.

"It's OK. There's a bucket. Over there." Hannah nodded to a corner of the cellar between the two mattresses, where a solitary metal bucket sat among the cobwebs. "The chain just about stretches far enough."

Hannah glanced behind her, back to her own mattress, seeing the stains she knew were there, only visible to her own eyes. "But it doesn't matter if you don't make it in time."

Zoe raised her head and stared out from beneath long, luscious eyelashes, rapidly blinking away fresh tears. "We are going to get out of here, aren't we?" She looked pleadingly at Hannah, her lips trembling. "There has to be a way out, right?"

Hannah glanced around the windowless, coffin-like cellar. She hoped Zoe couldn't see the scratches around the heavy oak doorframe — evidence of desperate fingernails trying to gnaw and scrape their way out of their hell-like prison. Had they been Georgie's fingernails? Someone else's? Hannah shuddered and pushed the thought from her mind. Instead she knelt down at Zoe's side and reached out to grab her hand, squeezing it as if it were their only lifeline.

"I hope so."

CHAPTER SEVENTEEN

Time: 8.27 a.m.
Date: Sunday 22 July 2012
Location: Kettle's Yard Mews, London

The sound of repeated knocking made Jack wake with a start. He rolled off the bed and glanced at the clock.

08.27 blinked back at him.

He was late.

The night had been yet another one devoid of sleep. He'd lain awake for much of it, playing over the thoughts of Joseph Geraghty being back in the capital. Then he'd tried to make sense of the evidence, such as it was, that they'd accumulated for the Patricia Gordon and Georgina Dale murders. Very soon there was no room for sleep in his headspace.

But at least no sleep meant no nightmares.

The knocking continued.

"All right, all right — I'm coming." Jack pulled on his dressing gown and went to open his front door.

"Morning, boss!" DS Chris Cooper waggled a greasy-looking paper bag in the air. "The door's bust downstairs — I came straight up."

Jack stepped back to allow the detective sergeant to step inside. "What're you doing here, Cooper? I'm running late."

"I went to see the kids this morning to tell them I've managed to get some tickets for the Olympics — the cycling and the swimming. They're made up. As I was passing, I thought I'd grab us some breakfast — I saw your car still outside so wondered if you wanted a lift in."

Jack spied the almost empty bottle of Glenfiddich on the coffee table next to the PTSD leaflet. Images of the night before sped through his mind as if on fast-forward.

Stu.

Joseph Geraghty.

Stu.

He nodded. "Thanks, Cooper. I'll just jump in the shower and pull on some clothes. Help yourself to a coffee." Jack paused before disappearing into the bedroom. "But there's no milk."

* * *

Time: 9.30 a.m.
Date: Sunday 22 July 2012
Location: St George's Road, Lambeth, London

DC Amanda Cassidy placed the tea tray down on the coffee table in the living room. Tea that nobody had asked for, nobody wanted and nobody would drink.

The sound of deep, impenetrable silence hung heavily around them.

The sound of bereavement.

So quiet it was deafening.

The first time DC Cassidy had visited a bereaved family as a fresh-faced, wet-behind-the-ears PC, she hadn't known that bereavement could be so tangible. You could hear it. You could feel it. You could touch it, and even smell it. It was there, clinging to every surface, seeping into every pore.

DC Rachel Baxter, the Family Liaison Officer assigned to the Dale family, nodded gratefully at Cassidy as she began to pour the tea from the teapot. DS Carmichael merely stood by the door and watched. Sitting together on a two-seater floral sofa underneath the window were Mr and Mrs Dale, Georgina's parents. Clutching each other's hands, their faces raw with grief, Cassidy could tell neither had slept since being given the terrible news less than twenty-four hours ago.

The dull tick-tock, tick-tock from the mantelpiece clock sounded muffled in the heavy air. Death had that effect. It made everything feel heavier. The air around you took on the consistency of treacle, words sounded muffled, time seemed to stand still.

Cassidy handed a cup and saucer to Mrs Dale first, noticing how her hand shook as she took hold of the dainty china. The teaspoon rattled in the saucer. Cassidy wondered if mugs might have been a better choice. Mrs Dale looked up briefly and caught her eye, a faint glimmer of thanks and appreciation hovering behind the glassiness of grief which otherwise washed over her. Her face had that translucent look of someone almost ghostlike and not of this world; as though this were some macabre dream, a horrific nightmare from which she would awaken.

But it was no dream.

And it was no nightmare.

Except a living one.

Sitting next to her, Georgina's father had an equally ashen complexion, the laughter lines around his mouth devoid of mirth. Though they were both only in their fifties, Cassidy saw the grim realisation of bereavement add twenty years to them overnight.

A Sunday newspaper sat folded on the arm of the sofa — and Cassidy wondered if it'd been opened and read. With Georgina's name released to the media at yesterday's press conference, it would no doubt be splashed across many a front page. It was difficult to tell from the look on both Mr and Mrs Dale's faces whether they'd been brave enough to read the printed words documenting their daughter's violent death. In some ways, Cassidy hoped they hadn't.

DC Rachel Baxter accepted a cup of tea, and then began filling both DC Cassidy and DS Carmichael in on the developments so far.

"As you know, Georgina didn't live at home while she was studying at university, so a search of her room here hasn't revealed anything substantial. Her room at the halls of residence has been cordoned off and is currently being processed."

Cassidy made a note in her notebook to check what, if anything, had come of the forensic search of Georgina's university room.

"Mr and Mrs Dale," she began, her voice quiet and calm, "I know how terrible this must be for you, and how talking about Georgina must be deeply distressing at this time, but anything you can tell us at this point could be invaluable to our investigation. Is there anything out of the ordinary that you can recall over the last few weeks? When did you last see or speak to Georgina?"

Mr and Mrs Dale looked at each other, exchanging mirror-image expressions of haunted sadness. It was Georgina's father who eventually broke the silence.

"Georgie was a beautiful girl. A beautiful daughter. She had her issues . . . before. But she'd turned herself around. She . . ." He broke off suddenly and gulped back a sob. "She'd left all that behind. She was moving on with her life."

"Georgina had been involved with some minor drug use in her late teens," explained DC Baxter, catching Cassidy's frown. "A conviction for possession eighteen months ago." Cassidy nodded, remembering how the victim's DNA had been flagged up on the system, and flashed a sympathetic look at Mr and Mrs Dale while she wrote the details in her notebook.

"She got in with the wrong crowd at college," explained Mrs Dale, leaning forward and placing her cup and saucer back down on the coffee table to stop it rattling in her frail grip; the tea, predictably, was untouched. "We know she went off the rails for a while, but we'd got her straight again. She'd got her place at university, and was doing so well."

Cassidy nodded again. "Well, there's nothing at this stage to suggest that drugs had anything to do with what happened. Do you know if she still kept in touch with anyone from her past?"

Mrs Dale shook her head. "She didn't. I know that for a fact. She completely cut herself off from them, wanting a clean break."

Cassidy made a few more notes in her notebook. "And she was doing well at university? Enjoying it?"

Mr Dale gave a wan smile and nodded. "She loved it. She'd really found her element, I think. She was completely transformed. And living in halls, although it was more expensive for us than if she'd lived at home, it was what she wanted to do. To experience the full university life. She was thriving."

"And she was studying English?"

Mrs Dale nodded, continuing to wring her hands together as if they were a dishcloth. "English language and literature. She loved it. She wanted to go travelling next summer, learn as much as she could about other countries." Her voice caught and fresh tears slid down her already saturated cheeks.

"And when was the last time you saw her, or spoke to her?" Cassidy watched both Mr and Mrs Dale's faces visibly sagging even further under the weight of their grief, if that were possible. It was Mr Dale who finally found a voice.

"That would've been about a month ago. She came here for my birthday — we had lunch." Mr Dale broke off as the words became stuck in his throat, several fat tears trickling down his cheeks to match his wife's. "That was the last time we saw her."

Cassidy nodded, added the information to her notebook and then slipped it into the breast pocket of her jacket. "I think that's all we need for now, Mr and Mrs Dale. We'll leave you in peace." She nodded at Rachel and rose from her seat, heading towards the door to the hallway.

DS Carmichael followed on behind, only speaking when they were outside and suitably out of earshot. Smirking, he turned and said, "Well done, Detective Constable. You handled yourself well in there. Almost as if you were a proper detective. Not a bad cup of tea, either."

Cassidy stopped in her tracks, momentarily speechless. She itched to pick up her phone and call Jack, tell him she needed to come back to the station, anything to get out of the company of the pompous, holier-than-thou Carmichael.

But she knew that she wouldn't.

She was stronger than that.

Carmichael led the way back to the car. "Chop chop, Detective. We have places to be. Next stop — Patricia Gordon's son, I believe."

* * *

Time: 10.45 a.m.
Date: Sunday 22 July 2012
Location: Metropolitan Police HQ, London

"It's no use, boss." DS Cooper slumped back in his chair. "It's like looking for a needle in the proverbial haystack." Blown-up photographs of the black stiletto shoe found at the second murder scene were strewn all over his desk. "There are literally hundreds of places this shoe could've come from — pretty much every high street and online shop you can think of."

Jack sighed and rubbed his forehead. The shoe was a dead end. There was no way they'd be able to trace all the women who'd bought a similar shoe in the last few months, the pool would be far too vast and they'd risk drowning before they even got started.

"Would you go public with it? Put a picture of the shoe in the media?"

Jack had thought about it — he'd thought about it a lot — but cast the idea aside. "And instil more panic on the streets than DS Carmichael and the *Daily Courier* have managed on their own? Not yet, Cooper. Not yet." They needed to change their focus. "Missing persons?" said Jack, looking away from the photograph of the shoe. "Any joy there?"

Cooper shook his head. "We've got the unit on high alert — but they don't have anything that sets off any alarm bells at the moment."

Of course not, thought Jack. No missing person's report that he'd ever seen would record someone's shoe size. "We need to work with what we've got." Jack rose to his feet and nodded at Cooper to follow him. "While Amanda and Carmichael are covering the family liaison angle, we'll go over to Patricia Gordon's workplace — the last place we have a positive sighting of her."

DS Cooper grabbed the jacket he wouldn't need to wear. "Good job we came in my car today. It's got air con."

* * *

Time: 10.55 a.m.
Date: Sunday 22 July 2012
Location: Isabel's Café, Horseferry Road, London

Isabel threw the dishcloth into the sink and gave a sigh of relief — the early Sunday morning rush was subsiding. They'd been rushed off their feet since opening, and she was glad Sacha had turned up to help. She'd even brought in more home-baked supplies with her, and Isabel could've kissed her right there and then.

She watched Sacha load the dishwasher with the last of the morning's baking trays. "Coffee?"

"An iced tea would be fantastic." Sacha closed the door of the dishwasher and started to wipe down the surfaces next to the double oven. She ran a hand across her forehead, her cheeks tinged pink with the heat. "It's been a warm one this morning!"

"Coming right up." Isabel busied herself preparing their drinks while Sacha lined up the next batch of tantalising delicacies ready to bake for the lunchtime crowd. With drinks in hand, and her laptop tucked under her arm, Isabel took them through to an empty sofa at the front of the café, placing the cups down on the second-hand coffee table. She moved a pile of magazines and some well-thumbed paperbacks out the way, then flopped down in among the cushions. This was one of her favourite times of the day — in between the morning rush and the lunchtime scrabble, there was a delicious moment of calm.

Sacha deposited herself next to Isabel and mirrored her sigh of relief. "That was a busy one!" She took hold of her iced tea, cradling the coolness of the cup in her hot hands. "How on earth will we cope when the Olympics are on?"

Isabel took a sip of her own tea. "Well, your cakes and pastries are too delicious, that's the problem! And as for the Olympics . . ." She paused and shrugged. "You'll just have to bake twice as fast!"

Sacha took a well-earned mouthful of iced tea before fixing Isabel with a mischievous look. "So, how did it go?" Her tired eyes sparkled over the top of her glass.

"How did what go?"

"You know — entertaining that nice young man in your flat last night!"

Isabel found herself grinning, and her cheeks flushed. "Oh, don't be silly — that was just Mac. We chatted and had a coffee. That's all."

"Mmmm." Sacha gave her friend a knowing look and returned her attention to her iced tea. "Just don't look a gift horse in the mouth — isn't that what people say? He seems nice enough. Handsome in a bad boy kind of way. And you're not getting any younger . . ."

"Stop teasing, Sacha Greene!" Isabel felt her cheeks redden further, but she couldn't help smiling. "I'm not looking for any kind of romantic relationship right now. I'm far too busy with the café and everything else that goes with it."

"So, what's with the website then?" Sacha nodded at Isabel's laptop. "And don't deny it — I've seen you scrolling through it. What's it called — London something?"

"It's nothing, really." Isabel went to nudge the laptop out of reach, but Sacha was too quick.

"Not so fast," she grinned, taking the laptop and opening it up on her knees. "London Life, that's it." Sacha looked quizzically at the home page. "Looks like a dating website to me. Since when?"

Isabel's cheeks flushed with yet more colour as she tried to avoid her friend's gaze. "It's nothing. Just a bit of fun. I'm not going to actually *meet* anyone."

Sacha smirked and raised her eyebrows, handing the laptop back. "If you say so."

"I'm not, honestly! I'm just chatting with a few people, that's all. Like I said, I'm too busy to actually meet anyone." Isabel raised her tea to her lips to hide her glowing cheeks.

"The lady doth protest too much, methinks," smiled Sacha, enjoying seeing her best friend squirm. "Just you be careful," she added, a more serious tone entering her voice. "You don't really know who you're dealing with on these sites."

"It's just chatting, honestly," replied Isabel, her hot cheeks burning. "Sometimes I feel like I just want a chat. It can get a bit lonely upstairs on my own, with just a cat for company. That's all."

Sacha gave her friend a playful squeeze on the knee. "Just be careful," she repeated. "There are some weird people out there. Just stay safe."

Isabel nodded. "I will, of course I will. Like I said, I'm not planning to actually meet anyone."

Just at that moment, Patrick popped his head out from the art studio at the rear of the café. "Any chance of a cuppa?" His pale green eyes glinted mischievously from beneath the sandy fringe that flopped across his forehead. "Now the rush has died down?"

"Coming right up, Patrick." Isabel pushed herself up from the sofa and snapped the laptop shut, catching Sacha's gaze as she did so. "Sacha would love to make you a coffee."

Isabel headed towards the art studio, while Sacha quickly filled a mug with freshly brewed coffee. Upon entering the studio, Isabel went and stood next to one of the easels.

"How's your commission coming along?"

Patrick merely sighed and nodded towards the array of ad hoc, hastily drawn sketches that covered most the table. "It's going painfully slowly, my dear. Painfully slowly. I appear to have a crisis of confidence. A block in my flow of artistic genius." He looked up as Sacha bustled in with a mug of coffee and a tea towel draped over one shoulder. "Any ideas?"

Sacha laughed, placing the mug in front of Patrick. "Oh good God, don't ask me. I can't draw a straight line. Isabel is far more artistic than me. Or even my Dominic, for that matter."

"Yes, where is young Dominic today?" Patrick picked up a charcoal pencil and added more strokes to a half-finished, or half-started, sketch. "We were having a good old chat yesterday. He's really into his languages, isn't he?"

"He's into just about everything, Patrick," confirmed Sacha. "He exhausts me just trying to keep up with him. Once he fixes his mind to something, that's it. But yes, he's always been into languages — says he wants to learn every language in the world."

"So he told me. Seems like I may have offered to give him a helping hand." Patrick raised an eyebrow. "Does he always manage to do that? Get people to agree to do things before they've even thought about it themselves?"

"Yes," smiled Sacha, ruefully. "He always manages to do that. I'm so sorry!"

Patrick held up a hand and shook his head. "No problem, no problem at all. I have a general knowledge of a smattering of languages — I'm more than happy to feed the knowledge-hungry young Dominic. We've started already, as it goes. He's got a brain like a sponge, hasn't he?"

"Thank you, Patrick." Sacha gave a grateful nod. "It means a lot. Someone taking the time to be with him — to interact with him. It really does bring out the best in him when people make the effort. I appreciate it. We *both* appreciate it."

Patrick waved away the compliment and took several deep mouthfuls of his coffee. "He's a pleasure to be with, my dear." After several more gulps, he pushed himself off his stool and grabbed the small knapsack hanging from one of the easels. He glanced at his watch. "Well, I need to be on my way. Time to go and get some inspiration from somewhere." He cast his eyes back down to the charcoal scribbles in front of him. "Right now, I'm pretty desperate."

After Patrick had left, Isabel and Sacha returned to the café. Soon the influx of Sunday strollers would be upon them, in desperate need of some chilled iced tea, or a cool and refreshing frappé, as they sought to escape the heat of the day. Isabel had seen the sales of the cooler drinks, such as milkshakes and smoothies, far outstrip her usual hot offerings over the last few weeks due to the heatwave. People had been known to even just ask for iced water.

Even Livi was finding the heat too much and after spending the morning lazing beneath the shade of her favourite bush in the rear courtyard, she'd padded back inside to lap up some fresh water from her bowl by the back door. Leaving the cat to find a cool corner of the café to resume her napping, Isabel slipped back behind the counter just as the bell jangled to announce another customer seeking respite from the heat.

CHAPTER EIGHTEEN

Time: 10.55 a.m.
Date: Sunday 22 July 2012
Location: The Briars Residential Care Home

DS Cooper pulled up outside the entrance to The Briars Residential Care Home. In the passenger seat, Jack peered out to see a rather imposing Victorian facade. All it needed, he mused, were some metal bars on the windows and you'd have yourself a Victorian lunatic asylum or workhouse.

The red-brick building rose up three storeys high, with a large wooden double-fronted door set above five concrete steps, a huge brass knocker in the centre. Each level of the building had eight arched windows looking out onto the narrow gravel driveway. As Jack got out of the car, he found himself looking up at each window, checking for any signs of life. Even in this heat, he noticed none of the windows were open.

The sound of Cooper slamming the driver's door jolted Jack's gaze away from the windows, and he followed his partner up the five steps to the vast front door. Three knocks from the brass knocker echoed loudly in the breathless air.

Before the last echo had subsided, the door creaked open. Greeting them was a middle-aged woman dressed in a black matron-style uniform, belted at the waist, with a silver fob watch attached to her ample breast. Her greying hair was scraped back into a harsh-looking bun, her legs encased in thick black tights and sensible black shoes. Despite her rather austere attire, she greeted the detectives with a warm smile that reached her eyes, causing them to twinkle.

"Police?" she enquired, her voice as warm and comforting as her smile. She held out a hand towards Jack, which he found himself taking in his own, noting her soft, pliable skin and reassuring squeeze.

"Indeed. Detective Inspector Jack MacIntosh." Jack tried to return the smile as best he could. "Metropolitan Police. And this is DS Cooper. Thank you for seeing us."

"No problem at all, gentlemen. Please come in. I'm Marion Masters, matron here at The Briars." Mrs Masters stepped sideways to allow Jack and DS Cooper to enter the building.

Once inside, Jack felt the temperature drop a rather comfortable ten degrees or so, the thick Victorian brickwork doing its job of keeping the heatwave outside at bay. They stepped into a large entrance hall, the high ceiling stretching up above them with ornate Victorian-style cornice plasterwork. At their feet was an expanse of what looked like original Victorian parquet flooring, buffed to a healthy shine. To the side, an imposing mirror covered one wall to give the hall an empty, cavernous feel. Jack gave an involuntary shiver, and not just because of the temperature drop. The hall enveloped its visitors with a stark coldness, conjuring up images of harsh treatment, ragged clothing, starving Victorian workhouse children pleading for another bowl of thin gruel-like soup. Jack's mind flipped back to the unopened windows outside, wondering how many of its current residents were desperate to escape its confines.

"If you'd both like to follow me." Mrs Masters' voice dragged Jack's attention back to the present. She turned on her comfortable heels and began walking towards the rear of the hall, her shoes squeaking on the polished floor. Jack and

Cooper did as they were bidden and dutifully followed the matron through another oak door, where they were greeted by an altogether unexpected transformation.

Gone was the sparse frostiness of the vast entrance hall. Similarly gone from Jack's imagination were the rows of hungry, ragged children, clamouring at the windows desperate for a better life. Instead, they moved into a newly carpeted foyer, complete with modern lighting, smooth plastered walls painted in invitingly warm tones, a range of indoor plants and comfortable-looking furniture giving the space a lived-in, homely feel.

"We have four wings to the building," explained Mrs Masters, gesturing to the four corridors fanning off from the foyer. "The residents' rooms are all accessed via these corridors. We have three floors — the most bedridden and least mobile are given rooms on the first and second floors. Our most mobile residents have rooms on the ground floor, so that they can access the outside space more easily." Mrs Masters turned to face Jack and Cooper. "Shall I take you through to the office?"

Jack nodded and followed the matron a short way down one corridor, immediately noticing how the soft, grey pile of the carpet underfoot absorbed the harsh squeaking from her comfortable shoes. Jack and Cooper were shown into a compact open-plan office space, housing several desks.

"Please take a seat." Mrs Masters nodded towards a couple of visitor chairs opposite a desk overladen with paperwork. They dutifully slipped into the seats, while Mrs Masters moved a pile of papers from the swamped desk out of the way, tutting to herself as she did so. Tucking herself behind the desk, she squeezed her ample frame into the small swivel chair. "So, how can we be of help, Inspector? I was so shocked when I heard the news about poor Patricia. I don't think any of us here can really quite believe it yet."

Jack gave a small nod and what he hoped was a sympathetic smile. "Indeed, Mrs Masters. It must've been, and still will be, a huge shock for you all."

"We're all like one big happy family here, you see, Inspector." Mrs Masters' eyes clouded over, and Jack thought he could see the beginnings of watery tears forming at the edges.

"Well, we won't keep you any longer than we have to." Jack nodded at DS Cooper to get his notebook out. "We just need to get a few more background details on Mrs Gordon — Patricia: her usual routines, her contacts, anything anyone can remember about the last time she was seen here."

Mrs Masters nodded, a slight tremble playing on her lips.

"I know you've already spoken at some length to one of our liaison officers," continued Jack. "But I wanted to come and visit myself, see if there was anything else you could tell us."

Again Mrs Masters nodded, the tremble on her lips intensifying. She reached into a side pocket of her starched uniform and pulled out a neatly folded handkerchief. She dabbed at the corners of her eyes. "Of course. Anything to help."

"We've been told that the last time anyone saw Mrs Gordon was here at about four o'clock on the afternoon of Friday sixth July. Is that correct?"

Mrs Masters finished dabbing her eyes and nodded, returning the handkerchief to her lap. "Yes. Her shift usually finished at two p.m. — she does an early shift, you see — but on occasion she would stay on a bit longer, to help out. She was like that, you see. Always willing to help." Mrs Masters paused, her voice cracking. "She left at about four o'clock, or just after. I know because that gardening programme had just started on television in one of the residents' rooms when she popped her head in to say she was off."

Jack nodded. He remembered reading this from the family liaison officer's notes. "And she didn't turn up for work the next morning?"

Mrs Masters shook her head, sadly. "She wasn't due in the next day. She'd booked a week's leave, so we weren't expecting her. If she'd been due to come in, we would've known that something was wrong much earlier. She was never late for work, you see. Never ill. Didn't even take the paid holiday she was entitled to, sometimes."

"And how long had she been working for you?"

"About four years." Mrs Masters returned the handkerchief to her eyes, dabbing away the newly erupting tears. "She'd recently separated from her husband, needed a full-time job, I think. She came to us with exceptional references from working in the hotel industry. To be honest, she was more than a bit overqualified for a simple housekeeping role, but she was so enthusiastic and really wanted the job. We're so lucky to have her." The words caught in the matron's throat. "We *were* lucky to have her," she whispered, a lone tear sliding down her cheek.

"Her husband," enquired Jack. "Have you met him?"

"Frank? Oh yes. He's a lovely man. Very caring. Used to give Patricia a lift to work when the weather was bad, pick her up again, too."

"Really?" Jack frowned, nodding to Cooper to make a note. "That sounds rather strange, for an ex-husband?"

"Oh, not really," continued Mrs Masters, wiping another stray tear from her cheek. "They were still very amicable with each other. Stayed good friends. Just better off apart — I think that's what they said. They never actually divorced, just separated. Nothing acrimonious, I don't think."

"Hmmm." Jack made a mental note to check out Mr Gordon. Amicable or not, marriages usually didn't disintegrate without a little disharmony along the way. "And did you see him at all on that Friday — the sixth of July? Did he come to pick her up?"

Mrs Masters shook her head. "No, I haven't seen him in a while. As I said, it was usually when the weather was bad. In nice weather like this," she gestured towards the window at the side of the office, "she liked to walk. She'd hop on a bus for some of the way and then walk through the parks."

"Is there anything else you can tell us, Mrs Masters? Anything at all? Anything out of the ordinary that happened in the last few weeks or months? She didn't mention anyone new in her life? Any new places she'd been to? Anything different to her usual routine?"

Mrs Masters shook her head. "No, not that I can think of. I've been wracking my brain ever since it happened. She didn't have that much spare time — always working. Such a hard worker, she is. Sorry, was." Mrs Masters took a deep breath, fighting back more tears. "Determined to keep a roof over her head and have nice things, without claiming a single penny in support. I've never met anyone who worked so hard."

Jack indicated to Cooper that they were finished and he could close his notebook. "Well, thank you very much for your time, Mrs Masters. You've been most helpful. If there's anything else you think of in the next few days or so, no matter how small, you just let me know." Jack reached into his jacket pocket and handed over a business card. "All my contact details are on there."

"Is it true?" Mrs Masters looked at the card before slipping it into her breast pocket.

"Is what true, Mrs Masters?" replied Jack, as he got to his feet.

"What they're saying in the papers this morning?" Mrs Masters paused, before raising her watery gaze to meet Jack's. "That it's a serial killer?"

Jack hesitated, noting the frightened look on the matron's face. But he couldn't hide her from the truth — no matter how much he might want to. "It would appear so, Mrs Masters. But please don't be alarmed. We're doing all we can to apprehend the person responsible."

"You will catch him, won't you?"

Jack hesitated for a split second. "Yes, Mrs Masters. We will."

* * *

135

Time: 12 p.m.
Date: Sunday 22 July 2012
Location: A cellar in London

Zoe Turner stretched out from beneath the scratchy blanket. She'd lain with her legs curled up underneath her and now felt a numbness spreading down her calves and into her ankles. She flexed her feet and shuddered.

She had no idea how long she'd slept for. The last thing she remembered was drinking a bottle of water that'd appeared earlier that day — or was it yesterday? She had no idea what time it was, or even what day it was.

There was one thing she did remember, though — going with him for that iced tea. How could she have been so stupid? Seeing him outside the Shard — he'd appeared out of nowhere, accosting her as soon as she crossed the street.

She was a professional woman.

She was intelligent.

Why had she gone with him?

The remnants of what looked like breakfast still sat next to her mattress. Cold toast, now stiff and stale. A banana she appeared to have nibbled at. Yawning, she rubbed her eyes, still feeling groggy.

Her eyes rested on the empty water bottle. Did he drug her? Was that why she felt so tired? She glanced over towards the other side of the cellar, where the other girl was curled up underneath a mound of blankets. Hannah, she'd said her name was. Had Hannah been drugged too?

Zoe shuddered again, and not because of the cool, damp air that clung to her skin. All she could visualise was him — bending down over her, that sickening smile plastered over his face. His cold touch against her skin. Another shudder wracked her body, and she pulled the blanket back over her legs.

What were you meant to do in situations like this? Were you meant to comply? Or were you meant to scream and shout? Zoe's usual confidence and composure had left her the minute she'd been overcome — the minute she'd been swiftly subdued and brought to this place, this prison.

Her mind scrabbled for clarity. What should she do? Escape seemed impossible — there were no windows, and only one door that was permanently locked. And then there was the chain. She moved her left leg and heard the metal clunking against the stone floor. Her mind continued to race, and it took her a while to acknowledge the voice that floated through the still air.

"Are you there? Zoe? I'm scared."

CHAPTER NINETEEN

Time: 12.45 p.m.
Date: Sunday 22 July 2012
Location: St James's University, London

Dr Rachel Hunter's office was light and airy, the floor-to-ceiling blinds on the window blocking out the searing heat of the afternoon sun. Jack could feel the welcome ripple of chilled air from the air conditioning system as he lowered himself into a soft leather armchair facing a low glass-topped coffee table.

"Coffee?" Dr Hunter gestured towards a complicated-looking coffee machine nestled in the corner, but Jack shook his head.

"No thanks, I'm fine." Jack felt himself sinking further into the plush leather — reminiscent of his visit to Dr Riches yesterday morning, her rooms being on the other side of the university campus. "Thank you for seeing me at such short notice, and on a Sunday."

Dr Hunter, the Metropolitan Police criminal profiler, settled herself into another leather armchair opposite Jack, smoothing out her skirt and tucking her legs to one side as she did so. Her light grey suit fitted her slim figure neatly, a cool, crisp white blouse contrasting with the light sun-kissed tan that glowed from her skin.

Jack glanced down at his creased shirt and trousers, possibly still yesterday's, and ran a hand over his roughly shaven chin. He crossed one leg over the other to hide the worst of the creases.

Psychologists made him nervous.

He felt the familiar feeling of inadequacy begin to resurface.

Even her office was tidier than his — although when you shared an office with DS Cooper that wasn't hard to achieve.

"So, your killer," began Dr Hunter, nudging her wire-rimmed glasses with a well-manicured finger. "Would you like to hear what I've got for you?" Her light green eyes twinkled from behind the lenses of her spectacles.

Jack gave a faint shrug and a nod at the same time. "Sure."

Dr Hunter reached forward, selecting a thin manila folder from the coffee table. Upon opening it, she slid out two pieces of paper, passing one across to Jack. "I would say your perpetrator is aged between thirty and fifty-five."

Jack lowered his eyes and saw a list of typed bullet points. "Thirty to fifty-five? That's quite specific."

"I don't believe your killer is a particularly young man, Detective Inspector. The details of the two crimes you sent over to me indicate a more mature killer. His crimes are well thought out, carefully planned."

Jack shrugged and returned his gaze to the list.

"Capable of intimate relationships, but with some difficulties." Dr Hunter read out the second characteristic. "Possibly divorced or separated."

"So single, then?" suggested Jack.

"Not necessarily," replied Dr Hunter, giving a slow shake of her head. "He could be in a relationship, but any relationship is likely to have its difficulties."

Jack suppressed a sigh. This was exactly the reason why he didn't like using profilers. He might be single. He might be married. He might be divorced. He might find relationships difficult. *Who didn't?* thought Jack.

"There is something I should add, though, which isn't yet in my report." Dr Hunter nodded at the list. "He's likely to be well presented, attractive. Charming, even."

"Charming?" Jack frowned. "What makes you say that?"

"These women trusted him. As far as I can tell, there were no defensive marks on either body, just abrasions around the ankles from the restraints. There are no witnesses to a forced abduction — no indication they were taken forcibly from their homes. Whoever he is, they went with him willingly. They *trusted* him." Dr Hunter paused. "Initially, at least."

"You say 'he'." Jack glanced up from the list. "So we're definitely looking for a male killer?"

Dr Hunter met Jack's gaze, her pale green eyes continuing to twinkle behind her glasses. "I think both you and I know the chances of a serial killer being female are pretty remote. I'd be most surprised if your killer was a woman."

Jack nodded, breaking Dr Hunter's gaze to cast his eyes back down to the list. Characteristic number three. "Educated. Intellectual. Intelligent. White-collar worker."

"Indeed," confirmed Dr Hunter. "Neither crime was impulsive. Both were meticulously carried out, to a high degree of precision — both in the abduction and the dumping of the bodies. Your killer is highly intelligent. Certainly not a manual labourer."

"Can't manual labourers be intelligent? That doesn't seem very politically correct."

Dr Hunter smiled in Jack's direction, a perfect row of sparkling white teeth set against a pair of pale pink lips. "You know what I mean, Detective Inspector. This killer is clever. I'd put him in a job that equated to his high intelligence level."

Jack shrugged, moving on to the next characteristic, which intrigued him the moment he read it. "Doesn't kill for pleasure. What makes you say that?"

"The method of killing is very clinical. I've studied both post-mortem reports that you kindly sent through. Both victims died as a result of strangulation via a ligature around the neck. To perform this, the killer would need to be standing behind his victim at the point of strangulation. This is a very cold method of killing. He doesn't want to look into his victim's eyes at the time of death."

Dr Hunter paused, the sparkle in her eyes dimming. "He has some other motivation for killing these women. It's not done for pleasure, I'm sure of it. If he gained pleasure or excitement from his acts, he'd want to be facing them, seeing the fear and horror in their eyes as he ended their lives. If that were so, he'd strangle them manually, facing them at the point of death. Your killer uses a colder and more clinical method. He distances himself from the actual act of killing — he's emotionally detached. Which leads me to believe he doesn't get pleasure from it — at least, not in the traditional sense."

Jack conceded the issue. She had a point.

"You haven't mentioned the shoes." Jack nodded back down at the list. "The shoes found at the scene."

Dr Hunter gave a slow, methodical nod. A faint frown creased her temples. "Yes, the shoes." Silence hung in the air between them.

"And?" pressed Jack, nodding once more towards the list.

"The shoes worry me." Dr Hunter gave a shrug. "I haven't commented on it in my report because I just don't know. I'm sorry."

"Isn't it some sort of fetish?" Jack had already googled shoe fetishes, and had been quite intrigued at what he found. "Retifism, isn't it called? Sounds the most likely, to me."

Dr Hunter nodded. "Yes, it can be known as retifism. But I don't believe that's what we have here."

"You don't?" It was Jack's turn to frown. "Why not?"

"As I mentioned before, this man kills for some other reason than pleasure. He's an emotional void at the moment of killing. I don't believe he's using the shoes for some form of sexual gratification."

"So why leave it at the scene? Are we looking at a trophy killer?"

Dr Hunter shook her head again, a stray lock of her auburn hair brushing her jawline. "Not in the traditional sense, no. He isn't taking the shoes as a trophy. You said it yourself. He left the shoe of the next victim at the scene. He doesn't want to keep them."

"So why do it? There must be a reason, surely?" Jack felt a hint of irritation seeping into his tone. "I need to get inside this man's head."

"I can assure you, Detective Inspector, that is the *last* place you want to be." Dr Hunter shifted in her seat. "It isn't a fetish. And it isn't a trophy." She looked up and locked Jack in her gaze. "I think he might be leaving them as clues."

"Clues?" The irritation in Jack's voice deepened.

"Yes, clues. He's teasing you — maybe playing games. He wants you to find him."

"A killer that wants to be caught?" The irritation had morphed into more of an exasperated tone. "Why would he want to be caught? It makes no sense. I thought you said he was intelligent?"

"Your killer is a complex character." Dr Hunter looked back down at the list of characteristics in her hand. "We've already established that he's educated, intelligent — and he kills for some other reason than pleasure. It wouldn't surprise me if he's testing your powers of detection."

Jack sighed.

A complex character.

Great.

"Number five," he continued. "Location — living in or having a good working knowledge of London." He tried to stop frustration creeping into his voice. "That goes without saying, surely?"

"Indeed it does. Your killer certainly knows his way around London. I understand you haven't had many leads from the CCTV images?"

Jack had to concede that they hadn't. DC Cassidy had organised a team to work through the night analysing hours and hours of footage. As yet, nothing had shown up. "Not as yet, no. We're widening the search."

"So, your killer is either very lucky and has avoided the CCTV cameras by accident or . . ." Dr Hunter let the question hang in the air.

"Or he knows where they are," finished Jack, nodding. "I get the picture, Doctor."

"Which takes us back to my third point. He's an extremely clever man. These are not random or opportunistic killings. They are well thought through, even to the point of when and where to dump the bodies."

Jack sighed again.

A clever killer.

Even better.

He let his eyes wander back down to the next characteristic and instantly felt a shiver course through his bloodstream, but this time not caused by the deliciously cool waft of air circulating around the warm room. Two words which would make any detective's blood run cold.

Forensically aware.

Dr Hunter noticed the expression that had crossed Jack's face. "Yes. Your killer is very forensically aware. Again tying in with the belief that he's an intelligent individual. The post-mortem reports both confirm that there was no trace of any foreign DNA, or any other trace evidence, left on either body. Nothing to connect the victims with any other person or location. I strongly believe your killer has an in-depth knowledge of forensics, taking special precautions to ensure no traces of himself, or where he kills his victims, are found."

Jack knew from experience the problem the words "*forensically aware*" posed. And it worried him. Like it worried every detective. Even with the growth of the multitude of CSI programmes available on TV these days, crime scenes would almost always give up some form of evidence, no matter how small, to tie the victim to the killer, or at least to the location where they were killed. Every contact leaves a trace — isn't that what they said? But a *sterile* forensic scene? Bodies being *cleansed*?

That worried Jack.

That worried Jack a lot.

The next characteristic on the list didn't lift Jack's mood much either.

"No criminal record." Dr Hunter read out the last of her conclusions. "I doubt he's ever come onto your radar before. I feel he's far too clever for that."

Jack sighed and tucked the piece of paper into his shirt pocket. He wasn't sure any of this brought them any further forwards, and the expression on his face showed it.

"I know you don't think much of profiling, Detective Inspector." Dr Hunter slipped her copy of the profile report back inside the manila folder.

"Why do you say that?" Jack met her gaze, noticing the softening of her eyes and the mischievous sparkle returning.

"Your reputation goes before you." Dr Hunter paused, a smile teasing her lips. "I'm not going to give you the name and address of your killer, Jack. That's a job for you and your team."

The use of his Christian name caused Jack's skin to prickle, feeling the psychologist's eyes tunnelling into his from behind the protective lenses of her glasses. A twitch at the corner of her lips revealed a tongue dancing briefly across her perfect white teeth.

Was she flirting with him?

Jack felt instantly uneasy.

Women never flirted with him.

Dr Hunter got to her feet. "All I can do is help to narrow down the pool of suspects." She inclined her head towards the door, motioning that Jack was free to leave. "It's up to you to catch him now."

CHAPTER TWENTY

Time: 2 p.m.
Date: Sunday 22 July 2012
Location: St John's Wood, London

Clean.

Neat.

Tidy.

Everything in Patricia Gordon's flat was in its rightful place.

Jack and DS Cooper carefully wiped their feet on the mat as they entered, even though the owner was no longer there to see. Visiting the homes of murder victims was always difficult; the warm, welcoming feel of a well-loved and well-cared-for home was always tinged with a cold emptiness, as if the very walls could sense the loss.

The scene-of-crime team had been and gone some time ago. Nothing had been found to suggest the victim had met her killer within these four walls. Her laptop and mobile phone had been taken away to be analysed by the tech team, but everything else had been left in situ, frozen in time.

"Nice place." Cooper peered out through the venetian blinds onto a tidy courtyard area at the rear of the flat.

"Indeed." Jack noted the expensive-looking widescreen TV and cinema surround sound system, iPod docking station and satellite set-top box. A low-rise, soft leather cream sofa stretched along one wall, with a plush terracotta coloured rug at its feet. A floor-to-ceiling bookcase hugged the opposite wall, its shelves full of well-known paperback bestsellers, a series of Encyclopaedia Britannica and a small collection of CDs. "This is what we had before Google, Cooper." Jack bent down to take a closer look at the impressive row of thirty-two hardback volumes of the encyclopaedias. He pulled out a volume, letting it fall open at a random page charting the history of the Egyptian Gods.

Cooper looked over his shoulder. "Encyclopaedias? They can be worth a pretty penny these days. Especially the full set."

Jack returned the volume to the shelf and continued his search, not entirely sure what he was looking for. A feeling, an instinct, a gut reaction — anything to provide him with a clue as to how a seemingly ordinary middle-aged care home worker could cross the deadly path of a serial killer. Was it simply a case of wrong time, wrong place — or was there more to it? He noted the framed photographs of Mrs Gordon and a similarly aged man; a man Jack assumed to be her ex-husband. A couple more photographs showed a young boy in various locations — beaches, forests, school uniforms and Christmas dinner tables.

A son.

That meant a family — a family that would no doubt be missing Patricia Gordon.

Jack wondered how they were coping with the news.

As his eyes swept the rest of the room, he couldn't help but notice how normal everything looked.

Ordinary.

But nothing ordinary had happened to Patricia Gordon.

The only bedroom in the flat was equally well-kept. The bed neatly made, nightclothes folded up and placed beneath the pillow. A dressing table housed the usual mundane items

— hairspray, deodorant, perfume bottles, various pots of face cream that claimed to make you wrinkle-free.

Jack sighed with hidden annoyance. Nothing was standing out — nothing to help them flush out the killer. He returned to the living room where Cooper was rifling through some paperwork inside a small bureau next to the sofa. There was the usual stack of bills, invoices and junk mail and, from what Jack could see, Mrs Gordon was in credit with her gas and electricity provider and her credit card balance was zero.

Jack picked up the most recent credit card statement. He saw the previous balance of £1,550 had been paid off in full. To Jack, it looked like the balance for a holiday — paid to SunSeekers Ltd, three weeks before she died.

A holiday that Patricia Gordon would never get to take.

"Let's go, Cooper. I don't think there's anything here to help us. Take some photos, then we'll go and see the husband." Jack slipped the credit card statement back into the pile and headed towards the door. DS Cooper dutifully snapped a few shots of the living room layout, the bureau and paperwork, then joined Jack in jogging down the communal steps to the front door.

* * *

Time: 2.10 p.m.
Date: Sunday 22 July 2012
Location: White Horse Road, Southwark, London

DS Carmichael held the passenger side door open while shielding his eyes from the baking sun overhead. Cassidy slipped into the passenger seat, giving him a sideways glance as she did so. It was an oddly charismatic gesture — not many people held doors open for women these days.

After she'd tucked her legs inside, the door slammed shut and Carmichael jogged round to the driver's door. He'd been very quiet during the interview with Patricia Gordon's son, letting Cassidy do all the talking. And on the drive over he'd seemed unusually distracted. Several times he'd braked at the last minute, or drifted over the white line into the opposite lane, his mind clearly elsewhere. She'd tried to make conversation during the journey from the Dales' family home, but most of her questions went unanswered or elicited a monosyllabic yes or no response. She'd tried to ask about his family — where they came from, where they lived — but that in itself seemed to make him clam up even more. Whenever she caught his eye, those beady bird-like pupils gave nothing away.

Determined not to have another silent journey back to the station, Cassidy pulled out her notebook.

"James seems to have built a good rapport with the son," she commented, flipping over the pages. James Anderson, the FLO assigned to the Gordon family, was someone Amanda knew well. They'd started their careers and completed their initial training together at Hendon, followed by periods of working alongside each other on various investigative teams. She knew him to be a thorough and reliable detective; if there was anything worth knowing about the Gordons, Anderson would discover it.

Carmichael appeared to grunt a reply, turning his head away while he tried to pull out across the two-lane carriageway.

Cassidy continued. "The son seemed to be quite close to his mother, don't you think? But I detected a bit of hostility towards the father. Did you sense that too?" She looked up from her notebook, trying to catch Carmichael's eye. "Well, did you?"

Carmichael flashed her a sideways look and merely shrugged. "I guess."

"Maybe there's more to the separation than we thought?" Cassidy made a note to herself at the back of her notebook. "Maybe it wasn't as amicable as Frank Gordon wants us to believe?"

Again Carmichael gave a non-committal shrug in response.

"Could be a motive?" Cassidy refused to give up.

"I wouldn't read too much into it," replied Carmichael, finally engaging in conversation as he pulled into a steady flow of traffic heading towards Waterloo station. "Families can be complex structures. Not everyone comes from the perfect home."

"No, but . . ."

"Some people get dealt a raw deal by the families they happen to be born into — some parents aren't exactly the best role models for their offspring. But it doesn't necessarily mean they're monsters."

"I still think it's a line of enquiry," persisted Cassidy. "There was definitely something off between the son and his dad."

Carmichael conceded the point. "Well I'm sure you'll raise it with Jack when we get back."

Cassidy turned her attention back to her notebook. James Anderson had done a thorough job, obtaining all the relevant background on the family. Other than the strained relationship with his father, the son, David, didn't reveal any other potential lines of enquiry. As far as he knew, his mother had no known enemies, hadn't befriended anyone in recent weeks, and pretty much kept herself to herself. The likelihood that the killer was someone that the family knew was looking less likely by the second. After the usual platitudes and routine tea-making and promising they would keep the family informed of any developments, Cassidy had led Carmichael out of David Gordon's well-kept three-bedroomed semi, and made their retreat.

"So, what made you become a police officer, Detective?" The question came out of the blue, just as Cassidy was resigning herself to another silent drive back to the station.

"I'm sorry?" she frowned.

"The police," repeated Carmichael, as they turned off the main road. "What made you join up?"

"I don't know, really. It was just something I'd always wanted to do as a kid. Maybe there were too many Miss Marple books around the house when I was growing up."

Cassidy smiled at the memory. "And my mum was always watching Juliet Bravo on TV — although I was too young to watch it and would get sent to my bed when it was on. But I can still remember the theme tune." She paused and turned to Carmichael. "What about you?"

She'd asked this question on the journey over and received nothing in response — but it was worth another shot. "What made you want to be in the police?"

The question hung in the air as Carmichael followed the Sunday afternoon traffic across Westminster Bridge. He pulled up at a set of traffic lights and stared directly ahead, chewing at his bottom lip while fixing his eyes on the red light in front of them. Eyes that Cassidy could see starting to soften.

"Were your family in the force?" Now she had him talking, Cassidy was determined to keep up the pressure. "Your parents?"

The lights turned green and Carmichael stepped heavily on the accelerator, lurching the car forwards. He glanced in his rear-view mirror and quickly pulled over to the side of the road.

"I've just remembered — I need to be somewhere." He nodded at the passenger side door. "The station's only a ten-minute walk from here. Do you mind hopping out?"

As he glanced over, Cassidy noticed the steeliness had returned to his eyes, replacing whatever softness she'd thought she'd seen before. He raised his eyebrows and nodded once again at the door. "Please?"

She mumbled a reply and scrambled to get out. Before slamming the door behind her, she bent down and poked her head back inside the car. "Don't forget we have a briefing at four."

Without replying, Carmichael sped off as soon as the door was shut.

* * *

Time: 3.15 p.m.
Date: Sunday 22 July 2012
Location: Kennington, London

"I still can't believe it." Frank Gordon sat on the edge of the stiff leather sofa, his hands knotted together in his lap. His face had a translucent, ashen hue, his eyes red-rimmed, as if sleep had evaded him for many days and nights.

"I still can't believe it," he repeated, his voice hoarse and grating. "I really can't." His thinning hair was closely cropped, but his face looked as though it'd been a while since its last contact with a razor. Jack instinctively rubbed a hand over his own prickling chin.

"We're very sorry for your loss, Mr Gordon." Jack again found himself spouting the standard textbook phrase all rookie policemen were taught during their initial training. He'd long since forgotten how many times he'd had cause to say it. "We're doing all we can to find the person responsible."

"Is it true?" Fresh tears brimmed at the corner of Frank Gordon's eyes. "What they said in the papers today?"

Jack knew exactly what he was referring to, but chose not to look at the folded copy of the *Mail on Sunday* sitting on the coffee table. "The papers?"

"About Patricia. And the other girl." Frank Gordon hesitated. "They say there's a serial killer on the loose." His voice cracked, painfully, as he spoke.

Jack lowered his gaze to the floor, studying his less-than-polished shoes, comparing them with the gleam that shone from DS Cooper's. "I'll be honest with you, Mr Gordon," he replied, raising his eyes to meet the tear-stained face opposite. "We do believe we're looking for one person — the same person responsible for both crimes."

Frank Gordon nodded miserably, silent tears sliding down his unshaven cheeks.

"We'll try not to take up too much of your time, but there are a few questions we'd like to ask you." Jack perched on the edge of the simple terracotta sofa. "I appreciate you've already spoken to officers about this — the family liaison officer DC Anderson has been round to see you? I believe he's currently with your son and his family?"

Frank Gordon nodded once again.

"There are just a few additional questions that might help." Jack noted the man's nails were bitten down to the quick. "When did you last see your wife . . . ex-wife?"

Frank Gordon's eyes misted over as he cast his mind back to a time before the nightmare began. Opening his mouth to speak, his tone was so soft it was hard to discern what he was saying. Both Jack and DS Cooper inched closer, inclining their heads to catch the hushed words. "The day before . . . the day before she . . ." Gordon broke off, lowering his gaze once again to his lap. "I went round to help her set up her new TV."

Jack remembered the state-of-the-art TV and cinema surround sound system sitting in the corner of Patricia Gordon's flat.

"I don't know why she'd bought herself a new one — her old one is just as good. Waste of money if you ask me, but Patricia always likes the good things in life. Sorry . . ." Gordon broke off, his voice cracking once again. "*Liked* the good things in life. Sorry, I just can't believe she's gone."

"That's OK, Mr Gordon, you've nothing to apologise for." Jack motioned for DS Cooper to continue the line of questioning they'd agreed in advance while he slipped out, seemingly unnoticed, to look around the rest of the house.

With the sound of Cooper's voice in the background, Jack quickly jogged up the stairs. Three bedrooms opened off the landing — only one of which was clearly in use. Another looked like a guest bedroom, and one a junk room. Jack popped his head into all three. Nothing seemed out of place. All tidy. All orderly — even the junk room. Jack headed to the far end of the landing where he found an equally spotless bathroom.

Stepping inside, Jack sniffed. The bath looked like it'd recently been cleaned, the cloying smell of detergent heavy in the air. The closer he bent towards the bath, the stronger the aroma of bleach. Straightening up, he turned towards an equally clean and gleaming sink. No splash marks, no limescale, no dried-up toothpaste around the plughole.

Opening the mirror-fronted cabinet above, Jack noted the usual array of toiletries, painkillers, plasters and razors. Again, nothing out of the ordinary. Nothing out of place.

Ordinary.

Clean.

Very clean.

* * *

Time: 4.10 p.m.
Date: Sunday 22 July 2012
Location: Isabel's Café, Horseferry Road, London

The hint of a welcoming breeze rippled in through the open patio doors, beginning to gently wash away the heat and stifling humidity of the day. Isabel smiled as she leaned against the door frame, watching Livi curled up fast asleep underneath the shadow of the ornamental grass nestled in the corner of the walled garden.

Isabel treasured moments like these. She closed up early on a Sunday, to make up for all the early starts throughout the week. Turning the sign to "Closed" at four o'clock on the dot, she'd sent Dominic and Sacha home to enjoy the rest of their Sunday. Sacha had been teasing her about Mac all day — Jack's brother having stopped off again that morning for a cold drink to take with him on his bike.

"Twice in two days — he's keen," she'd grinned, as soon as Jack's brother was out of earshot.

"Don't be silly," Isabel had replied. "He just came in for a drink — we *are* a café, after all!"

Sacha had given her a knowing look before disappearing back inside the kitchen. "Well, it's better than that London Life nonsense."

Isabel turned away from the patio doors and saw Patrick packing up his work for the day, washing his paintbrushes at the small, porcelain sink.

"Do you think I should stay open later, Patrick?" she asked. "Once the Olympics start?"

Patrick shook the brushes dry and stacked them in a waiting jam jar. "I don't know. Do you want to?"

Isabel sighed and slipped onto one of the stools next to the art table, which she noticed was still littered with Patrick's sketches. "I'm not sure. I know we aren't on the doorstep of the Olympic Park or anything, but there'll be more tourists in London over the next few weeks, which means more customers. And there are actually some venues a bit closer to us." Isabel started to gather up some of the abandoned charcoal pencils. "I probably should've thought about it sooner — the Games start on Friday."

"Do you need to?" Patrick turned and gave Isabel an enquiring look. "Open later, I mean? How's business doing?"

"Oh, you know. Up and down. It has its moments." Isabel straightened some of the sketches, avoiding Patrick's gaze.

"Really?" Patrick eased himself onto the stool opposite. "I know the rent along this road isn't cheap."

"It isn't, but I'm doing OK. Keeping my head above water. Dominic and Sacha are a godsend — they refuse to let me pay them what they'd get elsewhere. I'm really not sure what I'd do without them."

"You could always increase what I pay you?" Patrick let the question hover in the air while he joined Isabel in collecting up the pencils and chalks scattered across the table. "You don't charge half as much as other art studios would. And we *are* in Westminster."

"Oh, good God, no." Isabel reached for a stray pencil and lightly tapped Patrick on the wrist with it before popping it into the tray with all the others. "Don't you even think about it. Your rent is fair. You're not here all the time. I'm doing fine, honestly." She looked up and gave him what she hoped was a warm smile. "Truly."

"Well. If you're sure." Patrick made a move, gathering up his jacket from where it was draped over one of the easels. "You don't owe me any favours, Isabel. You know that."

"I know." Isabel smiled once again, and reached across the table to pick up Patrick's wallet and keys. As she went to hand them to him, the wallet fell open, spilling its contents. "Oh, sorry. Butterfingers." As Isabel gathered up the loose bank cards and receipts, her gaze fell upon a small two-inch by two-inch photograph. She noted its roughened edges were curled at the corners, suggesting it was well loved. The photograph showed a woman with strawberry-blonde shoulder-length hair, laughing and smiling towards the camera. A younger girl, with the same strawberry-blonde hair pulled back into a neat pony-tail, stood by her side, their arms wrapped around each other.

"That's a nice photo." Isabel handed the picture over the table, along with the wallet and keys. "Family?"

She realised she didn't really know much about Patrick's private life. She assumed he wasn't married or with anyone, as he never seemed to mention anybody special. But maybe he just kept his private life exactly that. Private.

Patrick took the photograph along with his wallet, but didn't reply. Isabel noticed the way he handled the worn picture, carefully smoothing out the edges before slipping it back inside his wallet. Such love. Such care. She also noticed how he continued to avoid her gaze.

"I'm sorry." Isabel realised she might've stumbled across something she wasn't meant to. "I didn't mean to pry."

Patrick returned the wallet to his pocket and managed a weak smile. "It's fine. Don't worry."

Isabel noticed Patrick's eyes had dimmed — as if a dark storm cloud had snuffed out any light and cheerfulness inside, the laughter lines that usually graced his skin disappearing in seconds.

It was a look Isabel knew well — one of pain and overwhelming sadness.

"I'll get us a coffee." Isabel quickly slipped back out into the café, returning moments later with two steaming mugs.

Patrick accepted the mug gratefully, affording Isabel another weak smile. They sipped their drinks in comfortable silence before Patrick began to speak.

"I miss them every day, you know? Not a day goes by when I don't think about them." Reaching back into his pocket, he drew out the battered photograph from his wallet. Holding the picture gently in between his fingers, he ran a fingertip across their faces, feeling the roughened paper beneath his touch. "This is all I have left of them."

Isabel felt her stomach lurch as she saw the raw grief still etched upon Patrick's face. "It's a beautiful photograph," she replied, thinking of her own photographs upstairs that held treasured memories bound tightly together with heartache.

"It was a while ago now." Patrick's soft voice cracked like old leather. "One minute they were there . . . the next they were gone."

"Your wife?" Isabel nodded towards the photograph.

"My wife, yes. And my daughter, Eleanor." Patrick stared at Eleanor's smiling face, taking a sip of coffee before he carried on. "It was a house fire. And it was all my fault. I only popped out to put some petrol in the car. By the time I got back . . ."

Isabel felt her breath catch. She slipped off her stool and rounded the table to take the seat next to Patrick. Without speaking, she wrapped an arm around his shoulders and pulled him close.

They stayed like this for a while, two kindred spirits lost in sadness — time having no meaning for either of them. Patrick's head rested lightly against her shoulder, her comforting squeeze letting him know that she understood his pain.

She understood his sadness.

She understood his loss.

She knew.

"I lost my parents." Isabel's voice was quiet, her heart squeezing painfully as images of her parents filled her head. "Nothing can prepare you for losing the ones you love or the grief you feel at their loss — the space they leave behind." She gave Patrick's shoulder another squeeze. "But it wasn't your fault — you can't hang on to that. It'll eat you up."

Patrick lifted his head from Isabel's shoulder and gave a small shrug. "Maybe not. But things could've turned out differently — if I hadn't gone out that night."

"Maybe. But maybe it would've happened anyway." Isabel squeezed Patrick's arm again. "Either way, it still wasn't your fault. You didn't start that fire. Things happen that are outside our control. Awful things. Dreadful things. And it's a test of our own courage as to how we carry on afterwards. We can't spend our lives blaming ourselves, or blaming others. Instead, we should spend this time showing our loved ones how strong we are, how courageous we are, and why we loved them so much. Blame only taints their memory."

Patrick gave a small smile. "Have you ever heard of the expression 'crying at the moon'?"

Isabel frowned. "No, I haven't. Sounds like something to do with werewolves."

A faint sparkle returned to Patrick's eyes. "It means asking for something that's impossible to have."

"So what are you asking for that's so impossible to have?"

"Peace. Forgiveness."

"And you think that's impossible?"

Patrick shrugged and looked away. "At the moment, yes. No matter what I do, I can't seem to find it — maybe I don't deserve it."

Isabel wished she could say something to bring Patrick what he so desperately searched for. But she knew from her own bitter experience that peace only came when you were ready — it could never be hurried. Instead she nodded at the cup of coffee sitting on the table in front of him. "Drink your coffee and get yourself home. I want to see you bright and early tomorrow with some more ideas for your commission." She gestured towards the random sketches still littering the centre of the table.

Patrick managed another small smile. "Thanks, Isabel. I'll see you tomorrow." With that, he gulped down the remaining coffee and shrugged himself into his jacket. With one last look at the photograph in his wallet, he turned and made his way to the front door.

Isabel followed, waving him goodbye through the window. Making sure that the sign was still turned to "Closed", she secured the bolts and turned the heavy key in the lock, watching Patrick's sombre frame disappearing along the pavement towards the Tube.

After disturbing Livi from her peaceful slumber underneath the shade of the ornamental grass and shooing her inside, Isabel secured the patio doors and climbed the stairs up to the flat.

* * *

Time: 4.30 p.m.
Date: Sunday 22 July 2012
Location: Metropolitan Police HQ, London

Jack pulled the blinds down over the window and switched on the fans. "I guess we won't wait any longer for DS Carmichael to grace us with his presence — let's get started."

DS Cooper sat at one of the desks, while DC Cassidy stood by the open window trying to create the illusion of a breeze where none truly existed.

"Amanda, tell us about the Dales."

Cassidy brought out her notebook and began to update Jack and DS Cooper on the meeting at the Dale family home earlier that morning. "Not much that we didn't already know, to be honest. She doesn't live at home. Had a pretty chequered past until a couple of years ago. Some minor dabbling in the drug scene. One conviction for possession eighteen months ago but seemed to have sorted herself out. Parents are adamant she wasn't back on the drugs or even in contact with anyone from her shadier days." Cassidy flicked over a few more pages. "Studying English. Plans to travel. Parents last saw her about a month ago. No contact since, but that

158

wasn't unusual. We know she was last seen on Thursday twelfth July — a week or so before her body was found at her halls of residence. Failed to turn up for lectures the following Monday. Although the academic year had finished, she'd signed up for some summer classes. No real alarm was raised when she failed to show up, as she could be a little sporadic in her attendance."

Jack nodded. "Anything else?"

"Nothing as yet, no. Rachel is doing a great job — the family are, understandably, devastated."

"OK, so what about the Gordons?"

Cassidy flicked over another page in her notebook. "We went to see David Gordon — Patricia's son. Again, understandably distressed at the loss of his mother."

"I can sense there's a but coming."

Cassidy nodded. "I sensed there was a tension between him and his dad — Frank Gordon. Nothing was actually said, but I felt maybe the son didn't get on too well with him. There was just some faint hostility when Frank's name was mentioned. Maybe the split wasn't as amicable as we're being led to believe."

Jack rubbed his chin. "Cooper, I don't recall Frank Gordon mentioning his son, do you?"

"I'm pretty sure he didn't mention him at all, boss."

"Hmmm. You would've thought he'd be concerned about how his son was coping. Would you not?"

Cassidy moved to stand directly in front of the fan. "Did you get anything else from him? The husband?"

"Upset," answered Cooper. "And very weepy. Which is understandable if they were as close as we're told they were."

"He had a very clean home, though." Jack remembered the smell of bleach. "And a clean house bothers me a little. We know our killer is forensically aware and leaves his crime scenes impeccably clean. Mr Gordon's home wasn't just tidy. It was *clean*. His bathroom was *sterile*."

"Some people are like that." Cassidy fanned herself with her notebook. "Especially when they live on their own."

Jack recalled the stacks of washing-up left in the kitchen back at his flat — the overflowing washing bin and the less than sterile bathroom. He pushed the thoughts from his head. "Let's just bear it in mind. Where are we on the CCTV and phone records? Any updates?"

"Phone records not showing anything interesting yet, boss." Cooper clicked the mouse and the whiteboard flickered into life. "Patricia Gordon's phone was left in her flat — forensics already worked through her recent messaging and call history. She didn't use it much and nothing stands out as unusual. Georgina Dale's phone is missing. It wasn't in her room at the university, and wasn't found with her body. Last activity was at her halls of residence on the day she disappeared. Either switched off or ran out of battery. Forensics will see what they can pull out of her messaging and call history."

"CCTV?"

"Still playing through," replied Cassidy. "The team are compiling lists of vehicles seen in each location and cross-checking them against each other — seeing if any vehicles appear in both locations. It's a massive job. We might know more tomorrow."

"I want to know the minute anything suspicious turns up."

"Any more thoughts on making the black stiletto shoe public?" Cooper nodded at the photograph of the shoe found close to Georgina Dale's body. "Asking if anybody recognises it?"

"I've thought of nothing else, Cooper, but I think it'd be a one-way ticket to mass hysteria. And not necessarily helpful. We've already established it's a very common shoe — so all we'll do is attract several thousand calls identifying everyone's wife, sister, mother and lover as having owned a pair." Jack paused. "I don't think our system can cope with that."

"And keeping the shoes out of the press is our one way of excluding prank callers," added Cassidy. "Only the killer knows he leaves a shoe at the scene."

"Exactly." Jack moved away from the window. "We'll keep it out of the media for now. Can you both make sure your notes are uploaded onto the system before you leave tonight?"

Both DS Cooper and DC Cassidy nodded.

"How did it go with the profiler? Anything useful?" Cassidy stepped away from the fan and slipped into a vacant chair.

Jack paused, feeling the weight of Dr Hunter's profile in his shirt pocket. He hadn't briefed the team yet on her observations — most probably because he wasn't sure what he made of them himself. But he knew he couldn't hold off much longer. He might not like it, but profiling sometimes did hit gold. He pulled Dr Hunter's list out of his pocket and handed it across to Cassidy.

"Knock yourselves out. Make a couple of copies and get the info uploaded onto the system. We'll go into it in more depth if and when we get a suspect." Jack glanced down at his watch. "Let's wrap things up — briefing at nine a.m. tomorrow." Hesitating only briefly, he pulled his mobile from his pocket. "I'll text DS Carmichael — in case he wishes to join us." The sarcasm in Jack's voice wasn't lost on anyone. "Do we even know where he is?"

Cassidy shook her head. "He just let me out at the traffic lights and said he needed to be somewhere."

"The place he *needed* to be was *here*." Jack sighed and waved at the door. "Get the notes uploaded onto the system and then get yourselves off home. Cooper — I'll need a lift home. It's been a long day."

CHAPTER TWENTY-ONE

Time: 6.35 p.m.
Date: Sunday 22 July 2012
Location: Kettle's Yard Mews, London

Shrugging off his shirt and unbuckling his trousers, Jack headed towards his small bathroom. The shirt had almost welded itself to his back during the course of the day, and peeling it off was like shedding another layer of skin. He'd listened to the radio in Cooper's car on the way home — officially the hottest July on record, beating even the summer of 1976. Not a millimetre of rain had fallen since May and most water companies were about to issue severe drought orders, imposing a swathe of hosepipe bans across much of the country. Everyone was being urged to conserve water wherever possible.

No baths. No car washing. No dishwashers. Use your washing machine with a full load, and only on an energy and water-saving programme. Jack glanced back towards the kitchen and noticed the full sink of dirty dishes. And then the washing bin full to overflowing with clothes that had yet to be anywhere near the washing machine.

Just doing my bit to conserve water, he thought, as he stepped into the shower.

He hit the button and sent a deluge of water down onto the top of his head. Remaining there for fifteen minutes, he savoured the cool water pulsating rhythmically against the back of his neck.

An illegal power shower.

But at least he wasn't doing the dishes.

Half an hour later, dried and refreshed, Jack pulled on an old pair of Hawaiian shorts that hadn't seen the light of day for many a year, and his last clean T-shirt. As he sank down onto the sofa, he already started to feel hot again. He hadn't quite been quick enough to buy a fan from any of the local shops, and everything was sold out online.

At least his fridge was full of ice-cold beer.

That was something the shops didn't seem to be running out of.

On the way home, he'd instructed DS Cooper to stop by a convenience store so he could stock up with essentials. Beer, another bottle of single malt, and several microwave meals that would probably lurk in the freezer for another six months.

He closed his eyes and leaned back against the softness of the sofa. As he settled, he felt something buried beneath one of the cushions behind his back. Wriggling to the side, he reached behind and pulled out an old, battered teddy bear.

Stu's teddy bear.

It'd been the only thing belonging to his brother that Jack had managed to salvage before the welfare system ripped them apart. A constant reminder of the past, Jack could've donated it to a local charity shop or hospital, or even just put it out with the rubbish.

But the past would still be there.

So the teddy bear stayed.

With another long evening stretching out in front of him, Jack reached for the pile of papers he'd brought home with him. The link between Patricia Gordon and Georgina Dale had to be there — somewhere. Which might just lead to their killer being found in time to save the owner of the black stiletto shoe.

Without bothering to get a glass, Jack unscrewed the lid of the Glenfiddich bottle and settled down to work.

* * *

Time: 9.15 p.m.
Date: Sunday 22 July 2012
Location: Isabel's Café, Horseferry Road, London

With Livi purring contentedly on her lap, Isabel stifled a yawn. The evening had slipped past so quickly, but she'd done nothing more than put a ready meal in the microwave for dinner and pour herself a glass of wine. The vegetable pasta bake had been all right, nothing to write home about, but the wine had gone down nicely. She'd resisted pouring a second glass, knowing it was likely to be the beginning of a steady road to ruin. Another five o'clock start in the morning beckoned and she knew her morning self wouldn't thank her for indulging in one more Chardonnay.

Leaving the empty wine glass on the coffee table, she rested back against the cushions and watched the sun disappear behind the buildings opposite and the light begin to fade. The beginnings of a faint breeze stirred the curtains — a welcome respite from the heat of the day.

Despite the King's Road being one of the busiest roads in London, there was very little sound wafting in from outside. The heat was draining everyone of what energy they had — no one venturing very far when the working day was over.

Closing her eyes, Isabel began stroking Livi's soft fur, feeling the tabby cat's rhythmic purring beneath her fingers. Just as she felt herself begin to doze off, a noise from outside caused her eyes to snap open.

It sounded like the sandwich board she used for chalking up the daily specials had fallen over on the pavement outside.

But she'd already brought it inside when she'd locked up, hadn't she?

A frown crossed Isabel's brow as she sought to cast her mind back — but the fog of tiredness merely confused her more. Patrick had left not long after she'd closed the café — and she'd watched him disappear towards the Tube — but did she bring the sandwich board back in then?

Maybe I didn't, she thought to herself, glancing towards the open window. *Would it matter if I left it outside? It's not as if it's likely to rain anytime soon.*

But what if someone steals it?

Knowing she wouldn't sleep tonight until she'd checked it out, Isabel dislodged a rather unimpressed cat and hauled herself to her feet. Slipping on a pair of flip-flops, she descended the stairs to the café beneath.

Everywhere was bathed in a subdued light — that special kind of light that is neither day nor night. The café sat in a peaceful slumber, just a faint hum from the fridge and freezer in the kitchen behind her. Isabel headed towards the door, a quick glance around telling her that the chalkboard wasn't inside where she usually kept it.

Peering through the window, Isabel saw the sandwich board collapsed onto the pavement just outside the door.

Damn, I did forget to bring it in after all. Sighing, Isabel turned the key in the lock and pulled back the bolts, giving the door a firm tug to open it. The bell above jangled, making her jump a little.

Stepping out onto the pavement, Isabel's attention was drawn to a departing figure across the street. With the fading light, it was difficult to see properly — but, despite the gloom, Isabel was once again certain about what she saw.

Or rather, *who* she saw.

The microwave meal from earlier solidified in the pit of her stomach.

Surely not again?

She'd thought she'd seen him before — the day Mac had taken a tumble from his motorbike outside the café. But she'd dismissed it as absurd. There was no way he'd come back — no way he'd come anywhere near her. Not after what had happened.

But here he was again; close to the café — and close to *her*.

As she blinked to clear her vision, the figure was gone. Shivering, despite the sultry feel to the evening air, Isabel picked up the sandwich board and hurried back inside.

* * *

Time: 10.15 p.m.
Date: Sunday 22 July 2012
Location: A cellar in London

Pausing at the top of the stone steps, he listened to his own quickening breath. It was always the same; always the same feeling whenever it was "time". With a familiar gleam in his eye, he began to descend the steps, holding onto the banister at the side to steady himself. His knees felt weak at the thought of what was to come — of what he had to do.

But it had to be done.

Jess needed to go to a better place.

It was the only way to protect her from this vile and sickening world.

He turned the heavy wrought-iron key in the lock and, placing one shoulder against the oak door, he shoved hard. The darkness and dampness enveloped him as soon as he stepped inside the cellar. He sniffed the air — it was tinged with a mixture of perspiration and the less than pleasant aroma coming from the metal bucket in the corner. He wrinkled his nose.

Maybe he was keeping them too long.

Neither Jess nor Carol were making a sound. Through the dense blackness it was hard to even make out their forms, but he knew they'd be huddled beneath their blankets, shutting out the world. He followed the outline of the metal chains from the radiator — one chain to his left, the other to his right.

Walking towards the chain on the right, he edged his way towards the threadbare mattress. As he approached, he heard sobbing sounds coming from underneath the thin blanket that was draped over Jess's crumpled body. He watched closely as the blanket shuddered up and down with each tear-ridden cry.

Next to the shrouded figure were the remnants of the Sunday lunch he'd brought them both. Jess had mostly eaten hers — a chicken and sweetcorn sandwich — with only the crusts remaining. He glanced over his shoulder towards Carol's mattress — noting the untouched sandwich and drink on the floor by her side.

"Ssssh now, Jess. Everything's all right." He turned back towards Jess's mattress and knelt down by her side, gently pulling the blanket away from the trembling figure beneath. The paleness of her skin and the whites of her eyes stood out in the dark. "Ssssh, Jess. Daddy's here."

Taking another key from his pocket, he took hold of Jess's slim ankle. If she'd had any strength left then she would've kicked out violently, and maybe started screaming and yelling.

But Jess had no energy left to do anything.

Hannah watched, silently, as the man unlocked her ankle restraint and placed the heavy chain to one side. She was surprised at the strength of his grip, feeling his bony fingers clasped around her wrists. She lay still, not moving, not intending to get to her feet, but he dragged her up with ease. With a wiry arm encased around her neck, he began dragging her across the stone floor towards the door.

Once through the door, she saw a light at the top of the stone steps — and, as they ascended, lighter and fresher air greeted her. Her heartbeat quickened, panic rising alongside the bile in her throat. Where were they going? As she was dragged further and further away from her prison cell, Hannah looked back over her shoulder and all of a sudden craved the darkness, the dampness, the smell of sweat and fear. She longed for the hard, cold ground and sense of hopelessness.

Take me back.
Take me back to the rotten cellar.
She'd rather have that than this.
Whatever *this* was.
And who is Jess?

CHAPTER TWENTY-TWO

Time: 6.15 a.m.
Date: Monday 23 July 2012
Location: Green Park, London

The fluttering blue-and-white police tape had been wound around two conveniently placed tree trunks and stretched lengthways along a section of the quietest part of Green Park. Jack nodded at the police officer standing guard at the outer cordon of the crime scene, ducking under the tape once he'd given his details for the police log and donned his protective suit.

His heart sank as he stepped cautiously along the improvised walkway, snapping the elasticated hood over the top of his head. He could tell from the white-clad bodies in the distance that the crime scene manager and forensics team had already been called.

Number three.

It had to be.

The owner of the black stiletto shoe.

Jack hoped with all his heart that he'd be proved wrong, but his head was telling him otherwise. And his head usually won.

As he approached the inner cordon, Jack saw the familiar white tent — the flaps parting as Dr Philip Matthews made his exit. It wasn't long before the pathologist caught Jack's eye.

"Jack." Dr Matthews ducked under the inner cordon tape and nodded in greeting, shrugging off his protective suit as he did so. He motioned for Jack to step to the side, away from the quiet hustle and bustle heading towards the tent.

"Doc," replied Jack, shuffling across in his blue plastic overshoes. "I'm guessing we have our number three."

Dr Matthews nodded, grimly, a haunted expression crossing his cleanly shaven face. Jack couldn't begin to imagine how many shocking scenes this seemingly unassuming and placid man had had to witness in his career. But his demeanour was always one of cool professionalism — appearing to be able to detach himself from the horrors he witnessed up close; able somehow to compartmentalise the violence and evil that cruelly ended the lives of the bodies he examined. But Jack was now seeing a layer of humility and sadness that he'd never quite detected before in the ageing pathologist. Maybe it'd always been there, and Jack just hadn't been looking quite hard enough.

"Female — young. No more than eighteen, I would suggest. Slightly built." Dr Matthews spoke in a hushed, respectful tone, while Jack gazed over his shoulder at the shrouded tent.

"Cause of death?"

"Preliminary — *very* preliminary — strangulation by ligature. You'll have to wait for my full report to confirm."

Jack nodded. "Of course."

"And yes," added Dr Matthews, anticipating Jack's next question. "Wearing just the one shoe. A black stiletto."

Jack nodded. A black stiletto shoe that no doubt matched the one found alongside Georgina Dale's body only three days before, the one that was currently in an evidence bag back in the incident room.

"If we can get her away from here soon, I'll ensure I schedule the post-mortem examination for later this afternoon." Dr Matthews turned to go, heading back towards the cordoned-off section of road where he'd parked his trusty Volvo. "You may want to send someone along this time, Jack. Now we're getting a pattern."

Jack raised a hand in acknowledgment as the pathologist backed away and headed towards the sanctuary of his car. Breathing deeply, he turned towards the white tent and the sombre dance being played out before him; white bodies moving in synchronised sequence to the inaudible tune of death. Turning to duck under the tape, he noticed DS Cooper waving at him from a distant corner of the park.

Changing direction, Jack headed in Cooper's direction, his already heavy heart sinking further when he noticed the pensive expression on the sergeant's face as he approached. Cooper nodded his head towards the longer grass at the edge of the park — no words were necessary. The look on his face told Jack everything he needed to know.

Nestling among the sun-baked grass was a solitary shoe. Jack knelt down, careful not to disturb the surrounding area. Snapping on a pair of protective gloves, he gently parted the wispy strands to reveal a patent black court shoe with a low heel.

"Number four?" DS Cooper stepped back as one of the crime scene investigators appeared, snapping several photographs of the shoe in situ, before lifting it gently into a plastic evidence bag.

Jack nodded. "Number four."

* * *

Time: 6.45 a.m.
Date: Monday 23 July 2012
Location: A cellar in London

Zoe had pretended to be asleep when he'd opened the door before, waiting for him to shuffle across to her mattress and kneel down by her side. She'd held her breath and waited for the touch of his cold fingers on her bare skin, recoiling

171

underneath her blanket at the very thought. But although she knew he was there in the cellar, she didn't hear his heavy breath by her side. Instead, she'd heard the scraping of Hannah's chain on the concrete floor, before hearing the door open and close.

And then there'd been nothing.

She'd lain frozen beneath the blanket for what seemed like hours afterwards; not daring to move or breathe in case he was still there, hiding in the shadows — playing some kind of warped game. How long it'd been she could only guess — it must've been hours; long, painfully slow hours — but eventually she found the courage to peek out from beneath her cocoon to only be confronted with the same darkness as before.

But this time she was alone.

Completely alone.

Hannah had gone.

* * *

Time: 7.35 a.m.
Date: Monday 23 July 2012
Location: Green Park, London

"You head on back." Jack walked beside DS Cooper as they headed towards their cars. "Get yourself some breakfast and freshen up." Jack knew there was little point in them hanging around much longer. The crime scene manager was in charge now, and two detectives would just get in the way. The scene would be expertly processed, evidence bagged and logged — and the body removed in a nondescript black private ambulance to be taken to the mortuary where, no doubt, Dr Matthews would be waiting. "I'll meet you back at the station. Get everyone together for a briefing at ten thirty — make sure Amanda and Carmichael are there."

DS Cooper nodded and headed towards his small silver Golf. Jack watched the young detective reverse out into the early morning traffic before making his way back towards the white tent.

Inside, he saw the body positioned on the grass — her arms were draped across her chest, her legs tucked to the side. One black stiletto shoe on her foot. She looked peaceful — serene, even. But everyone in the white tent knew the end to her life had been anything but peaceful and serene.

Jack saw the markings around her slim neck — markings that would become more visible as time progressed. But apart from that, she appeared to be untouched. Her pale eyes stared lifelessly skywards, her face empty of emotion.

Having seen enough, Jack exited the tent and ripped off his protective suit. He needed a change of clothes.

And then he needed coffee.

* * *

Time: 9.35 a.m.
Date: Monday 23 July 2012
Location: Westminster Coroners Court, Horseferry Road, London

Anthony Saunders pushed open the wrought-iron gate of the Westminster Coroners Court and glanced at his watch. The case had been adjourned for the third time, and was beginning to grate on his nerves. He'd been up for hours already; the early start making itself known by the dull, throbbing headache pounding at his temples. Turning right, he began walking towards the river — the day was already hot and sticky and he didn't fancy being cooped up in his stuffy office for any longer than necessary. As far as his secretary was aware, he was meant to be in court all day — and he wasn't about to put her straight.

With his stomach rumbling, his thoughts turned to breakfast. On his previous visits to the Coroners Court he'd noticed a new coffee shop had sprung up close to the entrance to St John's Gardens. Keeping in the shade as much as possible, he headed in its direction.

It didn't take long to arrive at Isabel's Café and a comforting draught greeted him as he stepped over the threshold. A mixture of the rich scent of coffee, cake and pastries went hand in hand with a faint aroma of sweet cinnamon. It made his stomach give a low rumble. The short walk from court had awakened his appetite.

He was then greeted by an even warmer, richer smile.

"Morning!" The smile belonged to an attractive woman whom he guessed to be in her early thirties, dressed in a pair of dark-blue denim dungarees, with a white T-shirt underneath; everything wrapped up in a red and white checked apron. Her light, sun-kissed hair was scraped away from her face into a high ponytail, her cheeks glowing rosily from the heat of the coffee machine steaming behind her. "Coffee?"

Anthony Saunders found himself returning the smile and nodding. "Yes, thanks. That would be great."

"Anything in particular? We do a great cappuccino, or if you fancy something different, a cinnamon latte?" Isabel wiped her hands on a nearby tea towel and smiled once again at her new customer. Her new, very handsome customer. "Or iced? If you need cooling down?"

Swinging his laptop bag off his shoulder and placing it on one of the comfortable-looking sofas, the defence solicitor gazed up at the blackboard behind the counter. "Um, a latte would be great. Sounds good." He paused while he cast his eyes around the rest of the coffee shop, noting he was the only customer. "Do you mind if I just sit here and do some paperwork? I don't fancy going back to the office just yet."

Isabel smiled, gesturing towards the empty sofas. "Be my guest. We've plenty of space. I'm Isabel, by the way. You've not been here before?"

"Me? No. I've not been out this way for a while." Anthony Saunders slipped off his jacket and folded it over the back of one of the sofas, seating himself among the soft cushions. He took in the homely-looking armchairs and beanbags, and the bookcases rammed full of paperbacks. "This place is amazing."

Isabel's rosy cheeks flushed a little darker. She turned towards the coffee machine, a jet of hot steam exploding from the spout and filling the room with the rumble of hot milk being steamed to its frothiest. Once the steam subsided, the aroma of sweet cinnamon floated through the air.

Bringing the coffee over to where Anthony Saunders was sitting, Isabel noticed his laptop was already open and a pile of paperwork sat next to it. Careful not to spill any of the coffee onto what looked like very important papers, Isabel set the tall glass down on a hessian coaster. Straightening herself up, she tried to imagine what this tall, dark, handsome stranger did for a living.

Writer?

Journalist?

Film critic?

"Thanks." Anthony Saunders nodded towards the coffee, inhaling the heady scent of cinnamon. "It smells lovely."

Isabel was about to turn away when she spied the man's mobile phone on the arm of the sofa. She recognised the mobile app open on the screen.

London Life.

She then noticed his ringless left hand.

Did that mean he was single? A strange fluttering sensation began to ripple through her stomach. She'd felt something similar when Mac had turned up in his bike leathers on Saturday, and she wasn't used to it. Her social life had been non-existent since setting up the café, and here were two eligible men turning up on her doorstep at the same time. Just like buses — you wait around all day, and then two come along at once.

Isabel's jumbled thoughts were interrupted by Dominic appearing from the kitchen.

"I've put fourteen pastries into the second oven," he informed her, already carefully recording the information in his notebook. "They'll be ready in exactly nineteen minutes."

Isabel smiled and returned to the counter. "Thanks, Dominic." She glanced at her watch. There would now be a lull until the pre-lunchtime rush started. "How about you take a break while it's quiet? I know Livi would probably like some fussing."

Dominic raised his head from his notebook, noticing their lone customer for the first time. He took in the stranger's appearance — medium build, dark-coloured neatly cropped hair, dark brown eyes, smart Savile Row suit — a jacket lying across the back of the sofa displaying the Gieves & Hawkes label. Working from an HP laptop; an iPhone 4S on the arm of the sofa. Freshly made cinnamon latte on the table. Dominic made the appropriate entries into his notebook and then, satisfied, he left in search of Livi.

Turning back to the counter, Isabel began straightening the napkin holder and cutlery tray. She hadn't managed much sleep after discovering the sandwich board outside last night — and then the figure she was certain she'd seen in the shadows. It had unnerved her and made sleep virtually impossible.

"Are you sure you don't mind me sitting here and working?" The voice jolted Isabel back to the present, away from her thoughts of last night.

"Of course not." Isabel slipped out from behind the counter and perched herself on the arm of the chair opposite her new customer. "As you can see, we're not busy. You've got at least another hour before the pre-lunchtime rush begins. Stay as long as you want. I can give you the Wi-Fi password if you need it?"

Anthony Saunders looked up, his gaze meeting Isabel's. Before he knew what was happening, he was introducing himself.

"I'm Anthony Saunders." He held out his hand. "Pleased to meet you."

"Isabel." Isabel leaned forward and found herself taking his warm hand in her own. She laughed. "Sorry, I already told you that when you came in."

Anthony smiled. He must've passed by this café several times on his way to and from court, and each time he hadn't realised what beauty lay within. "How long have you been here?" Clearing his throat, he reached for his coffee and lowered the lid of his laptop — suddenly the lure of paperwork wasn't so strong.

"Oh, must be about three or so months now," replied Isabel, feeling the blush still tingling at her cheeks. "I have a small art studio out the back, too." She nodded towards the rear of the café. "Artists can rent space from me, and sell their paintings in the café."

"And you live above?" Anthony nodded towards the ceiling and the flat above.

Isabel nodded. "It's only small but it's big enough for us. It's just me . . . and my cat." Isabel felt a fresh wave of heat cross her cheeks. Why had she just told a perfect stranger where she lived, and that she lived alone? With a cat. Before she could stop, she felt herself ask the next question. "You?"

"Me? Oh. I live along the Embankment. Alone. Just me. No cat." Anthony smiled, his chocolate eyes twinkling.

Feeling brave, Isabel nodded at the man's mobile phone still sitting on the arm of the sofa. "I couldn't help but notice the app on your phone. London Life. Do you use it?"

Anthony's gaze flickered towards his phone. Putting his coffee cup down, he swept the phone up and closed the app down, slipping the phone into his trouser pocket.

"I do. And I don't. It's a little embarrassing." He gave a short chuckle and reached for his coffee cup again. "A dating app at my age. If anyone knew at work, I'd be a laughingstock."

"Me too," Isabel blurted out, a little louder than she'd anticipated. "I mean — I use it sometimes. And it makes me feel a little like that, too. I daren't tell anyone!"

"Really?" Anthony raised an eyebrow and smiled. "That makes me feel a whole lot better! I just find my job keeps me so busy, I don't have time for meeting anyone. I'm divorced. Live on my own. I don't usually have much luck at relationships. And London is so . . . well, it can be a quite unfriendly place sometimes."

Isabel felt herself relax. "I feel exactly the same. I work here seven days a week, often until quite late. I never really get time to meet anyone, either."

"Well, today you've met me." Once again Anthony held out his hand and grinned, his smile reaching his chocolate-brown eyes and making them sparkle. Isabel laughed and shook his hand once again.

Over the next ten minutes, Isabel quickly found out that he'd been married just the once, was now divorced, originally came from Oxford but moved to London when he got a job as a solicitor. No pets. Liked pasta and Indian takeaways. Not keen on Chinese. Had a gym membership but rarely went. Didn't smoke. Tried weed at college once. And couldn't swim.

Suddenly, the bell on the coffee shop door jangled, and Isabel got to her feet to welcome her next customer. "Jack! Good to see you again." Leaving Anthony to his coffee, she returned to the counter. "Twice in one week. What brings you out this way?"

"Just a flying visit." Jack closed the door behind him, letting the enticing aroma of freshly baked pastries and coffee fill his nostrils, replacing the unpleasant scent of death from the morning's discovery at Green Park. The low rumble in his stomach reminded him that he hadn't eaten yet today — but the combination of the early start and the partially clothed dead body had gone some way to dampening his appetite. "Just in the area. Thought I'd treat the team to a proper coffee rather than the muck from the vending machine."

As Jack stepped towards the counter, he noticed they weren't alone. Glancing towards the sofa, he nodded at the defence solicitor, noting the pile of paperwork and laptop next to him. "Saunders."

"Detective." Anthony Saunders returned the recognition with a short, curt nod of his own.

"DC Cassidy tells me you got everything you needed from the unused material in the Hansen case." Jack pulled out his wallet and handed a twenty-pound note across the counter towards Isabel's outstretched hand. "Give me four coffees — whatever you recommend. I have no idea what any of this means." He nodded at the blackboard menu behind her.

"Indeed we did," replied Anthony, draining the last of his now-cooled latte. "We're good for trial."

Isabel busied herself behind the counter, placing four recyclable takeaway coffee cups into a cardboard tray. "The skinny latte is for Amanda." She tapped on top of one of the lids. "I've given you and Chris a cinnamon latte each. And then a mocha."

Jack nodded, lifting the tray from the counter. "Keep the change. Put it in your charity box." He pointed at the Marie Curie Cancer Care money box sitting by the cutlery tray. "I'd better get back before these get too cold."

With a brief smile at Isabel, Jack turned away and headed for the door.

"Cheerio, Inspector." Anthony Saunders didn't lift his eyes from his laptop. "See you in court."

CHAPTER TWENTY-THREE

Time: 10.50 a.m.
Date: Monday 23 July 2012
Location: Metropolitan Police HQ, London

A third victim.

Jack pinched the top of his nose as DS Cooper added details of that morning's grim discovery to the interactive whiteboard. The case was starting to get out of control.

"Regarding the body found this morning — Amanda, make a note to put a call in to Missing Persons when we're done here. The body itself is on its way to the mortuary — and this is one we're going to attend at the request of Dr Matthews. But, for now, we concentrate our efforts on Patricia and Georgina. How are we getting on with the CCTV?"

"We've got two teams trawling through the images." Cassidy sipped her skinny latte. "A list of vehicles seen at each vicinity in the hours before the bodies were discovered is now being followed up, the owners being traced. They'll be spoken to and ruled in or out as appropriate. I'm expecting an update later this afternoon, but so far we haven't been able to find a vehicle that shows up at both sites."

Jack nodded. It was as he'd expected. The road traffic division had already informed him that roadworks around the capital meant that traffic in some areas was being diverted away from its usual course, and many CCTV cameras were out of action. "Let's add this morning's scene to the CCTV. And widen the area — search more streets in and around each dump site. He has to have got the bodies to the sites somehow. He needs a vehicle. Let's focus on vans or large estates."

Cassidy nodded and made a note in her notebook. "I'll go through it again when we're finished here."

"So, then we have Frank Gordon."

"But why would he kill his wife?" Cassidy frowned towards the whiteboard where Gordon's face filled the screen.

"*Ex*-wife," corrected Jack, sipping his coffee.

"Ex-wife," conceded Cassidy, taking another sip of her skinny latte and inclining her head towards the screen. "Although they were technically still married. I still don't see his motive."

"You know the stats," replied Jack. "People are usually killed by someone they know. An ex-husband will always be a prime suspect until proven otherwise. And you said yourself — his split from Patricia might not have been as amicable as he wants people to believe."

"I agree." DS Carmichael had been sitting quietly at the far end of the incident room. "Statistically, most murders are committed from within the close family unit."

"Single murders maybe, but not for serial killers," continued Cassidy, shaking her head. "The son was off with him, but that doesn't prove anything. Let's say he did kill his ex-wife — why on earth would he kill Georgina as well? There's no connection to her — it makes no sense. And now we have a third."

"He's only up there as a suspect — nothing more." Jack drained his coffee and tossed the empty carton into the bin behind him. It was too milky for his liking and he wasn't a big fan of cinnamon. "He stays there until he can be eliminated."

In reality, Jack's gut feeling matched Cassidy's. Frank Gordon was an unlikely serial killer. If he'd had a falling-out with his son, then it was likely to be unconnected. Most families had some kind of splintered fractiousness underneath the surface if you scratched hard enough. But the list of profile characteristics given to him by Dr Hunter was burning a hole in his shirt pocket.

Frank Gordon fit the age range.

He was divorced, or as good as.

He was an educated man.

But there was one other thing that really alerted Jack's detective instincts.

The cleanliness of the house.

And the smell of bleach.

"I guess he does fit some of the psychological profile characteristics from Dr Hunter," conceded Cassidy, finishing her latte. "But I still don't think he did it."

Jack sighed inwardly. "So he stays there until we rule him out. For the rest of today — Amanda, if you and DS Carmichael focus on the CCTV for now, and touch base with Missing Persons about the body from this morning. Then I'd like you both at the mortuary for this afternoon's post-mortem — Dr Matthews has confirmed it'll be around three o'clock." Jack watched Cassidy give a slow nod. Carmichael merely raised his eyebrows above the rim of his mocha. "Cooper — later on, you and I are going to visit Georgina Dale's halls of residence. But, for now, give forensics a call and see if there's anything outstanding for either Patricia Gordon's or Georgina Dale's samples."

DS Cooper deposited his empty coffee cup in the wastepaper bin. "What about the shoe found this morning, boss?" A photograph of the shoe found in Green Park had already been uploaded onto the whiteboard.

Jack was well aware three pairs of eyes were now trained on him. "The shoe found at the scene in Green Park has been bagged up and is now with forensics."

"So we're pretty sure he has another." Cooper's voice was sombre as the realisation hit them all.

"Yes," replied Jack. "He has another."

* * *

Time: 1.30 p.m.
Date: Monday 23 July 2012
Location: A cellar in London

He looked at his watch and grimaced. He was later than he'd anticipated. It'd been harder to slip away today — people were starting to miss him, notice his absence. Filling the water bottle at the sink with tap water, he picked up the fresh packet of sandwiches and banana, placing everything inside a plastic carrier bag.

The door to the cellar was locked, as it always was. From the outside it looked like a door to a broom cupboard, somewhere you might keep your ironing board or vacuum cleaner. Somewhere to store muddy boots or a dog's lead. He chuckled to himself as he slid the metal bolt across and turned the heavy, wrought-iron key in the lock. It was strange how first impressions could deceive.

A cold rush of air greeted him as he began to descend the stone steps. He snapped on the overhead light which illuminated the stairwell with a dim glow. Reaching the bottom, he was faced with yet another door; once again the door was locked. Always locked. Even though he knew Carol could never escape, he couldn't take any chances.

Carol was clever.

The key turned easily in the lock, the grating sound echoing against the stone walls. He gently pushed the door open with a foot, hearing the wood scrape noisily on the stone floor beneath. Another rush of cold air enveloped him as he stepped forward into the cellar.

Cold air tainted with something else.

Could you smell fear?

If you could, then this was almost certainly what it would smell like.

* * *

Time: 2.15 p.m.
Date: Monday 23 July 2012
Location: St James's University, London

The room looked just like any other typical student digs — or as typical as Jack assumed they'd look. A single bed took up most of the space, with a single wardrobe and built-in desk opposite. Standard cheap flat-pack furniture, Jack mused, as he turned around, spying the compact shower room and en-suite completing the layout.

Georgina Dale's room had already been processed by the forensic team, the bedding bagged and taken away for analysis, along with her laptop and other possible items of evidence. So far, nothing had come back from the labs as showing up anything suspicious — no unusual fibres or DNA other than those of the victim herself. The crime scene manager was reprocessing some items to be doubly sure, but Jack didn't hold out much hope.

Walking over to the small window, Jack looked out onto a patchy triangle of grass bleached white by the sun. A handful of students was lazing beneath the trees, dozing between summer lectures or trying to catch up on coursework. Jack looked across the grass to the building opposite, to where both Dr Hunter and Dr Riches had rooms.

Glancing back around the room, Jack searched for anything out of place. Anything that might lead them to how Georgina met her fate.

And her killer.

But there appeared to be nothing.

Textbooks were stacked up neatly on the desk, a half-finished essay on A4 lined paper in the centre. Jack leaned in closer. An essay on Daniel Defoe's *Journal of the Plague Year* — destined never to be finished.

"Anything, boss?" DS Cooper joined him at the desk.

After one last sweep of the room, Jack shook his head. "No. Just do the usual photos, Cooper, then let's get out of here."

* * *

Time: 3.05 p.m.
Date: Monday 23 July 2012
Location: Westminster Mortuary, London

The chilled air caused DC Amanda Cassidy's arms to prickle with goosebumps. She shivered and wished she'd brought a jacket with her; her shirt doing nothing to protect her from the fridge-like atmosphere of the Westminster Mortuary.

Maybe I should be thankful, she mused, as she slipped on a pair of rubber overshoes — the temperature was soaring once again outside.

But then again, this was a mortuary.

Nothing to be thankful for in here.

Other than not being the one on the metal slab.

Pushing open the door that led from the female changing room out into the corridor, she saw DS Carmichael waiting for her.

"What took you so long?" he frowned, adjusting his own protective rubber apron. "Nice outfit."

Cassidy made a face, ignoring the remark and pushing past to head towards the main post-mortem room doors. "I could say the same to you. Where were you this morning? We were supposed to go over the CCTV together. Where did you slink off to?"

"A meeting." Carmichael avoided Cassidy's enquiring gaze, falling into step behind her. "Nothing important."

Cassidy pursed her lips but let it go, pushing open the heavy swing doors that led into the examination room. "Let's just get this over with, shall we?"

Carmichael followed. "Something tells me you're not all that thrilled to be here. This your first time?"

Cassidy swung round mid-step, almost causing Carmichael to collide with her. He quickly sidestepped, holding his hands up in mock defence. "Careful now! Looks like I touched a nerve, there."

Cassidy opened her mouth to reply, but found the words catching in the back of her throat as the smell of antiseptic mixed with death filled her nostrils. She could almost physically feel the colour draining from her face. She swallowed and tried to clear her throat.

"No, this is not my first time, thank you very much. And even if it was, it's none of your business."

Which was true.

It wasn't her first time.

But her first time was not something Cassidy wished to dwell upon.

It hadn't been her greatest moment — being carried out mid post-mortem by two mortuary assistants wasn't exactly something you wished to remember.

She raised a hand to cover her nose and at least attempt to shield her senses from the smell.

That mortuary smell.

A smell like no other.

During her training, some of the supervising officers had described it as the smell of decay. But it was much more intense than that. Putrid. Fetid. There weren't enough words in the dictionary to encompass the unique aroma of a mortuary.

Cassidy felt her stomach give a familiar lurch, regretting the hot sausage roll she'd consumed on her way into the station earlier that morning, and then the skinny latte from Isabel's.

"Just asking." Carmichael shrugged and strode across to the far side of the room where Dr Matthews was hovering next to a stainless-steel bench.

Cassidy inhaled a deep breath, recoiling at the taste of death invading her airways, and followed on behind.

"Ah, Detective Constable Cassidy, nice to see you again." Dr Matthews smiled warmly — his brow crinkling beneath the tight protective cap covering his head.

He remembers, thought Cassidy, feeling her cheeks glow. *He remembers.*

"And who else have we here?" Dr Matthews turned his attention to DS Carmichael.. He raised his eyebrows and let his eyes twinkle. "A stand-in for DI MacIntosh, are we?"

Carmichael held out his hand. "DS Robert Carmichael, Doctor. Here to supervise." He gave a small, sideways glance at Cassidy's green-tinged complexion. Cassidy baulked at his tone, her pulse rate quickening at the clearly intended jibe.

If she hadn't felt so queasy she would've retorted with a clever quip of her own, but she knew full well that opening her mouth right now might give her stomach contents an excuse to make their exit.

Dr Matthews waved away Carmichael's proffered hand and turned towards the table that housed the shrouded body of Hannah Fuller. "Time to crack on."

* * *

Time: 3.15 p.m.
Date: Monday 23 July 2012
Location: Metropolitan Police HQ, London

DS Cooper thrust open the door to Jack's office.

"The body from this morning, boss? We've got a positive ID."

Jack raised his gaze from his desk, glad to look at something other than the ever-growing mountain of paperwork in front of him. "Already?"

"Well, it's a potential ID — nothing confirmed as yet because the next of kin haven't been contacted. But Amanda spoke with Missing Persons this morning and they've just phoned through with a potential match."

Jack held his hand out for the folded piece of paper Cooper was flapping in his hand. He flicked it open to reveal a passport-sized photograph and list of brief details.

"Hannah Fuller," read Jack. "Age seventeen. Reported missing by her social worker last Thursday after failing to pick her daughter up from nursery."

"You think it's her?" Cooper nodded at the photograph.

Jack let his eyes rest on the passport picture. It showed a young woman's face, almost child-like in appearance — certainly no older than a teenager. Pale and gaunt-looking, with blonde hair scraped away from her face, a faint scowl hovering. Jack thought back to the white tent from earlier that morning.

The face staring lifelessly towards the sky.

The pale face.

The hollow eyes.

The wispy blonde hair.

Jack slowly nodded. "It's her. Next of kin?"

Cooper shook his head. "There's nothing on record. Missing Persons are in touch with social services to see if they can trace anyone. From the brief notes they have, she lived in a mother-and-baby unit out in Camden. No family support."

"Keep in touch with them. Upload what you have onto the system and find out what you can about her."

"Will do, boss." Cooper headed for his desk. "You thought any more about DS Carmichael?"

"Carmichael?" Jack frowned, moving a pile of paperwork from one side of his desk to the other. "In what sense?"

"Finding out why he's here. And where he really came from?" Cooper picked up the remnants of what looked like a bacon sandwich from his own cluttered desk, giving it a tentative sniff before taking a bite. "You still want me to do some digging?"

Jack sighed. "Something isn't right about him, but I guess we've got bigger and better things to worry ourselves about right now."

"Have you mentioned it to the chief super?"

Jack paused, watching Cooper demolish the rest of the sandwich and wash it down with a cold cup of coffee. He imagined turning up at Chief Superintendent King's office to raise his suspicions about their new member of the team. He could guess the response he might receive in return.

"No, I don't think that's a good idea, Cooper. But do that digging — see what you can find out. Keep it between ourselves for now, though — we need to concentrate on catching this killer."

But Jack wasn't going to forget about DS Carmichael.

Killer or no killer.

CHAPTER TWENTY-FOUR

Time: 3.15 p.m.
Date: Monday 23 July 2012
Location: Westminster Mortuary, London

Dr Matthews angled the overhead light in order to take a closer look at the deep ligature marks around Hannah Fuller's neck.

"We have a Caucasian female, well nourished, one hundred and sixty-five centimetres tall, weight sixty kilograms." He spoke into a dictation machine that was suspended on a thin wire above his head.

DS Carmichael leaned in closer, a look of morbid fascination on his sharp features. DC Cassidy hung back, averting her eyes from the pale-skinned, naked body lying before her, fixing her gaze instead on a bright red plastic bucket beneath the table.

"Clear ligature marks to the neck, compressing the trachea. X-rays taken prior to the examination show a hairline fracture to C1. The skin is broken, indicating extreme force. Classic haemorrhaging spreading from the site of compression." Dr Matthews cleared his throat and glanced up at Cassidy. "Everything all right there, detective?" His kind eyes found her gaze. "Let me know if you need to step outside for a breather."

Cassidy responded with a shake of her head, a faint smile shadowing her blue-tinged lips.

"In that case," nodded Dr Matthews, "I will continue with the upper body dissection."

The pathologist reached for a slim scalpel from the instrument trolley by his side, and made a long, slow incision along each side of Hannah's upper torso, just below her clavicle. The two incisions met just below her neck, then continued with one single incision down towards her pubic bone.

Cassidy felt her eyes unwittingly drawn to the macabre showcase in front of her. She bit her lip, willing herself to break the gaze and go back to studying the red plastic bucket beneath — but her eyes remained locked in focus, watching Hannah's chest and abdomen being peeled back like the rind of a ripe orange.

After he'd finished dissecting and exposing Hannah's skin and subcutaneous tissue, Dr Matthews' soft tones once again filled the room. "Normal-sized chest cavity — ribs and sternum intact."

Cassidy didn't need to watch to know what came next — the rib cutters giving that unmistakable sound of splitting bone.

"Heart and lungs look healthy." Dr Matthews proceeded to remove each organ from the chest cavity, recording their measurements and weight. "Diaphragm, liver and spleen — no abnormalities detected. Moving down into the abdomen and pelvic cavities — kidneys and bladder appear undamaged. As does the uterus."

Cassidy watched as Dr Matthews reached inside Hannah's abdomen, her ears unable to block out the squelching sound as he rummaged unceremoniously among the organs inside. "Bringing out the colon now." The pathologist slowly withdrew his hand from the cavity, bringing with it a length of sausage-like organs, folded and intertwined. The organs slipped through his gloved hands, blood and mucus staining them a russet red. Cassidy felt her own intestines clench involuntarily, and fought the overwhelming urge to retch.

"What about the stomach contents?" DS Carmichael had stepped even closer, his inquisitive eyes following each and every move and sweep of the pathologist's hands.

"You're ahead of me, Sergeant," commented Dr Matthews, his attention still firmly locked on the length of colon in his hands. "Large intestines intact, no abnormalities detected." He paused and flashed his new spectator an inquisitive, yet appreciative gaze. It was unusual for a member of the police force to be so interested in his work. Usually they would stand at the back of the room, on the fringes of the examination, and leave at the earliest opportunity to await the formal post-mortem report rather than stopping to ask questions.

But DS Carmichael was different. And different could be both good and bad. "Coming to the stomach now," Matthews continued, replacing Hannah's colon back inside her abdominal cavity.

Once again, the scalpel soundlessly sliced through the tissue. Reaching inside the cavity, Dr Matthews brought out a surprisingly large J-shaped organ encased in strands of bloody mucus. "Weight, please." He passed the organ to a mortuary assistant who placed it into a metal bowl and quickly took it to the stainless-steel workstation behind them.

"1406 grams," came the reply.

With the bowl returned to him, Matthews carefully slit the organ open, allowing the stomach contents to run out into the base of the bowl. Reaching for the overhead light, he used a spatula to move and inspect the contents.

"Some undigested food contents are present. Looks like meat — possibly chicken — and some type of corn. Sweetcorn, most likely. Some starch-like substance, most probably bread."

"A chicken and sweetcorn sandwich," murmured DS Carmichael, edging closer so he could see the contents for himself.

"Indeed," replied Dr Matthews, tipping the bowl at an angle for his avid viewer.

"Are we talking M&S or a homemade variety?"

The pathologist let a faint frown cross his brow. "Whichever it was, Sergeant, it was the last meal this unfortunate lass was to eat."

Cassidy brought a hand up to cover her mouth, trying to force the bile back down into her own stomach. She tried her hardest not to breathe in, the smell of undigested food and stomach acid mixing in with the already stale odour of death making a toxic mixture. She forced her eyes to look away, anywhere but the body on the table before her.

The red bucket.

She focused once again on the red plastic bucket.

But the red bucket was no longer a welcome source of distraction. Cassidy watched helplessly as the blood and other fluids released from Hannah's body flowed slowly along a deep rutted channel on the examination table, and then dripped down into the bucket.

Drip.

Drip.

Drip.

Cassidy's cheeks lost even more colour, if that were possible. She felt a fuzziness engulf her head, her vision clouding over as if someone had dropped a veil across her face.

Suddenly, Carmichael tore his gaze away from the display of stomach contents, noticing the swaying figure standing several feet behind him. With a quick lunge, he leapt backwards and wrapped his arms around the slumped shoulders of DC Cassidy, stopping her falling at his feet and crumpling to the floor.

He looked down at the ashen face staring back up at him, her eyes wide open but the pupils disappearing up into the top of her head.

"Whoa, there you go." Carmichael eased Cassidy backwards, her body a dead weight in his arms. "Let's get you out of here."

With a quick nod at Dr Matthews, Carmichael scooped up the young detective's small frame and carried her out of the examination room. As soon as he'd backed out through the heavy swing doors, they were both greeted with a welcoming rush of cooler and fresher air.

Carmichael made his way through the fire exit to a small courtyard at the rear. Propping Cassidy up on a low wall, he gently pushed her head down between her knees and held onto her shoulders to keep her steady.

The sun was now starting to dip behind the tall trees that circled the mortuary grounds. Thankfully, the rear entrance was shaded from the intense glare and, judging by the cigarette butts littering the paved ground, it appeared to be the designated smoking area for the mortuary staff. As much as he hated smoking, he couldn't begrudge them this small act of normality.

"Nice deep breaths now," he murmured, patting Cassidy's shoulders. "Nice deep breaths."

Very slowly, Cassidy felt her vision clear. Everything that had been blurred was now swimming back into focus. As clarity returned, she saw she was staring down at a baking hot, dusty pavement and not a red plastic bucket filling with blood and guts. A repeated wave of nausea washed over her which made her retch, her shoulders rising sharply. She fought once more to keep her breakfast down, not wanting to embarrass herself even more than she had already. The hot, acrid taste of bile at the back of her throat burned.

As she looked up, she found a pair of black, beady eyes watching her. Eyes that she'd previously associated with haughtiness and self-importance, she now saw displayed something else. Was it concern? Compassion? Sensitivity? Even kindness? The longer she looked, the more she was convinced that there was something else beneath the cold, hard exterior she'd seen before. She'd seen a brief glimpse of it when returning from visiting the home of Georgina Dale — and now she saw it again.

"Are you OK?" Carmichael's tone was soft. "You look a bit pale. Shall I get you some water?"

Cassidy shook her head. "No, it's fine. Thanks. Just give me a minute."

"You had me worried there for a moment." Carmichael released his grip of her shoulders, and once he was satisfied she wasn't about to collapse, moved to the side to sit on the low wall. "Why don't you stay out here. I'll go and finish up in there."

Cassidy took in a deep breath of fresh air, feeling the stale odour of decay finally leaving her lungs. "Thanks. That would be great."

Carmichael pushed himself up off the wall, heading back towards the fire exit.

"Carmichael? Can we . . . er . . . can we keep all this to ourselves?"

DS Carmichael turned to face her, his hand resting on the door handle. "All what?"

Cassidy nodded towards the building in front of them. "What just happened . . . in there."

Carmichael hesitated before pulling open the fire exit door. "What happened? I don't know what you mean." He gave a small shrug. "Nothing happened, did it? Nothing that I can recall anyway." With a quick flash of a smile, he disappeared back inside the mortuary.

* * *

Time: 4.30 p.m.
Date: Monday 23 July 2012
Location: Metropolitan Police HQ, London

"Show me what we've got so far." Jack sat down next to DS Cooper in the tech suite and nodded at the screen. The room was dark, the lights dimmed to help them scour through hours and hours of CCTV footage.

"It's not great, boss." Cooper manipulated the mouse and let the cursor dance over the screen. "Amanda and Carmichael have been through most of it. It hasn't thrown up many leads."

Jack glanced at his watch. "When did they say they'd be getting back from their jaunt to the mortuary?"

Cooper shook his head. "Not sure, boss. Anytime soon would be my guess. Dr Matthews doesn't normally hang around once he gets started."

"OK, so let me see what we have here while we wait." Jack nodded again at the screen in front of them and watched as Cooper brought up various images of CCTV footage.

"Cameras are on all the main roads around the three dump sites. Inevitably some weren't operational, but we've pulled the images from every camera that was working." With another click of the mouse, DS Cooper brought up the first set of camera footage, black and white images that jumped and flickered. "The quality isn't great."

"You're telling me," sighed Jack, squinting through the dark to try and make sense of the poor-quality, grainy images on the screen. "Anything useful?"

Cooper paused, clicking the mouse again. "From what Amanda tells me, none of the vehicles we see on the footage show up in more than one location. So, either none of the vehicles belong to the killer, or . . ."

"Or he has access to more than one car or van," finished Jack, sighing even more deeply. He'd thought as much. They weren't going to be that lucky. If the killer did want them to catch him, as Dr Hunter seemed to be suggesting, then he wasn't going to make it easy. And he definitely wasn't going to make the mistake of being caught on CCTV.

"All the drivers seen on camera in any of the three locations are being traced. Amanda has extra uniforms helping out on that as we speak. Everyone traced will be interviewed to see if they saw anything. Anything useful will be uploaded onto the system and forwarded to you directly."

Jack nodded. "Anything else?"

DS Cooper once again clicked the mouse and the grainy images in front of them changed. "Just this one, boss." He nodded his head at the screen where one of the images was frozen — Berkeley Street in Mayfair, close to where Hannah Fuller had been found that morning. "It might be nothing, but Amanda highlighted it as a potential line of enquiry. You see that van there?" Cooper pointed at a blurred image of a dark-coloured transit van. "The van behind the ambulance?"

Jack followed Cooper's finger towards the van and nodded. "Right kind of size for transporting a body. Have we run the plates?"

"It's bearing false plates, boss. That's why Amanda flagged it up before she went to the mortuary. It's the only suspicious thing the images have thrown up."

Jack peered more closely at the screen. "Can you enlarge it?"

Cooper clicked the mouse and the image grew larger, filling the entire screen. And sure enough, behind the London Ambulance Service vehicle was the blurred image of a dark-coloured transit van. Two small windows at the rear appeared to have curtains pulled across. The registration plates were clearly visible — MK12 YZK.

"And the plates are false?"

Cooper nodded. "Yep. Traffic have traced them to a silver Peugeot stolen in Greater Manchester last week."

"Do we have any images from the front?" Jack let his gaze linger on the fuzzy image. "Can we see the driver?"

Cooper minimised the image and replaced it with another from a different angle, this time with a front-end view. "Not much clearer, I'm afraid."

Jack saw the front of the van looked slightly dented, with one headlight out, but the image was so blurred it was impossible to see anyone inside. He sighed once again. "And it's not been seen at any of the other two locations, just this one?"

"Just this one, boss," confirmed Cooper. "I know it's a long shot, but Amanda thought it suspicious enough to warrant further investigation."

"She's right. We're probably looking for a van and there's no saying that this isn't the van our killer was driving — that night at least." Jack's eyes lingered on the image. "He may have just got lucky with the other cameras. See if you can get it to ping up on any other CCTV or ANPR systems across the capital." Jack paused, keeping his eyes on the van. "Let's see if we can't trace where this son of a bitch went."

"There's some CCTV from around the university," continued Cooper, leaving the image of the grainy van on the computer screen. "But only one decent camera at the entrance. Shows Georgina Dale leaving — but isn't really helpful as to what direction she went in. And there's no CCTV in or around The Briars Care Home."

Jack nodded and made to get up. "Anything yet from Patricia or Georgina's bank statements or cashpoint activity?"

Cooper followed Jack out of the tech suite. "Nothing unusual for either of them. No transactions after they went missing, as we would expect. The only thing they did have in common, though, was a direct debit to London Life."

"London Life? What's that? Sounds like an insurance company to me." Jack held the door open for Cooper to follow him through to the stairs. "Message Amanda to get onto it — they must be back from the mortuary by now. Then we'll have a briefing before we go home for the night."

* * *

Time: 4.45 p.m.
Date: Monday 23 July 2012
Location: Metropolitan Police HQ, London

DC Amanda Cassidy's phone pinged as Carmichael parked the car in the rear car park. Having spent the journey back from the Westminster Mortuary with the window down and a slight breeze caressing her face, she felt far less queasy. The green tinge to her skin had paled. Glancing down at her phone, she noticed it was a message from DS Cooper.

"Chris wants me to check out London Life. You ever heard of it?" She glanced up at Carmichael as he turned off the engine. "The boss reckons it sounds like an insurance company."

Carmichael shook his head and released his seat belt. "No, never heard of it."

"Both Patricia Gordon and Georgina Dale had direct debits with them." Cassidy slipped out of the passenger seat and joined Carmichael as he started walking towards the rear entrance of the police station. She felt a little lightheaded but jogged to keep up with him. "Looks like it's the only link between them so far."

Carmichael held the door open but remained outside, hovering on the top step. When he didn't follow her inside, Cassidy turned around and frowned at him. "Coming in?" she enquired. She watched Carmichael glance at his watch. "The boss'll be waiting upstairs."

Carmichael took a guarded step backwards. "If you're feeling better and can make your way up on your own, I just need to pop out somewhere. Cover for me?" Without waiting for a response, he turned on his heels and headed back towards his car.

Cover for me? Cassidy watched as he reversed out of the parking space and headed back out onto the road.

How can I cover for you when I have no idea where you're going?

CHAPTER TWENTY-FIVE

Time: 6.35 p.m.
Date: Monday 23 July 2012
Location: Metropolitan Police HQ, London

DS Cooper closed the door to the incident room behind him and hurried over to where Jack was leafing through some of the paperwork. "Boss?" He looked, hesitantly, over his shoulder at the closed door. "I managed to do that digging you wanted — about our new friend, Carmichael?"

Jack's head snapped up. "Yes? Anything?"

Cooper frowned. "It's all a bit strange. You said he came from *Sussex* Police, right?"

Jack nodded, fearing where this conversation might be going. "That's what the chief superintendent said."

"Well, nobody at Sussex has ever heard of a DS Carmichael. I even checked with Surrey in case the names got mixed up — Surrey and Sussex." Cooper paused. "Still nothing."

Jack let the bank statements drop from his hands. "You're saying *nobody* has heard of him?"

"No one that I managed to get hold of, no. I even got someone to run the name through their database. Nothing.

I then made a search for any DS Carmichael on the force throughout the country — the only DS Carmichael registered is from Strathclyde Police, and he's aged sixty-seven and long retired." Cooper glanced over his shoulder at the closed door once more. "It's like he doesn't exist, boss."

Jack absorbed the words in silence.

It's like he doesn't exist.

Before he could reply, the door flew open and DC Cassidy breezed in. "Good, you're both here."

"How was the PM?" Jack rubbed at his temples in an attempt to massage away the threat of the impending headache about to engulf his brain.

Cassidy hesitated slightly, her cheeks turning pink. "It was fine. Dr Matthews said you'll get his report by the morning. But you asked me to look into London Life?"

"What did you manage to find out?"

"Well, for starters, it's not an insurance company." Cassidy closed the door behind her. "It's a dating site."

"A *dating* site?" Jack's frown deepened. "What do you mean, a dating site?"

"A dating site, guv. It's how everyone mingles and meets people these days, what with social media and all that." Cassidy placed her mobile phone on the desk, open at the London Life homepage. "And both Patricia and Georgina look like they belonged to it."

"Bring it up onto the screen, Cooper."

DS Cooper dutifully brought up the home page of London Life onto the interactive whiteboard, navigating the screen with a few more clicks to bring up twenty or more thumbnail pictures of lonely Londoners seeking friendship and love, and goodness knows what else. Happy faces. Smiling faces. Faces that wanted to be your friend.

Not the London I know, mused Jack, rubbing his chin and feeling the ever-growing prickles jabbing at his fingertips. "I want a list of all subscribers to this site. I want to know who they are, where they are, and I want to see their messages."

"Not sure they'll give that info out without a fight, boss." Cooper scrolled through several more pages of the website.

"Then a fight we will have, Cooper." Jack pushed himself up out of his chair and stretched, feeling his back creak. "Get onto them pronto and see what you can do. Get a warrant if they won't cooperate — and while you're at it, check if Hannah Fuller was a member too."

"Will do." Cooper scrolled back to the home page to obtain the dating site's contact information.

"And as much background as you can find on Hannah Fuller for tomorrow's briefing. Anyone seen DS Carmichael?" Jack made a point of looking around the room, noting the obvious absence of their new DS.

"He said he needed to be somewhere once we got back from the mortuary," replied Cassidy.

"Did he now." Jack didn't bother to hide his irritation. "How good of him. Right in the middle of an investigation and he goes AWOL. *Again.*"

"Give him the benefit of the doubt, guv. He seemed genuine. I don't think he's slacking off."

Jack cast a bemused look in Amanda's direction. "You've certainly changed your tune. You thought he was a creep yesterday."

"Yeah, well." Cassidy avoided Jack's inquisitive stare. "Maybe he's not so bad after all."

"Well, I need him here first thing tomorrow for the briefing. As you two are such good mates after your trip to the mortuary, I'll leave it to you to tell him the good news — it's an eight o'clock start. No excuses." Picking up the jacket that he wasn't going to need to wear, Jack headed for the door. "Update the system with what's happened today, then get yourselves off home — we've an early start in the morning. And good work on that stolen van — I've actioned an ANPR search to track its movements. It could be just the breakthrough we need."

* * *

Time: 7.30 p.m.
Date: Monday 23 July 2012
Location: Isabel's Café, Horseferry Road, London

Sighing, Isabel stretched her legs out along the length of the sofa and closed her eyes.

Finally.

Peace at last.

Her legs ached. Her feet throbbed. Her back twinged every time she moved. Any thoughts she might have had of opening in the evenings when the Olympics started were unceremoniously thrown out of her head in an instant.

Although she loved the café when it was busy, the afternoon had been frantic. It'd been the last day of school for a lot of children in the borough, and they'd all descended on the café on their route home, snapping up sausage rolls as if they hadn't eaten all day. Both Sacha and Dominic had stayed until closing time and Isabel hadn't a clue how she'd have coped without them.

Just then, she felt a familiar furry bundle jump up from the floor and nestle into her lap. Opening her eyes slightly, she was greeted with the twitching, quivering nose and whiskers of her favourite companion.

"Livi, sweetie," murmured Isabel, letting her eyelids close once again while stretching out a hand to begin to rub the cat's cheeks, just below her whiskers. "How was your day?" Isabel's question was greeted with a low, rhythmic purring, increasing each time she stroked underneath the tabby cat's chin. "Sleeping and eating? Eating and sleeping?" Isabel smiled to herself. "You poor thing, you must be exhausted."

Livi rubbed her head up against Isabel's hand, her whole body vibrating with each purr. Isabel could feel the wetness of Livi's nose as she rubbed her furry head against her fingers. There was something quite comforting and relaxing about feeling the soft fur of a cat against your skin. Once Livi had tired of being petted, she set about giving her paws a good clean, flicking her tiny pink tongue in and out between her claws.

Isabel could sit and watch her precious pet for hours. Having rescued her from a stray cat sanctuary when she was only seven months old, she'd watched the frightened, timid creature slowly become accustomed to her and then the busy café — now strolling around as if she were the one that was really in charge.

The TV was playing in the corner of the room, but Isabel had turned the sound down. Every news channel led with the gruesome story of the two women found murdered in London parks, and a possibility of a third this morning.

The thought made Isabel shiver.

Then she found herself thinking about Anthony Saunders.

He'd left after an hour or so and when he'd shyly asked for her number, Isabel had been momentarily struck dumb. Men didn't ask for her number — not these days. She couldn't remember the last time it'd happened — or the last time she'd actually handed it over. Although that wasn't strictly true — she'd given her number to Mac just yesterday when he'd called in for a cold drink. She'd felt a strange fluttering sensation when he'd turned up in his bike leathers.

Two numbers in two days — the thought made her blush.

She knew there was more to Mac than met the eye — the estrangement from Jack was all too clear to see — but she didn't know either of them well enough to ask. People were entitled to their secrets.

Livi had now finished her ritualistic washing and had hopped down off Isabel's lap, padding over towards her food bowl. Isabel made to get up, but as she did so she felt her phone vibrate in her pocket.

Pulling it out and glancing at the screen, she gave a sly smile.

* * *

Time: 9.30 p.m.
Date: Monday 23 July 2012
Location: Kettle's Yard Mews, London

Placing the Indian takeaway cartons on the coffee table, Jack headed back to the kitchen in search of plates and cutlery. "Beer?" he called back over his shoulder, already pulling open the fridge.

"Beer," agreed Mac, ripping the lid off one of the cartons. "I'm starving."

Jack brought the plates and forks, plus two bottles of Budweiser, through to the sofa. He'd seen his brother more times in the last few days than he had in the last twenty years — but there was something about it that felt right.

They sat in companionable silence, the only sound being the scraping of forks as they set about the two-person Monday night special banquet from the Taj Mahal takeaway around the corner. But Jack found his appetite waning, and merely pushed his beef madras around his plate with his fork.

London Life.

He couldn't quite get the idea of a dating site out of his head. He knew they existed — had done for some years now — but he could never quite get his head around the idea. It made him shudder that this was where they were all headed eventually — touting for potential partners online. An old police colleague of his had tried to lure Jack into speed dating a few years ago — they were no longer friends.

Three minutes to find a potential life partner.

Jack hadn't managed that in as many decades.

"Come on, bruv, eat up." Mac tipped the remains of the chicken biryani onto his plate. "I'm eating your share."

Jack waved his hand towards the cartons. "Go ahead — I'm not all that hungry. I think I'll start the washing up."

Jack retreated to the kitchen and began filling the sink with hot, soapy water. Seeing Mac again tonight brought all manner of images of Joseph Geraghty back into his thoughts, jumbled up with those of London Life and the investigation.

He still hadn't told the chief superintendent Geraghty was back on the streets of London — and Jack knew that with every hour that passed, he was digging an ever-bigger hole for himself. But he needed proof. It wasn't that he didn't believe his brother — but he just needed something tangible, so there could be no doubt.

CCTV.

Jack made a mental note to request images from around the café — if any existed.

"Bugger!"

The exclamation from the sofa jolted Jack away from his thoughts. He turned to see his brother's T-shirt covered in a generously sized dark brown stain.

"Bloody chucked that madras all down me. You got a spare T-shirt I can borrow?"

Jack suppressed a smile. "In the bedroom. You might find something in the wardrobe."

Mac wiped his mouth on the bottom of his now ruined T-shirt, and headed for Jack's bedroom door. He hadn't been in his brother's bedroom before, and wasn't surprised to see how sparsely it was furnished. Just a bed, a wardrobe and small bedside table.

On the bedside table sat a glass of water, a packet of paracetamol and a book on the Police and Criminal Evidence Act. Next to a lamp was a small black and white photograph housed in a silver-plated frame. The picture was of a young woman with soft, dark eyes and a warm smile. Mac didn't have a picture of their mother, but he knew instinctively that it was her. He didn't remember too much about her and for that he was sometimes grateful. Would he be in a better or worse place now if he did remember?

But Jack slept with her by his side, night after night. He didn't like to think what state his brother's headspace might be in — finding your mother's dead body swinging from a light fitting when you were four years old must mess you up in some way.

Hence the shrink.

Or the psychotherapist, as Jack called her.

Maybe they both needed one.

He hadn't been an easy child, of that Mac was certain. Various social workers had given him labels such as "*destructive*", "*rebellious*", "*attention-seeking*" and even "*violent*" made an appearance at times. "*Delinquent*" was also a popular term. No wonder he'd only ever lasted a few months in any one place. It wasn't something he was proud of.

Pulling open one of the wardrobe doors, Mac found a lone T-shirt hanging up. It was becoming clear to him that his brother lived a sparse and empty kind of life. There was no evidence of any female company and, from what he'd learned about Jack during the last few days, he seemed to live a solitary existence.

But then again, so did Mac.

Two apples from the same tree.

Although one seemingly more diseased than the other.

A knock at the door made him jump and Jack's head appeared around the door frame.

"Coffee? I've got milk this time."

CHAPTER TWENTY-SIX

Time: 8.15 a.m.
Date: Tuesday 24 July 2012
Location: Metropolitan Police HQ, London

"Fill me in on the post-mortem." Jack nodded towards DC Cassidy and DS Carmichael, whom he noted were sitting close together by the window in the incident room. Both fans were already humming, the sun outside promising yet another blisteringly hot day to come.

Cassidy flashed a look at Carmichael, her cheeks colouring.

With a faint flicker of a smile, Carmichael gave a curt nod. "You take the lead on this one, Amanda," he said. "I was only there as backup."

With her cheeks flushing a shade darker, Cassidy cleared her throat. "Well, now we have a positive ID, I can confirm that Hannah Fuller died from strangulation. Missing Persons managed to get in touch with her next of kin — the family are based in Leeds." Walking over towards the whiteboard, she clicked the mouse to bring up Dr Matthews' typed post-mortem report. "Strangulation by ligature. So forceful it broke one of the bones in her neck." Cassidy paused, scrolling down to the conclusion at the bottom of the report. "No defensive wounds. Abrasions to one ankle — suggestive of being held in a restraint. No other visible injuries. No sign of sexual assault." Clearing her throat again, she went on. "Dr Matthews commented on the lack of fibres and forensic material on the body — it's his opinion the body was cleaned or washed before being dumped."

There it was again — that word.

Cleaned.

"So Hannah's post-mortem report basically mirrors those of Patricia Gordon and Georgina Dale. The same cause of death. The same ankle abrasions." Jack nodded his thanks to Cassidy. "And the same lack of forensic detail. We now have three murders linked to the same killer — and we need to find him before he makes it four."

Jack let his eyes stray to the blown-up colour photograph sitting on one of the desks — the black court shoe found close to Hannah's body. "I think we all know the owner of that shoe is in significant danger."

"A FLO is making contact with Hannah's family." DS Cooper brought up a photograph of the seventeen-year-old onto the interactive whiteboard screen. "Social services might help, too. According to the missing person's report, she's still under regular review at the mother-and-baby unit."

Jack nodded. "We have two tasks for this morning — Amanda and Carmichael, I want you both to concentrate on liaising with social services — get as much background as you can on Hannah and her life here. Friends. Acquaintances. Places she visited. And see if we can get the local force in Leeds to assist liaising with the next of kin."

"Boss," nodded Cassidy, opening her notebook.

"Cooper and I are going to swing out to Camden and take a look at Hannah's room at the mother-and-baby unit. Everyone back here for another briefing at one."

* * *

Time: 10.30 a.m.
Date: Tuesday 24 July 2012
Location: Blackfriars Crown Court, London

"Ladies and gentlemen of the jury, I am now going to sum up the facts of the case and then direct you on some matters of law." His Honour Judge Geoffrey Campbell-Smythe paused and let his heavy-lidded eyes roam across each and every member of the twelve-strong jury sitting to attention at the side of courtroom number one.

Sitting high up upon the bench, his bright red robes stood out against the dark mahogany wood panelling of the courtroom walls. As he shifted in his seat to pick up his legal notepad, the bench creaked beneath his weight.

"I want to start with the facts as set out by the prosecution in this case . . ."

Anthony Saunders stifled a yawn. Six weeks this trial had lasted and at last they were on the home stretch. He glanced at the old-fashioned clock mounted on the wall behind His Honour, and calculated how long the summing up might take. With any luck, they could be out within the hour. Hopefully less than that if the old man hurried up. But His Honour Judge Geoffrey Campbell-Smythe was not renowned for being speedy.

He felt the trial had gone well. His client stood a reasonable chance of a not-guilty verdict. Whether he deserved one was an entirely different matter, and not one that troubled Anthony Saunders. He hadn't become such a sought-after defence solicitor by troubling himself with such minor details. The law wasn't about the truth — and it wasn't about justice, either.

It was about who could play the best game on the day.

And Anthony Saunders was backing his team.

Yes, there was circumstantial evidence that could possibly place his client at the scene, and yes, he didn't really have an alibi. And, unbeknown to the jury at this present time, due to the quirkiness of the English legal system, he had a list of convictions as long as his tattooed arm. But did that make him guilty in this game called the law?

Not if you played the game well enough.

Collecting up a pile of loose papers, Anthony Saunders quietly slipped them inside his laptop bag, not taking his eyes off His Honour Judge Geoffrey Campbell-Smythe for one second. The old man was moving on to the defence facts now.

Not that there were many of those to trouble the jury.

With nothing left to tidy away that wouldn't draw the disapproving scowl of the judge, Saunders picked up his pencil and began outlining a sketch on a spare page in his legal pad. Anything to pass the time. He glanced up at the wall clock, wondering if time was actually going backwards instead of forwards.

And there were still the judge's directions on points of law to go.

His pencil made little or no sound on the blank white paper, certainly nothing that could drown out His Honour's monotonous tones. As he sketched, he kept an ear open to gauge the progress the judge was making to bring the case to a close.

Moving onto points of law now.

Anthony Saunders groaned inwardly.

This could take some time.

The law on theft in England had many constituent parts, each of which had to be proven by the prosecution beyond a reasonable doubt — and the judge was keen to set out each and every one in turn.

Beyond a reasonable doubt.

Saunders smiled to himself as his pencil skimmed across the page. It was such a far-reaching statement. Given long enough, most experienced and wily barristers could implant at least one seed of doubt into most jurors' heads.

All it took was one simple seed.

And they'd scattered plenty of these over the last six weeks. It was just a case of waiting to see if any had taken root.

Forty-five minutes the judge had been speaking for now, and he didn't look like stopping anytime soon. Letting his eyes sweep over the jurors' faces, Saunders noticed they were all hanging onto every word that spilled from the distinguished judge's mouth. He wondered what was going on inside their heads right now. What questions were they asking themselves? What opinions had they already formed about the defendant? Were they even thinking about the case? Maybe they were, like Anthony Saunders, merely passing the time until they could get out of the stuffy courtroom.

Saunders' pencil continued to skip silently over the paper, the drawing beginning to take shape. He liked drawing. Sketching. He'd been told that he was quite good at it. When he was younger, there'd been talk of him going to art college, something that'd both excited and appealed to him. But his overbearing father, the Right Honourable Bernard Saunders QC, was having none of that.

"*You cannot make a living from colouring in, my boy.*" Anthony could almost hear his father's words as he sketched. "*No son of mine will be a penniless artist.*" And so, dutifully, Anthony had gone to university to study law, just like his father. All thoughts of pursuing his artist's dream extinguished. And although he'd excelled at university, achieving a first, Anthony felt he'd never quite lived up to his father's expectations. Having chosen the solicitor route, and not the Bar, Anthony felt his father's dismissive disappointment every time they met for Sunday lunch. Which wasn't often, it had to be said. Something that suited them both.

But at least the Right Honourable Bernard Saunders QC didn't have a layabout son at art college.

Fifty-five minutes now.

When would it end?

Anthony studied the drawing in front of him and wrinkled his nose. Hmmmmm, not one of his best. Ever so quietly, he detached the page from his legal pad — it wasn't a masterpiece he would be keeping. There was a glimmer of light at the end of the tunnel as His Honour Judge Campbell-Smythe closed the legal pad on his bench and cleared his throat.

"Ladies and gentlemen of the jury, you will now retire to consider your verdict."

With a nod of his head and an "All rise" from the court usher, everyone in the courtroom rose to their feet and the jury solemnly filed out, one behind the other, to be ensconced in the jury room.

Saunders glanced again at the clock and mentally calculated what time he could get home. It would be tight, but he should just about make it. Technically he should wait at court with his client, as the jury could come back very quickly with their decision. But Anthony Saunders didn't intend to hang around for their verdict. There was a good chance they'd get sent home for the night and resume again tomorrow. But even if they did reach a verdict before the end of the day, Saunders didn't feel the need to support his client with the guilty or not-guilty decision. The defendant had enough experience in front of the courts, as his lengthy previous convictions showed. He'd be fine either way — he didn't need his hand holding.

Anthony gathered up his things, ramming his court folder and legal pad into his bag and zipping it up. Swinging the laptop bag up onto his shoulder, he eased his way out from behind the counsel benches. He nodded his thanks to his defence barrister and hastily made his way to the exit, queuing behind the throng of family members from the public gallery and several court reporters.

Another glance at his watch.

If he got a move on, he'd get back home in time.

* * *

Time: 11.45 a.m.
Date: Tuesday 24 July 2012
Location: St Joseph's Mother and Baby Unit, Camden, London

The room was small, with just a tiny window tucked away above a chipped sink. A narrow single bed hugged one wall, a smaller cot bed by its side. The walls themselves were bare — the washed-out pale grey paint peeling off in strips.

Jack and DS Cooper both cast their eyes around the inside of Hannah Fuller's room. The bed was unmade, as was the cot. Greying sheets and a stained duvet were rolled up in a heap on Hannah's bed; a smaller, milk-stained baby blanket lay hanging over the side rails of the cot.

There was no wardrobe; instead, a hanging rail ran along the opposite wall. A selection of clothes hung from the rail, but most were piled in a heap on the floor beneath. A separate mound of baby clothes and a selection of toys sat in the corner.

A small fridge hummed behind the door. Upon opening it, Jack only found a few cans of cheap lager and an unopened packet of cheese. On top of the fridge were empty cartons of baby milk and a sterilising machine.

The room had already been processed by forensics — working through the night. Fingerprint dust was still evident on the door frame, the door handles and other surfaces in the room. With no suggestion that Hannah had met her killer within these four walls, the examination had been concluded relatively quickly.

"Not much here, boss." Cooper confirmed Jack's own suspicions. But before he could make any form of reply, a figure appeared in the doorway behind them.

"Felicity Walker." The figure stepped forward and held out a hand. "I'm Hannah's social worker."

Jack shook the social worker's hand and stepped back to allow her enough room to enter the confined space. "DI MacIntosh," he greeted her, and nodded towards his partner. "And this is DS Cooper. You knew Hannah well?"

Felicity Walker hesitated before giving a faint nod. "As well as anyone, I guess. She wasn't always an easy person to get to know. She didn't trust people very easily, and she especially didn't trust anyone in a position of authority. So we had a fairly fraught relationship."

"And how long had she been here?"

"Since Hope was born." Felicity gestured towards the only personal item in the sparse room — a small photograph pinned to the wall above Hannah's bed. It showed Hannah with a small baby in her arms, wrapped in a pink knitted blanket. "They came here straight from hospital — Hope would've only been a few days old. That would be about eighteen months ago now."

"And what can you tell us about Hannah's time here at the unit?"

Again, Felicity hesitated before replying. "As I said, Hannah didn't trust people easily. She had a very poor upbringing and things weren't easy for her. The staff here at the unit tried their best — and for the most part, she was doing well. But sometimes she would have lapses."

"Lapses?"

Felicity sighed. "At times she would forget to feed Hope. Or forget to wash her clothes. Sometimes forget to pick her up from nursery. Hannah had secured a place for Hope at a local nursery, so she could look for a job. Everyone in the unit receives help with nursery funding to support them finding employment and eventually their own place to live. Living here is only meant to be temporary." Felicity paused and shook her head. "But Hannah was so young — and she struggled."

"She had no family support?" Jack had already been told by DC Cassidy that Hannah's family had effectively washed their hands of her — and their grandchild.

Felicity continued to shake her head. "Hannah ran away from home at fourteen, her home life being very unstable. Her family are from Leeds and throughout her time here at the unit, none of them have wanted to become involved in her care." Felicity gave another sigh. "It's sad, really. Hannah was just a child herself, trying to make her way in an adult world. She could've done with a lot more support than we were able to give her."

"Did she have any friends? Anyone she would see on a regular basis? You mentioned she might've been looking for a job?"

Felicity gave a wan smile. "A seventeen-year-old mother living in a local authority unit isn't usually at the top of the interview shortlist. And as for friends, she was friendly with a couple of the other mothers in the unit, but beyond that no. There was no one else in her life other than Hope."

"So you don't remember seeing her in the company of anyone else recently? Especially around Thursday nineteenth July?"

"Not that I recall. You can have a word with the staff here — I'm sure they'd be happy to help."

"What about boyfriends?"

Felicity shook her head. "No one I saw. But I know she'd signed up to some dating site. I told her it was a bad idea and a waste of money — but she didn't listen."

"Dating site?" Jack raised an eyebrow in Cooper's direction. "That wouldn't be London Life, would it?"

Felicity paused. "Now you say it, yes. I'm pretty sure that was the name."

Jack began moving towards the door. "I don't think we need to take up any more of your time. Where's her daughter now? Hope, did you say?"

Felicity nodded. "Hope is being well looked after. She's with temporary foster carers at the moment."

Raising a hand as he departed, Jack stepped out into the corridor, the words "temporary foster carer" echoing inside his head. Visions of himself and Stuart being taken to their first foster placement flooded his brain. He wished Hope all the luck in the world, praying she followed his own path instead of that of his brother.

"Come on, Cooper," he breathed. "Let's get back to the team."

* * *

Time: 11.45 a.m.
Date: Tuesday 24 July 2012
Location: Blackfriars Crown Court, London

Daphne Holbrook loved the quiet; first thing in the morning, last thing in the evening, or when a jury left to consider their verdict. She revelled in the peace they left behind in her courtroom.

Because it was *her* courtroom.

Judges and juries came and went. Barristers and solicitors appeared and then disappeared among a flurry of robes and wigs. Defendants would sit in the dock — some nervously, others not so much — until their fate was decided. Then they, too, would be gone. Either home to their families, rejoicing in their liberty, or taking the solemn steps down to the cells beneath the court to await their transport to prison.

But Daphne Holbrook, court usher in courtroom number one, always remained. And she ran a tight ship. Everyone who appeared in her court knew the behaviour she expected. With the commotion surrounding the most recent case to be tried in her court now died down, she could quietly start to reclaim some form of order.

Tutting to herself, she picked up a discarded wig from the front bench. No doubt the barrister to whom it belonged would be frantically searching the robing room at this very minute, trying to remember where he'd left one of the most important pieces of his courtroom attire. She placed it carefully back down on the prosecution bench. There was a chance the jury would return later that day and the wig would be needed.

She continued tidying the counsel's benches, tutting once more at the number of pens and pencils that'd fallen to the floor beneath. Picking them up, she popped each one into her pocket. She then collected the glasses and jugs of water, stacking them on the trolley by her side.

Just as she was turning away, about to push the trolley towards the door, she saw it.

A discarded piece of paper which had floated to the floor behind the defence counsel's bench. She bent down as much as her arthritic hip would allow, and grabbed the wayward piece of paper. Running her enquiring eyes over it, she arched her eyebrows in wonder.

Unusual. Intriguing. Very intricate and detailed in parts. Shading in the right areas. Certainly a very good drawing.

But who would draw such a detailed picture of a shoe?

* * *

Time: 1.15 p.m.
Date: Tuesday 24 July 2012
Location: Acacia Avenue, Wimbledon, London

Mac slid the package from the carry box on the back of his motorbike, then removed his helmet. Customers often didn't like to be confronted by a biker with their helmet on — something about not being able to see their face.

He made his way up the short gravel drive, enclosed between smartly trimmed leylandii hedges. The drive ended in front of an impressive-looking house, two large bay windows either side of the front door. Next to the house stood a wide, double garage, its roll-top door open. Tucking the parcel underneath his arm, Mac leaned into the porch and rapped on the heavy wooden door using the brass door knocker. The sound echoed in the sultry air. Frosted glass panels either side of the door showed no signs of movement or life from within. Mac leaned forward once again and gave the door another rap.

The sound echoed emptily around him once more, but just as he was about to turn away, a different sound reached his ears.

The sound of a hedge trimmer.

Mac stepped off the porch, spying a narrow paved pathway leading around the side of the house. With the parcel still tucked under his arm, he walked in the direction of the hedge trimmer.

At the end of the path, a gate swung open into a beautifully well-kept back garden. Just inside the gate stood a man kitted out in worn gardening overalls, a hedge trimmer grasped in his hands. As soon as he spied Mac heading towards him, he pulled the set of ear defenders off his head and waved the hedge trimmer in the air.

"Sorry. Can't hear a thing with these on."

Patrick Mansfield stepped forward, laying the hedge trimmer down on the grass, and took the parcel from Mac's outstretched hand. "Thanks. I've been waiting for this."

"No problem." Mac held out the electronic device for Patrick's signature. "You rent a space at Isabel's café, don't you?" Mac watched as the man scribbled his name. "In the art studio?"

A quizzical look crossed Patrick's face. "Yes, yes I do. So you must be . . . ?" He frowned, clearly unable to put a name to the face in front of him. "Sorry, have we met?"

"I'm Mac. I met you briefly on Saturday."

"Ah yes. Forgive me. I don't have a great memory for faces. You're the one whose brother works for the police?"

Mac pocketed the electronic device. "That's right."

"How's she doing? Isabel?" Patrick bent to pick up the hedge trimmer again. "She sometimes looks a bit down — as if she's got the weight of the world on her shoulders. She got quite emotional last night."

Mac turned to go. He still had another two deliveries before he could clock off for the day and was desperate to get out of his leathers. "I don't really know her all that well. I think she's OK. She's going on a date tonight, anyway."

"A date?" Patrick raised his eyebrows. "Who with?"

Mac shrugged and started walking back down the path. He'd drummed up the courage to message Isabel earlier that day, to ask her out for a drink — but she'd told him she was meeting someone. He'd felt a pang of disappointment mixed with jealousy at the news. "Some defence solicitor. Said his name was Saunders, or something. Got some swanky apartment on the Embankment."

Raising a hand as a departing gesture, Mac left Patrick to attend to his hedge cutting and rammed his crash helmet back on his head, instantly feeling the hair starting to stick to his scalp. As he swung his leg over his motorbike and started the engine, he could hear the whine of the hedge trimmer spluttering into action.

* * *

Time: 1.30 p.m.
Date: Tuesday 24 July 2012
Location Metropolitan Police HQ, London

"We're missing something." Jack saw the piles of paperwork stacked up on various desks and sighed. "The answer has to be here somewhere. Let's go back to the beginning. Victim number one — Patricia Gordon."

DS Cooper brought up a picture of Patricia Gordon onto the whiteboard screen. "Scene of crime have released their formal report. No evidence she met her killer at her flat. It's clean."

Clean.

Jack heard Dr Rachel Hunter's soft tones once more. *"Your killer is very forensically aware." "No trace of any foreign DNA or any other trace evidence were left on either body."* He pushed the thoughts away, turning his attention back to the screen. "Then where did she meet him, Cooper? Where did she meet her killer if not at her flat? Between leaving work on sixth July and her body being found a week later, where did she go that meant she crossed the path of our killer?"

"A date?" Cooper nodded back to the piles of bank statements and London Life paperwork littering the desk. "We know she was a subscriber to London Life — like the others."

Jack shook his head. "London Life are digging their heels in about releasing confidential information, but they did tell us she hadn't been active on the site for some time, and definitely not in the weeks leading up to her disappearance. Her last interaction on the site was back in April."

"Maybe it was someone she'd met from the site before? And they messaged privately, rather than through the website?" Cooper shrugged. "Text messages, emails?"

"The forensic trawl of her mobile phone records didn't flag up anything unusual." Jack nodded at another pile of paperwork. "She didn't text very often. Only the odd message to the care home about work, or to her ex-husband. And on the day of her disappearance, her phone was switched off."

"The ex-husband, then?" Cooper clicked the remote control and Frank Gordon's image filled the screen.

"I don't know. They seemed to get on well — surprisingly well for exes." Jack thought back to when they'd met Mr Gordon. His grief at the murder of his ex-wife had seemed genuine. Despite the son insinuating that all was not well with the separation, Jack increasingly felt that Frank Gordon wasn't their man. "I think his grief was real, Cooper. And we can't link him to any of the other victims." He picked up the copy of Patricia Gordon's last bank statement. "But we're definitely missing something." He paused, and then nodded to the sergeant. "OK, let's move on. Georgina Dale and Hannah Fuller."

Just then DC Cassidy burst into the room, DS Carmichael not far behind.

"You'll never guess what, guv," she breathed, slightly out of breath from hurrying along the corridor. "It's Anthony Saunders — the defence solicitor."

"What about him?"

"He subscribes to London Life."

"And?" Jack eyed the young DC as she approached. "Although interesting, I don't think being a member of a dating site is classed as a crime. Yet." Although maybe it should be, he mused silently.

"Maybe not." A smile twitched at the corners of Cassidy's lips. "But in the last six months, he's sent messages to all three of our victims."

CHAPTER TWENTY-SEVEN

Time: 2.30 p.m.
Date: Tuesday 24 July 2012
Location: Metropolitan Police HQ, London

DS Carmichael clicked the remote control and the interactive whiteboard screen went blank. Picking up a whiteboard marker, he stepped forward.

"Here we have Saunders." Carmichael drew a box in the centre of one of the adjacent whiteboard screens. He then drew three lines at angles away from the box and wrote *Patricia Gordon*, *Georgina Dale* and *Hannah Fuller* next to each. "On April second, fifth and twenty-seventh, he messaged Patricia Gordon. London Life are resisting making the content of the messages available, but will confirm that messages were sent."

Jack followed Carmichael's pen as he wrote the dates next to Patricia Gordon's name.

"And then we have Georgina Dale, our second victim. Messages again from Saunders, on May fifth, thirteenth and most recently twenty-seventh June." Again, he wrote the dates next to Georgina's name.

"And lastly Hannah Fuller." Carmichael wrote June sixth, eighteenth and thirtieth next to Hannah's name on the whiteboard. "He messaged her three times — the last one very recently."

Jack frowned at the whiteboard. "Are we seriously thinking he could be our killer? A *solicitor*?"

"I like him for it," Carmichael continued. "He's been in touch with all three victims. He knows police procedures inside out, forensic procedures too. He'll know about DNA transference and how to keep a crime scene clean. And he's likely to know where the CCTV cameras are and how to avoid them. He's local — he knows London."

"But *seriously*?" Jack could feel alarm bells ringing. What Carmichael had outlined was true, but there was something still gnawing at him. There was something that still didn't fit. "I'm not so sure. What possible motive could he have?"

"Maybe there isn't one," replied Carmichael, the hint of irritation in his tone plain to all that were listening. "Maybe he's just a psycho. They do exist."

"We need more than this." Jack shook his head. "We don't have realistic grounds to arrest him based on the fact that he's a member of a dating site, even if he has been in touch with the victims at some point. Without knowing what those messages actually contain, it's not enough. It could be anything."

"But, boss." Cassidy stepped in. "Although I hate to say it, he does fit a lot of the characteristics in the forensic profile."

I fit the profile, thought Jack, thinking back to his meeting with Dr Rachel Hunter. Christ, pretty much everyone in this building fit the profile. He shook his head again. "Still not enough. Bring me details of exactly what the messages said — lean on this London Life to disclose them — go and work your magic, get that warrant served. Then, and only then, will I consider approaching Saunders."

Cassidy and Carmichael left to twist the long arms of London Life. Once they were gone, Jack eyed the paperwork littering the incident room. "We're still missing something, Cooper."

"If Patricia Gordon didn't go out on a date, maybe she went out to a club or evening class? Or maybe she was just on her way to the shops?" Cooper suggested.

Jack picked up another of Patricia Gordon's bank statements. Casting his eyes down the columns he noticed she was a very careful spender. Never overdrawn — always with a healthy balance in the account at all times. Jack scanned the regular monthly deposit from The Briars. Not much to live on once you took the regular bills into account. And then the rent on the flat — it was in a nice area, so wouldn't have been cheap. His eyes wandered across the withdrawals column and noted what looked like the rent payment — confirming his suspicions that it would've been a big drain on such a modest income. And then there were all the furnishings in the flat — Patricia Gordon had a taste for good quality. None of it would've come cheap. Jack also remembered the credit card bills that were paid in full each month.

"Where did she get her money from?"

"Boss?"

"Patricia Gordon. Where did she get her money from? She lives in a nice area of London. All the expensive furniture and gadgets we saw in her flat. She's never overdrawn. The care home doesn't pay much more than minimum wage. Where did it all come from?"

Cooper came round to Jack's desk where they spread out the last six months of Patricia Gordon's bank statements. Together, two pairs of eyes scanned the figures.

And it wasn't long until the answer presented itself.

"There." Jack pointed to the credit column on the page closest to them. "Cash deposit, two hundred pounds." He then stabbed a finger on another page. "And another two hundred pound cash deposit."

Two hundred pounds cash.

Every Friday.

Without fail.

Jack looked up at the bemused expression on the sergeant's face. "Our victim had a second job, Cooper."

"A second job?"

"Has to be." Jack pointed again at the cash deposits on Patricia Gordon's bank statements. "She was earning two hundred pounds a week, cash in hand — for something."

Cooper flicked open his notebook. "Nothing came up in any of the reports from DC Anderson — neither the ex-husband nor the son mentioned anything about a second job."

"Maybe they didn't know." Jack got to his feet. "We need to find out what she was doing for the extra cash — and more importantly, who was paying her."

At that moment, the door opened.

"DI MacIntosh?" A young PC's head peered around the doorjamb.

"That's me," answered Jack, still focusing on the bank statements in his hand.

"Message from downstairs. You're needed over at Blackfriars Crown Court."

Jack looked up and frowned. "I'm needed where? And why?"

The PC shrugged. "Sorry. The message was just that you needed to meet with QC John Fortmason — about the Hansen case. He'll be outside court two in about thirty minutes."

Jack grimaced. He nodded at the PC, letting him know the message had been received and understood. "Great," he muttered, as the door to the incident room swung shut. "Just great." Pausing to grab his mobile phone, Jack turned to Cooper. "Right, while I'm away on this wild goose chase, I need you to collate everything we have on Saunders — ready for when Amanda and Carmichael return. If we seriously think it's him, I need to see everything we've got. And keep tracking that Ford Transit."

"Boss." Cooper sat back down at one of the desks, pulling what paperwork they had towards him. "And what about Patricia Gordon's second job?"

Jack made for the door. "Put that on hold, Cooper. For now, we concentrate on Saunders. We rule him in — or we rule him out."

* * *

Jack jogged up the steps of Blackfriars Crown Court. *As if I don't have enough to do.* A patrol car had been able to drop him off outside the court, so he wouldn't be away from the investigation for long, but it was still time he couldn't really spare. The only good thing about the crown court on a day like today, however, was that it was cool. Its thick walls and air conditioning meant that the oppressive heat from outside stayed exactly there — outside. Stepping over the threshold, Jack breathed in a lungful of cool air.

Courtrooms one to three were to the left so, after clearing the security checks, Jack walked briskly along the left-hand corridor. As he approached the first courtroom, the heavy oak-panelled door creaked open and a court usher he knew as Daphne hurried out. Jack carried on walking towards courtroom two, giving Daphne a brief nod as he did so. But instead of returning the greeting, she stood in the corridor, barring his progress, waving a piece of paper in her hand.

"Detective," she began, still waving the piece of paper, "have you seen the defence solicitor, Anthony Saunders, on your way in?"

"Saunders?" Jack looked back over his shoulder, his stomach shifting a little at the mention of the solicitor's name. "No, sorry, I haven't. Is there a problem?"

"No, no, not a problem as such. He just left something behind in my courtroom. I just wondered if he needed it. It's rather good."

Jack frowned, letting his eyes fall to the piece of paper in the court usher's hand. The unsettled feeling in his stomach intensified. *Saunders.* "Something to do with the case? Evidence?"

Daphne shook her head. "Oh, no, nothing like that. Just a picture. A drawing. And a pretty good one at that. Have a look for yourself."

And so Jack did.

And suddenly his meeting with John Fortmason QC slipped out of his mind.

"Do you mind if I take this?"

Daphne handed the drawing over without comment. At least she could now go back to her courtroom and resume her rightful position. Jack swiftly turned back towards the entrance. John Fortmason would have to wait.

* * *

Time: 4 p.m.
Date: Tuesday 24 July 2012
Location: A cellar in London

As he bent down to pick up the discarded wrapper at the side of Jess's mattress, he noted most of the sandwich had been eaten, but she'd left the crusts behind which were now hard and crispy beneath his fingertips.

Jess never did like to eat her crusts.

He smoothed and straightened out the moth-eaten blanket over the thin mattress. It looked flat and deflated now Jess had gone. Casting a glance over his shoulder to the other side of the cellar, he saw Carol propped up against the damp wall, a look of horrified resignation mixed with panic on her pale face.

Poor Carol.

She looked so sad.

But it was all her own fault — she'd brought all this upon herself.

All of it.

Placing Jess's rubbish and the stale bread crusts into a plastic carrier bag, he slowly crossed the stone cellar floor. As he approached, Carol seemed to shrink even further back into the wall — hugging her knees up tightly to her chest, pulling the scratchy blanket taut around her legs. Her stockinged feet poked out of the bottom, raggedy holes allowing her toes to peek through.

"Now, now Carol, my dear." He knelt down in front of her. "There's no need to be like that."

"What . . . what do you want from me?" Zoe's voice was barely audible, her lips hardly moving.

"Shush now, Carol. You just stay here and eat your dinner." He nodded at the as-yet untouched packet of sandwiches by her side — he'd chosen prawn and mayonnaise this time. Nothing was too good for his Carol. "And drink your water. I don't want you getting ill."

Zoe shuddered at the thought of food, imagining it would stick in her throat and make her gag. But water — she needed water. She reached out to grab the plastic water bottle, snapping off the lid and drinking thirstily.

"That's more like it, Carol. Not too fast, though, you don't want to choke." He laid a hand on her wrist, pulling the bottle away from her lips.

Zoe physically recoiled from his touch, his fingers ice-cold against her skin. She could almost feel the evil transferring from his hand to hers. She began to retch.

"You see, Carol? You need to listen to me. Drink it more slowly. That's what used to make me so mad." There was a hard edge creeping into his hushed tones. "You never listened. Just do as you're told for once, Carol."

Zoe watched as he backed away towards the door.

Who was Carol?

And more importantly — what had happened to her?

* * *

Time: 4.15 p.m.
Date: Tuesday 24 July 2012
Location: Metropolitan Police HQ, London

Jack added the pencil drawing to the rest of the pile and frowned.

Shoes.

Why was this case becoming all about shoes?

Cassidy passed him a bottle of chilled water. "Chris has gone back down to the tech suite to see what else the CCTV throws up — and to get the guys to track that transit van through the ANPR system." She switched on both floor fans and fanned her face.

Jack gulped down several mouthfuls of water before he spoke. "How did you get on with London Life?"

"Still refusing to answer. They're quite rude. I've filled out the details for the warrant. We'll see what the response is."

"And Carmichael?" Jack noted the lack of DS Carmichael's presence in the room. Again. "Where's he got to?" He noted Cassidy's hesitation. "He *is* still here, isn't he?"

DC Cassidy perched on the windowsill by the open window and sipped her water. "He popped out a while ago."

"Popped out? What do you mean *popped out*?" Jack massaged his temples in frustration. "That man is never here."

"I'm sure he'll be back soon, guv. He said he wouldn't be long." Cassidy pushed herself off the window ledge and approached the table. "What's that?" She pointed at the sketch Jack had just added to the pile.

Jack passed the drawing over. "A drawing of a shoe — sketched by none other than our friend Anthony Saunders."

"Saunders?" Cassidy took hold of the sketch, her eyes widening. "He drew *this*?"

Jack nodded. "At court today. Left it behind as he rushed away, apparently."

"So, what are you thinking?"

"I don't know what I think right now." Jack rose from the desk and made his way towards the door. "Get Cooper up here as soon as he's done with the CCTV and ANPR. And track down Carmichael. He's starting to get on my nerves with his disappearing acts."

Jack made his way back to his office, feeling his shirt sticking to his back as he walked. The air inside was worse than the incident room, and he immediately threw the window open as much as health and safety allowed. It wasn't much, and all he inhaled was a lungful of exhaust fumes.

Saunders.

Could it really be him?

Slumping into his chair, Jack closed his eyes and rubbed his throbbing temples. Another headache was brewing and he was craving a cigarette. It'd been forty-three days now — and he *was* counting.

In among his tangled thoughts, Jack found himself thinking about Joseph Geraghty. Ever since Stu had mentioned who'd knocked him off his bike, he'd been plagued with thoughts of the gangland leader. Surely he wasn't so stupid as to set foot back in the capital just months before one of the biggest criminal trials they'd seen in years? And a trial involving his own? Jack had the man down as having more intelligence than that.

But that was a distraction he didn't need. With three bodies and a fourth imminent, he needed to be thinking about the investigation — not Geraghty.

Remembering the mental note he'd made last night, Jack picked up the desk phone and stabbed in the number. He didn't need to wait long for it to be answered.

"Will? It's Jack — Jack MacIntosh. I need to request some CCTV from Horseferry Road."

CHAPTER TWENTY-EIGHT

Time: 6.45 p.m.
Date: Tuesday 24 July 2012
Location: Buckingham Street, Embankment, London

Clutching the chilled bottle of Chardonnay in her hand, Isabel rang the doorbell to Flat 1B. No audible sound emerged. As she waited on the pavement, she nervously bit her lip.

A date.

Was she really going on a date? When she'd received the text from Anthony yesterday evening, it'd seemed like a good idea. A harmless dinner date. A chance to get away from the café for a change.

But a *date*?

Her stomach gave an involuntary flip as she waited. She felt a little sorry for Mac — he'd sent a garbled message to ask if she'd like to have a drink with him at a new bar in Soho tonight. Part of her wanted to say yes but, by that time, she'd already agreed to dinner with Anthony.

Dinner with Anthony.

Her stomach gave another flip.

The Buckingham Street flats were housed in an old converted grain merchant's building, a short step away from the banks of the River Thames. Sleek, energy-efficient windows had replaced the rotting wooden eighteenth-century frames, but the original brickwork remained. The words "*Ernest Baker — Grain Merchant 1725–1899*" had been chiselled into the solid russet-red bricks above the communal door.

After what seemed like an eternity, Isabel heard the intercom buzz.

"Come on in — push the door."

Isabel's heart gave another leap, her stomach clenched into knots. She tentatively pushed the heavy glass-fronted door, which clicked and swung open, and then stepped into a huge, cavernous space. Her eyes were instantly drawn towards the high vaulted ceiling above.

A curved staircase to the right hugged the eighteenth-century walls, and Isabel took several hesitant steps towards them. As she did so, a face appeared underneath the stairwell.

"Hey — I'm just through here."

Anthony Saunders' face beamed as Isabel crossed the flagstone floor, her three-inch heels clicking with every step. She smiled shyly when she reached the entrance to Flat 1B, nervously smoothing down her skirt as she approached.

"For you." She thrust out the wine bottle, hoping he'd take it before the glass slipped through her clammy fingers.

"Thanks," smiled Anthony, glancing at the label. "A Chardonnay. Excellent choice." He flashed another smile, Isabel noticing the faint dimple that appeared in his cheek as he did so. "Just through here, follow me."

* * *

Time: 6.45 p.m.
Date: Tuesday 24 July 2012
Location: Metropolitan Police HQ, London

DS Carmichael took the stairs, two at a time. A glance at his watch told him that he'd probably been gone too long this time. But he hadn't accounted for the roadworks and diversions that added at least half an hour to his journey. He knew it wouldn't be long before Jack lost his patience. The text from Cassidy had been brief, but to the point.

Get here. *Now.*

Jogging along the corridor towards the incident room, he straightened his tie. Despite the heat of the day, he continued to wear a shirt and tie — appearances were very important. Appearances were *very* important indeed.

Plastering a suitably haughty expression on his face, Carmichael pushed open the incident room door and breezed in. He was met by three pairs of eyes — Cassidy and Cooper quickly lowered theirs to their coffee cups, which left one pair boring into him.

"Nice of you to join us." Jack didn't even bother to hide the sarcasm from his voice this time.

Seemingly unflustered, Carmichael took one of the vacant seats, his eyes instantly drawn to the pencil sketch in Jack's hand. "What's that?"

"*That* is a drawing by Anthony Saunders. Something you would've known about several hours ago if you'd bothered to be present. Where've you been?"

Carmichael ignored the question and reached for the sketch. "Anthony Saunders drew this?" He looked up, all three pairs of eyes now on him.

"This changes things a bit, doesn't it? Surely we have to bring him in now?"

* * *

Time: 6.50 p.m.
Date: Tuesday 24 July 2012
Location: Buckingham Street, Embankment, London

The first thing Isabel could sense upon entering the flat was an intoxicating aroma of garlic and rosemary. Her stomach flipped again — but this time more from hunger and the anticipation of delicious food than nervous trepidation of going on her first date in over six years.

Anthony closed the door behind them and lightly touched her arm.

"I hope you don't think it's odd, but would you mind taking off your shoes?" He nodded down towards Isabel's feet.

Isabel noted Anthony had already slipped off his brogues which were now neatly tucked away at the side of a plush door mat.

"Er, no . . . of course not. Not at all." Isabel felt her cheeks turn pink and hot as she bent down to unbuckle the thin straps around her ankles. She stepped down from the three-inch heels and tidied them away by the side of the door.

"Sorry — new carpet." Anthony nodded at the soft, deep-pile oatmeal carpet that stretched away from the front door and into the flat beyond. "Only had it laid last week."

"It's really no trouble," smiled Isabel, feeling the pink tinge to her cheeks begin to fade. "I'd be the same."

Anthony's smile deepened, as did the dimple on his cheek. He cast his eyes down to the discarded shoes. "Nice shoes, though. They look like Christian Louboutin."

Isabel's own smile widened in surprise. "They are! I picked them up while I was travelling in France last year. I never usually get the chance to wear them — I can't exactly wear them in the café."

Anthony bent down and picked up one of the shoes, turning it over in his hands. "These are really well made. The stitching on the leather is remarkable — so intricate." He trailed a finger along the delicate ankle strap, following the natural curve down to the elegant, tapered heel. "And these heels are exquisite. The French really do know how to make a good shoe!"

Isabel watched as Anthony continued to marvel at her shoe, turning it over and over in his hands. The feeling of hunger in her stomach subsided a little, allowing the underlying trepidation to resurface.

Why is he so interested in my shoes?

Anthony looked up and caught Isabel's confused gaze. He smiled, sheepishly, the dimple reappearing. "Sorry. Listen to me." He placed the shoe back down next to its partner and gestured for Isabel to follow him. "You must think I'm some kind of weirdo, pouncing on your shoes like that. Come through. I've got some wine already open."

* * *

Time: 7 p.m.
Date: Tuesday 24 July 2012
Location: Metropolitan Police HQ, London

"There's enough here to pull him in." Carmichael leaned against the windowsill, the faint breeze doing nothing to unstick his shirt from his back. "The sketching of the shoe seals it."

Jack drained the dregs from his water bottle and rubbed his eyes. "It just seems too convenient for me." He hadn't had the stomach to touch any of the Chinese takeaway Cooper had ordered in — most of it still sitting in cartons on one of the central desks.

"He's not above the law just because he's a solicitor." Carmichael loosened his tie and unbuttoned the top button of his shirt. "He's just as capable of committing crimes."

"I realise that." Jack tried to stop the sarcasm and hostility from returning to his voice. "I just feel there's something missing, that's all. Something we're not seeing."

"I say we pull him in anyway." Carmichael fixed Jack with a beady stare. "*Right now.*"

"I'd feel better if London Life had responded to our questions — I need to see the content of those messages."

"Doubt we'll get that until tomorrow, guv." Cassidy flicked open a page in her notebook. "They still won't voluntarily disclose anything. I've tried, and so has Chris. They won't budge. The warrant's being issued."

Jack shook his head at Carmichael. "I just need more."

* * *

Time: 7.25 p.m.
Date: Tuesday 24 July 2012
Location: Buckingham Street, Embankment, London

The wine began to seep effortlessly into Isabel's bloodstream, its numbing effect finally allowing a wave of relaxation to take hold. Leaning back in the soft leather armchair, she glanced around Anthony's living room. It was elegant and stylish, nothing cheap or out of place. She could instantly tell he must be doing well for himself — a sleek HD TV sat in the corner with some sort of surround sound cinema system; a towering bookcase hugged one wall, crammed full of DVDs and books. A large abstract painting faced her on the wall opposite — something that wouldn't look out of place hanging in the Tate.

Anthony had lit several candles that now glowed and glimmered, circulating a sweet, fresh fragrance. The blinds were drawn across the large floor-to-ceiling windows, keeping out the heat of the dying day and giving the room a fresh coolness. Isabel took another sip of wine and smiled. The scent of roasting lamb was stronger now, the rich aroma of garlic and rosemary filling her nostrils each time she breathed in. Her stomach was aching to taste it. The small galley-style kitchen was across the hallway, where she Isabel could hear Anthony quietly humming to himself as he moved around the pots and pans.

Isabel pushed herself up out of the armchair and headed in the direction of the mouth-watering aroma. *I should at least ask if I can help*, she thought to herself — although she'd been very much enjoying just allowing herself to be enveloped in soft leather and letting the mellow alcohol work its way through her body. She couldn't remember the last time she'd spent an evening like this.

"Anything I can do?" Isabel entered the galley-style kitchen, sipping her wine as she did so. Anthony had just removed the roasting tin from the oven and was busy basting the succulent lamb with the cooking juices. The scent that hit Isabel was just as intoxicating as the wine in her hand. She breathed in deeply and quietly gasped. "My God, that smells divine."

"Fresh garlic and rosemary from the street market this morning," replied Anthony, flashing another smile, his dimple popping out once again. "Can't beat it." He drizzled the sizzling meat once more with the heady mixture. "And the meat came from that organic farm shop that just opened. Not too far down the road from you?"

Isabel nodded and took another gulp of wine. She swayed a little with the alcohol. If she had her Christian Louboutin heels on right now, she would've been tottering precariously. "Well, it smells gorgeous. Do you need a hand with anything?"

"All under control." Anthony slipped the roasting tin back into the oven. "Another twenty minutes or so and it should be ready. You just make yourself comfortable." He picked up the nearly empty wine bottle and poured another generous measure into Isabel's glass. "I'll be through in a moment. Just need to steam the vegetables."

Isabel giggled and obediently sipped more wine. "OK. This wine is delicious, by the way."

"There's a cellar underneath the flats — I keep a few bottles down there for special occasions." He winked as he refilled his own glass.

Isabel returned the smile, aware she was starting to feel a little giddy. She backed out into the hallway. "Can I use your bathroom?"

Anthony pointed over her shoulder. "Sure. Door at the far end."

Isabel turned on her stockinged feet and left the heat of the kitchen, heading in the direction of the bathroom. It was, indeed, at the end of the hallway. Just as she was about to push the door open, she glanced across at the slightly open door adjacent to it. Sipping more wine and swaying a little, she glanced mischievously over her shoulder to check that Anthony was still ensconced in the kitchen. She then turned back towards the second door and tiptoed cautiously through.

CHAPTER TWENTY-NINE

Time: 7.30 p.m.
Date: Tuesday 24 July 2012
Location: Buckingham Street, Embankment, London

For a man's bedroom it was tidy. Extremely tidy. Worryingly tidy. Isabel thought back to her own bedroom in the flat above the café, and the tangle of bedclothes, nightwear and other clothing that seemed to occupy each and every surface and most of the floor space.

Anthony had a large double bed in the centre of the room, the duvet neatly smoothed, pillows plumped and straightened on both sides. A small bedside table housed an iPod docking station, a lamp and a glass of water.

Isabel stepped further inside, giving the room a full three-hundred-and-sixty-degree sweep. Some tasteful prints were hung on the walls, and low-level lighting recessed into the ceiling gave the room a soft hue.

As she was about to turn back and head for the bath-room, Isabel noticed a slatted door on the wall opposite the bed. It looked like some sort of built-in wardrobe, or maybe an en-suite. Isabel hesitated momentarily, taking another sip of wine while listening to see if Anthony had ventured out of the kitchen yet. Hearing the crashing of pans and the sound of the oven door opening and closing, she turned back and stepped silently across the bedroom towards the door.

* * *

Time: 7.30 p.m.
Date: Tuesday 24 July 2012
Location: Metropolitan Police HQ, London

"He could be out there, right now." DS Carmichael had rolled his sleeves up to his elbows, beads of sweat visible on his brow. "Taking another victim off the street." He deposited a half-eaten carton of noodles into the bin. "We can't afford to hesitate on this one."

"I do know that," replied Jack, tersely. "But we also have to make sure there is actual evidence before we wade in with our size nines and arrest him."

Carmichael refused to give up. "He already has one in his clutches — he could be doing almost anything to her, right now. The consequences of us getting this wrong . . ."

"I'm well aware of the consequences," Jack cut in, his voice taut. He looked around the room. "What do you both think? Is Saunders our man?"

"I can't really believe it'd be him." Cassidy directed her gaze towards Carmichael. "I mean, *really*? He's a solicitor — and a well-respected one at that."

"Just because you fancy him doesn't mean he isn't our killer."

Cassidy felt her cheeks burn and threw an uneaten carton of vegetable chow mein onto her desk. "I don't *fancy* him, for your information," she retorted. "I was only giving you my opinion."

Jack held his hands up. "Look, less of the bickering. It's getting late — we're all hot, tired and grumpy."

"I'm hot and tired, but I'm not grumpy," replied Carmichael, his face telling a different story. "I just need to know if we're together on this one. If we get this wrong and we leave him out there . . ."

Jack rubbed his eyes. Something wasn't right, he could feel it. But what choice did they have? "Look, *this* is what we'll do." He paused to ensure he had everyone's attention. "First thing in the morning, we see if London Life have coughed up the details we need about the messages. Ideally, we need that before we decide to do anything. If they haven't, you put your case before the chief superintendent, Carmichael. If he's in agreement, we go in."

"But delaying it until the morning . . ."

"Is my *final* answer," replied Jack, hotly. "End of discussion."

* * *

Time: 7.35 p.m.
Date: Tuesday 24 July 2012
Location: Buckingham Street, Embankment, London

Shoes.

Isabel stepped into the small walk-in wardrobe, unsure if she should be feeling intrigued or slightly concerned. The racking on either side housed shelves upon shelves of women's shoes.

Each pair were arranged with similar colours grouped together — on the bottom shelves there were racks and racks of black styles, ranging from ankle boots to delicate strapless stilettos. From what Isabel could see, peering through the haze of alcohol that was now descending, they all looked to be of good quality, and many from well-known fashion houses and designers. She was sure she could see some Jimmy Choo, Louis Vuitton, Walter Steiger, even some Alexander McQueen.

Then the racks changed colour — groups of russet reds, bright blood-red scarlets, muted chocolate browns; then pale pastels, verdant greens and sunburnt oranges. Cool ice whites and glistening silvers adorned a further rack. Isabel's curiosity

240

was piqued, drawing her in to pick up the pair closest to her — a pair of plum-purple velvet Gucci court shoes with a modest heel. She ran her fingers over the soles. They looked brand new. They smelled brand new.

Isabel hastily returned the shoes to the rack and backed away.

What was Anthony doing with a wardrobe full of women's shoes?

Taking a large sip of wine, she decided that she really did need the bathroom after all.

* * *

Time: 8 p.m.
Date: Tuesday 24 July 2012
Location: A cellar in London

Zoe eventually ate the prawn and mayonnaise sandwiches — hunger taking over from the nausea she felt. He'd left a banana and apple by her side, so at least he wasn't starving her. Her stomach rumbled once again, but the thought of more food made her feel sick.

The cellar felt deathly quiet without Hannah. Although the pair of them hadn't talked much, now she was alone, Zoe felt suffocated in the silence. The only sound was the occasional scrape of the metal chain as she changed position. She'd tried shouting for help, but the thick walls merely swallowed her words. Tired and hoarse, she'd eventually succumbed to the dark and the silence once again.

She had no idea what time it was. The gloom of the cellar dissolved any semblance of day or night.

With a shuddering sob, she turned over and faced the damp wall. Closing her eyes, she welcomed sleep to block out the rising terror that threatened to consume her.

How would she ever get out?

* * *

"You don't mind, do you?" Anthony Saunders paused, his fork midway between his plate and his mouth. "Eating in the living room, I mean? I don't have a separate dining room."

Isabel shook her head, savouring a particularly moist piece of well-cooked lamb. She washed it down with another sip of wine. They'd moved on to their second bottle of Merlot.

"Not at all. I always eat with a tray on my lap at home." Isabel smiled from her seat on the sofa. "And usually a cat."

"Maybe I should get a cat. It can get quite lonely rattling around here on my own."

Isabel cut a slice of roast potato and dipped it into the garlic and rosemary gravy on her plate. She popped the crispy forkful into her mouth and let her eyes wander again, putting the thought of the shoe collection out of her mind. She'd already given the room a good once-over while Anthony was busy cooking, noticing there weren't many personal possessions or mementoes to be seen. All she could see were a handful of photographs on a bookcase — all of the same person.

"Is that your daughter?" Isabel nodded at the photograph closest to them. The picture was in a simple silver-plated frame and showed a young girl sitting astride a pony. Her face was full of delight, grinning towards the camera. Standing either side of her, Isabel assumed, were Anthony and his ex-wife.

Anthony placed his fork down and turned towards the photograph. Although the wine was turning her vision a little hazy around the edges, Isabel thought she saw his eyes cloud over a little, their brightness snuffed out like a dying candle. After a while, he simply nodded.

"Yes, she was about eight when we took that." A sad smile returned to his lips. "Always loved her ponies."

"Does she live with her mother?" Isabel wasn't quite sure why she was asking. She took another large gulp of Merlot, hoping she hadn't put her foot in it and trodden unceremoniously onto painful territory.

"She's with her mother, yes. I don't see much of them anymore." Anthony lowered his eyes to his plate where he began to slowly cut through another piece of meat.

Isabel scoured the rest of the photographs on the bookcase. There were more pictures of Anthony's daughter with her mother, and one of a newborn baby wrapped tightly in a blue blanket. Another one that caught her eye was of Anthony's daughter, a little older than the other pictures — possibly teenage years — sitting on a bench next to a life-size Mickey Mouse. Isabel inched forwards in her seat a little. She had her father's smile, that was evident; the signs of a small dimple on the girl's cheek gave it away. She was dressed in blue jeans with a light grey sweatshirt that featured a large letter "J" in the centre — her hair was scraped back off her face and held in a high ponytail.

The "J" matched the "J" Isabel had noticed on a signet ring on Anthony's left hand. She usually didn't like jewellery on a man, but this seemed different somehow.

"She's very pretty." Isabel noticed Anthony staring sombrely into the remains of his dinner. "You must be very proud of her."

Anthony looked up and slowly nodded.

"Always," he said, simply. "Always."

* * *

Time: 1.45 p.m.
Date: 21 November 1997
Location: The Forest of Dean, Gloucestershire

"Come on, slowcoaches!" Jess hurried on ahead, shrieking with delight every time she jumped over a fallen tree branch. Her laughter filled the air, echoing and bouncing off the trees that lined their forest path. "Race you to the river! Last one there buys the ice cream!" Her voice tailed off as she disappeared out of sight.

Jess's mother lengthened her stride and picked up the pace, following in her daughter's footsteps. She swung the rucksack a little higher up onto her shoulder, feeling it bounce rhythmically between her shoulder blades as she walked.

"Come on, Carol. Don't be like this." His voice was strained and had the hint of long-suffering impatience bubbling underneath the surface like the babbling brook that flagged their route.

"Me?" she thundered, feeling her own anger bristling. "I'm not being like anything." She continued striding ahead, her walking boots making light work of the moss-covered pathway. The weather had been kind to them so far — the late autumn Indian summer they'd been promised had extended into November, meaning that their week's holiday in the Forest of Dean had been full of trips out for forest walks, exploring deserted caves and even some wading in the rivers.

"Carol." This time his voice was hard and threatening. He picked up his pace and caught up, easily matching her stride for stride. He deftly made a grab for her arm, catching her tightly around the wrist and pulling her roughly to a stop.

"Ow, stop it! You're hurting me." Carol tried to wrestle her arm free of his grip, but he was too strong for her. "Let go. Jess might see."

"Stop fighting, Carol. Just calm down." He made no attempt to loosen his grip, if anything it tightened even further. "You know why things are like this. You know what you did."

Carol flashed him a hot look, full of hatred, and once again tried to twist herself free. She dug the heels of her walking boots into the dirt track underfoot and twisted her body violently in towards his. Caught momentarily off guard, he stumbled and lost his footing.

It was enough to break free.

This time.

CHAPTER THIRTY

Time: 1.15 a.m.
Date: Wednesday 25 July 2012
Location: A cellar in London

The hardest part was negotiating the steps. They didn't look very steep when you were climbing up and down, with the banister to help, but dragging a body to the top always made him sweat. He paused halfway, resting against the handrail, and wiped the sweat from his brow with the back of his hand. He hadn't remembered Carol being so heavy before. Maybe she'd been putting on weight without him realising.

She obviously hadn't been listening to him.

Again.

Carol *never* listened.

Breathing deeply, he placed his hands once again between her shoulders and began hauling her up the final few steps. Her legs bounced against the roughly hewn stone, but Carol remained quiet and didn't utter a sound. The sedatives had worked. Once they reached the top, he placed her onto the kitchen floor and glanced at his watch. The sun would be coming up soon — he'd need to get moving if he wanted the protection of darkness to mask Carol's final journey.

But first she needed to be cleaned.

They always needed to be cleaned.

Dragging her towards a small utility and washroom at the rear of the kitchen, he placed her in the shower cubicle. Everything he needed was at hand. Nailbrush. Antibacterial wipes. Bleach. If he moved quickly, he could be finished in half an hour.

Donning a pair of thick rubber gloves, he turned the shower to hot.

* * *

Time: 2.45 a.m.
Date: Wednesday 25 July 2012
Location: Kettle's Yard Mews, London

Jack sat on the window ledge, his head resting against the cool glass. Sleep had been predictably hard to find, so he'd given up and taken to night watching. Various lights were on in and around Kettle's Yard Mews, evidence that maybe he wasn't the only one struggling with sleep on this hot, sticky night.

Dr Riches had urged him to try meditation and mindfulness techniques to deal with his insomnia — Jack had only just managed to swallow the laugh before he'd left the building.

He rolled the bottle of once-chilled water across his forehead and thought about Anthony Saunders. Had he been right to quash Carmichael's suggestion they pick him up tonight? Or had he merely dismissed the idea as a way of getting back at the new detective sergeant?

It was a dangerous ploy if he had.

Pushing himself off the window ledge, Jack headed to the kitchen to make a coffee. The fresh bottle of Macallan sitting on the side had caught his eye, but he knew the answer to his problems — current or otherwise — wouldn't be found there tonight. Instead, he snapped on the kettle.

As he waited for the water to boil, he heard the all-too-familiar "ping" of yet another incoming message on his laptop. He'd tried to sort through his outstanding emails earlier, but abandoned the idea as time went on.

Sloshing boiling water into his mug and adding the last of the milk, Jack headed for the sofa, tapping the laptop keyboard as he passed to see what further delights had landed in his inbox. He quickly saw that Will had come good with the CCTV from Horseferry Road.

Taking a sip of the too-hot coffee, Jack clicked on the attachment and settled back to watch. The images didn't look too bad — much better than some they had to wade through — and clearly showed the traffic and pedestrians making their way along the street that morning.

Jack already knew the time of day he was interested in, so fast-forwarded the recording until a minute or so before Stu came off his motorbike.

His eyes searched the pavement for any sign of Joseph Geraghty. Anticipation mixed with more than a hint of exhaustion sank to the bottom of Jack's stomach. Maybe Stu'd made a mistake.

Jack had been involved in several cases where Joseph Geraghty was their prime suspect — and each time the man managed to evade justice. Witnesses were suddenly reluctant to make statements, or rapidly changed their sworn evidence; sometimes they even disappeared altogether. Evidence started to get itself lost — and Jack soon suspected it was down to more than just sloppy police work. Police corruption existed, everyone knew that, no matter how many task forces were created to root it out. Jack suspected more than a few took backhanders from time to time — Joseph Geraghty could be very persuasive when it came to retaining his liberty.

Jack turned his attention back to the laptop screen, taking another mouthful of his caffeine-laden drink.

And then he saw it.

Almost dropping the boiling hot coffee in his lap, Jack quickly rewound the footage and watched again.

Stu's motorbike came into view, and a split-second later Joseph Geraghty sprinted across the road directly in front of him. Stu'd been quick to react — avoiding colliding with the man by the skin of his teeth and taking out the bollard in the centre of the road instead.

Jack froze the image on the screen.

Joseph Geraghty was back.

CHAPTER THIRTY-ONE

Time: 6.05 a.m.
Date: Wednesday 25 July 2012
Location: Battersea Park, London

Jack shuffled along the hastily constructed walkway, his white protective suit rustling as he did so. The early morning dew clung to his bright blue plastic overshoes. The call had come through to his mobile at 5.04 a.m. He hadn't been asleep — he'd continued to watch Joseph Geraghty on the CCTV outside Isabel's café until the sun came up.

Déjà vu engulfed him.

They had another one.

The discovery had been made by a jogger in Battersea Park. It always seemed to be a jogger. Or sometimes a dog walker.

Which was why Jack avoided outdoor exercise and had never owned a pet.

The body lay in a section of open grass flanked by mature trees. It was daring. It was brazen. Jack noted that the main road, a busy arterial route across the river towards Chelsea, wasn't far away.

The familiar white forensic tent had already been erected to screen the grisly discovery from prying eyes and protect it from the elements. Dr Philip Matthews was in attendance, exiting the tent just as Jack approached the end of the walkway.

The pathologist nodded towards the tent flaps behind him. "DI MacIntosh. We really must stop meeting like this."

"Morning, Doc," replied Jack, noting once again how impeccably turned out the pathologist was, even beneath his protective suit. He would've received the dawn-chorus phone call at roughly the same time as Jack, but still seemed able to have donned an expensively cut three-piece suit, cravat and also polish his shoes. Jack had barely managed to run a hand through his bed-hair. "What've we got?"

"Female. Approximately thirty-five to forty-five. Hair colour, dark. Clothing undisturbed. Found positioned on her back." Dr Matthews paused, knowing what piece of information Jack was waiting for. "And yes, ligature marks around the neck."

"Same as before," stated Jack.

It wasn't a question.

"Same as before," concurred Dr Matthews.

"Restraints?"

"Abrasions to the left ankle," conceded the pathologist.

"Any idea how long she's been here?"

"I can't answer that, Jack. Not now. But I'd say not long, not long at all. Let me get her back to the mortuary. It was a warm night, so time of death might be difficult to pinpoint even with further tests."

Jack nodded and waved Dr Matthews on his way. Stepping forward, he peered inside the tent, feeling the need to see for himself.

The body lay just as Dr Matthews had described. Her eyes were open, staring up at what would've been a cloudless sky were it not for the tent acting as her tomb. What did those eyes see at the very end? mused Jack. What face had filled her last moments when the life was being choked out of her? What secrets would she never tell?

The woman was pale-skinned, slim and well dressed. Her legs were bent modestly to the side, but Jack quickly saw all he needed to see.

One shoe.

A black court shoe with a low heel.

Jack already had the other in an evidence bag back at the station.

Stepping out of the tent, Jack felt his heart sink — a familiar gnawing feeling gripped his stomach. DS Cooper was hovering by the cordon, plastic evidence bag in hand.

Silently, the pair of them began scouring the immediate vicinity.

Looking for a shoe.

A shoe belonging to the next victim.

* * *

Time: 6.45 a.m.
Date: Wednesday 25 July 2012
Location: Isabel's Café, Horseferry Road, London

Angus McBride peered in through the window, cupping his hands against the glass.

CLOSED.

The sign hanging up in the front door confirmed his suspicions, but a deep frown creased his forehead nevertheless. Isabel's was never closed at this time — not on a Wednesday morning. He let the heavy Royal Mail postbag sink to the pavement by his feet and took a step back. He quickly glanced up and down the street, wondering if he would spot a slightly harassed figure rushing towards him, apologising profusely for making him wait but she'd just run out of milk and had to make an emergency dash to the corner shop further up the street.

But there was no such figure, harassed or otherwise.

Angus then glanced up at the window above the café, which he knew was the flat where Isabel lived. The small window that overlooked the road gave nothing away. The curtains were open, but the window itself remained closed.

An unsettling feeling began to creep into Angus's stomach, replacing the rumbling hunger pangs that'd begun when he'd thought about the freshly baked sausage roll he'd be having for breakfast.

He peered once again through the window into the café. But nothing had changed. The closed sign was still hanging. The lights were still off. The counter still deserted.

Isabel was nowhere to be seen.

* * *

Time: 6.50 a.m.
Date: Wednesday 25 July 2012
Location: A cellar in London

Isabel's eyes fluttered open. Her head felt groggy, her tongue felt dry. Her vision remained blurred as if her eyelids were still glued together.

How much did I have to drink last night, she wondered, as a snapshot of several glasses of Merlot entered her head. One bottle? Two? More? She then saw Anthony's face, and the smell of roast lamb with rosemary and garlic filled her nostrils.

Except she couldn't really smell lamb.

She couldn't smell rosemary or garlic, either.

She could smell something entirely different.

What was it? Vomit? Sweat? Urine?

Isabel's eyes snapped open. Now fully awake, a quick glance confirmed that she wasn't at home — this wasn't her bed; this wasn't her flat. With her heart thumping, she pushed herself up into a sitting position as memories started tumbling through her mind, slotting together like a badly fitting jigsaw puzzle.

The meal.

The photographs.

The shoes.

Anthony.

Isabel's eyes flickered towards the other side of the cellar, where she saw an identical threadbare mattress. Had there been someone there before? Isabel frowned, trying to make sense of the foggy memories jostling for position inside her head. There'd been a woman, she was sure of it. She took in the empty blanket draped over the mattress. But she was sure she'd spoken to someone — and she was sure she'd said her name was Zoe.

But Zoe was no longer there.

Isabel was alone.

Where was she? She couldn't even remember leaving Anthony's — everything was such a distorted haze.

She tried moving her legs, and as she did so, a loud scraping sound accompanied the movement. Looking down, she saw her left ankle was encased in a heavy, metal clasp with a chain snaking its way into the darkness and beyond, in the direction of a rusty radiator on the wall.

She also noticed that one of her shoes was missing.

CHAPTER THIRTY-TWO

Time: 7 a.m.
Date: Wednesday 25 July 2012
Location: Isabel's Café, Horseferry Road, London

Dominic sprinted as fast as he could along Horseferry Road. He was late. And he was *never* late. His heart thudded in his chest, partly from the exertion of running, but partly from his fear of being late. He knew Isabel wouldn't mind — but Dominic *hated* being late.

He had to have routine — and his routine said he arrived at Isabel's at six thirty, not seven.

Anxiety began to multiply with every stride as he ran the last fifty metres towards the café. Even before he got there, Dominic sensed that something was wrong.

He slowed to a jog as he approached the front door, immediately noticing the "Closed" sign hanging in the window.

Isabel had forgotten to turn it over.

Just as she'd forgotten to turn on the lights.

And forgotten to put the chalkboard outside advertising the day's specials.

Dominic tentatively stepped forward — Isabel had also forgotten to unlock the door.

Except she hadn't forgotten — not really.

Dominic knew in an instant.

Isabel wasn't there.

Panic welled up inside him. This wasn't how the day was meant to start. He began to sidestep, foot to foot, clutching his notebook as if his life depended on it. After what seemed like an eternity, Dominic thrust his hand into his jeans pocket and brought out his key.

His emergency key.

For use in an emergency.

This was an emergency.

He forced the key that he'd never had to use before into the lock and twisted it clockwise, hearing the heavy "click". Pushing the door open, he stepped over the threshold and peered into the dim café.

"Isabel?" he called out, his voice quieter than the stillness of the sleeping café. "Are you there?"

"She's not there, sonny."

Dominic whirled round to see Angus McBride hovering outside, a concerned look on his wrinkled face. His greying beard twitched as he spoke, his slate-grey eyes having lost their usual twinkle. "I came for my usual coffee and sausage roll — but there's no sign of the lass."

Dominic took another small step into the silent café. No hissing sound of the coffee machine warming up; no humming sound from the ovens as they baked their first batches of the day. No sound. No sound at all. Everywhere was deathly quiet.

"I've been coming here at quarter to seven every day for three months, sonny," continued Angus, depositing his Royal Mail bag at his feet. "Never has the wee lass not been here to open up."

Anxiety soaring, Dominic reached for his phone.

* * *

Time: 7.35 a.m.
Date: Wednesday 25 July 2012
Location: Islington, London

Mac was about to put his motorbike helmet on when he felt his phone vibrating inside his heavy leather jacket. Momentarily considering whether to let it ring out, he sighed and placed his helmet at his feet. It might be work, cancelling or rearranging one of his deliveries. Better to answer it.

He shrugged out of the jacket and reached inside for his phone. Glancing at the screen, he almost hit the ignore button — an unknown number. An unknown number at this time of day usually meant a PPI call, or someone trying to sell him life insurance. His finger hovered over the top of the red button; he was already late for work as it was.

But what if something had happened to Jack?

He hit the green button and brought the phone to his ear.

But it wasn't a PPI call. And it wasn't an insurance company asking about his plans for retirement and death. Neither was it anyone from work, ringing about his schedule.

And it wasn't about Jack.

Instead, it was Sacha from the café. Mac had only met her a couple of times, and she spoke very quickly, panic evident in her tone.

Did he know where Isabel was?

The café and the flat were empty.

Isabel was missing.

* * *

Time: 7.45 a.m.
Date: Wednesday 25 July 2012
Location: Metropolitan Police HQ, London

Jack eyed the ever-increasing pile of files on his desk before slipping into his chair. Various other open investigations still needed his attention — but Operation Genevieve had to be his priority. He ran a finger inside his shirt collar, feeling the stickiness of the day starting in earnest already.

It had taken two long, cool showers to rid himself of the cold sweat ingrained into his skin from yet another restless night thinking about Joseph Geraghty and Anthony Saunders, and then the smell of death from their earlier trip to Battersea Park. He was down to his last shirt. And yesterday's trousers would have to do. Again.

But at least he smelled good. Two showers and a liberal encasement in deodorant made sure of that.

Deodorant was another item the shops had yet to run out of — cold beer and deodorant. Electric fans, yes. Dehumidifiers, yes. Air conditioning systems, yes. But deodorant and cold beer — there were plenty of those to go around.

Jack drained the dregs of the black coffee he'd grabbed from the vending machine downstairs and checked his watch. DC Cassidy was on her way in; Cooper was already in the incident room. Where DS Carmichael was, nobody knew.

As Jack got to his feet, about to head towards the incident room, his mobile rang. Stuart. Another glance at the time told him his brother should be at work by now, weaving in and out of the congested commuter traffic.

"Hey, Stu?" Jack answered the call on the third ring. "What's up?"

CHAPTER THIRTY-THREE

Time: 8.25 a.m.
Date: Wednesday 25 July 2012
Location: Metropolitan Police HQ, London

Jack sat staring at his desk phone, unable to move.

The image of the shoe found at the scene at Battersea that morning had immediately been sent through to Sacha at the café. And it hadn't taken long for her tearful confirmation to be relayed back to him.

His stomach churned.

Isabel.

Any thoughts that she might've merely overslept, or taken the day off, disappeared in an instant.

Jack held his head in his hands. When he'd taken Stu's call earlier that morning, the whole axis of the world around him had instantly shifted.

Why hadn't he agreed to go and pick up Saunders last night? A delay of twelve hours…

Jack didn't want to think about what that might mean.

They had to find her.

He had to find her.

But, right now, he had to go and face his team. With sickness spreading, he grabbed his jacket and headed for the door.

* * *

Time: 8.30 a.m.
Date: Wednesday 25 July 2012
Location: A cellar in London

Isabel could feel the hard concrete beneath the thin mattress. Pulling the coarse blanket off her legs, she lay there in the shadows, pain shooting through her aching limbs with every slight movement she made.

She had no idea what time it was but knew she must've drifted back to sleep at some point.

Fear started to grow as she lay in the dark — but she knew she mustn't panic. She mustn't shout out or scream; that was right, wasn't it? That was what you were told do in situations like this? She needed to keep her head, to keep her self-control. Only then would she be able to find a way out.

As she fought to get her breathing under control, she lay back against the thin mattress and stared up at the ceiling.

I must find a way out.

* * *

Time: 8.45 a.m.
Date: Wednesday 25 July 2012
Location: Metropolitan Police HQ, London

Chief Superintendent Dougie King drummed his fingers on the desk. A pensive look darkened his features. Neither Jack nor DS Carmichael had sat down in the vacant chairs — they hadn't been asked to. Instead, they both stood to attention awaiting their fate like a schoolboy awaits his punishment from the headmaster.

"And you're sure about this?" The chief superintendent held Jack's gaze without blinking. "This is our man?"

Jack hesitated, about to reply, when Carmichael stepped in.

"Absolutely, sir. One hundred per cent."

Chief Superintendent King transferred his gaze to Carmichael. "Talk me through the evidence once again. We have to be more than sure on this one."

Jack allowed Carmichael to take the lead, his own mouth devoid of speech. He should've acted sooner — agreed to bring Saunders in last night. His mouth felt bone-dry, nausea welling up from within.

Carmichael cleared his throat before addressing the chief superintendent.

"Firstly, he fits the demographics of the profile. Right age. Right background. He's educated. He's intelligent. He's charming — so the women say." Carmichael began to count the points of evidence off with his fingers. "He lives in the right area. He has knowledge of London. He's single. And he has an expert knowledge of forensics." Pausing, Carmichael made sure he had the chief superintendent's undivided attention. "Secondly, he's a subscriber to a dating site which the first three victims also subscribed to and he's sent messages to all of them — although the content of those messages is something we're unsure of at present. We haven't got an ID yet for the woman found this morning but, as soon as we do, checks will be made to see if she was a member of the site, too. And thirdly, we have a potential fourth victim. A woman by the name of Isabel Faraday had a date with Saunders last night and hasn't been seen since. She failed to open her café this morning and doesn't appear to have come home. Her mobile phone is switched off. Sacha Green — who works at the café with Miss Faraday and is a close friend — has been shown a photograph of the shoe found at the scene in Battersea this morning. She confirms it closely resembles one Miss Faraday herself owns."

Chief Superintendent King sat back in his chair, the leather creaking under his weight.

But Carmichael hadn't quite finished. "And there's one final piece of evidence that suggests we have the right man." He glanced at Jack. "You have it, Jack?"

Still somewhat shell-shocked, Jack brought out the plastic evidence bag he'd had clasped behind his back.

"In here, we have a drawing made by the suspect." Carmichael handed the evidence bag across the chief superintendent's desk. "It's an intricate drawing — a sketch — of a shoe."

"I can see that, Sergeant." Chief Superintendent King let his eyes rake over the pencil drawing. "And we're saying this is evidence of what, exactly?"

"Our killer has a shoe fetish, sir," continued Carmichael. "He leaves shoes at the scene. Saunders clearly has an unusual interest in shoes."

"It shows he has an interest in drawing, Sergeant — in art. Not necessarily in shoes." The chief superintendent handed the plastic evidence bag back across the desk. "What's your view on it all, Jack?"

The sickness in Jack's stomach continued to spread. He could almost taste the acrid stomach acid in his mouth as he swallowed.

Isabel.

"Is Anthony Saunders our man?" pressed the chief superintendent.

Jack took a deep breath and nodded. "He certainly fits the profile, sir. DS Carmichael is quite correct about that."

"I know he fits the profile, Jack, but does he fit the *evidence*? Do we even *have* any evidence? Real evidence?" Chief Superintendent King shifted his gaze between Jack and Carmichael. "Enough for sending an armed response team in to arrest him? Are we sure she hasn't just stayed over at Saunders' place?"

The possibility had fleetingly entered Jack's head after Stu's distressed call that morning, but he'd dismissed it just as quickly. Isabel never failed to open her café. And then there was the shoe . . .

Images of Isabel flooded his brain. She was out there, somewhere — held against her will. Kidnapped. Or worse. He had to do everything within his power, and beyond, to find her. Before it was too late. "We're sure, sir. Saunders is the only suspect we have. And if we don't act now, we might have another murder on our hands." The words stuck in Jack's throat.

"You do know who his father is?"

Jack nodded. "I'm fully aware who his father is, sir. But Anthony Saunders has to be our man."

* * *

Time: 10.30 a.m.
Date: Wednesday 25 July 2012
Location: A cellar in London

Isabel ran her tongue over her dry, chapped lips and shuddered. The air around her in the cellar was stale and warm, but she still felt ice cold.

Was this what it felt like — waiting to die? Was this how her parents had felt just before their car left the road? Had they known they were about to die?

She choked back the lump in her throat. She'd always wondered, but had been afraid to ask.

Correction: she'd been afraid to hear the answer.

She hoped with all her heart that they'd been oblivious to what was coming.

Unlike what was happening to Isabel right now.

She knew exactly what was coming.

She wasn't stupid — she read the papers.

She knew what this man was capable of.

* * *

262

Time: 11 a.m.
Date: Wednesday 25 July 2012
Location: Buckingham Street, Embankment, London

"He's in Flat 1B — ground floor." DS Carmichael led the team of four armed officers to the front of the converted grain merchant's building. A quick call to the solicitor's office had confirmed that Anthony Saunders was working from home that day. "I want two of you around the back, in case he makes a run for it, and two of you remain out here."

Two officers, kitted in their heavy police armed response protective gear, nodded and immediately jogged around to the rear of the building, their Glock 17 pistols held loosely but firmly by their sides. Radio communications crackled in their earpieces as they disappeared out of sight. "Jack?" Carmichael glanced back over his shoulder to the pavement where Jack was standing with DS Cooper and DC Cassidy. All three had bulky police-issue stab vests on. "You ready?"

Cooper and Cassidy cast concerned looks in Jack's direction, noting how his forehead knotted with an ever-deepening frown. He didn't move or utter a sound.

"Boss?" Cooper broke the silence. "We going in?"

Jack ran a finger around the neck of his stab vest. It was already beginning to chafe and irritate his skin. His feet remained firmly planted by the kerb, his vision swimming in and out of focus.

None of this felt real.

He'd hoped it was just another one of his nightmares — that he'd wake up in a cold sweat, feeling nauseated, with Isabel safely tucked away in her café, serving her early morning customers as usual.

But Jack knew this particular nightmare was real.

He gave the nod.

"Sure. Let's do this."

Carmichael approached the communal door.

"Mr Saunders? My name is Detective Sergeant Carmichael from the Metropolitan Police. Open the door."

Silence.

"If you don't open the door I have authority to force entry." Carmichael paused, listening to the continued silence. "If you don't open up in the next ten seconds, the door will be forced."

More silence.

Just as Carmichael was about to give the nod to the two accompanying officers to use the enforcer, a sharp buzzing sound filled the quiet street.

The communal door was open.

Motioning for the two armed police officers to enter ahead of him, Carmichael radioed his command to the officers stationed at the rear of the building to hold their ground — and be ready.

They were going in.

Jack, together with DS Cooper and DC Cassidy, followed on behind, each with their uncomfortably bulky stab-proof vests weighing them down. *Stab-proof*, mused Jack, as he moved ahead of Cassidy. He eyed the Glock 17 pistols in the hands of the armed officers up ahead. *But not bulletproof.*

"Mr Saunders? Open up." Carmichael's voice echoed outside Flat 1B. "You have ten seconds — otherwise armed officers will break down the door. I repeat. Open up, Mr Saunders. Ten seconds."

Jack held his breath for what seemed like longer than the aforementioned ten seconds, but a discernible click was heard almost as soon as Carmichael had finished giving the command. The door to Flat 1B swung open.

Carmichael motioned for the armed officers to enter, flattening himself against the outside wall, and indicated that Jack, Cassidy and Cooper should follow suit. Only when the confirmatory "clear" was heard emanating from inside the flat did they move towards the door and enter.

Carmichael strode into the hallway to see an ashen-faced Anthony Saunders standing against a wall with his hands raised above his head. Dressed in a loose-fitting dressing gown, shampoo suds still clinging to his hair, it appeared that the raid had interrupted the defence solicitor's morning shower.

"Anthony Saunders." Carmichael stepped further into the flat. "I am arresting you on suspicion of murder. You do not have to say anything. But it may harm your defence if you do not mention when questioned something that you later rely on in court. Anything you do say may be given in evidence. Someone cuff him and let him get dressed."

Jack gave the ground-floor flat a cursory glance while Cooper and Cassidy filed past to take Saunders to put something more substantial on than a flimsy dressing gown. "Have a look round but don't touch anything."

Carmichael arrived back at Jack's side. "Let's get him shifted back to the station for interview. Then get the forensics lot in to go over the place."

Jack nodded, watching Saunders emerge from his bedroom in more appropriate attire and be led away towards the waiting police van outside. Was he looking at the man who'd kidnapped Isabel? The man who'd killed four other women? Nausea welled up inside him. If he was, then the chief superintendent could breathe a sigh of relief and the Olympics could go ahead as planned.

As Saunders disappeared outside, Cooper joined Carmichael at Jack's side. "Full of shoes, boss." He nodded back towards Saunders' bedroom. "There's a wardrobe in there full of shoes."

Shoes.

Jack lowered his eyes to the floor as his growing nausea was joined by something else.

Fear.

Because, if Anthony Saunders was indeed their man, then where was Isabel?

"We're in a ground-floor flat, Cooper. We need to check if this building has a cellar."

CHAPTER THIRTY-FOUR

Time: 2.30 p.m.
Date: Wednesday 25 July 2012
Location: Metropolitan Police HQ, London

"Patricia Gordon. How well did you know her?" Jack fixed Anthony Saunders with a searching stare. Interview room one was a small and stuffy windowless space — the submarine-grey walls flecked with drips of long-discarded coffee and other stains Jack didn't wish to dwell on. The previous occupant's body odour issues still lingered in the stagnant air.

Saunders sat with a straight back on an uneven-legged wooden chair. His eyes widened at the question posed to him. "I don't even know who that is." He reached for the plastic cup of water that he'd asked for.

Jack had watched the defence solicitor's demeanour alter slightly at the mention of the first victim's name. He let the question hang tantalisingly in the air for a moment or two longer than necessary before continuing. "Really? The evidence begs to differ." Jack nodded at DS Cooper, who slid an A4-sized document out from a thin folder in front of him.

"You are being shown item reference CC-001 — a message inventory from London Life." Cooper slid the piece of paper across the table.

The defence solicitor took the document in his hand, his eyes immediately scouring its contents.

"For the sake of clarity, Mr Saunders," continued Jack, casting his eyes down to an identical piece of paper sitting in front of him, "this document shows an itemised list of messages sent by you on the dating site London Life — the recipient of those messages is Patricia Gordon."

Jack let the information hang for a moment, jostling for room among the stale body odour and an ever-increasing tension that electrified the air around them. "I put it to you again, Mr Saunders. How well did you know Patricia Gordon?"

Anthony Saunders let the document fall back onto the table, and lifted his gaze to meet Jack's. "And I repeat my earlier response, Detective Inspector. I didn't know her. I *don't* know her."

Jack began to sense the wariness and nervousness Saunders had initially exhibited upon being arrested and read his rights slowly being replaced by a self-assuredness bordering on the cocky. The shift was subtle, but even the humid and heavy air of the interview room couldn't mask it from the experienced detective.

"This document would appear to suggest otherwise." Jack nodded back down at the paperwork. "A total of three messages sent to Patricia Gordon between the second and twenty-seventh April this year. How do you explain that, Mr Saunders, if, as you claim, you didn't know her?"

Saunders leaned back in his chair, the uneven legs causing it to wobble, and folded his arms across his chest. A flicker of a smile crossed his lips as he took another sip of the warm water in his cup. "And what do these messages say?" he enquired, theatrically raising an eyebrow and giving a small shrug. "You don't seem to have a printout of the content of these so-called messages."

Jack shifted in his seat and caught DS Cooper's eye. They'd anticipated this question coming up during their hastily arranged interview strategy meeting, but not quite this early on. Jack eyed the man sitting across the table — Anthony Saunders, ever the seasoned defence professional, was clearly no pushover when it came to police interviews. He would've sat in on enough of them to pick up more than an adequate knowledge of police tactics.

Jack hated interviewing lawyers.

And he was beginning to hate interviewing this one more than most.

Clearing his throat, Jack continued. "We are requisitioning the content of these messages as we speak." London Life had continued to politely decline to disclose the content of its members' private messages. They'd quoted a number of privacy and data protection laws. Without a warrant, they would disclose nothing.

Something Saunders obviously knew.

The warrant had been served that morning and DC Cassidy was monitoring London Life's response from the room next door.

"But as yet, you don't have them." The defence solicitor continued to rest back in his chair. The cocky edge to his tone was growing. "Shall we move on?"

"You don't deny that you *have* sent messages to Patricia Gordon, three times between second and twenty-seventh April?" Jack refused to let the man gain the upper hand. "The evidence is there in black and white."

"Indeed it is, Detective Inspector," replied Saunders, nodding slowly. "But I send messages to lots of women." A smile crossed his face. "Between you and me, I'm known to be a bit of a flirt." He winked across the table at Jack. "Is this all you have? Some messages?"

Jack felt the tell-tale sensation of his hackles rising on the back of his neck. The heat of the interview room was doing nothing to help keep a lid on his increasing temper. He avoided the solicitor's taunting gaze and slid the London Life document back into his folder, at the same time as pulling out two more. He nodded silently at Cooper.

"You are now being shown two further documents with item reference CC-002 and CC-003." Cooper handed two almost identical documents across the table towards Saunders.

"These documents contain further evidence from London Life showing messages between yourself and Georgina Dale and also Hannah Fuller." Jack paused, allowing Saunders time to scan the printouts. "Bit of a coincidence, don't you think? These two women, plus Patricia Gordon, have all been abducted and murdered within the last twelve days. And you've been in contact with all three of them. I'll ask you one more time — how do you know these women?"

Saunders flicked through the two documents, casting his eyes down each list of dates. Jack could see a film of perspiration forming on the solicitor's upper lip, the first sign that he was becoming agitated. Saunders placed the two pieces of paper back down on the table and resumed his stance with arms folded across his chest, hands tucked away out of sight — hands that Jack sensed were beginning to show a slight tremble. "I've never met any of these women before."

"But you have messaged them." Jack tapped a finger on the documents in front of him. "It says so right here."

Saunders merely shrugged. "If it says I did, then I did. But I refer you to my previous answer. I've messaged lots of women on this site. But I don't necessarily meet any of them. And I don't keep records."

Jack conceded the point. "Duly noted. It's a good job someone does, though, isn't it? As soon as London Life respond to the warrant and disclose the content of these messages, I'm sure we'll return to it." Cooper returned documents CC-001 to CC-003 back inside their folders. "Forensics, Mr Saunders." Jack decided on a change of subject. "You have a lot of knowledge and understanding of police procedures with regards to the collection of forensic evidence at crime scenes, don't you?"

"Are you asking me or telling me?" Saunders remained seated with his arms folded.

"I'll rephrase." Jack noted an element of hostility creeping into the defence solicitor's tone. "What exactly is your knowledge of police procedures for the collection of forensic evidence at crime scenes?"

Saunders shrugged. "I have a basic working knowledge. It comes with the job."

"A basic knowledge, Mr Saunders?" Jack raised an eyebrow. "I put it to you that you have a much more in-depth knowledge than just the basics."

Another shrug in response. "Where are you going with this, Detective Inspector?"

"On eighteenth March this year you attended a conference held in Birmingham — the title of that conference was 'Police procedure and the collection of crime scene evidence — the defendant's perspective'."

"Indeed I did." A darkness began to descend across Anthony Saunders' features. "Along with several hundred others."

"So you must concede that your knowledge is a little more than the basic level you intimated to us before?"

"Must I?" Saunders levelled his gaze at Jack. "If I recall correctly, the conference was a little disappointing, offering nothing more than any half-decent solicitor would already know, or any fan of the many CSI programmes on TV these days. I left early."

"But you do know how to keep a crime scene forensically clean?" Jack knew he was pushing it with this line of questioning, but as Saunders had waived his right to any legal representation, he thought it worth the risk. Anything was worth it if they could find Isabel alive.

A throaty chuckle emanated from Saunders as he shook his head. "An interesting line of questioning, Inspector. One that will be automatically thrown out if this goes any further. But yes, in answer to your pathetic question — obviously I am aware of what evidence can incriminate a suspect at a crime scene, and I am therefore aware of how to avoid it. Was that the answer you wanted?"

Jack glanced up at the video camera blinking in the corner of the room. Being unsure exactly who might be watching, and not wanting to attract unwanted attention, he changed his tactics.

"Isabel Faraday. How well do you know her?"

* * *

Time: 2.40 p.m.
Date: Wednesday 25 July 2012
Location: A cellar in London

Isabel had drained the last of the water from the plastic bottle some time ago. How long had he been gone? When was he coming back? Time meant nothing in this deep, dark cavern.

She felt herself begin to shake. *I need to get a grip*, she told herself. *I need to stop panicking*. Someone would have raised the alarm by now. Poor Dominic would've arrived for work and found the café empty and locked up. She could just imagine the panic that would've overtaken him and hoped he hadn't been too distressed.

But surely he would've said something to someone? He would've rung Sacha, at least, wouldn't he?

Surely *someone* was looking for her?

* * *

Time: 2.40 p.m.
Date: Wednesday 25 July 2012
Location: Metropolitan Police HQ, London

"I met Isabel at her café — on Horseferry Road."
"And subsequently?"

271

"She came to my flat for dinner last night." Anthony Saunders unfolded his arms, leaning forward onto the wooden table. "Why?"

"When was the last time you saw Isabel?" Jack watched as the cockiness that'd been adorning the defence solicitor's face earlier began to slowly recede, replaced by unease.

"When she left my flat." Saunders' voice was controlled, his tone level. Gone was the mocking distaste at Jack's line of questioning. "I don't know exactly what time — about half past eleven, maybe quarter to midnight at a guess. I'd had a little too much to drink. Why are you asking?"

"Isabel Faraday didn't open her café this morning, and as far as we can tell she didn't return home last night." Jack paused, watching the solicitor's reaction, trying to read the man behind the facade. "What can you tell us about that?"

"Nothing!" Saunders exploded, his eyes wide with shock. "I told you, she left to go home about half eleven, or just after."

"So you say. Were there any witnesses to that effect?"

"Witnesses?" Saunders ran a hand through his hair, visibly flustered. "What are you getting at? I thought this was about me messaging women on a dating site."

"Witnesses," repeated Jack, continuing to hold the increasingly uncomfortable-looking solicitor in his stare. "Did anyone see Isabel Faraday leave your flat last night?"

"No, of course not. It was late. But she got into an Uber. I know, because she went outside to meet it."

"An Uber?" Jack frowned and looked at DS Cooper. "What the hell is an Uber?"

"It's a taxi — they're new." Cooper tried to suppress the smile on his lips as he watched the bemused expression on Jack's face. "You book them with an app on your phone."

"So, she got into a taxi, or whatever an Uber is," continued Jack, shaking his head. "You have any idea who picked her up? You have the number?"

Saunders shook his head. "No. She used her own phone."

"You have CCTV outside your flat?"

Another shake of the head. "No, it's never been necessary."

"Is there a basement or cellar at the Buckingham Street flats?"

Jack detected a flicker of unease cross Saunders' features. "Yes," he replied, warily. "There's a cellar. Why?"

Jack made a mental note to check in with the forensics team when they decided to give Saunders a break from interrogation. But the silence from the team so far didn't fill him with much confidence.

"Let's try something else." Opening his folder, Jack slid a photograph across the table. "Tell me who's in this picture."

Saunders took hold of the photograph, the slight tremble in his hands visible. The perspiration on his top lip remained. "That's a photograph of my wife — and my daughter."

The photograph showed a young woman with her arms lovingly enveloped around a girl of approximately eight years of age.

"And these?" Jack slid three more photographs across the table.

Saunders picked them up, the tremble increasing in severity. "Again, there's a photograph of my daughter on a pony. And another of her at Disneyland." He traced a finger over the image of his daughter sitting next to Mickey Mouse in her favourite sweatshirt with the letter "J" emblazoned across the front. "And that one there — that's a photograph of my son, just after he was born."

Jack watched the defence solicitor's face drain of colour.

"Mr Saunders. Where are your wife and children now?"

* * *

Time: 7.15 p.m.
Date: Friday 12 June 1998
Location: Arundel, West Sussex

"Jess, go to your room." His voice, deep and stern, almost caused the plates to vibrate on the dinner table.

Jess looked up, her fork hovering over the as-yet-untouched chicken casserole. The tension in the dining room caused any feeling of hunger to instantly disappear. She glanced warily from her father's thunderous face to her mother's pensive one, her own heart quickening inside her chest.

She hated it when they argued.

"I said, go to your room," her father repeated, emphasising each word clearly. "Now!"

Jess let the fork crash down onto her plate, specks of gravy peppering the clean white tablecloth. She leapt from her chair and ran from the room.

She'd known this was coming.

Dad had had 'that look' on his face ever since Mum came home from work. They'd started arguing almost straight away and Jess had immediately excused herself, running down to the bottom of the garden on the pretext of going to feed the chickens — even though she'd already fed them when she got in from school.

Jess shuddered and ran up the stairs, two at a time.

Now up in her room, she could feel her father's deep-throated booming voice vibrating up through the floorboards from the dining room below. Curling up on her bed, she reached for the tatty teddy bear that sat by her pillow. She hugged it tightly to her chest and began to cry.

Silent tears cascaded down her flushed cheeks, dripping onto the bear as she pulled him closer and closer with each sob. The sound of dishes crashing to the floor beneath her made her clamp her hands over her ears and pull the duvet over her quivering body. She wanted to wrap herself up and disappear. Sobs escaped her mouth as she gulped in air in between each shudder, her pillow quickly sodden with her salty tears.

Although she was hiding underneath her duvet with her head buried under a pillow, nothing could drown out the blood-curdling scream and thud that followed.

Jess sat bolt upright in bed, hardly daring to breathe.

* * *

Time: 2.55 p.m.
Date: Wednesday 25 July 2012
Location: Metropolitan Police HQ, London

"So, where are they?" repeated Jack, watching Saunders' expression as he continued to hold the photographs in his hand. "Your wife? Your children?"

"We don't live together anymore." Saunders' reply was blunt as he dropped the photographs back onto the table.

"We know that. That's not what I asked." Jack nodded back down at the photographs. "I want to know where they are now."

Saunders breathed in deeply and raised his gaze. "Can I have some more water, please?"

Jack felt a flash of annoyance. "In a moment. I want you to answer the question, Mr Saunders. Where are your wife and children?"

"I really need some water." Saunders averted his gaze from both Jack and the photographs. "And then maybe I need that solicitor after all."

* * *

Time: 8.30 p.m.
Date: Friday 12 June 1998
Location: Arundel, West Sussex

Jess crept downstairs to find her father on his hands and knees clearing away the broken crockery from the dining room floor. She hovered in the doorway, unsure if she had the courage to step through. She glanced around the room.

Where was Mum?

He must've sensed her presence, because within seconds he'd turned around and plastered his face with a reassuring smile. "Oh, Jess. It's you." He motioned for her to come forward. "Mind your feet. We had a bit of spillage."

Jess flashed a quick look at the dining table and noticed the dish that had housed the homemade chicken casserole was missing — she could only assume that was what her father was attempting to clear up from the floor beneath. Large ceramic shards littered the floor, in between gooey lumps of chicken, gravy and vegetables.

Jess also noticed that the water jug and glasses lay smashed to smithereens in another corner of the room. Her father saw her shocked expression.

"Ssshhh, it's OK," he soothed, beckoning her towards him. He pushed himself up off his knees and held his arms out wide. "Come here."

Jess took a hesitant step towards her father, her terrified eyes still searching frantically around the room.

Where was Mum?

"Sssshhhh, it's OK," he repeated. "It's OK." He took a step forwards, carefully sidestepping the broken casserole dish and closed the gap between them. Wrapping his arms around her shoulders, he pulled her close. "Everything's all right now, Jess."

Jess stood rigidly in her father's arms.

Where was Mum?

Jess stayed in her room for the rest of the evening. She could hear her father continuing to clear up the mess in the dining room. He'd placed the broken shards of the casserole dish into the outside bin, and swept up the shattered water jug and glasses. She then heard the mop and bucket being taken out of the understairs cupboard.

She didn't dare go downstairs again.

Not yet.

She'd yet to hear anything from Mum. Dad said that she'd got upset, bringing on one of her migraines — so she needed to go and lie down. She got a lot of those these days. Migraines.

But Jess hadn't heard her mother come upstairs to lie down. She hadn't heard her parents' bedroom door open or close.

All there'd been was silence.

CHAPTER THIRTY-FIVE

Time: 5 p.m.
Date: Wednesday 25 July 2012
Location: Metropolitan Police HQ, London

"For the purpose of the tape, Mr Anthony Saunders now has legal representation." Jack cast his eyes across the table once they were all seated. "Please introduce yourself."

"Caroline Beachcroft, from Messrs Ogden, Peters and Staff."

Jack acknowledged the seasoned solicitor who sat opposite. In her early fifties, with greying fair hair clasped neatly back in a loose bun, she had an unblemished face, adorned with a smattering of freckles across the bridge of her nose and cheeks. He knew Caroline — liked her, even. Knew her to be fair, with no hidden agendas. And she was smart, too; she knew her stuff, and certainly knew her way around a police interview. She'd been a very wise choice on behalf of Anthony Saunders. *He* certainly knew what he was doing.

"You've now had time to consult with your solicitor. Before the break, we were asking you about your wife and children." Jack picked up where they'd left off before Saunders had summonsed his lawyer. A fresh round of water, chilled this time, had furnished the table, with coffee for both Jack and Caroline Beachcroft.

"My client will not answer questions about his family, Inspector." Beachcroft's voice was light and crisp. "Nothing you've disclosed prior to this interview means his family circumstances are relevant to his arrest."

Jack was forced to suppress the smile that teased his lips. Oh, she was good — she was very good. He eyed Saunders across the table, noting that the man still stared down at the table in front of him, a pensive look on his face. "In that case, we'll move on." Jack opened his folder once more. "Mr Saunders. A further woman was found murdered in the early hours of this morning. During the break, I was informed that she's been identified as Zoe Turner. Do you know someone by the name of Zoe Turner, Mr Saunders?"

Saunders continued staring at the table, refusing to meet Jack's eyes.

"These four women went missing on sixth July, twelfth July, nineteenth July and twenty-first July, respectively. Please tell us where you were on each of these dates. Let's start with sixth July."

Saunders glanced sideways to his solicitor. She gave him a discreet nod, at which point he returned his gaze to face Jack and DS Cooper. "I'm afraid I can't tell you. I don't remember."

"It was a Friday," added Jack, after consulting the folder. "If that helps at all."

Saunders' face remained impassive. He merely shook his head slowly from side to side. "I don't remember. Without my work diary, I can't possibly . . ."

"Well, it's a good thing that we've already checked with your employers and got a copy of your diary, isn't it?" Jack pulled out another piece of paper and slid it across the table.

"Item reference CC-004," confirmed DS Cooper, pulling out an identical copy from his own folder.

"This document, Mr Saunders," continued Jack, "confirms that on the afternoon of Friday sixth July you cancelled a meeting with a new client at two p.m. You then cancelled a conference with Counsel at Pump Court Chambers, which had been due to take place at four p.m. Your employers confirm you left your office at 1.45 p.m. and didn't return. Where did you go, Mr Saunders?"

Anthony Saunders stared at the copy of his work diary entry for Friday sixth July, while Caroline Beachcroft hastily cast her eyes over the damning entries. Silence filled the stuffy interview room, the break for refreshments having done nothing to extract the stale odours from the air.

Jack glanced across at Cooper and then turned his attention back to Saunders. "Well? Where were you going that was so important that you had to cancel an important barrister's conference at such short notice and clear the rest of your diary?"

Saunders carried on shaking his head, accompanied this time by a small shrug.

"Surely you'd be able to remember something like that?" pressed Jack. "It wasn't that long ago, Mr Saunders. What was so important that you had to cancel all your engagements that afternoon?"

The silence continued.

"The suspect has not provided an answer," stated Cooper, eyeing the tape recorder sitting at the side of the table.

"I . . . I just don't remember," stuttered the defence solicitor, still shaking his head. Jack noticed that Saunders was jiggling his leg up and down under the table. A sign of agitation, he mused. A sign that he was uncomfortable with the line of questioning.

A line of questioning that Jack fully intended to continue with.

"Let's try another." Jack reached back inside the folder and retrieved another document. "How about twelfth July? Where were you that day?"

Saunders looked up, eyeing the piece of paper in Jack's hand. His leg continued to jiggle uncontrollably beneath the table. He glanced at Caroline Beachcroft who, once again, gave a curt nod towards her client. He opened his mouth, then closed it again without a sound.

"Mr Saunders? The afternoon and evening of twelfth July. Where were you?" Jack paused. "Again, if it helps, it was a Thursday."

More silence.

Saunders continued to fidget in his seat, whether it was from the uncomfortable silence or the uncomfortable wooden chair, Jack couldn't be sure. To prolong the agony, Jack sat back and fixed the increasingly worried-looking defence solicitor with his best penetrative stare. He noticed that Beachcroft was still casting her expert gaze over the extracts from Saunders' work diary, her expression giving nothing away.

Jack waited a few more seconds before deciding to turn the screw a little more.

"Again we've been in touch with your employers, and obtained a copy of your diary for the day in question." Jack nodded once more towards DS Cooper, who promptly handed over another sheet of A4 paper.

"Item reference CC-005," Cooper announced. "Desk diary entry for Thursday twelfth July."

Once again, the now established pantomime of Anthony Saunders staring at the diary entries followed by questioning glances towards his solicitor played out in interview room one. And Jack was happy to sit back and watch, letting himself start to enjoy the now obvious displeasure that his tactics were causing.

"Where did you go, Mr Saunders? Why did you cancel your commitments *again* that afternoon?" Jack nodded towards the document on the table. "Once again, more client meetings cancelled at short notice. What was so important?" Jack's questions were met by more silence.

"Again, the suspect has not given an answer." DS Cooper reached back into his folder and passed two more documents across to Jack.

"How about nineteenth and twenty-first July? A Thursday and Saturday respectively."

"Item reference CC-006 and CC-007," confirmed Cooper. "Desk diary entries for both dates."

"I again ask you, Mr Saunders, to account for your movements on both of these dates." Jack tapped a finger on the copies as he slid them across the table towards Saunders and his solicitor.

The accustomed silence prevailed.

Jack could almost hear the ticking and whirring of the tiny wheels and cogs inside Anthony Saunders' head, as he either tried to remember his movements or tried to concoct a suitable-sounding explanation.

Neither was forthcoming.

"As before," continued Jack, "we've approached your employers, who confirm that you cleared your diary on Thursday nineteenth July at short notice, without explanation, again cancelling important meetings. Tell us where you were, Mr Saunders."

* * *

Time: 1 p.m.
Date: Thursday 19 July 2012
Location: Blackfriars Road, London

Anthony Saunders glanced at his watch and then at the traffic inching, nose-to-tail, along the Blackfriars Road, heading towards the Thames. The heady smell of diesel fumes from the idling buses snarled up in the lunchtime traffic began to infiltrate and irritate his nostrils. He could feel a headache coming on.

The heat didn't help either. The temperature had continued to climb all day, the non-existent breeze meaning there was no respite from the incessant heat beating down onto the bone-dry pavement beneath. Pedestrians went about their business with increasingly uncomfortable frowns on their faces, clutching bottles of water and fanning themselves with their hands.

There was no chance of hopping onto a bus, he mused, as he took another glance at the crawling traffic. It would take too long. With a sigh he headed towards the underground station — the thought of even a short journey cooped up in a stifling carriage with tightly packed, sweaty bodies made him shudder.

But he needed to get home.

And fast.

His secretary had pursed her lips when he'd told her to clear his diary for the rest of the day. *Again.*

This is becoming a bit of a habit, Mr Saunders, she'd muttered through her tightened jaw, peering disapprovingly at him over the rim of her spectacles.

He pushed her image from his thoughts and concentrated on negotiating the steps down into the Southwark underground entrance.

He had things to do.

* * *

Time: 5.30 p.m.
Date: Wednesday 25 July 2012
Location: Metropolitan Police HQ, London

"Tell me about your wardrobe, Mr Saunders." Jack returned the extracts from the solicitor's work diary to his folder.

"My wardrobe?" Anthony Saunders stared blankly at Jack. "What about my wardrobe?"

"The one in your bedroom with all the shoes in it." Jack slid a photograph from DS Cooper's folder across the table. The photograph showed multiple shelves stacked full of shoes in a variety of styles and colours.

"Item reference CC-008," announced Cooper, taking out an identical copy for himself.

Saunders continued to stare blankly down at the photograph.

"Tell me why you have so many pairs of women's shoes in your wardrobe, Mr Saunders."

"Relevance, Inspector?" Caroline Beachcroft peered closely at the photograph, a frown crossing her freckled face. "How is this connected with the murder of four women, the basis of your arrest of my client?"

Jack took a deep breath. They'd managed to keep the fact of a shoe being found at each murder location out of the press so far — a feat in itself, considering the propensity of internal leaks springing up during even the lowest-profile investigations. But Isabel was still missing, and potentially still alive, so Jack had decided that now was the time to place all their evidence on the table. Plus, Caroline Beachcroft was no pushover; unless they divulged the relevance of their line of questioning she would advise her client not to answer.

"A shoe was left at each scene by the killer," confirmed Jack. "A shoe belonging to the next victim. *That* is the relevance of the shoes, Miss Beachcroft."

"This is new information, Inspector. You haven't disclosed this in any of the press releases so far and you certainly didn't disclose it as part of the discovery when I arrived today." Beachcroft raised her head and fixed her pale blue eyes on Jack. "How do we know this is even true?"

As much as Jack liked and respected Caroline Beachcroft, he was starting to become irritated. He reached for his coffee, but realised that it'd now become tepid with a film of stagnant milk on the surface. Instead, he turned his attention back to the defence solicitor across the table.

"As you will be well aware, Miss Beachcroft, certain details, *pertinent* details, during a murder investigation can and are often kept out of the press for operational reasons." Jack opened the folder and took out a series of four photographs, each depicting an abandoned shoe at one of the crime scenes.

"Item reference CC-009 to 012," confirmed DS Cooper, handing out identical copies.

"These shoes were found at the sites of the discovery of the bodies of Patricia Gordon, Georgina Dale, Hannah Fuller and now also Zoe Turner this morning. So my question still stands, Mr Saunders. Why have you got a wardrobe full of women's shoes?" Jack tapped a finger on each of the photographs, feeling his pulse quickening. "I need an answer. Now."

* * *

Time: 1.45 p.m.
Date: Thursday 19 July 2012
Location: Buckingham Street, Embankment, London

Anthony Saunders breathed a sigh of relief as he finally arrived outside his flat. He was on time. The Tube journey had been just as horrific as he'd anticipated — hot, stuffy, and smelly. He'd shared a far too intimate space with a heavyset man covered in body hair and tattoos, neither of which ordinarily bothered him, except the dense covering of body hair was a haven for odour-heavy droplets of sweat to be captured, releasing their toxins freely into the enclosed carriage space throughout the journey. Mixed with the stomach-churning aroma of greasy fried chicken and onions that'd been left behind in a discarded takeaway box, Saunders couldn't wait to be released into the relatively fresh air of the ground above.

He reached the entrance to his flat and couldn't open the door quickly enough, shuddering at the memory of the Tube journey. Once inside, he wrenched off his sweat sodden shirt and tie, wriggled out of his suit trousers and underwear, and headed straight for the bathroom. Leaving his clothes strewn across the floor, he stepped into the shower and turned the dial to "cool".

A few minutes later, cleansed and freshened, he gathered up his discarded clothes and rammed them straight into the washing basket. He padded through to the front room with a towel wrapped around his waist, letting the last of the shower's water droplets dry naturally on his skin.

Just at that moment the doorbell buzzed. He picked up the intercom and immediately pressed the button releasing the main door.

At last.

He'd been waiting for this all week.

A short, sharp rap on his front door followed, and Saunders pulled it open to take delivery of the large parcel that'd been manhandled through the entrance by a frazzled, pink-cheeked delivery driver.

"Parcel for Saunders," the man announced, breathlessly, from behind the parcel.

"Sure thing, thanks." Saunders took the parcel from the grateful delivery man, scribbled a rough signature on the proffered delivery note, and backed away towards his front room.

His eyes gleamed.

This was the one he'd been waiting for.

This was the one that was going to make all the difference.

He skilfully sliced through the parcel tape using a knife that he'd abandoned on his breakfast plate earlier that morning. Folding out the flaps of cardboard, Anthony Saunders' face glowed with delight. He reached inside and picked out an elegant ruby-red stiletto, the ankle straps adorned with diamond-like stones.

They were exquisite.

They were expensive.

They were *perfect*.

* * *

Time: 5.45 p.m.
Date: Wednesday 25 July 2012
Location: Metropolitan Police HQ, London

Anthony Saunders buried his face in his hands and gave a shuddering sigh. He tried to suppress the sobs that were gathering in his throat, but it was a battle he was always going to lose.

The time had come.

He would have to explain.

He would have to tell all.

He had no choice.

Raising his head, he breathed in the deepest breath he could muster and settled his focus on Jack. Slowly, he gave a nod.

"OK, I can explain." Saunders' voice was shaky as he nervously wrung his hands together in his lap. "I know I've done wrong, and that it may have pretty dire consequences for me."

Jack and Cooper exchanged an expectant look. Were they now about to get their long-awaited confession?

"I've done wrong, I admit it," continued Saunders, locking eyes with Jack across the table. "But I'm no killer." He paused again, taking in another deep breath. "I have never met any of those women. And Isabel really did leave my flat alive and well last night. I swear. You've got the wrong man."

* * *

Time: 11.35 p.m.
Date: Tuesday 24 July 2012
Location: Buckingham Street, Embankment, London

Isabel hovered over the threshold of the door to Flat 1B. She felt a little tipsy from the wine they'd drunk, and then the "one for the road" brandy afterwards. She swayed a little as she stepped back into her shoes and smothered a giggle behind her hand.

"Oops," she laughed, steadying herself against the door frame.

"Let me." Anthony Saunders knelt down and gently buckled the straps around Isabel's slim ankles. "These really are lovely shoes."

"Well, thank you, kind sir," Isabel chuckled, straightening her shoulder bag across her chest.

"Thank you for coming," replied Saunders, the smile on his lips triggering the boyish dimple on his cheek. "I had a great time."

"Me too," smiled Isabel, her cheeks colouring as she tucked a stray lock of hair behind her ear. "Dinner was lovely."

"Are you sure you don't want me to wait outside with you?" Anthony motioned towards the door. "When is your taxi coming?"

Isabel glanced down at her phone. "It says it's five minutes away. I'll be fine." She turned on her heels and began to totter across the flagstone hallway.

"Well, if you're sure." Anthony gave another dimple-smile and watched as Isabel carefully made her way past the stairs, holding onto the banister as she did so, the red wine still having its effect. "Call me sometime."

Isabel raised a hand in reply, concentrating on putting one foot in front of the other. The evening had been great, the food and wine had been divine; the company, she had to shyly admit, had also been good. She didn't fancy him or anything — he was a little too self-centred for her liking, and she got the impression he was a bit of a flirt — but he was pleasant enough company. So the last thing she wanted to do was round off such a perfect evening by turning a somersault and face-planting the floor.

Pulling open the communal door, she felt the welcome rush of cool evening air hit her face. Carefully stepping over the front step, she glanced back down at her phone to check the location of her Uber.

"Damn," she muttered, as the screen suddenly turned to black. "And now you choose to die on me." She pressed a few random buttons in the hope of injecting some hidden power, but all they did was confirm to her that her battery had died.

Stepping onto the pavement outside the converted Ernest Baker Grain Merchants building, she looked along the road to where she hoped she would see the taxi emerging in a moment or two. The evening air was balmy and she quietly hummed, happily, to herself as she waited.

It wasn't long before two headlights approached from the end of the road and headed in her direction.

CHAPTER THIRTY-SIX

Time: 6.15 p.m.
Date: Wednesday 25 July 2012
Location: Metropolitan Police HQ, London

"Interview recommenced with Anthony Saunders at 6.15 p.m." DS Cooper started the tape recording.

After requesting a short break to consult with his solicitor, Saunders had returned to his seat and nodded he was ready to continue. A fresh cup of water was placed in front of him, from which he took a sip and cleared his throat.

"I swear. She got into that taxi."

"But you didn't actually *see* her, did you?" Jack eyed the defence solicitor across the table. "You weren't actually outside with her."

"No," admitted Saunders, glumly. "She left my flat and the last I saw of her was when she stepped outside to wait for her taxi."

Jack nodded. A search of Isabel's phone records had confirmed her last location was in the Buckingham Street area when either the battery had died or the phone had been switched off. The last activity on her phone had been accessing the Uber application. Hurried checks during the break confirmed a driver had shown up at Flat 1B, but there'd been nobody at the address to pick up. Due to roadworks, they'd been a few minutes late. After waiting a while, they'd put it down to a crank call and the Uber was reallocated elsewhere.

"OK, go on." Jack nodded at Saunders to continue.

"The shoes — I can explain the shoes. But it's not what you think." Saunders paused and drew in a deep breath. "I buy and sell women's shoes. Larger sizes for the transgender and transvestite community. I have a website."

"Details, Mr Saunders." Jack motioned to Cooper to take a note of the address.

"Um, it's www.biggershoes.co.uk." Saunders buried his head in his hands, his shoulders shuddering as he fought back the tears that were again threatening to engulf him. "I know this'll mean trouble for me. And my father, he . . ." Saunders broke off, shaking his head. "God knows what my father will say. But I swear to you, that is all I do with the shoes."

Jack frowned. "Why will buying and selling larger-sized women's shoes mean trouble for you, Mr Saunders? As far as I know, that hasn't been made a crime."

Saunders glanced up at Caroline Beachcroft by his side, and she gave a small nod, giving her silent permission for her client to answer. "Well, I may not buy them from the most authorised of channels."

"Meaning?" probed Jack, although he knew exactly what the man was getting at.

"OK, so some of them may be stolen." Saunders hung his head.

"*Some?*" Jack raised his eyebrows.

"OK, so most of them."

Jack exhaled loudly and caught Cooper's eye. They both looked down at the photograph from Saunders' wardrobe.

And then the penny dropped.

It'd stared them in the face and they'd both been too blind to see it.

Pairs of shoes.

Pairs.

Anthony Saunders wasn't their man.

"But why, Mr Saunders?" Jack rubbed his chin, pushing away the ever-increasing sense of panic within. "You're a successful defence solicitor. You work in a prestigious law firm in central London. You must be pushing a pretty decent salary. You come from a privileged and moneyed background. Your father . . ."

"Yes, I know who my father is," interrupted Saunders, hotly. "You don't need to remind me."

"So why?" Jack stood his ground. "I don't follow. Why would you get involved in this kind of business on the side — buying and selling stolen goods? What on earth is worth taking such a risk for?"

Saunders reached for the pile of evidence that had slowly been accumulating on the table in front of him. He leafed through the documents, placing some to the side. Spreading the rest out on the table, he selected the series of photographs showing his daughter riding the pony, the one of her sitting on the bench at Disneyland, and the one of his new-born son.

"Them," replied Saunders, his voice barely above a whisper. "I do it for them."

* * *

Time: 8 p.m.
Date: Tuesday 24 July 2012
Location: Buckingham Street, Embankment, London

"I'm sorry," breathed Isabel, softly, taking another sip of Merlot. "I didn't mean to upset you."

Anthony Saunders shook his head and hastily wiped away a solitary tear that was sliding down one cheek. "No, I'm the one that's sorry. I'm being all soppy and maudlin and we're meant to be having a good time!" He raised his wine glass and took a large mouthful of the deep burgundy wine, thankful for the anaesthetizing effect of the alcohol. He'd drunk more since the children had been born; a lot more.

"Well, I'm sorry anyway," repeated Isabel, giving what she hoped was a sympathetic smile in his direction. "She's really pretty."

Anthony nodded, looking towards the photograph of his beaming daughter riding a pony.

"She loved ponies — ever since she was small. Still does." He smiled at the memory. "And despite her condition, and her problems, we did everything we could to make her feel like any other child — to give her the same experiences and opportunities."

Isabel felt a frown forming. Her condition? Her problems? She looked once again at the photograph on the bookcase, this time looking more closely and more intently than her earlier cursory glance had allowed.

And it was then that she saw it.

She still saw the same happy, grinning child sitting astride a brown and white pony, an unmistakable look of glee on her heart-shaped face — but what Isabel hadn't seen the first time around were the callipers on her legs, and the small, thin tube leading to her nostrils. Isabel followed the tubing to an oxygen cylinder being supported in the crook of her father's arm.

Both parents, one either side, had steadying hands around their daughter's waist, helping her to sit high and proud atop her pony.

Just like any other child.

Isabel felt her eyes begin to swim with newly forming tears. As she silently brushed them away, she watched Anthony's face crumple around the edges, the pain very much still evident.

Letting her gaze drift across to the next photograph, Isabel again looked at the picture of a slightly older girl, sitting on the bench next to Mickey Mouse. At first glance, she'd assumed it was merely a family photograph taken while on holiday in Disneyland — which it was. Except a closer look this time revealed much more than that.

The girl in the photograph had the same heart-shaped face — the same warming smile beaming out towards the camera. Her teeth now sported braces, but the same hazel eyes twinkled with intense happiness. Isabel looked more closely, and again saw the same callipers on her legs, the same oxygen tank attached to tubing that curled across the "J" on her sweatshirt, delivering oxygen to her nostrils.

Mickey Mouse was sitting close up against her, close enough to offer the teenager the support she needed in keeping upright on the bench.

"Cerebral palsy." Anthony answered the unspoken question on Isabel's lips. "It was a traumatic birth. She was premature — just thirty weeks — and the cord was wrapped tightly around her neck. Her brain was deprived of oxygen for too long — she suffered severe birth asphyxia."

"I'm so sorry." The words seemed so insufficient, but Isabel didn't know what else to say.

"Babies aren't usually affected by having the cord around their neck — it happens a lot, but . . ." Anthony broke off, his voice shuddering. "We were unlucky. Jasmine now needs twenty-four-hour care. She lives with her mother." He took another long swig from his wine glass. "We separated when she was small."

Isabel choked back the fresh tears that were forming and she, too, settled on another slug of wine. Across the top of her wine glass, she watched as Anthony got up and refreshed both of their glasses with the rest of the Merlot. Before returning to his seat, he reached up to the shelf above and brought down the other photograph Isabel had briefly seen on her first inquisitive sweep of the room.

Anthony held the photograph in his hands for a moment and Isabel watched as the pain intensified across his face. Clearing his throat, he passed the photograph across to her.

"This is Sonny. He was Jasmine's twin brother."

Isabel brought a hand up to her mouth to stifle a gasp.

"He didn't make it." Anthony's voice caught, and the rush of tears that he'd been successfully damming up until now broke though. "Jasmine was born first, and they managed to resuscitate her. But by the time they got to Sonny

. . ." He broke off for more Merlot to take away the pain. "This is our only picture of him."

Isabel glanced back down at the photograph, noting the tiny baby wrapped tightly in a blue blanket. He was firmly swaddled with just his face visible; his tiny face perfectly formed, eyes closed as if in peaceful slumber.

A slumber from which he would never wake.

Isabel rose from her seat and crossed over to where Anthony was slumped in his chair, placing a comforting arm around his shoulders.

"I'm so sorry," she repeated, once again. "I'm so sorry."

* * *

Time: 6.45 p.m.
Date: Wednesday 25 July 2012
Location: Metropolitan Police HQ, London

"With Jasmine needing twenty-four-hour care, it doesn't come cheap." Saunders stared vacantly down at the photograph on the table. "They live in the States and nothing comes cheap over there. My wife — she's American. When we split, she went back home and took Jasmine with her. Hydrotherapy really helps with her mobility. But it's expensive. That's why I set up the website to try and earn something extra to help pay for all her medical bills. They don't have the NHS — everything has to be paid for."

Silence hung like a noose in the stale air of the interview room. Jack was devoid of words, and a quick glance across at DS Cooper beside him confirmed that his sergeant was equally moved. Cooper passed Jack his mobile phone, logged into the www.biggershoes.co.uk website.

It was, indeed, a website selling shoes in larger sizes.

Across the table, Caroline Beachcroft dabbed at the corners of her eyes.

"Interview terminated at 6.45 p.m." Jack motioned for Cooper to turn off the tape recording. "Mr Saunders, you are free to go."

* * *

Time: 7 p.m.
Date: Wednesday 25 July 2012
Location: A cellar in London

He cautiously shouldered open the heavy oak door and peered into the inky blackness beyond. He'd left her for longer than he'd intended, but events of the day had been spiralling. As he pushed the rest of the door open, a shaft of light illuminated a strip of the cellar floor, catching the edge of her mattress.

He could see a faint bundle at the far end, pushed up against the wall. The metal chain from the radiator was pulled tight. She'd been trying to cram herself into the farthest corner of the room again, as far away from reality as possible.

They'd all tried to do that at some point.

But it didn't make any difference in the end.

He stepped forward, his soft-soled shoes making no sound on the stone floor. He noticed the water bottle was empty and on its side by the end of the mattress, and it looked like she'd at least tried to eat some of the sandwich.

Good girl.

Carol was finally starting to listen.

He brought a hand up to the side of his cheek where there were several red marks starting to show. Carol had been quite feisty when he'd got her inside the car, and when she'd realised that she wasn't going home. That was most unlike her. Carol didn't normally show such physical strength towards him. It was something he was going to have to watch — and control.

He placed the thin twine and masking tape that he'd been carrying by the side of the discarded water bottle, and bent down onto his knees. The others hadn't needed to be subdued like this — they'd been good girls, compliant.

But this one was different.

* * *

Time: 7.05 p.m.
Date: Wednesday 25 July 2012
Location: Metropolitan Police HQ, London

"Where's DS Carmichael?" Jack shot down the corridor leading away from the interview rooms. "He's got some explaining to do."

DC Cassidy, who'd been viewing the interview from the room next door via a two-way mirror, quickened her stride into a jog to keep up. "He's not here, guv."

Jack came to an abrupt halt, causing Cassidy to almost run into the back of him. "What do you mean he's not here? We're in the middle of a bloody murder investigation."

Cassidy shrugged, a worried look crossing her face. "He left soon after the break — when the solicitor arrived and once you started interviewing Saunders again. I don't know where he's gone."

"Jesus," muttered Jack, glancing at his watch and running a hand through his hair. "Everything goes belly-up and he's nowhere to be seen. Arresting Saunders was his idea, you know. He was the one pressing for it, convincing us all we had the right guy."

Cassidy merely nodded, unsure what she should say. They carried on along the corridor and just as they were approaching the main reception area, DS Cooper caught up with them from behind.

"Boss? Chief Superintendent King wants to see you."

"I bet he does," muttered Jack, knowing that the catastrophic farce that had just been played out in the interview room would've already been brought to the senior officer's attention. News like that never did take long to spread.

"Should we ring him?" asked Cassidy, bringing out her phone. "DS Carmichael, I mean. Find out where he is?"

Jack shook his head. "No, it's too late for that. Leave him be. Wherever he is." Holding the door open, he let Cassidy and Cooper walk ahead of him. "If I speak to him now I don't think I'll be responsible for my actions. He'd just better show his face tomorrow,"

"So, if we're ruling out Saunders, where do we go from here?" Cassidy slipped her phone back in her pocket. "Forensics found a cellar at the Buckingham Street flats but there's nothing down there but wine bottles and boxes of shoes."

"Add Saunders' address to the CCTV trawl. And any cameras in neighbouring streets. We need to find that taxi."

"Uber," corrected Cooper, ripping the top off a packet of ham sandwiches he'd managed to find.

"Uber," conceded Jack, with a grimace.

* * *

Time: 8.30 p.m.
Date: Wednesday 25 July 2012
Location: A cellar in London

In the end, she'd been surprisingly compliant.

The sedative in the water bottle had helped.

Glancing back down at the limp form stretched out on the mattress, he placed the thin blanket over the top of her, tucking it in around the edges. It could get quite chilly down here at night-time, despite the hot weather. And Carol always felt the cold.

He picked up the masking tape and remains of the twine, and backed away towards the door. Carol would sleep peacefully for a while now. As he reached the door and turned to head back up the stairs, he passed the empty mattress opposite and frowned.

Jess.

He needed a new Jess.

CHAPTER THIRTY-SEVEN

Time: 9.30 p.m.
Date: Wednesday 25 July 2012
Location: Kettle's Yard Mews, London

Mac handed Jack another bottle of ice-cold Budweiser and sank down onto the sofa next to him. "I won't be able to sleep tonight, Jack. Not while she's still out there." Mac's voice cracked and he took another slug of beer to mask it.

Join the club, thought Jack.

"I don't think many of us will be sleeping tonight, Stu. Crash here if you want. I'll be up early — I've to go and see the chief superintendent first thing. And that won't be pretty." Jack had avoided the repeated messages from Dougie King and managed to slip away from the station unnoticed. But he was going to have to face the music at some point. The thought gnawed away at his insides.

Mac rolled the cool beer bottle across his forehead. "Thanks. But I feel I should be out there, you know, looking for her."

Jack shook his head. "We've got officers on patrol all night. We're doing everything we can to find her." He heard his own empty promises echoing around the flat and took a mouthful of beer to wash them away. Had he really just said that banal statement out loud? The textbook standard response you always gave to the worried family. '*We're doing everything we can.*' It sounded so lame. So inadequate. So meaningless.

And it was.

Jack hadn't really wanted to leave the station, prepared to work through the night if it meant they would find Isabel, but the thought of the chief superintendent tracking him down and giving him the bollocking he probably deserved had persuaded him to make his retreat. Cooper and Cassidy had refused to go home — planning to review the CCTV footage in the hope of tracking down the Uber and finding the evidence everyone else had so far missed.

"So, it really wasn't Saunders then?" Mac downed the rest of his beer in a second gulp.

"Nope." Jack gave another shake of his head. "He looked good for it on paper, but there was always something about him that didn't quite fit. I should've stood my ground. If I'd been more on my game . . ."

"Not your fault, Jack. You and your team, you've all been working like dogs on this. Everyone can see that."

Everyone maybe except Chief Superintendent King, thought Jack.

"I just hate waiting around." Mac got up and crossed over to the fridge, pulling two more beers out. "I can't go to work. I can't go home. I can't do anything."

"Stay here tonight and keep your phone switched on tomorrow." Jack drained his bottle and accepted the fresh one.

"You'll call me if you hear anything? Anything at all?" Mac turned away from his brother, blinking rapidly.

"I promise — I can see she means a lot to you."

Mac swallowed down a sad laugh. "We hardly know each other."

"Sometimes it doesn't take much — some things are just meant to be."

Mac shook his head and turned his attention back to his beer bottle. "Yeah well, she's not likely to feel the same, is she? Not about me."

Jack frowned, trying to catch his brother's eye. "I don't see why not."

Mac gave a throaty chuckle. "You don't know why not? Why would someone like Isabel be even remotely interested in someone like me?"

"What do you mean — '*someone like me*'?"

Mac swallowed another mouthful of Budweiser. "Let's face it, Jack. I'm hardly the best prospect, am I? I've got a string of convictions, spent more time in young offenders' institutions than I care to admit. Time in adult prison. I'm not exactly ticking all the boxes, am I?"

"That's all in the past, Stu. You were young. You've straightened yourself out now."

"But I'm damaged, Jack. You know it. I know it." Mac paused and hung his head. "I'm damaged."

"I'm sure she wouldn't see it like that. I don't."

"Yeah, well, I do. It makes me ashamed, Jack — ashamed of what I used to be." Mac rolled the half-empty beer bottle between his palms. "Do you remember that day in court? When I got sent down for the first time?"

Jack nodded, slowly. "Of course I remember."

"You want to know why I didn't look at you? The whole time, throughout the whole trial, I never once acknowledged you?" Mac paused. "I was ashamed, Jack. I was a hot-headed kid who thought he knew better than everyone. I gave the impression that I didn't care. But I was just ashamed. I couldn't look you in the eye because I was ashamed."

* * *

Time: 3.30 p.m.
Date: 31 October 1982
Location: Bournemouth Crown Court, Dorset

"All rise."

The court usher solemnly announced the return of His Honour Judge Charles Trowbridge. The wooden seats creaked as everyone in court number two at Bournemouth Crown Court obediently got to their feet.

Shuffling in from the door that led to his chambers, the judge sat down heavily in his seat — pale blue eyes peering over the top of the horn-rimmed spectacles perched on the end of his bulbous nose. He gave a curt nod to the sea of heads in front of him, some bearing wigs, others not, and everyone obligingly sat down. Except for the defendants in the dock.

Jack resumed his seat with the others in the public gallery. His foster mother, Mary, sat next to him and gave his hand a reassuring squeeze. He'd sat through every minute of the five-day trial, listening to the evidence that was going to spell the end of his brother's life as he knew it.

"Members of the jury — will the foreman please stand." The court usher turned towards the twelve members of the jury, nodding as a gentleman from the front row got to his feet. "For each of the defendants, have you reached a verdict upon which you are all agreed?"

The foreman of the jury gave a slow nod. "We have."

The court usher then turned towards the four defendants standing in the dock. "In respect of the defendant Jason Alcock, on the charge of robbery, do you find the defendant guilty or not guilty?"

"Guilty."

"In respect of the defendant Jason Alcock, on the additional charge of manslaughter, do you find the defendant guilty or not guilty?"

"Guilty."

"In respect of the defendant, Stephen Byers, on the charge of robbery, do you find the defendant guilty, or not guilty?"

"Guilty."

"In respect of the defendant Kyle Williams, on the charge of robbery, do you find the defendant guilty, or not guilty?"

"Guilty."

"And in respect of the defendant Stuart MacIntosh, on the charge of robbery, do you find the defendant guilty, or not guilty?"

Jack held his breath.

But he knew what was going to be said before he actually heard the fateful word.

"Guilty."

Jack felt his stomach lurch, and the grip his foster mother had on his hand tightened. Hot tears pricked at the corners of his eyes, but he used his free hand to rub them furiously away. He mustn't cry. He'd promised Stu he wouldn't cry.

Jack watched as all four defendants remained standing in the dock. The jury were dismissed and thanked by the judge for their dedication and professionalism over the last five days. His Honour Judge Trowbridge then turned towards the front bench of lawyers who were now all on their feet, wigs bobbing up and down in synchronicity.

The judge held up a hand to quieten the throng. "Jason Alcock, Stephen Byers, Kyle Williams, Stuart MacIntosh. You have all been found guilty of the crime of robbery — contrary to Section 8(1) of the Theft Act 1968. In addition, Jason Alcock, you alone have been charged and found guilty of the offence of manslaughter, contrary to common law. I will be deferring sentence for probation reports to be prepared on each of you. However." The judge paused and peered at each defendant in turn over the lenses of his spectacles. "I must warn you that the offences of manslaughter and robbery are serious crimes. You were sent for trial at the Crown Court due to the seriousness of these offences. And therefore it is certain that only a custodial sentence will be passed." He then turned his attention to the wigged lawyers still on their feet in front of him. "I trust there will be no applications for bail?"

It was more of a statement than a question, and not a question that the judge expected an answer to.

"Take them down." His Honour Judge Charles Trowbridge nodded at the security personnel flanking the defendants.

Jack craned his neck from his seat in the public gallery, straining to catch a glimpse of his brother before he disappeared. But try as he might to gain his attention, Stuart MacIntosh refused to raise his head, keeping his eyes cast downwards to the floor. He shuffled in line behind his three co-defendants and disappeared from sight.

* * *

Time: 9.45 p.m.
Date: Wednesday 25 July 2012
Location: Kettle's Yard Mews, London

"You did your time, Stu. No one thinks anything less of you because of it." Many a time, Jack had wished he could turn back the clock, forcing his brother onto a different path; any path other than the one he took. "You just fell in with the wrong crowd — boys from that children's home. It was inevitable where it would lead."

A rueful smile crossed Mac's lips. "They weren't all bad news. Most were decent kids beneath it all. But at the time I didn't care. And to be honest, being banged up — even in that youth detention place — was better than being in that children's home. Anything was better than that place." Mac took another large mouthful of beer to take away the memories.

"You were lucky only one of you got charged with manslaughter," added Jack. "The prosecution didn't seek to get you all under the joint enterprise law, which they could've, easily. I'm surprised they didn't, to be honest."

Mac shrugged. "I don't feel lucky, Jack. Prison taught me all I needed to know about crime — so even when I got out I didn't stop."

"But you did eventually, Stu. That's what counts."

Mac's face contorted in pain as he held his brother's gaze. "You have to find her, Jack. You have to find Isabel."

"I will, Stu. I promise."

A promise I hope I can keep, mused Jack, finishing off his beer.

* * *

Time: 10.45 p.m.
Date: Wednesday 25 July 2012
Location: Metropolitan Police HQ, London

DS Cooper rubbed his eyes and forced his blurred vision to refocus on the monitor. The lights in the tech room were dimmed, giving the place a calm and serene feel. But Cooper was feeling anything but calm and serene. Isabel had been missing for almost twenty-four hours now and, with the release of Anthony Saunders, they were back to square one.

Where was she?

Cooper navigated the screen and pulled up the CCTV images for all four victim locations. The images had been viewed countless times, with nothing useful being gained — but he couldn't help feeling there must be another clue somewhere.

Anywhere.

So far, the only credible lead the CCTV images had thrown up had been the black transit van with cloned plates. The registered owner of the Peugeot, the true owner of the registration plates, had been interviewed. A seventy-six-year-old partially sighted gentleman from Manchester, who was now bedbound after a recent stroke, was quickly eliminated from the enquiry. Whoever had cloned his registration plates wasn't known to him.

Cooper brought up the images of the transit van and watched its progress, in slow motion, approaching Hyde Park. No matter how many times they'd enlarged the images, or looked at the van from other angles, there was no way of see-ing inside. Whoever was driving remained hidden from view.

Cooper sighed and let the images play out. He'd watched them so many times he could recite the vehicle sequences in his sleep. The grainy progression played out before him once more — the black transit van again passed through and turned right at the junction ahead, then disappeared from sight. ANPR checks had followed its route out of London, losing it somewhere east of Oxford. Where it was now was anyone's guess.

Just as he was about to give up, something caught Cooper's attention. What was that? Reaching for the mouse, he started the CCTV sequence from the beginning once again. The usual progression of vehicles commenced — a white Ford, followed by a dark BMW, then a mini with two motorbikes in close proximity behind. A gap, then, until an ambulance came into view, followed by the black transit van with the cloned plates. Once the transit van had turned right, the next vehicles to enter the CCTV screen were a Land Rover followed by a VW Golf. All as expected. All checked out and eliminated — other than the stolen black transit van.

But this time Cooper noticed something that'd escaped him before — and everyone else who'd viewed the tapes. A slight flicker on the screen as the vehicles moved through the sequence — so slight it was almost undetectable.

But it was there.

Cooper rewound the scenes once again and noted the clock in the lower right-hand corner giving the timings for the images. He let the scene play out one more time, finishing with the Land Rover and VW Golf.

And there it was.

The clock jumped forwards by approximately one hour in between the Land Rover and the VW Golf passing in front of the camera.

Cooper frowned, replaying the images once more to be absolutely sure.

But it was plain for all to see.

And there could only be one explanation.

* * *

305

Time: 11.05 p.m.
Date: Wednesday 25 July 2012
Location: Kettle's Yard Mews, London

Jack rose from the sofa and collected the empty Budweiser bottles from the coffee table. Stuart had managed to sink a fair few before passing out, and Jack couldn't really blame him. He watched his brother curled up at one end of the sofa, mouth open and a faint snore rumbling from his nostrils. Hopefully he would sleep all night, putting off the nightmare that would greet them both in the morning.

Despite craving sleep, Jack hadn't felt like drinking, waving away the third bottle his brother had offered him. He needed to keep himself alert, and alcohol wouldn't be his friend tonight.

Sitting alone in the dark, his mind had shifted from the investigation to thinking about Joseph Geraghty — and the CCTV evidence of him outside Isabel's café. There was no doubt it was him — Jack had watched the images a dozen or so more times just to be sure. Up to now, Jack — along with everyone else — had assumed the gangland leader had emigrated abroad and was soaking up the sun on a Cuban beach, laughing at the chaos he'd left behind.

When the chief superintendent finally caught up with him tomorrow, he knew he should impart this latest bit of intelligence — but he also knew he more than likely wouldn't.

Padding over to the sink, he placed the empty bottles in the recycling. As he did so, his mobile began to ring.

Jack answered the call. "Cooper? What's up?"

* * *

Time: 11.45 p.m.
Date: Wednesday 25 July 2012
Location: Metropolitan Police HQ, London

Jack threw open the tech room door and hurried inside. "Show me what you've got." He grabbed a chair and sat down.

DS Cooper quickly navigated the screen and brought up the first set of grainy CCTV images.

"I was running through the images, looking for the black transit van, when I spotted it. Hyde Park on the evening of twentieth July. The images run through as expected until 9.04 p.m." Cooper let the screen play out before them, pausing the reel at precisely 9.04 p.m. "The vehicle you see passing through is a Land Rover." He nodded at the screen and Jack saw the aforementioned vehicle paused in the camera's view. "But when I resume the recording, note the time in the bottom right-hand corner."

Jack's gaze flickered to the digital clock in the corner of the screen and gave a quick nod for Cooper to continue. When the screen resumed the sequence, the Land Rover disappeared and was replaced with a VW Golf jerkily crossing the scene. Jack immediately saw the time jump — to 10.05 p.m.

"Show me again, without the pause."

Cooper rewound the images and let them play. Once the VW Golf had exited the screen, he paused the images. "So, as you can see, we have an hour of missing footage between the Land Rover and the VW Golf."

"Plausible explanation?" Jack could almost feel the colour draining from his face as he asked the question.

"It's possible there could've been a technical problem with the camera," began Cooper, closing down the CCTV images for location two.

"But?" Jack could sense there was a "but" coming. He knew his DS too well. Cooper wouldn't have called him out so late at night just to tell him one of the CCTV cameras was faulty.

"But, after seeing that, I went back and looked at the CCTV for the other locations too."

Jack almost didn't need to ask. "And?"

"There's missing footage on all of them." Cooper pulled up more CCTV images on the screen. "I'm no technical expert, boss, but looks to me like someone's been deleting evidence."

CHAPTER THIRTY-EIGHT

Time: 7.30 a.m.
Date: Thursday 26 July 2012
Location: Metropolitan Police HQ, London

Chief Superintendent Dougie King forcibly threw the newspaper into the middle of his desk, narrowly missing a tumbler of water. Jack felt himself flinch.

"Jesus, Jack," he breathed, easing himself back into his chair and nodding at Jack to take a seat. Jack decided to remain standing. "It's all over the front pages."

Jack nodded, eyeing the front page of the *Daily Courier* and Jonathan Spearing's exclusive report on the wrongful arrest of a prominent London solicitor. "Yes, sir."

"You told me he was our man." The chief superintendent turned his head away from the newspaper print. "You both stood right there before me, and swore blind that he was our killer."

Jack hung his head, lowering his eyes to the floor. He had no words to justify their actions; no words to explain the almighty cock-up that had occurred under his watch. It wouldn't serve any purpose to mention how he'd had his own doubts at the time that Anthony Saunders might not be their man. It was *his* investigation. *He* was the senior officer. *He* was in charge. He'd given his backing to the arrest — that was the bottom line.

And now look where it'd gotten them.

"Tomorrow, Jack," continued the chief superintendent. "Tomorrow is the Opening Ceremony. And I've promised the powers that be that we'll have the killer in custody before then. Please tell me you have a plan B?"

"I know." Jack found his voice. "We're working round the clock, I promise." Jack knew it was a feeble and empty gesture, but he didn't really have anything else to give.

"This has created such a backlash upstairs, Jack. I'm having dinner tonight with the Right Honourable Bernard Saunders QC, our wrongly accused's father. And he's not a happy man, Jack. Not a happy man at all. Hopefully I'll be able to smooth things over a little and repair some of the damage — prevent any future embarrassment. But it's not going to be pretty." Chief Superintendent Dougie King exhaled loudly again and closed his weary eyes. "I need you to get the right man, Jack. And fast."

"Sir."

"But first, you need to warn this reporter off." Chief Superintendent King pushed himself out of his chair and started pacing behind his desk, coming to a halt by the window. He gazed out at the uninspiring view of the rear staff car park. "I don't know where he's getting his information from, but this needs to stop. Now."

Jack nodded. "I'll have a word." Jonathan Spearing's exclusive article had leaked the fact that the killer was leaving shoes at the scenes of his crimes. It was the one clue they'd purposefully kept from the media — but now it was open season. The advantage had been lost. "*A source close to the investigation*" was all the article had spoken of.

"Make sure you do." The chief superintendent turned back to face Jack across his desk. "I can't have the press printing things that not even our own officers are party to. The shoes — that was evidence we were meant to be suppressing.

If there's a leak in the department, Jack, you need to plug it. And quickly."

"Sir." Jack knew Jonathan Spearing relatively well. They'd had their run-ins in the past, but he was a decent reporter. He was old-school and respected the work of the police — most of the time. If he was receiving information from a source within his own team, Jack needed to get to the bottom of it. And in the words of the chief superintendent, he needed to do it fast.

"He's still out there, Jack." Chief Superintendent King tapped the glass in the window frame with the tip of his finger. "Our killer. It's embarrassing enough to have arrested the son of a prominent QC — but it's even worse to be seen to be running around like Keystone Cops. It's not like you to be so off your game, Jack. You need to pull this all together." He paused, then turned back around. "This killer is still in my city, Jack. And I need you to find him."

* * *

Time: 8 a.m.
Date: Thursday 26 July 2012
Location: A cellar in London

The masking tape stretched across her mouth made it difficult to breathe — she could feel herself starting to hyperventilate. She tossed her head from side to side to try and rid herself of the scratchy blanket that irritated her skin, and to get her head out into the open air.

It seemed to still be dark, but that meant nothing down here. She had no idea what time it was, or what day it was. Her stomach rumbled. She couldn't remember the last time she'd eaten. Today? Yesterday? She saw the empty packet of sandwiches had now been removed — replaced by a fresh packet and a fresh bottle of water.

He must have been back — but Isabel couldn't remember when.

Her mind felt foggy, her thoughts jumbled and incoherent. She tried to sit up but found her arms tied behind her back, wrapped at the wrists with some sort of thin twine. It cut painfully into her flesh every time she tried to move.

So, eventually, she stopped moving.

* * *

Time: 8.10 a.m.
Date: Thursday 26 July 2012
Location: Metropolitan Police HQ, London

"I'll go." DS Carmichael held up a hand, silencing any protests. "I'll go and warn off the reporter."

"I'm not sure that's a good idea, Sergeant." Jack closed the blinds to block out the early morning rays of sun that were already causing the incident room's temperature to soar. He rolled his shirtsleeves up and undid the top button of his shirt, feeling the sweat bristling underneath his collar. "I think you could do with keeping a low profile for now. Plus, I know the man better than you. Might be better coming from me."

Carmichael shook his head and rose to his feet, picking up the suit jacket he'd slung across the back of his chair. "I really need to do this, Jack. I ballsed up. I admit it. Jumped to the wrong conclusions — and took you all down with me." He gave Jack a weak attempt at an apologetic smile. "I need to make amends."

Jack exhaled and rubbed his eyes. He could still feel the chief superintendent's wrath like an open wound.

They'd messed up.

Correction.

Jack had messed up.

And now the whole world knew, too.

The *Daily Courier* had led with the story first thing that morning. How they'd got their information was anyone's guess — the Metropolitan Police could be a leaky ship at the best of times, and working out how to plug it would be a fool's errand. They were on a damage limitation exercise now, the first step of which was to silence the reporter who'd broken the story.

An hour after Anthony Saunders had been escorted from the building, London Life had responded to the warrant asking them to disclose the content of their members' messages. The messages Saunders had sent to each of the women were scrutinised — and found to be harmless. Advertising messages regarding his outsize shoes website; nothing more, nothing less. As soon as Jack had read the documents, he screwed them into paper balls and vented his frustration on the wastepaper bin. If they'd received this information earlier, maybe they wouldn't have gone in all guns blazing and arrested Saunders.

And they wouldn't be in the mess they were in now.

"I don't know, Sergeant. We can't afford for anything else to go wrong. The chief superintendent is not a happy man. We've got the threat of a wrongful arrest claim hanging over us now." Jack paused and sighed. "I should really go myself."

Carmichael continued to walk towards the door, slipping his suit jacket on as he did so. He shook his head. "I *really* need to do this, Jack. Let me try and repair the damage."

Jack exhaled another sigh, but before he could reply DC Cassidy stood up and began to cross the room. "Maybe give him a break, guv? Let him go?" She'd been sitting, quietly, in the corner by the window. "Might be for the best in the circumstances?"

Jack opened his mouth to protest, but found DS Cooper was also nodding in agreement. "Go on, boss. We need you here. We still have an investigation to run." Cooper flashed a look at Cassidy, a look that only the two of them would understand. But it didn't go unnoticed by their detective inspector. "And we still need to run through that CCTV with you again."

Jack frowned. Hadn't they sat through the CCTV late last night? What else could there be to see? He raised his hands in defeat and gave Carmichael a nod. "OK, OK, off you go. You know where to go and what to say?"

Carmichael patted his breast pocket. "Got the address right here. I'll call when I'm on my way back."

"All right. But you come straight back, mind. No more vanishing tricks."

Jack gave a dismissive wave to Carmichael's back as he slid through the incident room door and disappeared. He then turned a curious eye to Cooper and Cassidy. "So, what's so urgent with the CCTV that I need to see it again?"

CHAPTER THIRTY-NINE

Time: 9.15 a.m.
Date: Thursday 26 July 2012
Location: Home of Jonathan Spearing, London

Carmichael pulled up outside Jonathan Spearing's home address and checked his watch. The drive hadn't taken as long as he'd expected, and he'd made good time — flicking the blue lights and sirens on from time to time had helped. Leaving the car at the side of the road, he made his way up the short, paved garden path that was flanked by welcome bursts of colour in the flowerbeds. Bright yellow rudbeckia mirrored the scorching heat of the sun overhead. Spiked spears of red-hot pokers interspersed with clumps of lilac and salmon-pink petunias softened the edges of the path. The heady, sweet smell of the potted geraniums tickled Carmichael's nose as he approached the front door.

He rang the doorbell, hearing the faint tinkling sound echoing into the depths of the house beyond. Sources at the *Courier* had confirmed Spearing was working from home that day, and it wasn't long before Carmichael could see the faint outline of a figure approaching the door through the mottled glass side panel.

The door opened to reveal a lean-framed man dressed in casual tracksuit bottoms and a faded REM T-shirt. "Can I help you?"

Carmichael held out a hand showing his warrant card. "DS Carmichael, Metropolitan Police. Are you Jonathan Spearing?"

The man glanced at the warrant card, a faint frown creeping onto his forehead. He nudged his spectacles further up onto the bridge of his nose. "Yes, yes I am. What's this about?"

Carmichael pocketed his warrant card and nodded over the reporter's shoulder. "Maybe we could step inside?"

Spearing allowed his frown to deepen slightly, and a shadow of suspicion tinged with curiosity edged into his features. "Well, I was just on my way out, Sergeant, so if you don't mind I think it's best that we do this here?" He looked directly into Carmichael's eyes, a flicker of a smile dancing on his lips. "Whatever *this* is?"

Carmichael nodded. Great. A defensive reporter. The last thing he needed right now was to draw attention to himself and be the subject of tomorrow's front pages. He plastered a suitably sarcastic smile on his face.

"Of course, Mr Spearing. Here is fine. I'll try not to keep you too long."

The reporter kept his eyes on Carmichael as he stepped out onto the porch, pulling the front door closed behind him. Carmichael instinctively took a step backwards.

"I'll be frank, Mr Spearing. I'm here concerning a newspaper article that appeared in this morning's edition of the *Daily Courier*. An article that contained some fairly classified information." Carmichael waited to see the reporter's reaction. There was none. "Information that could be damaging to an ongoing murder enquiry."

A smile crossed Spearing's face and a small chuckle escaped his lips. "Has DI MacIntosh sent you to rap me across the knuckles, Sergeant? Do his dirty work for him?" The smile widened, reaching eyes that twinkled in the glare of the overhead sun.

DS Carmichael cleared his throat and continued. "As you can appreciate, the leaking of sensitive information to the press . . ."

"Are you admitting you have a leak, Sergeant?" Spearing folded his arms across his chest and rocked back on his heels. "Tut, tut. Oh dearie me."

Carmichael bristled underneath his suit jacket and fixed the reporter with a hard stare. "At times like this, we need the national newspapers to work *with* us, not against us. Reporting sensitive information could have a detrimental effect on our investigation — you could be responsible for allowing a serial killer to remain at large, putting more women at risk."

"Oh, I think you're managing to keep this serial killer on the streets all by yourselves — you don't need my help. You arrest and question an entirely innocent man?" Spearing shook his head and allowed another chuckle to form. "Surely that has a far more damaging effect on your investigation than me simply reporting the truth? I think the bigwigs at the Met are getting all hot under the collar because they now face a wrongful arrest claim — could cost them a pretty penny, too. Especially if Daddy QC wades in."

Carmichael drew in a deep breath, fighting against the bait Spearing was dangling in front of him. He needed to maintain his composure and not lose it with a reporter who wouldn't think twice about making him tomorrow's headline news. "It would be very much appreciated if such classified information was left that way — classified. Just let us get on with our jobs."

Spearing took a step forward, the smile slipping from his lips. "Look, I only report what I'm told. Maybe you should concentrate on arresting the right people in future."

Carmichael nodded his head and took a matching step forwards towards the reporter. The two men stood face to face. Another inch and their noses would've been touching.

"I'm not sure if you quite heard me." Carmichael's black eyes bored into the reporter's equally stony stare. "If any more classified information reaches the front pages, then things could become very difficult for you. Take this as a friendly warning."

Jonathan Spearing held Carmichael's beady gaze for a few seconds before taking a step backwards and nodding. "Friendly warning received and understood, Sergeant."

Carmichael returned the nod and mirrored the retreating step — the space between the two men restored. "Then I'll be on my way." As he turned to leave, a man headed up the garden path towards them.

"Ah, I was about to pop round and see you." Spearing bent down to retrieve the parcel that had been sitting on his porch between the geranium pots. "Parcel for you — delivered while you were out."

Carmichael obligingly stepped out of the way as Spearing handed the box to his neighbour.

"Thanks, Jon. They always deliver when I'm not at home. Thanks for taking it in."

"No problem. Anytime." Spearing watched as his neighbour turned to go back down the garden path. "See, Sergeant. I *can* be a responsible neighbour. You plug your leaky ship and I'll be a good boy and only report on things I'm meant to. Deal?"

Carmichael grunted in response and followed Spearing's neighbour and his parcel back down the garden path, heading for his car. Slipping into the driver's seat, he watched the reporter head back inside his house and close the door behind him. Had the message been received and understood? He hoped so. He really hoped so. He could ill afford to make any more mistakes.

Taking his notebook out of his pocket, Carmichael updated his notes on his confrontation with Spearing. Slipping it back inside his jacket, he glanced at his watch. He just had enough time to take a detour on his way back to the station.

* * *

Time: 9.15 a.m.
Date: Thursday 26 July 2012
Location: Metropolitan Police HQ, London

Jack followed DS Cooper into the darkened tech suite. DC Cassidy was already seated and getting the footage ready to view.

"Chris called me early this morning." Cassidy eyed DS Cooper and gave a half-hearted smile. "He showed me where the scenes had been deleted from the CCTV." Cassidy nodded at the screen in front of her as Jack and Cooper took their seats. "And the tech guys worked on the images overnight."

"They find anything?" asked Jack, more out of hope than anything else.

"Well, don't ask me how, but they've managed to recover the deleted scenes from all four locations. They worked through the night — gave Chris the results early this morning." Cassidy clicked the mouse and the first set of grainy images flooded the screen. "This is from the first location. The deleted scenes were between 9.30 p.m. and 10.45 p.m." She let the frames play out, cars and vans making their way through the camera's view. At 9.47 p.m., she paused the screen.

At the centre of the monitor was a dark-coloured Ford Mondeo, registration plate clearly visible. AK09 BVZ. Cassidy let the image remain on the screen for several more seconds before clicking the mouse and bringing up a different set of images.

"These are from location number two. Hyde Park. Deleted images were between 9.04 p.m. and 10.05 p.m." As before, she let the images play out before pausing the screen at 10.01 p.m. The same dark-coloured Ford Mondeo, registration AK09 BVZ, hovered in the centre, caught on camera.

Jack's eyes widened as the realisation hit home.

"And locations three and four?" His voice was taut.

Cassidy nodded, loading up the CCTV images for location number three. "Deleted scenes were between 9.20 p.m.

and 11 p.m." The scene played out until 9.44 p.m. when the Ford Mondeo graced the screen once again. She quickly followed suit with the most recent murder location, at Battersea Park. "Here we have the fourth location from yesterday's discovery. Deleted scenes were again found between 9.25 p.m. and 10.58 p.m. of the night before." After playing on for a few seconds, the image of the now familiar Ford Mondeo was frozen in the centre of the screen.

Jack sat back in his chair, his heart thumping. This was it. This was the break they'd been searching for. The black transit van had been a costly red herring. *This* was the guy they were after.

Ford Mondeo AK09 BVZ.

"Please tell me they aren't cloned or stolen plates," breathed Jack, not taking his eyes from the image of the vehicle in front of him. "Please say we can trace him."

Cassidy paused, and flashed a look at Cooper. Cooper gave a discreet nod — but not so discreet that it escaped Jack's attention.

"What? What is it?" The tension gave Jack's voice a gravelly hoarseness. "What is it you're not telling me?"

Cassidy took in a deep breath before clicking off the computer screen. The room darkened even further as Ford Mondeo AK09 BVZ disappeared from view.

"We can trace the vehicle, guv," she replied, keeping her voice even and controlled. "That's not a problem. We even know where it is right now."

Jack let out the breath that he hadn't been aware he'd been holding in. "Well, that's good news, right?" He continued to eye his junior officers' faces, not liking the expressions they were trying their hardest to hide. "Right?" he repeated.

"Vehicle AK09 BVZ is a Metropolitan Police pool car, boss." This time it was Cooper who cut through the silent tension.

"A pool car?" Jack's face froze. "It's one of *ours*?"

Cooper nodded, feeling his mouth turn dry. "And we traced who it's currently booked out to." He paused, before dropping the bombshell Jack already knew was about to land. "Currently, vehicle AK09 BVZ is booked out to DS Robert Carmichael and has most recently been tracked to the address of the *Daily Courier* reporter, Jonathan Spearing."

* * *

Time: 9.50 a.m.
Date: Thursday 26 July 2012
Location: St James's University, London

Dr Rachel Hunter opened the door and stepped aside to let Jack into her office.

"We could've dealt with this over the telephone, Inspector," she began, closing the door behind him. "I have an appointment in ten minutes."

Jack nodded, out of breath from the rushed journey from the station. "I know, I'm sorry. I just need to say what I've got to say in person."

Dr Hunter nodded her acquiescence, motioning for Jack to take a seat in the comfortable chairs by the coffee table. "Glass of water?" She inclined her head towards the iced water machine nestled next to the coffee. Despite the ever-increasing humidity, Dr Hunter looked impeccably cool and unflustered.

Jack shook his head and remained standing. "Could it be a police officer?" He came straight to the point, seeing little or no sense in beating around the bush. "Our killer. Could he be a serving police officer?" The words seemed to stick in his parched throat.

Dr Hunter paused, seating herself behind her uncluttered desk. Jack found himself comparing it to his own desk which seemed to visibly groan under the weight of files and paperwork being deposited on it with relentless regularity. He shook his head to rid himself of the distraction. He watched as Dr Hunter reached into the top drawer and pulled out the thin manila folder Jack recognised from their initial meeting.

Opening the folder, she slid out the single sheet of paper that listed the characteristics she'd compiled for the investigation. She ran a well-manicured finger down the headings.

"A police officer, you say?" Dr Hunter slowly let her gaze flick up to meet Jack's. "You have someone in mind, or are you talking theoretically?"

"Let's say theoretical, for now," replied Jack, nodding his head towards the list in her hand. "Is it possible, though?"

Dr Hunter returned her attention to the list of characteristics. "Well, if your *theoretical* police officer is male, aged thirty to fifty-five — is single or has difficulties making relationships, is charming, intelligent, forensically aware with no criminal record . . ." She paused and held Jack in her gaze. "Then I would say you have a potential match. *Theoretically.*"

CHAPTER FORTY

Time: 11.30 a.m.
Date: Thursday 26 July 2012
Location: Metropolitan Police HQ, London

"He's on his way." Jack looked at the message on his phone. "We need to be ready for him."

"Are you really going to arrest him, boss?" DS Cooper asked the question that was on both his and Cassidy's lips. "DS Carmichael?"

Jack shook his head. "Not at this stage, Cooper. We've got some questions that need answering, that's for sure. If he cooperates."

"And if he doesn't?" Cassidy let the question hang in the air.

Time was running out to find Isabel. The interval between victims was shortening all the time. Dr Hunter had explained to Jack how serial killers often escalate their behaviour, ultimately killing more frequently — the initial euphoria felt after each kill lasting for a decreasing amount of time. The information did nothing to calm the unease he felt. If DS Carmichael knew anything about Isabel's disappearance, then Jack was going to get it out of him one way or another. DS or no DS.

He'd shared the information gleaned from his impromptu visit to Dr Hunter with both DS Cooper and DC Cassidy as soon as he'd returned to the station. Predictably, neither seemed willing to believe Carmichael could be the killer.

"But, one of us, boss?" Cooper's face was ashen. "Surely not?"

"Is he, though? One of us?" Jack raised a questioning eyebrow. "You did the searches yourself, Cooper. We've no idea where the hell he's from — or even if he *is* a police officer. You found no trace of a DS Carmichael — *anywhere*."

Jack had gone through each and every characteristic of the criminal profile, and both Cassidy and Cooper had to admit that he seemed to fit. Everyone was still stinging from the rebukes their arrest of Anthony Saunders had caused from the higher echelons of the Met; this time they had to get it right.

Making their way down to the main entrance, they didn't have long to wait.

* * *

DS Carmichael walked briskly through the front doors, smiling at his good fortune of securing a privileged parking space out front rather than the rear car park, but within a split second he knew something was wrong.

To his immediate left, he saw Jack standing alongside DS Cooper, their faces pale and tense. He flashed his gaze to the right where the lobby was flanked by a further four officers. The two closest to him he noted to be armed, with steady well-trained fingers hovering millimetres above triggers — the faces that belonged to the fingers trained on his every move.

Carmichael's stride faltered. He froze, standing stock-still in the centre of the entrance lobby, his feet sticking like glue to the parquet floor below. Feeling his pulse quicken, he took a backwards glance at the doors that had swung shut behind him. Two more armed officers blocked off any retreat.

Carmichael raised his eyebrows. "Is everything all right?"

Jack's eyes momentarily flickered to the armed officers who had now entered the lobby at Carmichael's rear. Their body armour seemed to creak with every movement they made.

Carmichael edged away from the gun barrels pointed in his direction. "What's happened, Jack?"

"You need to step this way, Sergeant." Jack motioned for Carmichael to move forward. "Nice and steady, no sudden movements. You know the score." He nodded at the two armed officers flanking Carmichael, each one taking a synchronised step towards him. DS Carmichael whipped his head to the side, his eyes widening.

"What's going on? You're starting to scare me now, Jack." Carmichael's arms rose slowly into the air, instinct taking over as he continued to eye the guns pointing towards him. "Let's not do anything hasty."

"Time to come with us, Sergeant." Jack motioned to Carmichael that he should follow him towards the custody suite behind them. "Let's not make this any harder than it needs to be."

Carmichael took another hesitant step forward. "Make what harder, Jack? What's going on?"

Jack paused, as if waiting for Carmichael to catch up. He placed a light yet firm grip on his fellow officer's elbow. "I think you already know."

CHAPTER FORTY-ONE

Time: 11.45 a.m.
Date: Thursday 26 July 2012
Location: Metropolitan Police HQ, London

"The time is 11.45 a.m. Present in the room are DS Cooper and myself, Detective Inspector Jack MacIntosh." Jack paused and looked up, his hollow eyes meeting Carmichael's. "State your name and rank for the purposes of the tape."

Carmichael remained wide-eyed, his coal-black pupils flicking from Jack to Cooper. "Seriously? We're really doing this?"

"Don't make it any harder than it already is, Sergeant." Jack eyed the video recorder tucked away in the top corner of the room, the red dot winking on and off. "Your name and rank."

Carmichael licked his lips. Reaching forward, he took a sip of water from the plastic cup, grimacing. He gave a discernible shake of his head before replying. "Detective Sergeant Robert Carmichael."

Jack let a sigh escape his lips. "You are not under arrest, but remain under police caution. Do you understand?" He avoided Carmichael's stony stare — it was never easy interviewing one of your own.

Carmichael mirrored Jack's sigh, but his tone now exhibited a degree of exasperation tinged with an edge of hostility. "Yes, I understand the difference between being under arrest and under caution. I'm a police officer."

Jack felt the hackles prickle at the back of his neck, but refused to rise to the bait. "And you've been offered legal advice and the opportunity to have legal representation, which you've declined. Is that correct?"

"Why would I need . . . ?" But Carmichael was cut short.

"Is that correct, Sergeant?" Jack was straining to keep his voice civil and emotionless. He could feel the anger welling up inside him; the man opposite him could be responsible for Isabel's disappearance, and the deaths of four women.

Anger that he had to keep in check.

Because anger wasn't going to get him the answers he needed.

Anger wouldn't get Isabel back.

"Yes, that is correct," replied Carmichael, icily. He sat back in his chair, his black beady eyes boring into Jack. "I don't need legal assistance as I've done nothing wrong."

We'll see about that, thought Jack, as he slid a series of four black and white grainy pictures, each seven inches by five inches, across the table. "For the purposes of the tape, items reference AC 001 to AC 004 are being shown to DS Carmichael."

Jack leaned forward, resting his elbows on the table. "Recognise the vehicle in each of these images, Sergeant?" He nodded at the stilled frames from the CCTV pulled by DC Cassidy, isolating the vehicle registration AK09 BVZ.

Carmichael's gaze lowered to the four pictures placed in front of him. From the other side of the table, Jack physically saw the colour ebb away from his cheeks. His skin took on a clammy, pallid tone, and if Jack was seeing things correctly, a few beads of sweat had popped up on his forehead.

Now we're getting somewhere. "Sergeant?" repeated Jack, nodding once again at the images. "The vehicle?"

Carmichael's eyes travelled from one image to the next, his lips thinning and the muscles in his jaw tightening. He looked up to meet Jack's questioning look.

"No comment."

The two words all police officers hated to hear echoed around the bare walls of interview room number two.

"Are you saying that you don't recognise the vehicle in these images, Sergeant?" Jack nudged each of the photographs a few centimetres closer to Carmichael. "Why don't you take a closer look?"

DS Carmichael shook his head. "What I am saying, Inspector, is no comment." His voice was as hard and steely grey as the walls around them.

And just as unyielding.

"The interesting thing is, Sergeant," continued Jack, unmoved by his fellow officer's refusal to cooperate, "this vehicle was seen at all four of our victims' locations, merely hours before their bodies were discovered. How do you explain that?"

Carmichael let a flicker of a smile tease at his lips. "I know what you're doing, and it won't work. I don't have to answer your questions, and you know I don't." He paused and nodded back down at the photographs. "If what you really want to ask me is did I have anything to do with the deaths of these four women, then the answer is simple. No, I did not." Carmichael broke off, even more colour seeming to drain from his face. "And I can't believe you're really asking me that, I really can't."

"This car is a Metropolitan Police pool car," continued Jack, tapping one of the images with his finger. "And as of Wednesday fourth July, who do you think it was booked out to?"

Carmichael maintained his silence, merely turning his head to the side and upwards to glance at the video camera, its red recording light still blinking.

"I'll tell you, shall I?" Jack carried on. "As of Wednesday fourth July, vehicle registration number AK09 BVZ was booked out to a Detective Sergeant Robert Carmichael. Your good self."

"Item reference AC 005," announced DS Cooper, sliding a copy of the pool car documentation across the table.

"So, here we have it, Sergeant. A car seen at each location, merely hours before the bodies of the victims were discovered. And said vehicle is booked out to yourself. How do you explain that?"

"No comment."

"Did anyone else have the use of your vehicle, Sergeant?"

"No comment."

"Where were you going on each of these dates, Sergeant?"

"No comment."

"Still you choose no comment." Jack failed to keep the irritation out of his voice. "We have the life of another young woman at stake here, for God's sake. If you know anything . . ." Jack broke off, his voice catching at the back of his dry throat. "You need to tell us where she is."

Carmichael shook his head, more urgently this time. "You're barking up the wrong tree here, Jack. Completely. Shit, you're in completely the wrong forest."

"Another interesting fact, Sergeant," continued Jack, clearing his throat, "is that these images of *your* car were found to have been deleted from the system. How much of a coincidence is that?"

Carmichael shrugged and avoided Jack's penetrating look. "No comment."

Jack raised his eyebrows. "From where I'm sitting it looks like a senior police officer has tampered with evidence. Evidence that incriminates him in four murders and a kidnapping."

Carmichael rubbed his hands over his face. "No comment," he replied.

"Luckily for us, the tech guys managed to retrieve it all. Who knew that was even possible, eh?" Jack let the question hang in the air. "So, I'm going to ask you again, one more time. Why is the vehicle that is booked out to you found to be at each of the four murder locations? And why were the images deleted?"

DS Carmichael pushed the images back across the table. "No comment."

"Did you delete them, Sergeant?"

"No comment."

* * *

Time: 9.20 p.m.
Date: Wednesday 25 July 2012
Location: Metropolitan Police HQ, London

DS Carmichael closed the door to the tech suite behind him. He was pretty sure no one else was around, but being pretty sure wasn't good enough. He knew Jack had gone home, but he hadn't seen DC Cassidy or DS Cooper leave.

Sitting down at one of the computer stations, he powered up the monitor and glanced at his watch. He needed to be in and out of here as quickly as possible — someone could come in at any moment — people worked 24/7 around here. The monitor sprang into life, casting a hypnotic glow out into the dimness of the suite.

Quickly, he pulled up the first set of CCTV images for the location of Patricia Gordon's body. Following the timeline through, he paused the screen when Ford Mondeo AK09 BVZ filled the screen at exactly 21.47. With a quick look over his shoulder, Carmichael entered the commands into the keyboard exactly as he'd been shown.

"Are you sure you wish to delete this file?" The box flashed up in the centre of the screen.

DS Carmichael hit "*yes*".

* * *

Time: 12.05 p.m.
Date: Thursday 26 July 2012
Location: Metropolitan Police HQ, London

"Are you married, Sergeant?" Jack's change of direction caught DS Carmichael momentarily off guard. A faint frown crossed his brow, his black eyes seeming to darken even further.

"I'm sorry? What's that got to do with anything?" He glanced from Jack's expressionless face to DS Cooper, then back again.

"I'm interested. Are you married?" Jack made a show of consulting one of the pieces of paper inside the manila folder still sitting on the table in front of him — Dr Hunter's criminal profile. "Maybe divorced? Wife run out on you?"

"I don't think that's any of your business," cut back Carmichael, a hotness creeping into his voice.

"Oh, it's my business all right." Jack closed the folder. "When I'm investigating four murders and at least one kidnapping, *everything* is my business."

"And while you're asking me senseless questions, you're wasting valuable time when you could be tracking down the real killer."

"I'll decide whether my questions are senseless or not." Jack inclined his head towards the table where Carmichael had placed both his hands. "Looks like you've got a mark where a wedding ring used to be."

Carmichael instinctively covered up his left hand with his right, and flashed a warning look at Jack. "No comment."

* * *

Time: 5.45 p.m.
Date: Friday 12 June 1998
Location: Arundel, West Sussex

He stared intensely at the third finger on her left hand. "You've taken your wedding ring off."

She gave no response.

"Carol. I said, you've taken your wedding ring off."

Carol whipped her head around in his direction, her eyes brimming with tears. She tipped the saucepan full of vegetables into the casserole dish with the chicken. "Can you blame me? After what you said to me last night?" She rubbed at her wet cheeks with the back of a hand. "What you accused me of?"

He was still staring at the third finger of her left hand. "Everything I said last night was true, Carol. Deny it if you want, but I know a lying bitch when I see one." His voice began to rise, the tone thick with condemnation and what sounded to Carol like pure and unequivocal hatred. "You've been lying to me for a long time. Do us all a favour and just admit it."

Carol glanced at the closed kitchen door behind them, praying that the thick oak panels would absorb the rising tempo of their latest argument. She bit her bottom lip, wondering if any door, any wood, could ever really be thick enough.

"Would you keep your voice down?" she urged, her voice low. "Jess might hear. She's only upstairs."

He either didn't hear her, or he didn't care.

Maybe it was both.

"Perhaps she needs to know the truth about her precious mother," he replied, the venom in his voice spilling out into the kitchen. "Perhaps she'd be better off knowing what a lying, cheating whore her mother truly is."

A trembling hand flew up to cover Carol's mouth as she tried to gulp back her sobs. "I've told you so many times — you're wrong. There's nothing going on between me and Brian. There never was." She rubbed again at her wet cheeks, trying to stem the steady flow of fresh, hot tears that continued to leak out of the corners of her eyes. "Why won't you listen to me? It's all in your head."

Enraged, he jumped to his feet, the wooden chair scraping violently behind him on the flagstone floor. "Don't you dare tell me I'm imagining it, Carol. I've *seen* you. I've seen what you're like together. You don't even have the decency to hide it."

Carol slammed the casserole dish into the oven and sat down at the kitchen table — a table made from roughly-hewn railway sleepers, back in the days when her husband would lovingly create anything for his growing family. She could barely remember those days now. Just like she barely recognised the man in front of her as her husband.

When had it all changed?

When had it all started to go wrong?

Before Jess was born?

After?

Carol's memory was as hazy as her tear-streaked vision. Accusing her of having an affair with someone at work had been the final straw. The weeks and months of bickering and fighting had culminated in such a showdown last night that Carol had ripped off her wedding ring and flung it across the bedroom. As far as she knew, it was still lying underneath the Victorian chest of drawers upstairs.

And the way she was feeling right now, that's where it could stay.

She heard him stomp across the kitchen towards the door, feeling him bump roughly against the back of her chair as he passed by.

"Don't forget we're meant to be going out for the day tomorrow," she murmured, her head in her hands. "Jess has been looking forward to it for ages. She can't see us like this."

She felt him pause by the door, and waited for the acid-laden retort to escape his poisonous mouth. Instead, his voice was quiet and calm — if anything, that worried her more.

"Don't worry — Jess won't see us fight. I won't let you hurt her the way you've hurt me. Jess won't see a thing."

* * *

Time: 10.35 p.m.
Date: Friday 12 June 1998
Location: Arundel, West Sussex

Jess mustn't see.

He shut the door that led to the back garden and turned the lock.

Things hadn't gone to plan.

They were meant to have been having a talk after dinner, a calm discussion about the future. *Their* future.

But now?

This was not supposed to have happened.

But it wasn't his fault, was it?

None of this was his fault.

She had been the one to start lying to him.

She had been the one to start going behind his back.

She had been the one to blame.

She had driven him to it.

And what had now happened, *she* had been the one to make him do it.

It was her fault.

It was all her fault.

The remnants of the broken casserole dish were now in the bin, and the floor had been mopped clean of the remains of the chicken casserole. He'd swept up the shards of shattered glass — everything was back to how it was before.

Except for one thing.

Carol.

He stepped out into the hall and glanced up the stairs, just in time to hear Jess's shrill voice cut through his muddled thoughts. "Dad? Where's Mum?"

* * *

Time: 9.05 a.m.
Date: Saturday 13 June 1998
Location: Arundel, West Sussex

"Isn't Mum coming too?" Jess slid into the passenger seat and fastened her seat belt. She glanced back over her shoulder towards the house. "The fresh air might do her good?"

He smiled and started the engine. "Mum has another of her migraines, Jess. It's best she stays home and rests for a while. But we can still go and have fun, right?" He flashed another smile at his daughter — one that almost reached his cold, lifeless eyes.

Almost.

But not quite.

Jess returned the smile, but quickly glanced back at the house again as the car moved off the drive. "OK. It's just that I haven't seen her since yesterday, at dinner. Is she all right?"

"I told you, Jess," snapped her father, tightening his grip on the steering wheel. "She has one of her migraines. She needs to lie down in the dark and not be disturbed. Now can we please stop talking about your mother."

Jess shrank back into her seat and clasped her hands together in her lap, quietly kneading them together to steady herself. She hated it when Dad got angry. It frightened her when Dad got angry.

And Dad got angry — a lot.

* * *

Time: 12.10 p.m.
Date: Thursday 26 July 2012
Location: Metropolitan Police HQ, London

"Seriously, Jack, you're wasting time." DS Carmichael turned round in his chair to face the video camera. "How long are you going to let this carry on for?"

"If you could address your answers to me, Sergeant."

"This is such a joke. A sick joke." Carmichael closed his eyes and shook his head. "Why won't you listen to me?"

"Was that why you were so keen to arrest Anthony Saunders?" Jack leaned back in his chair. "A useful diversion? Pin the crimes on someone else?"

"You're not listening," replied Carmichael, continuing to shake his head. "You've got this all wrong."

"There's something else you might be able to help us with, Sergeant. When you arrived here on my team, you claimed to have come from Sussex. So how is it that no one from Sussex has ever heard of a DS Carmichael?" Jack waited for a response from the other side of the table.

The muscles in Carmichael's jawline tensed and he flashed another look up at the video camera which was still blinking at them. Jack frowned slightly — for a second, it looked like Carmichael was mouthing something to the camera behind the cover of one of his hands. He cleared his throat to regain Carmichael's attention.

"It's like you don't exist — anywhere." Jack folded his arms across his chest and fixed DS Carmichael with a stony stare. "Why is that? Where are you really from?"

Carmichael sighed once again and shook his head. "No comment."

Jack tried not to let the exasperation he felt infiltrate his voice. "Are you even a police officer?"

Carmichael covered his face with his hands and rubbed his palms into his tired eyes. "Jack — you're not listening to me. You're wasting time asking me absurd questions, when you should be out there looking for Isabel. We all should be. Instead, you're in here asking damn stupid questions about nothing."

"I may be asking damn stupid questions, as you so eloquently put it, Sergeant, but you're not answering them." Jack's hands balled into fists by his side. "*That* is wasting us time."

Carmichael's patience snapped. "Look, turn that bloody tape recorder off and let's get out there and find him." He nodded at the tape recorder at the side of the table, the counter still ticking, marking each second of the interrogation. Kicking back his chair, he rose to his feet and leaned forward on the table. His face inched closer and closer to Jack's. "Isabel won't thank you for being holed up in here, when her life could be ebbing away as we speak."

Jack sprang to his feet and, before he knew it, one balled fist that had been resting loosely by his side suddenly thundered forwards and smashed into DS Carmichael's face. The force of the impact sent Carmichael reeling backwards, tripping over his own feet where he landed, sprawled on the floor.

"Don't you dare bring Isabel into this," roared Jack, his hand stinging sharply from its contact with Carmichael's nasal bones. The pain shot up his arm and into his shoulder. "She's worth a million of the likes of you."

DS Cooper leapt to his feet, and made his way around to the door, either to summon help or get the hell out of the interview room — he hadn't quite made his mind up which. As he wrenched the door open, he was confronted by the imposing figure of Commander Adam Forsyth.

The commander strode into the room, closely followed by a harried-looking Chief Superintendent Dougie King.

"DI MacIntosh." Commander Forsyth's booming voice echoed around the walls of the interview room. At a little under 6' 6" with broad shoulders to match, he seemed to instantly fill the snug confines of interview room two. His closely cropped dark hair, greying at the temples, sat atop stern and scowling features — a scowl that was being directed wholly at Jack. "Stand aside. Wait for me in Chief Superintendent King's office." He paused, his ice-blue eyes jabbing hotly towards Jack's. "Now, Inspector!"

Jack jumped as if he'd been hit with a bolt of electricity and strode from the room, his cheeks burning and his fist throbbing. As he exited the interview room and made his way out into the corridor, he heard the commander's voice continue in his wake.

"DS Carmichael, you are hereby immediately released from caution. Get somebody to see to your nose." There was a pregnant pause. "And somebody turn off this bloody tape!"

CHAPTER FORTY-TWO

Time: 1.15 p.m.
Date: Thursday 26 July 2012
Location: Metropolitan Police HQ, London

"Shit, Jack. What in God's name's got into you?" Chief Superintendent Dougie King ran a hand over his closely cropped hair, beads of perspiration clearly visible on his worried brow. "I've no idea how to unpick this unholy mess — and with the commander watching, too." He shook his head and exhaled loudly. "Shit, Jack," he repeated.

Jack frowned. "Why was the commander watching, anyway?" He remembered the furtive glances Carmichael kept making towards the video camera. Had he been aware all along that they were being watched? "That's not routine."

"Nothing about this is routine, Jack," replied the chief superintendent, exhaling noisily yet again. "Assaulting a fellow officer? On tape? Jesus, Jack . . ."

"But why was the commander watching? I don't understand."

"You think *that* is your main concern right now? That the commander was watching?" Dougie King wiped the sweat from his brow and nodded at the vacant chair in front of his desk. "I think you'd better sit down for this one."

Jack stepped forward and began to lower himself into the visitor's seat.

"On your feet, Inspector," boomed Commander Forsyth, striding into the room and sending the door crashing into the wall behind. Jack almost jumped out of his skin as he leapt to his feet. He winced as the fist that had thrown the punch continued to throb. "You've got some explaining to do, but first you are going to listen."

Commander Forsyth nodded curtly at Chief Superintendent King to step aside, and deftly slipped himself into the vacant swivel chair behind the desk. A snug fit for the chief superintendent's ample frame, the chair was dwarfed by the commander's imposing stature. He once again fixed his ice-blue eyes on Jack. Jack remained standing, planting his feet in a wide enough stance to withstand what he expected to be the mother of all ear-bashings.

"Before you give me your account, Inspector, of just *how* you came to assault one of our own officers — and if he escapes without a broken nose, I should be very surprised — you need to listen and listen well. Understood?"

Jack fixed his gaze on a section of the wall above the commander's left shoulder. He knew better than to try and return the stony stare that was boring into him. He gave a slow nod.

"You are one of my best officers, DI MacIntosh." The Commander spoke in a low and level tone, the initial anger having abated. "And for that reason I am possibly going to overlook the serious errors of judgment you've displayed recently." He paused, and flicked his ice-blue eyes towards Jack. "Detective Sergeant Carmichael has been seconded to our division by the Major Crime Unit at Sussex."

Jack tore his eyes away from the section of wall he'd been fixing his gaze upon and found his mouth starting to open. But any reply he was forming was silenced by the commander's raised hand.

"Yes, I'm well aware, Inspector, that your own investigations drew a blank concerning there being a DS Carmichael attached to Sussex Police. Or anywhere else, for that matter." The Commander's voice, although now devoid of anger, had lost none of its frosty tone. "And there is a very good reason for that, if you'd stopped to think before rushing in, all guns blazing."

And then the penny dropped.

"DS Carmichael is working as an undercover officer on Operation Evergreen. The reason his vehicle was captured on your CCTV was by pure coincidence. And the subsequent deletion of the images was authorised by myself. There was no ulterior motive connected to your case. Carmichael is not his real name, for obvious reasons."

"Undercover?" The cog wheels inside Jack's brain slowly started turning. "But how does that fit . . . ?"

"It doesn't, Inspector," interrupted Commander Forsyth, getting to his feet. "His brief with Operation Evergreen is to investigate historic child cruelty and the possible sexual assault of children in local authority care, dating back to the 1970s and 1980s. He's investigating possible police involvement and possible corruption of high-ranking police officers in association with these cases of abuse. He's working with our anti-corruption unit from the top floor."

"The ghost squad?" Jack raised his eyebrows.

Commander Forsyth flashed an irritated look at Jack and continued. "A new, much larger, investigation is due to be launched later this year — Operation Yewtree. Yewtree will be investigating child abuse claims involving some of the country's highest-profile figures of the entertainment industry. It's going to be one of the biggest, if not *the* biggest, investigation the Metropolitan Police has ever launched. It will be huge, Inspector. Unprecedented. And DS Carmichael's investigation will be working in tandem." Commander Forsyth paused. "As you can imagine, confidentiality is of extreme importance. Hence why nobody knew of DS Carmichael's true identity — not even the chief superintendent here, before you start casting aspersions in that direction."

Jack glanced across at Chief Superintendent Dougie King, whose bemused features mirrored his own.

"Only senior officers with the rank of commander or above have been privy to this information, DI MacIntosh. Your little antics in there a few moments ago have meant that such confidential information is now required to be disclosed to yourself — and, no doubt, the rest of your team." The ice-blue eyes again bored into Jack's. "For Operation Evergreen, and ultimately Operation Yewtree, to succeed, I need you and your team to keep this information to yourselves. Under no circumstances can any of the conversation within these four walls leak out. Do I make myself clear?"

"Crystal, sir," replied Jack, nodding his head curtly and flashing another look at the chief superintendent. "You can rely on my team's discretion, sir."

"Hmmmm." Commander Forsyth pushed the swivel chair back and strode purposefully towards the door. His towering frame filled the doorway. "You need to make your apologies to DS Carmichael. And quickly. He's a mighty fine officer and will be a credit to your investigation. And I could do without the complexities of an internal enquiry and criminal proceedings for assault taking up our valuable and already stretched resources."

And with that, he was gone.

"Did you . . . ?" Jack half-turned towards Chief Superintendent King, who was resuming his place behind his desk. He raised a hand and cut Jack off mid-sentence.

"No, I did not, Jack. You heard the commander." He eased himself into the newly vacated chair. "Only ranks of commander and above were privy to the information surrounding Operation Evergreen. It's all news to me."

"This Operation Evergreen, and Yewtree . . ."

"Is not your concern right now, Jack." The chief superintendent nodded towards the door. "You need to be gone. Go and apologise to DS Carmichael and then go and catch my killer, Jack. You have until tomorrow. The clock is ticking."

* * *

Time: 1.45 p.m.
Date: Thursday 26 July 2012
Location: A cellar in London

A pair of hands grabbed Isabel roughly by the shoulders and lifted her into a sitting position. Her eyes squinted through the murkiness of the cellar. She must've dozed off — again. Without warning, the masking tape was ripped from her mouth and then she felt something bang against her teeth.

It felt like a bottle.

Opening her lips, she felt the cool rush of water fill her mouth. She greedily gulped the liquid down as fast as she could.

"Slow down, slow down," he hushed, a faint chuckle to his voice. "You'll choke."

Isabel coughed and spluttered as the water went down the wrong way, but it didn't stop her thirstily draining more from the bottle. Water had never tasted so good. She felt as though she hadn't had a drink in days. So thirsty. So thirsty.

But it didn't last.

The bottle disappeared and the masking tape reappeared once again.

"Not long now, Carol — we'll soon have you out of here."

* * *

Time: 1.45 p.m.
Date: Thursday 26 July 2012
Location: Metropolitan Police HQ, London

"One more time, Cooper." Jack rubbed his roughened chin. "What are we missing? Give me a rundown on what we have so far. Again."

DS Cooper clicked the remote control and the interactive whiteboard screen flickered into life. It gave a faint hum as the images of the four victims were brought up in quick succession.

"Patricia Gordon, age forty-five, last seen on Friday sixth July. Body discovered at St James's Park on Friday thirteenth July. Cause of death, strangulation by ligature. Restraint marks on one ankle. Worked at The Briars Residential Care Home as a housekeeper. Had a second job, one that paid her two hundred pounds every Friday — but we haven't located where that was yet."

Jack nodded. "We need to figure that out." He motioned for Cooper to continue.

"Georgina Dale, age twenty-one, last seen on Thursday twelfth July. Body discovered at Hyde Park on Friday twentieth July. Cause of death also strangulation by ligature. Again, restraint marks on one ankle. Full-time student at St James's University, studying English. No known part-time jobs."

"With a shoe belonging to Georgina found at the first location," added Cassidy, "it suggests both were held captive at the same time."

Cooper flicked over a page in his accompanying notebook. "Hannah Fuller, age seventeen. Last seen on Thursday nineteenth July. Body discovered at Green Park on Monday twenty-third July. Cause of death the same as for the first two victims, strangulation by ligature. Same restraint marks to one ankle. Unemployed — full-time mother."

"And a shoe belonging to Hannah was found close to Georgina's body," added Cassidy.

"Again, suggesting the two women were held captive at the same time," mused Jack. "Where is he keeping them? He needs somewhere big enough to keep two people out of sight."

Cooper continued. "Final victim, Zoe Turner, age thirty-nine. Last seen on Saturday twenty-first July. Body discovered yesterday morning. Dr Matthews has verbally confirmed likely cause of death is strangulation by ligature, but a formal

PM report is to come. He also confirmed a similar marking on one ankle — the same as the others. News just in states she worked at a company due to move into the Shard. No other information yet — next of kin are still being traced. Visual ID made by her boss — he reported her missing when she failed to turn up for work."

"And her shoe was found close to Hannah's body." DC Cassidy hesitated slightly before continuing. "The shoe found close to Zoe's body yesterday has been identified as belonging to Isabel Faraday — current whereabouts unknown."

Jack swallowed past the lump that settled in his throat at the mention of Isabel's name.

"Do you want to run through the psychological profile again, guv?" Cassidy reached for the manila folder where Dr Hunter's report had been filed.

Jack shook his head. "No. We've gone off on two separate wild goose chases on the back of that report — let's leave it where it is. We need to find a link between the victims — there *has* to be one. He's too clever for it to be that random. It's buried, but it has to be there." Rising from his chair, he headed towards the door. "I'm going back to The Briars to find out where Patricia Gordon's second job might've been. They could know something. Cooper, give Frank Gordon a ring — see if he knows anything. While I'm gone, get all the crime scene photos together, and go through them. *Again.* We're missing something."

CHAPTER FORTY-THREE

Time: 2.45 p.m.
Date: Thursday 26 July 2012
Location: The Briars Residential Care Home

"Sorry to bother you again, Mrs Masters." Jack nodded and smiled at the matron, easing himself into a chair in the same small office as before. He noticed the desk was still piled high with paperwork, much like it had been on his first visit. In this sense, it bore a striking resemblance to his own desk back at the station. Jack pushed the thought from his mind.

"Not at all, Inspector." Mrs Masters once again squashed her ample frame into her swivel chair. It creaked beneath her weight. "How can I help you?"

"It's really just some more background information on Patricia Gordon. During our investigations, it's come to our attention that she may have had another job? A second income?"

Mrs Masters nodded. "Yes, yes, that's quite correct. She did."

Jack raised his eyebrows. "You don't happen to know what that would be? We noted from her bank statements there was a regular deposit each week in cash, so we can't trace where it came from." He paused. "Another care home, maybe?"

Mrs Masters shook her head. "No, not a care home, Inspector. She worked in the evenings, Monday to Friday, as a cleaner."

"A cleaner?" Jack frowned. "Would you happen to know where that was?"

* * *

Time: 3 p.m.
Date: Thursday 26 July 2012
Location: Horseferry Road, London

The bollard had been repaired already, and all other evidence of the unfortunate collision had disappeared. Joseph Geraghty watched from the other side of the road, eyes trained on the entrance to the café. He could see no lights were on, and the "Closed" sign was displayed in the café window. He thought he might've seen movement once or twice inside, but didn't dare get any closer.

He knew he was playing with fire even showing his face — it wouldn't be long before someone recognised him. A few years in the sun had lightened his hair and darkened his skin — but everyone recognised Joseph Geraghty.

He fleetingly wondered how the motorbike rider was, but dismissed the thought as irrelevant. He didn't really care — compassion wasn't one of his traits. All he cared about was himself.

Himself and Isabel.

He wondered if she still had her mother's eyes.

One day he hoped to get close enough to find out.

* * *

Time: 3.45 p.m.
Date: Thursday 26 July 2012
Location: Metropolitan Police HQ, London

Jack handed DS Carmichael another tissue. "I guess saying sorry again doesn't really cut it."

345

Carmichael took the tissue, throwing the blood-tinged one in his hand into the waste bin by his side. He dabbed at his nose, the blood flow finally showing signs of abating. He shrugged and shook his head.

"You had your reasons, Jack. Forget it."

Jack gave a somewhat rueful smile. "Maybe. But I should never have hit you. I don't know what came over me. I don't do that."

"She's your friend," replied Carmichael, dabbing at his top lip where Jack's fist had split the skin on its upward trajectory towards his nose. "I get that. It's fine, honestly. I'll live."

"Not broken, then?" Jack nodded at Carmichael's nose. He received a shake of the head and a faint grin in response.

"No, badly bruised and swollen, I think, was the verdict. And I still have all my teeth." He raised his split lip, wincing in pain as the open wound oozed blood.

Jack grimaced and passed him another tissue. "And I shouldn't have said those things about your personal life." His eyes flickered towards DS Carmichael's bloodstained hand — the faint mark of a wedding ring band still visible. "You were right — it was none of my business."

Carmichael flexed his left hand and gave another shrug. "We're police officers, Jack. Since when did any of us retain the ability to maintain a stable relationship? Show me a happily married police officer and I'll let you have another go at breaking my nose."

"Fair point." Jack rose to his feet and headed towards the door. "When you've finished pampering yourself, we could do with you back upstairs. We've still got a killer to catch."

* * *

Time: 3.50 p.m.
Date: Thursday 26 July 2012
Location: A cellar in London

He'd seen the perfect Jess walking her dog on Wimbledon Common. A creature of habit, she walked the animal every

morning at 6.30 a.m. It was one of those little yappy things —
a terrier of some description. It made a lot of noise so he knew
he'd have to silence it pretty quickly when the time came.

And the time was coming soon.

Tonight.

He'd followed her home from her dog walk that morning and noted she lived in a very secluded ground-floor flat
not far from the Common. Access was easy — she never
seemed to lock her front door.

At least Carol wouldn't be alone anymore. Mother and
daughter reunited once more.

For a while, at least.

Carol needed to go — like the rest of them.

And then Jess.

It was just the way it had to be.

* * *

Time: 3.55 p.m.
Date: Thursday 26 July 2012
Location: Metropolitan Police HQ, London

As Jack returned to the incident room, the wall of heat hit
him square in the face. DC Cassidy was busy trying to make
the standing floor fans provide more than a weak wave of air
movement; trying but failing. The only window in the room
was open as wide as it could go, and the blinds were drawn
to shut out the direct sunlight that was beating down from
outside. Despite this, the heat of the day still managed to
seep into the room.

Jack ran a finger around the inside of his shirt collar and
grabbed a bottle of water from one of the desks. Although not
chilled, it was better than nothing. "We need to go through
the CCTV again," he announced. "There's got to be something we're missing."

Cassidy turned her attention away from the floor fans
and reached for the remote control. The whiteboard screen

juddered into life, but then froze. "Not again," she breathed, tapping the mouse against the table. "This thing's been playing up while you've been gone. I think it's the heat."

"Ex-husband confirmed the evening job," said DS Cooper, rolling up his sleeves and discarding his tie. "An art gallery."

Jack nodded. "The matron at the care home said the same thing. Gladwins Art Gallery on Buchanan Street. She's been working there in the evenings for quite some time."

Cassidy cursed under her breath and tried switching the screen off and on again; the usual troubleshooting command for anything IT-related. Why it worked, no one ever knew. However, when the whiteboard screen jolted back into life, it remained frozen. "God give me strength . . ."

Just then, the door opened and DS Carmichael strode in, still dabbing a bloodied tissue to one nostril. "It's all kicking off downstairs. The Wi-Fi's down, due to the heat." He glanced at the stuttering pixelated images on the whiteboard screen. "Looks like you know about that already, though."

Jack opened his mouth, about to welcome Carmichael back on the team, when a deafening bang penetrated the room. Cassidy almost flew out of her seat, dropping the remote control as if it were on fire. The whiteboard screen went black with a hiss and crackle. The overhead lights snapped off and the floor fans ground lazily to a halt.

"Power cut," announced Cooper, stepping over towards the door and popping his head out into the corridor. "Yep. Lights off everywhere."

Great, thought Jack. *Just great.*

"OK, Cooper. Let's bring DS Carmichael here up to speed." Jack nodded at the folder and paperwork still on one of the desks. "I had wanted to go through the CCTV again, but . . ." Jack waved his hands towards the non-existent power supply. "Looks like that'll have to wait."

DS Cooper seated himself back down and reached for the manila folder.

"Look, why don't we go back to basics?" Carmichael strode over to the far corner of the room. "Time for a bit

348

of old-school policing, eh Jack?" He looked back over his shoulder, while dragging out the abandoned pinboard from where it'd been propped up against the far wall. "Sometimes, the old ways are the best, don't you think?"

A smile steadily crept across Jack's face as he watched Carmichael pull the pinboard to the centre of the room. He tossed a box of drawing pins onto the desk. "Off you go then, Cooper."

* * *

Time: 4 p.m.
Date: Thursday 26 July 2012
Location: Metropolitan Police HQ, London

It wasn't long before DS Cooper had pinned up photographs of all four women onto the cork pinboard. He also added a timeline for each, from the last time they were seen to the discovery of their bodies. Brief post-mortem results and cause of death accompanied each photograph, plus pictures of the shoes found at each location.

Jack let Cooper run through the evidence once again for DS Carmichael's benefit, taking the opportunity to go over the facts one last time in his own head. Facts that bounced around inside his brain, but seemingly failed or refused to organise themselves into any logical sequence. At times like this, Jack often tried to get inside the mind of his suspect — delve into the inner workings of whatever depraved soul they were trying to apprehend. But this one — this one was different. Try as he might, Jack couldn't make sense of anything. It was like trying to complete a jigsaw puzzle without all the pieces, while blindfolded.

Something was missing.

"Cooper, pin up the CCTV images." Jack walked over to the pinboard and spun it around on its wheels, so a fresh board faced them. Fortunately, he had insisted on printing off much of the evidence as hard copies — still somewhat reluctant to rely solely on technology, generally ignoring the emails that clogged up his inbox advising everyone they needed to do their bit to save paper. Jack wasn't against saving the environment — he proudly owned several "bags for life" — but, sometimes, technology couldn't replace good old-fashioned paperwork. Unable to mask the smug smile that shadowed his lips, he watched as Cooper slid the photographs out of the file.

The grainy camera shots from each of the four locations were pinned to the corkboard. Ford Mondeo registration AV09 BVZ, DS Carmichael's pool car, appeared in each image, along with other random cars and vans.

Four pairs of eyes scoured the photographs.

It didn't take long for the obvious to stare them full in the face. With the images pinned side by side across the pinboard, it was impossible to miss.

"Shit," mouthed Jack, as the penny well and truly dropped. He could tell from the expressions of the other three pairs of eyes in the room that he wasn't alone.

"Shit," repeated Carmichael, stepping closer to the board. "How did we manage to miss this?"

"How to hide in plain sight," added Cooper, shaking his head. "It's genius."

In each of the images where DS Carmichael's Ford Mondeo was pictured, a single vehicle could also be spotted — sometimes in front, sometimes behind.

But there.

Always there.

The same vehicle.

In each location.

As clear as day.

A vehicle that would raise no suspicion.

A vehicle that would never register in anyone's memory as it went about its lawful business.

As soon as this vehicle was seen, it was instantly forgotten.

Invisible.

A perfect choice.

Jack joined DS Carmichael in front of the pinboard. The vehicle in question was a London Ambulance Service NHS Trust ambulance.

CHAPTER FORTY-FOUR

Time: 4 p.m.
Date: Thursday 26 July 2012
Location: Metropolitan Police HQ, London

"We need to find a sodding PC that's working." Jack scribbled the ambulance's registration number onto a scrap of paper. "Aren't we meant to have some kind of generator system up and running by now?" He could've sworn that during one of his many major incident training seminars he'd dozed through, there had been the promise of a backup generator if the worst should happen. Any widespread power outage, whether caused by accident, divine intervention or a terrorist attack, reassurances were abundant that the police's work would be able to continue.

But so far, he couldn't see, hear or feel anything kicking in.

Except panic and his own rapidly increasing heartbeat.

"On it, boss." DS Cooper leapt into action and headed in the direction of the door. "None of the internal phones are working, and I've got no mobile signal either. I'll head downstairs and see what's what." Before he could reach for the door handle, however, the door was flung open.

Jack's eyes widened at the sight of his brother rushing into the incident room, closely followed by a harried-looking police constable.

"Sorry, sir," said the constable, still trying to get in front of Mac and bar his entrance. "The power cut has played havoc with all the security doors downstairs. And he wouldn't wait."

"I need to know what's happening, Jack." Mac's voice was on the verge of breaking. "I'm going mad just waiting around for news." He shrugged off the clutches of the police constable who was still trying to guide him back into the corridor. "I need to know, Jack."

"OK, OK. Just calm down." Jack turned towards the pink-faced police constable, giving her a reassuring smile. "He's fine. Don't worry about it. Leave it with me. I'll escort him from the building when we're done." He flashed her another of his smiles, and saw the constable's features relax, relief flooding her cheeks that she was now free from the responsibility of the unwanted intruder. She wasted no time in backing out of the incident room and leaving them to it.

"I don't know what to do, Jack," continued Mac, pacing up and down by the window, his trembling hands raking through his unruly hair. "I can't . . ."

"Look, Stu. Stop, you're making me dizzy." Jack grabbed hold of his brother's arm and guided him towards a chair. "Just sit down. But now really isn't a good time. You can't be here."

"Where else am I meant to go, Jack? I just want to help."

Jack placed what he hoped was a comforting hand on Mac's shoulder. "I know. But we're a bit busy here right now." Jack flashed a worried look at the pinboard, nodding towards the CCTV images that were still displayed. "We've got to try and track down an ambulance when all our computer systems are down. You need to let us get on with it."

Mac whipped his head up, his eyes drawn to the pinboard. "Did you just say 'ambulance'?"

* * *

Time: 1.15 p.m.
Date: Tuesday 24 July 2012
Location: Acacia Avenue, Wimbledon

After receiving the handheld electronic device back from the customer, Mac retreated from the garden. The houses around here were stunning — all detached with acres of garden. He'd never be able to afford anything like this, not on a courier's wage. As he stepped back through the garden gate, he saw the up-and-over garage door was open. One side of the garage appeared to be a workshop area, with a wooden bench running along the left-hand side. Mac squinted through the sun, seeing what looked like a variety of hand tools hanging from the wall above the bench. Hammers, several saws, and what appeared to be a power drill with its various attachments.

The right-hand side of the garage, however, housed a vehicle. Mac let his eyes run over the unusual occupant of the building. Not that the vehicle itself was unusual — it was pretty standard — but it just wasn't the type of vehicle you normally expected to see in a suburban double garage. Its signature yellow and green colouring reflected the sun's rays, shining brightly as if recently washed and polished.

* * *

Time: 4.05 p.m.
Date: Thursday 26 July 2012
Location: Metropolitan Police HQ, London

"I need that address, Stu," barked Jack, making a grab for the same piece of paper that he'd scribbled the ambulance registration number on.

"I'm not sure I remember it exactly. I'd need to check back with work."

"Think, Stu. Just think. Anything you can remember about it — the road name, the postcode. Jesus, even just the area of London would be a start." Jack picked up one of the internal phones, grimacing when the silence confirmed the systems were still down. "Where's this sodding generator?"

"It was in Wimbledon. That's all I can remember. The road . . . maybe something avenue?" Mac broke off and shook his head. "But surely you don't think it's him?"

"Him?" Jack frowned at his brother. "What do you mean *him*?"

"Patrick."

"Patrick who?" A sinking feeling began to creep into Jack's stomach. "Who are you talking about?"

"Patrick," repeated Mac, pausing while the others caught up with him. "The guy who rents space in Isabel's art studio. It was his house where I saw the ambulance. In his garage. I was delivering a package to his address."

Jack stood stock-still, his eyes widening. It was several seconds before he managed to find his voice, seconds that seemed to drag on for hours. "*Isabel's* Patrick? Are you sure?"

"Absolutely, no question," nodded Mac. "I even mentioned to him that I recognised him. From the studio."

"Whoa, let's back up a minute." Carmichael had been leafing through his pocket notebook, frantically flicking the pages until he found the one he wanted. "Would this have been Acacia Avenue, by any chance? Corner house, flanked by huge leylandii trees. Just down the road from the White Hart pub?"

Mac nodded. "Sounds like the place. There was definitely a pub close by. Patrick Mansfield lives there. Big double garage."

Carmichael snapped his notebook shut and shook his head, his throbbing nose and bleeding lip pushed from his thoughts. "No, he doesn't. But Peter Holloway does."

* * *

Time: 9.15 a.m.
Date: Thursday 26 July 2012
Location: Acacia Avenue, Wimbledon

Jonathan Spearing bent down to retrieve the parcel that had been sitting on the porch between the geranium pots. "Parcel for you — delivered while you were out."

DS Carmichael obligingly stepped out of the way as Spearing handed the box to his neighbour.

"Thanks, Jon. They always deliver when I'm not at home. Thanks for taking it in."

"No problem. Anytime." Spearing watched as his neighbour turned to go back. "See, Sergeant. I *can* be a responsible neighbour. You plug your leaky ship and I'll be a good boy and only report on things I'm meant to. Deal?"

Carmichael grunted in response and followed Spearing's neighbour and his parcel back down the garden path, heading for his car.

Patrick Mansfield. Carmichael had taken a quick glance at the address label on the parcel as he followed the man down the path. Patrick Mansfield, it had said.

As he made his way over to his car, Carmichael caught the neighbour's eye. Only fleetingly, and just for a split second — but it had been enough.

Enough for Carmichael to know that Patrick Mansfield wasn't who he said he was. It was the eyes that'd given him away. He'd seen them before. Hollow eyes — just like his real name — devoid of any form of emotion.

Eyes that Carmichael would never forget.

* * *

Time: 4.05 p.m.
Date: Thursday 26 July 2012
Location: Metropolitan Police HQ, London

"I knew there was something wrong about it," continued DS Carmichael. "But I couldn't put my finger on it at the time. It was over in a matter of seconds. That reporter, Jonathan Spearing, handed him the parcel, and then he was gone. But not before I caught his eye. I'd seen him someplace before — I just couldn't remember where. When I saw the name Patrick Mansfield on the address label, it grated with me. I just didn't know why at the time." Carmichael paused, flashing Jack an urgent look. "It came to me on the drive back to the station — but when I got here we were kind of distracted." He touched his bloodied lip, wincing as he did so. "But that guy's not Patrick Mansfield. He's Peter Holloway."

"Peter Holloway?" Jack felt the air around him thicken, every breath of oxygen squeezed from it. His throat felt scratchy and in desperate need of hydration. He swiped at the bottle of water and gulped down the lukewarm fluid inside. "Talk to me. Who is he?"

Carmichael grabbed an A4 sheet of paper from the manila folder on the desk and rushed over to the pinboard. He stabbed two drawing pins into it before swiping up a marker pen.

"Peter Holloway. When I worked at Sussex Major Crime, his wife and daughter disappeared — the summer of 1998 it was. I was just a rookie PC, but even I could see he was the number one suspect. But he came out squeaky clean — played the devastated husband and father very well."

"You didn't believe him?" Jack moved closer to the pinboard.

"Not a chance. He did it. I was sure of it."

"Details. Now."

Carmichael wrote as fast as his shaking hands would allow. "Peter Holloway. On a Sunday in June 1998, he reported his wife Carol and daughter Jess missing. He said they'd failed to come home after a shopping trip."

"And they were never found?"

"Never." Carmichael shook his head. "At the time they were living out in the Arundel area of West Sussex. We took that place apart, the garden too. The man's a liar and he's evil. Pure evil."

* * *

Time: 5.15 p.m.
Date: Sunday 14 June 1998
Location: Arundel, West Sussex

Peter Holloway clicked the padlock into place and turned his back on the shed. Walking briskly back towards the house,

357

he glanced at his watch. He'd need to move them soon; they couldn't be found here.

But before that, he had things to do.

Entering the kitchen by the back door, he immediately strode over to the American-style fridge housed in the corner, next to the gleaming range cooker. It'd been Carol's choice, the fridge. He hated it. Too big. Too cumbersome. Too *American*.

But Carol got her way.

Like she always did.

Although not anymore.

Pinned to the fridge, in among the shopping lists and photographs, was the calendar Carol used to plan their lives. Supermarket deliveries, hair and doctors' appointments, coffee mornings, school parents' evenings, hockey club for Jess, riding lessons on a Saturday morning, Carol's shift patterns, Carol working late.

Yes, Carol working late.

He knew exactly what *that* had meant.

She could deny it all she wanted.

But he knew the truth.

He grimaced as he cast his eyes over the latest entries. He hated the way his life was mapped out for him. Every minute of every day was planned and accounted for. What time was he going to work? What time would he be home? Was he going to take the car for its MOT next week? Questions, questions, endless questions.

But not anymore.

Peter picked up the marker pen Carol used to annotate the calendar. In small, neat handwriting, mirroring Carol's, he added an event to Sunday 14 June.

"Mum and Jess — London shopping. Back late."

The marker pen squeaked on the cheap, glossy calendar paper and felt clumsy in his latex-gloved hands. He stretched his fingers, the tight-fitting material making his hands feel hot and sweaty. But he couldn't remove them.

Not yet.

He still had things to do.

A quick scan of the front room located Carol's handbag. Inside, he deposited her purse, glasses and house keys. He picked up both jackets from the coat stand by the front door, and bundled everything together into a black bin liner.

He glanced again at his watch. Quarter past five. He had a few hours until he would become worried about his wife and daughter's whereabouts; concerned that they'd not been in touch and hadn't yet returned home. Concern that he would dutifully pass onto the local police station — not 999; I mean, it's not an emergency is it, Officer? They're just out late, enjoying the day shopping. It's nothing to worry about, really, is it? It's just, well, it's getting late now, Officer, and they haven't come home.

Peter Holloway snapped the latex glove back on his hand.

Three hours.

He would ring in three hours.

That would be enough time.

Time enough to clean the car and empty the shed.

CHAPTER FORTY-FIVE

Time: 4.10 p.m.
Date: Thursday 26 July 2012
Location: Metropolitan Police HQ, London

Suddenly, the overhead lights flickered into life, the fluo-rescent bars humming and buzzing. The floor fans whirred and picked up speed, ruffling the papers pinned to the cork pinboard.

"Looks like the generator has kicked in, or the power is back on," mused Cooper. "What do we do first, boss?" He nodded at the annotations and information on the board that Carmichael had hastily added only moments ago.

Patrick Mansfield. Could it be him?

"Get me a search on the address in Wimbledon. I want to know who owns it." Jack paced up and down by the win-dow. "And then we'll need a backup team — two teams — one for Isabel's café in case he's there, one for the Wimbledon address . . ." Jack broke off mid-sentence, his eyes falling on the scattered crime scene photographs on the table in front of him.

And then it hit him.

It was there.

The link.

The link they'd been searching for all along.

Jack spread the photographs out, separating them into four sections.

"Patricia Gordon." Jack pointed at the batch of photographs of her neat and tidy one-bedroomed flat. "We now know she had an evening job — at the Gladwins Art Gallery. Who fancies betting a certain artist we know frequented that gallery?"

* * *

Time: 6 p.m.
Date: Friday 6 July 2012
Location: Gladwins Art Gallery, Buchanan Street, London

Patricia Gordon pushed open the door to Gladwins Art Gallery and smiled at Roger, the security guard, standing to attention by the front window.

"Evening, Roger," she breezed, heading straight for a door at the rear of the ground-floor gallery, which led to the back offices and store cupboards. "Still hot out there today."

"Certainly is, Mrs Gordon," replied Roger. "Not looking forward to the journey home tonight."

Patricia smiled over her shoulder as she disappeared through the door, emerging a few moments later with her mop and bucket, pulling a cleaning trolley behind her. She'd placed a plastic apron over her clothes and swapped her shoes for a comfy pair of trainers. She headed for the lifts, usually starting her cleaning routine on the upper floors of the three-storey gallery, cleaning the exhibit rooms on level three first.

The lift pinged and the doors opened. With a final smile in Roger's direction, Patricia pulled the cleaning trolley into the lift and hit the third-floor button. It only took a matter of seconds to reach the top floor, the doors opening once again onto level three. This was where the gallery exhibited its most prized and valuable paintings and sculptures. Most of the exhibitors were unknown local artists, but there was the occasional Damien Hirst or David Hockney to be found, which would draw in the crowds from time to time.

As she stepped out of the lift, Patricia noticed a slightly built man heading her way, a large canvas painting under his arm.

"Oh, hold the lift, would you, my dear," he called, breaking into a faster walk, the canvas banging against his leg. "This thing is very awkward to carry."

Patricia hurriedly turned back towards the lift doors and hit the button, but just as she did so the doors closed and the lift started its journey back down to the ground floor.

"Sorry." Patricia turned round, apologetically, and hit the button once again to recall the lift. "Just missed it."

"No problem, my dear." The man came to a halt by the lift doors, resting the canvas at his feet. "I'm in no real rush."

Patricia smiled, picking up the mop and bucket with one hand and starting to push the cleaning trolley with the other.

"Patrick. Patrick Mansfield." The man held out his hand, his watery green eyes twinkling. "I'm not sure we've met."

"Oh, er, Patricia. Patricia Gordon." Patricia placed the mop and bucket back down at her feet and politely took hold of his hand, noting it felt smooth and cool in her grip. "I'm just the cleaner."

"Never just a cleaner, my dear," cooed Patrick, continuing to smile at her as the lift doors pinged once again. "You're just as important as the artists on show here."

Patricia returned his smile and once again turned to leave.

"You remind me of someone," Patrick continued, ignoring the waiting lift and stepping in front of the mop and bucket. "I think it must be your eyes."

* * *

Time: 4.15 p.m.
Date: Thursday 26 July 2012
Location: Metropolitan Police HQ, London

"And Georgina Dale. It just came to me now — where I'd seen it before." Jack jabbed a finger at the series of photographs of Georgina's small bedsit in the halls of residence at St James's University, and at one photograph in particular, taken from her student desk. Among the open copy of Daniel Defoe's *Journal of the Plague Year*, and the half-finished essay, was a scrap of paper pinned to a Post-it notepad.

> *Evening Language Tuition — Italian, French, German, Portuguese, Russian, Japanese, Mandarin.*
> *All abilities — contact Patrick on 07700 900198.*

Jack's mind was instantly cast back to his first, and last, abortive attempt at hypnotherapy.

* * *

Time: 9.25 a.m.
Date: Saturday 21 July 2012
Location: Dr Evelyn Riches' office, St James's University

Jack emerged from the therapist's office, blinking rapidly as the full glare of the morning sunlight flooded in through the curtainless windows. Although Dr Riches had assured him that he was out of whatever trance-like state he'd slipped into, he still felt somewhat groggy, a little soft around the edges.

He wasn't convinced it was working, but he'd promised the chief superintendent he'd try. With the dreams picking up in their intensity over the last few months, he knew that something had to give. Work was draining him, and the sleepless nights were taking their toll.

"Same time in a fortnight," Dr Riches had said as her parting shot. "And remember to practice the meditation techniques in the meantime. Access those websites." He'd nodded his head, obediently, taking the leaflet on the "step-by-step guide to meditation" and forcing it into his back pocket along with the one on PTSD. "We'll get there, Jack," she added. "We will."

Jack remained unconvinced. He walked over to the chair where he'd left his suit jacket, folding it over his arm as he had no intention of wearing it on what promised to be another scorching hot day. The clock on the wall told him he needed to be at work.

Squeezing these fifty-minute sessions into an ever-decreasing window in his work day was going to be tricky enough — but with a live murder investigation underway it was likely to become untenable. Maybe he'd knock the sessions on the head for a bit — until things calmed down. He could always try the meditation in the meantime.

Jack felt a rueful smile cross his lips.

Jack MacIntosh — the Meditator.

Or not.

Jack knew the crumpled leaflet in his back pocket would most likely stay there.

Heading for the door, he glanced at the notice board adorning the wall as he passed — covered in motivational quotations.

Difficult roads lead to beautiful destinations.
Don't wait for opportunity. Create it.
Don't try to be perfect. Just try to be better than you were yesterday.
The pain you feel today is the strength you will feel tomorrow.

Other posters contained website addresses for mindfulness techniques and meditation, self-help groups and publications. Jack then noticed more posters that contained adverts with detachable strips of paper. One was calling for volunteers for a research study into the effect of playing computer games on the brain.

Are you aged 18–30? Regularly use computer games?
Take part in our research study and earn £50 per session.
Call Mark on 07700 900146

The next was calling for volunteers to assess the effectiveness of meditation techniques in giving up smoking.

Are you a smoker? Want to give up?
Take part in our research trial investigating meditation techniques.
Earn £25 per session.
Call Andrea on 07700 900957

Hmmm, thought Jack. Seems like there's more money to be made in computer games than giving up smoking. Figures. As he reached the door, one final advert caught his attention.

Evening Language Tuition — Italian, French, German
Portuguese, Russian, Japanese, Mandarin.
All abilities — contact Patrick on 07700 900198

* * *

Time: 4.20 p.m.
Date: Thursday 26 July 2012
Location: Metropolitan Police HQ, London

Patrick.

"I knew I'd seen it before." Jack stabbed a finger at the photograph from Georgina's student desk. "I'm betting that's our Patrick Mansfield. He was into languages, wasn't he?"

"Didn't her parents say she wanted to travel the world after leaving university?" Cassidy stood by Jack's shoulder. "Might explain an interest in languages. Are you thinking she contacted him — Patrick?"

"I think it's more than likely."

* * *

Time: 11.45 a.m.
Date: Thursday 12 July 2012
Location: St James's University halls of residence, London

Georgie dropped her biro onto the as-yet-unfinished essay on her desk and rubbed her eyes. She'd studied Daniel Defoe's *Journal of the Plague Year* for A-level English a couple of years ago — but it was like reading it for the first time again. She was struggling to concentrate, and the *thump thump thump* from the guy playing drum and bass in the room above wasn't helping either.

She got up and went to open the mini fridge next to her bed. Three cans of Red Bull and a half-eaten sausage roll. Sighing, Georgie considered ringing home — she was sure they'd be glad to see her. And she'd get fed. And get her washing done. And she'd be able to relax in a hot bath rather than make do with the lukewarm dribble from her en-suite shower room.

Tempting as it was, Georgie settled for a Red Bull and returned to her desk. She closed the Daniel Defoe book — she'd give it another go after a shot or two of caffeine. The summer classes she'd signed up for were, on the whole, interesting — and she didn't regret choosing to stay on in her halls of residence over the summer break. She'd be paying the rent on the room anyway — or at least her parents would be.

Taking another long gulp of the fruity, fizzy liquid, Georgie waited for the caffeine buzz to enter her bloodstream. She smiled at the way her life had turned around — when now the strongest substance she took was either caffeine or the occasional vodka and coke. She didn't even smoke anymore.

She glanced at her notepad and the Post-it note stuck in the corner. She'd placed it there as a reminder; she needed to give Patrick a call. He'd cancelled their lesson last week, due to some family crisis or other, so she needed to rearrange. They'd been working on some basic Mandarin, and she was keen to keep at it. She desperately wanted to travel when her studies were over — maybe even visit China. The thought thrilled her.

Reaching for her mobile phone, Georgie drained the last of her can of Red Bull and dialled the number. It was answered quickly.

"Georgie, my dear — how good to hear from you. I was only thinking about you a moment ago."

Georgie smiled into the receiver. "Hi, Patrick. Wondered if I could rearrange my lesson with you? Are you free over the weekend?"

Patrick confirmed that he was, indeed, free at the weekend — but as he had a few hours spare later on today, would that be acceptable? Georgie readily agreed; anything to get out of her stuffy room and have a change of scenery. Her essay could wait another day.

After arranging to meet later on that afternoon, Georgie ended the call and deleted the call history.

Patrick was quite insistent on that.

And cash payments.

Something to do with how he wasn't declaring his language tuition earnings to the tax man — so everything had to be done under the radar. Cloak and dagger. Secretive. No paper trail.

Georgie smiled.

She liked that about Patrick.

It felt exciting.

It felt dangerous.

CHAPTER FORTY-SIX

Time: 4.30 p.m.
Date: Thursday 26 July 2012
Location: Metropolitan Police HQ, London

"Patricia Gordon. Now Georgina Dale. What background do we have on our third victim? How could she have crossed paths with Patrick Mansfield?" Jack focused his gaze on the only photograph they had of Hannah Fuller. Said to be a fairly recent picture, it showed a very slim, waif-like young girl, with her blonde hair scraped back into a high ponytail. "Has anything come in yet from the family liaison officer?"

"Still a bit sketchy." Cassidy reached for the remote control. "Some more information was uploaded earlier today, but with the power cut no one's really had a chance to view it." The whiteboard flickered into life. "We already know she was estranged from her family — ran away from home at fourteen. They don't really know that much about her recent life — and to be honest, they don't appear to be that interested. The social worker was more helpful."

Cassidy used the mouse to navigate her way around the screen, pulling up a series of internal reports. "After leaving home, she lived on the streets or sofa-surfed with friends.

Minor drugs offences. Some shoplifting. Gave birth to a daughter in 2011 — when she was sixteen." Cassidy clicked on some images, showing Hannah together with her new-born baby. "Placed in a mother and baby unit soon after birth. The baby, Hope, has been the subject of several interim care orders. Hannah had been given one last chance to sort herself out, clean up her act, or her daughter was going to be removed from her care permanently." Cassidy paused while bringing up a series of separate documents onto the screen. "Hannah was diagnosed with a personality disorder before she ran away — her GP records show several overdoses and self-harm attempts. Her current address is still given as the mother and baby unit, where she attended weekly sessions with her social worker, Felicity Walker."

It was all information Jack had heard before — but then he spied something written at the very bottom of the white-board screen. "What's that? The addendum at the bottom?"

Cassidy enlarged the screen and read out the entry from the bottom. "Attends Art Therapy at the local community centre, one evening a week."

Art therapy.

* * *

Time: 8 p.m.
Date: Wednesday 18 July 2012
Location: Walton Road Community Centre, Camden, London

Hannah loaded the paintbrush heavily with thick, black paint and scored several wide, angry lines across the paper. Paint flicked onto her T-shirt and across her cheeks. She brandished the brush as if it were a sword and she were fighting for her life.

In a way, it felt like she was.

With her other hand she picked up a smaller brush, loaded it with a shimmering, metallic gold, and began stabbing and jabbing the paper in ferocious strokes. In among the smears of paint across her cheeks, angry tears trickled hotly from her reddened eyes, and dripped from the bottom of her chin. She rubbed them away with her arm, causing dark smudges of black and gold to smear across her face.

She loaded both brushes again. More paint. More smudges. More tears.

Her anger was at boiling point, ever since her five o'clock appointment with Felicity. Hannah was trying, really trying, but whatever she did it never seemed to be quite good enough. She wasn't keeping her room tidy enough; she wasn't washing Hope's clothes often enough; she wasn't feeding Hope the right food; she was smoking too much around Hope; she was drinking too much. Everything was just *too much*.

Hannah attacked the easel with the black paintbrush once again. Everyone expected so much of her, but offered her so little in the way of help. Mum and Dad were nowhere to be seen; not interested in helping to raise their only grandchild. Hannah knew she was struggling, but was determined not to give up. They could threaten to take Hope away as much as they liked — but she would never give up.

"Now, now Hannah." Patrick Mansfield appeared at her side and placed a calming hand on her shoulder. "Carry on like that and you'll go right through that paper."

Hannah shrugged Patrick's hand from her shoulder and resumed her stabbing strokes, more black and gold paint flicking towards her.

"I'm not done yet," she replied, fiercely, her eyes squinting towards her easel. "You can't stop me."

"No, no I can't," answered Patrick, his voice low and soothing. "And neither would I want to." He edged away from Hannah's easel and opened a nearby cupboard. "Here — you might be needing these."

Hannah watched as Patrick deposited two fresh pots of paint on the table next to her — one black, one gold. Plus, two extra paintbrushes. He nodded at her to continue, closing the cupboard door as he did so. Turning to leave her to it, he leaned in close to her ear and whispered.

"You remind me of my daughter."

Without another word, he merely winked and turned away.

* * *

Time: 4.50 p.m.
Date: Thursday 26 July 2012
Location: Metropolitan Police HQ, London

"Art therapy," confirmed Cassidy, putting down the phone. "Social Services have confirmed the sessions were run by local artist Patrick Mansfield."

"Do they not do any background checks for these kinds of things?" Jack's eyes were drawn back to the pinboard. Hannah Fuller's seventeen-year-old face stared back out at him.

"If they did, unless he's got a criminal record, I guess nothing would've flagged up," commented Cooper. "He wasn't using his real name."

Jack eyed his watch. Time was ticking away. "How long will those cars be, Cooper?" He walked over to the window and parted the blinds, the sun streaming in and momentarily blinding him. Despite the window being open, the air remained hot and still. He stepped back and stood in front of one of the floor fans.

"As soon as, boss," replied Cooper. "They'll let us know."

Jack eyed his brother, who was still slumped on one of the chairs close to the pinboard. "You shouldn't be here, Stu. None of this is for your ears."

Mac merely shrugged and avoided Jack's gaze.

Without the energy to argue, Jack turned his attention back to the evidence. "While we wait — what have we got on yesterday's victim? Zoe Turner." Walking back over to the pinboard, he tapped the crime scene photograph of Zoe

Turner's body lying in the grass in Battersea Park. "What do we know about her?"

Cassidy turned back to the whiteboard screen. "Dr Matthews emailed through a preliminary post-mortem report just an hour or so ago. Same cause of death — strangulation by ligature. Same abrasions to one ankle, consistent with being restrained. Approximate time of death, between ten o'clock Tuesday night and the early hours of yesterday."

"Anything else?" Jack resumed his seat at one of the desks, squinting at the whiteboard and Dr Matthews' draft report. "I guess it's too early for reports on her last known movements. Have next of kin been contacted yet?"

"Next of kin are being traced," replied Cassidy. "She was from Barnstaple originally, so we're liaising with the force in North Devon on tracing her family. She was reported missing by her boss when she failed to turn up to work yesterday morning, and he was worried due to the press coverage about the previous murders. She was single. Lived alone. A well-respected advertising executive, based in offices on London Bridge — due to relocate to the new Shard as soon as practical."

"The Shard?" Mac stirred in his seat, a frown crossing his forehead. "She worked at the Shard?"

"Well, not yet," said Cassidy. "The company she worked for had agreed to lease offices on one of the floors. But they hadn't actually moved in yet, building work still being finished off." Clicking the mouse, she brought up Zoe Turner's employment details. "Crawford Advertising Agency. Due to move into the Shard towards the end of the year or early 2013 — currently working with designers to kit the place out."

"He was working on a new commission." Mac got to his feet and moved closer to the whiteboard. "Patrick. He mentioned some advertising agency wanted him to design paintings for their reception area — they were moving into some new building in the city."

* * *

372

Time: 12.35 p.m.
Date: Saturday 21 July 2012
Location: The Shard, London Bridge Street, London

Patrick watched as Zoe Turner quickly stepped across the road, shielding her eyes against the glaring sun. She reminded him so much of Carol. *His* Carol. The trim figure. The sleek black hair. The air of confidence that seemed to surround her.

He headed after her, timing it to perfection so that they met on the pavement.

"Ah, Ms Turner," breezed Patrick, a welcoming smile flashing across his face. "Fancy bumping into you here." He held out his hand in greeting.

Zoe Turner hesitated, her stride faltering while she tried to place the man standing in front of her. A slight frown crossed her features until recognition finally filtered through. "Mr Mansfield. Patrick," she replied, taking his hand in hers and giving it a momentary shake. "What brings you out this way?"

"Nothing in particular, Ms Turner," replied Patrick, gesturing for Zoe to step to the side as two workmen carrying a heavy metal barrier sought to get past them on the pavement. "It's all happening around here, isn't it?" He nodded towards the Shard, where a flurry of activity was still evident. Workmen in bright-orange, fluorescent tabards were dragging barriers across the entrance; others were seated in cranes hauling heavy materials into place.

"Yes, indeed it is." Zoe pointed towards the skyscraper. "Our offices are to be on the seventh floor. I've just been allowed up to review the floor designs and office layout. I took your portfolio with me; I hope you don't mind. Our artistic director was there and he was most impressed with your work. He can't wait to see what you come up with for our reception area."

Patrick smiled. "Well, I'm going to make it my best work yet. I should have something for you to view in the next fortnight or so."

"That's super. We look forward to it." Zoe Turner turned to go, but found that Patrick had inched himself across her path.

"If you have a few minutes — we could grab a cold drink? They do a nice iced tea in that café over there." Patrick nodded back towards the vegan restaurant he'd vacated only minutes before, his quinoa noodles no doubt still warm in the bin.

Zoe hesitated for a moment and looked at her watch.

Patrick noticed her delicate wrists, her slender fingers.

So much like Carol's.

"Well, yes, I suppose I could do with something cool. An iced tea would be perfect." Zoe nodded her agreement and followed Patrick back across the road in the direction of the restaurant.

Patrick smiled to himself.

Carol had always liked iced tea.

* * *

Time: 5 p.m.
Date: Thursday 26 July 2012
Location: Metropolitan Police HQ, London

"What about Isabel?" Cassidy nodded at the pinboard where an additional photograph had been hastily tacked next to the four other victims. "Where did her path cross with this Patrick's?"

"Could've been anywhere," mused Jack. "They knew each other well — he rented space in her art studio and was there most days."

"Well, it had to be sometime soon after she left Anthony Saunders's flat," replied Cassidy. "Because she never made it home."

* * *

Time:11.35 p.m.
Date: Tuesday 24 July 2012
Location: Buckingham Street, Embankment, London

Isabel stepped onto the pavement outside the converted Ernest Baker Grain Merchants building and looked along the road to where she hoped she would see the taxi emerging in a moment or two. The evening air was balmy and she quietly hummed to herself as she waited.

It wasn't long before two headlights approached from the end of the road and headed in her direction.

Taking a step closer to the kerb so the Uber driver would be able to see her, she raised a hand in greeting. The headlights drew closer, momentarily blinding her as they swung across the road to pull up in front of her.

As she made to reach for the rear passenger door, the driver's door opened and a figure stepped out into the dark stillness of the night.

"Oh," exclaimed Isabel, stopping in her tracks. "I didn't expect to see you!"

Patrick Mansfield smiled and gestured along the road behind them. "There's an accident not far from here — the road is completely blocked and traffic's backing up all over. I thought I'd head down and rescue you. If you've ordered a taxi, there's no way they'll be getting through any time soon."

Isabel returned the smile. "That's extremely kind — but how did you know where I'd be?"

Patrick shrugged. "Lucky guess? Your friend, the motorbike delivery guy, he mentioned you had this date tonight . . . didn't take long to look up your lawyer friend in the phone book."

Isabel slowly nodded, and reached again for the passenger door. She was still feeling a little tipsy from the alcohol and needed to get her shoes off.

"Hey, come and sit next to me." Patrick took hold of Isabel's elbow and guided her towards the front. "You'll be much more comfortable up here."

Isabel was in no position to protest and soon found herself folded into the front passenger seat. She heard the heavy clunk of the door as Patrick got in, and then the click of the central locking. Feeling a little queasy as the car drew away from the kerb, Isabel felt a chill flutter through her veins.

"If my taxi can't get through, how come you did?"

* * *

Time: 5.05 p.m.
Date: Thursday 26 July 2012
Location: Metropolitan Police HQ, London

Jack looked up at the four other faces surrounding the table. "I don't think we've any doubt that he's our man — that he's our killer."

The internal phone rang, Cooper snatching it up on the second ring. He listened intently to the voice on the other end, briefly nodding his head. "Good. Fine. OK." He gave another nod. "I'll let him know." Replacing the receiver, Cooper reached for his jacket and turned towards Jack. "Two tactical teams will be in the rear car park in five minutes. Plus squad cars."

Jack nodded his thanks. "Good. You take one, Cooper — and head for Isabel's café. It's just possible he might be there. Take Amanda with you. I'll head to Wimbledon with Carmichael. Stu?" He looked towards his brother's haunted face. "You stay here. Don't go anywhere. And leave your phone on." After seeing Mac slowly nod his head, Jack turned to the rest of his team. "OK people. Let's go catch our killer."

CHAPTER FORTY-SEVEN

Time: 5.20 p.m.
Date: Thursday 26 July 2012
Location: Metropolitan Police HQ, London

Jack dived into the passenger seat and slammed the door behind him. "Go, go, go!" he yelled, using one hand to wrench his seat belt across his body and click it into place. In his other hand he pressed his mobile phone to his ear. "Cooper? Update me as soon as you get to the café. If this guy Patrick, or Holloway or whatever the hell he calls himself, is there — I want to know. And fast."

He snapped his phone shut and thrust it into his pocket. Steadying himself against the front dashboard, he felt the patrol car swerve around the exit of the rear car park and out onto the main road. It would take them approximately thirty minutes to reach Wimbledon. His stomach clenched as he tried not to think about what they might find when they got there. Part of him hoped Patrick was there; part of him didn't. If Cooper found him at the café, innocently working in the art studio, all this would be unnecessary.

But Isabel needed to be found. And Jack had to be the one to find her — no matter how traumatic that find might be. He picked up the police radio that had been sitting on the front dashboard, selecting the agreed radio frequency. "ETA thirty minutes," he informed the squad cars following in their wake. "Keep in formation." One further high-performance patrol car and an armoured police van were tailing him with blue lights flashing and sirens blaring. Worried road users hastily got out of their way, pulling over to the side of the heavily congested road; buses slowed down and waved them through. Taxis tended to carry on regardless.

The rapid response driver in control of Jack's vehicle concentrated on the road ahead, barely flinching as he sped through red lights and onto the opposite carriageway to reach their destination as quickly as possible. Jack could feel beads of sweat forming on his brow, but PC David Lyons was as cool as the proverbial cucumber. His eyes fixed, his face taut with concentration, both hands loosely on the wheel as he guided the car through a one-way system at sixty mph. Jack's own hands gripped his seat, the whites of his knuckles showing.

Jack's radio crackled into life. He risked taking a hand off the seat and grabbed it, knowing it would be DS Cooper with an update.

"Just arriving on scene, boss. Update to follow."

The radio went silent.

* * *

Time: 5.25 p.m.
Date: Thursday 26 July 2012
Location: A cellar in London

The huddled frame beneath the thin blanket was still, and had been for some time.

Despite the heatwave soaring outside, the thick walls of the cellar kept the air cool and dank. No heat to warm the limbs that rested beneath the blanket. No heat to bring colour to her wan cheeks.

She remained cold.
She remained still.
She remained motionless.
Not even her breath could be heard.

* * *

Time: 5.45 p.m.
Date: Thursday 26 July 2012
Location: Isabel's Café, Horseferry Road, London

Horseferry Road was curiously empty for the late afternoon rush hour. Maybe it was the heat keeping people indoors, or the excitement of tomorrow's Opening Ceremony causing workers to take time off work. The patrol car carrying DS Cooper drew up in a bus lane on the opposite side of the road, fifty metres away from the front entrance to Isabel's café. From his front passenger seat position, Cooper scoured the entrance using a pocket-sized set of binoculars. The door was closed.

From his previous visit to Isabel's, Cooper knew there was some kind of back entrance — patio doors leading out onto a small, walled courtyard garden.

"We'll take the front. Amanda — you and your guys take the back." Cooper's radio transmission was greeted by an affirmative confirmation. Looking in the rear-view mirror, he noticed the squad car behind discharging its occupants.

DC Cassidy, dressed in protective clothing, exited the front passenger seat while two armed officers emerged from the rear. An additional police van housing more armed officers came to a halt close to their rear bumper. The group quickly jogged across the two lanes of traffic and headed down a narrow alleyway between an organic wholefood shop and another shop selling retro second-hand clothes. Both shops were open for business, but trade was light — and nobody seemed to notice the procession of heavily armed police officers heading down the shaded alleyway to the rear of the buildings.

Each property along the passageway had a rear wall — some with access gates, others without. Cassidy took the lead, heading down the narrow alley until they came to a neat, well-maintained red-brick wall topped with ornamental spikes. There was no means of access to the walled garden beyond, but Cassidy knew this was the one they were looking for. She stopped and nodded at the wall in front of her.

The two armed officers at her rear scaled the wall as if it were a mere foot-high inconvenience, avoiding the lethal-looking spikes, and silently dropped themselves down into the courtyard below. Taking up positions either side of the rear patio doors, hidden in the shadows, they held their weapons steady, listening for further command.

Three more armed officers had followed them along the alleyway from the backup police van, and with the help of two conveniently located rubbish bins, they were now also training their loaded weapons on the rear entrance to Isabel's café.

Receiving a nod from each of the armed officers positioned on the wall in front of her, Cassidy brought her police radio to her lips. "In position — rear entrance secure."

* * *

Time: 5.45 p.m.
Date: Thursday 26 July 2012
Location: Wimbledon, London

Jack's stomach clenched tightly as he looked out of the passenger window, watching the nameless streets with their nameless occupants flash by — the blue lights and sirens affording them an uninterrupted run towards Wimbledon. The tightly packed streets of central London, with their terraced houses, one-room bedsits and two-up-two-down maisonettes, had now given way to much wider streets — mature leafy trees lining the pavements. The properties facing these streets were now spacious semis, or roomy detached houses sporting front and back gardens. Private driveways housed gleaming Range Rovers and shiny Mercedes. The street lighting looked as though it actually worked, dustbins remained hidden in back gardens until bin day, and there wasn't a mini-cab firm or kebab shop in sight. Jack had a distinct feeling that they weren't in Kansas anymore.

Welcome to suburbia, he thought, as they took a left and headed down yet another tree-lined avenue. The patrol car slowed down outside the White Hart public house — a well-maintained pub that sported a generous car park to the rear, wooden picnic-style tables outside the front entrance complete with umbrellas, and ceramic plant pots filled with sweet-smelling summer blooms either side of the arched wooden front door.

Jack's patrol car swept into the virtually deserted car park, pulling up next to a brand-new BMW. The following patrol car and police van did the same. Almost before the car engine had died, Jack pulled himself out of the passenger seat and quickly scanned the car park and beyond. He noticed the walls of the pub were graffiti-free, no broken bottles littered the ground, and no piles of dried-up vomit decorated the front steps. It was as far removed from the city as Jack could imagine.

There was only one couple sitting outside on one of the wooden picnic tables, nursing cold glasses of cider, plates of recently consumed late lunchtime salads and sandwiches discarded to the side. The procession of police vehicles, and then the heavily armed officers wearing bulky protective clothing that emerged from within them, afforded a raised eyebrow from the couple on the picnic table. However, Jack noticed that they continued to sip at their ciders, content to watch the scene play out before them.

As they passed by, Jack raised a hand and put a finger to his lips.

* * *

Time: 5.50 p.m.
Date: Thursday 26 July 2012
Location: Isabel's Café, Horseferry Road, London

Two pairs of wide, panic-stricken eyes stared at the barrel of the Glock 17 weapon, their hands rising instinctively in the air.

"H . . . he's not here," stammered Sacha, her voice quivering in harmony with her hands. Not taking her eyes off the gun, she reached out to clutch Dominic to her side. "I . . . I've not seen him . . . not for a few days. Dom?"

Dominic shook his head, his own anxiety building. "N . . . no. Not since yesterday."

Both Sacha and Dominic had instinctively screamed when the patio door exploded in front of them; Sacha dropping the stack of freshly washed baking trays to the floor as she emerged from the kitchen, Dominic diving beneath the art studio table.

"H . . . have you found her?" Sacha's voice trembled, her grip tightening on Dominic's arm. "Isabel?"

DS Cooper shook his head, raising the police radio to his lips. "Stand down. I repeat stand down. Suspect absent from the premises." Turning back towards Sacha and Dominic, he tried a reassuring smile. He wasn't convinced it was working. "Sorry, not yet." He tried ushering them towards a sofa, but only Sacha obliged. "Take a seat. Apologies we had to shock you like that."

The two armed officers who'd initially burst through the patio doors now retreated into the back courtyard, stepping through the jagged glass, their weapons lowered.

"Why are you looking for Patrick?" asked Sacha, her voice trembling.

"He's just someone we need to speak to about Isabel."

Sacha's shaking hand whipped up to cover her mouth. "Oh my God, you don't think . . . ?" She choked back the question. "He can't be involved, surely? *Patrick*?"

"As I said, he's just someone we need to speak to." Cooper glanced back through to the art studio, and the smashed patio door. "We'll get someone over to repair the door."

Dominic was still hovering by the archway, anxiously stepping from one foot to the other. One-two-three, one-two-three — right then left. Sacha knew she needed to get him home. "But . . . Patrick?" She shook her head. "No, he can't be. There must be some mistake."

Cooper headed towards the front door. "At the moment, we just don't know. But we need to find him. Jack's heading over to his house in Wimbledon as we speak." Sacha went over to unlock the door, and Cooper spied Amanda waiting outside on the pavement. "Sorry, I need to get going. As I said, we'll come back and repair the damage."

Just as Cooper went to step outside, Dominic came out of his mother's shadow, notebook in hand.

* * *

Time: 5.50 p.m.
Date: Thursday 26 July 2012
Location: Acacia Avenue, Wimbledon

DS Carmichael recognised the imposing leylandii trees from his last visit. They'd been recently trimmed, but still afforded cover as he and Jack approached the house from the side. Two armed officers stealthily inched their way up the gravel path and around the side of the house towards the back garden. The windows into the house gave no hint of life within.

Jack, with Carmichael at his side, followed in the wake of the armed officers, their protective body armour hanging heavily from their shoulders, making them sweat profusely in the incessant heat. Every movement they made seemed to generate a deafening creak. The only other discernible sound was of birds chirping in the surrounding trees and the distant noise of a tinny radio.

The double garage next to the house looked to be locked — would they find an ambulance hidden inside? Time would tell, but for now they needed to find Patrick.

Two further armed officers brought up the rear, four more remaining at the front of Acacia Avenue, loaded weapons trained on the front door. The heavy military-style boots of the officers leading the procession crunched lightly on the gravel as they made their way towards the back gate. The gate was shut, but unlocked. Looking through the wooden slats, the first armed officer gave a curt nod towards Jack.

Their man was at home.

Kneeling on a padded garden mat, Patrick Mansfield was busy clipping back the straggling, sun-singed tentacles of his perennial geraniums, depositing the clippings into a nearby recycling bin. The garden was well-tended and neat, the lawn freshly mowed, the flowerbed edges trimmed. He'd spent some of the morning deadheading all the patio containers that adorned the paved area outside the kitchen door, and was now tending to the bushes that'd sprung up and grown over the summer despite the intense heat and lack of rain.

He hummed to himself as he worked. When he was finished, he would make a fresh pot of coffee and relax in a garden chair. Maybe start a new painting or sketch. The sun was beginning its descent towards the horizon, but its heat still beat down on the back of his neck. There would be a good few hours of sunlight left yet. He felt a trickle of sweat making its journey down his back, in between his shoulder blades. Maybe a cool shower first?

He sensed their presence before the announcement came. The sweat on the back of his neck was now accompanied by a prickle — the unmistakable sense of being watched.

"Armed police — put your hands in the air where I can see them."

CHAPTER FORTY-EIGHT

Time: 6 p.m.
Date: Thursday 26 July 2012
Location: Acacia Avenue, Wimbledon

"Nothing." DS Carmichael emerged from the back door of Patrick Mansfield's house. "No sign of anyone inside."

The initial crude search of the house had revealed nothing untoward. A standard three-bedroomed house. Kitchen. Lounge. Dining room. No secret doors. No secret passageways. No basement or cellar. Nowhere to keep the kidnapped women. And, more importantly, no Isabel.

The outbuildings hadn't shown up anything either. The double garage did, indeed, house a refurbished London Ambulance. A quick search revealed that the registration number AK01 RPG was legally registered to one Mr Patrick Mansfield.

Jack hadn't authorised a detailed search inside the ambulance or the garage, wanting to wait for the forensics team to arrive and do a thorough job without any allegations of contamination. The rest of the garage housed a workshop, with the usual tools and paraphernalia that went with it. A cursory look around had revealed there were no secret spaces underneath the concrete floor; no secret steps down to a cellar or basement. And nothing in the loft space above.

Just a regular three-bedroomed house with detached double garage.

Jack began to feel deflated. He'd been so certain, so sure they were finally onto the real thing; that finding Patrick would lead them to Isabel. But now the all-too-familiar feelings of doubt were creeping in once again. This could be the third wrong suspect they'd targeted in as many days, and Jack didn't fancy having to explain that fact to the chief superintendent — not after last time.

"He recognised me as soon as he saw me." Carmichael followed Jack back along the garden path and around the side of the house. "He realises I know who he *really* is."

"Holloway? You really think it's him?" Jack approached the front patrol car, nodding at the driver that he was free to leave and transport the prisoner back to the station. Patrick Mansfield sat handcuffed in the back seat.

"No doubt in my mind." Carmichael peered into the rear window. "I'd never forget that face. Not in a million years."

* * *

Time: 2.45 p.m.
Date: Thursday 18 June 1998
Location: Sussex Police

Peter Holloway nursed a cup of hot coffee, his hands curled around the sides, letting the heat spread through his fingers.

"Is there anything else we can get you, Mr Holloway?" Senior Investigating Officer DCI Michael Broadbent sat on the opposite side of the table.

"No, thank you. This is fine." Peter Holloway's voice was calm and steady. He managed a small smile.

"Well, I won't keep you long. I'm sure it's been a long enough day for you already."

Holloway nodded and took another sip of his coffee. It tasted bitter and sour at the same time, as if the milk was on the turn. He wished he'd asked for sugar now.

"You reported your wife and daughter missing on Sunday fourteenth June — can you just run through the events of that day one more time for me? Just for our records."

Holloway dutifully nodded, placing his cup of coffee back down on the battered interview table. "It was about seven or eight o'clock that I started to get worried. They'd been out shopping all day, but I thought they'd be back by seven at the latest."

DCI Broadbent nodded. "And then what?"

"Well, I waited a little longer — as you do. But they still didn't arrive home." Holloway paused, breathing in deeply to compose himself. "So I went out in the car and headed down to the station to see if I could meet them from the last train. I wish we'd invested in some mobile phones — but Carol never wanted one."

"And they never arrived?" DCI Broadbent watched as Holloway shook his head, sadly.

"No. I waited until the last train and then contacted the police."

"Were there any difficulties in your marriage, Mr Holloway?" DCI Broadbent looked directly into Peter Holloway's eyes. Eyes that were unemotional — as empty as his name suggested. "Any recent arguments?"

"Arguments?" Holloway frowned, and shook his head. "No, none. We were very happy."

Broadbent nodded and added a note on the piece of paper in front of him. He glanced sideways at the two-way mirror where he knew the hastily arranged investigation team were watching. There was more to the disappearance of Carol Holloway and her daughter than Peter Holloway was telling them. Of that they were sure.

"And what about your daughter, Eleanor? Was she happy at home? Any problems at school?"

"No, no problems at school," replied Holloway. "Eleanor — well, Jess we called her. She hated her first name, preferred us to use her middle name, Jessica. But she was the perfect student. And the perfect daughter." He raised a hand to his eyes and made to brush away a stray tear — a tear that Broadbent was sure was fake.

"So, the two of them disappearing like that, without taking any clothes or personal items with them, would be completely out of character?"

"Completely." Holloway leaned back in his chair, his coffee cup abandoned in front of him. He flicked his eyes to the side, noticing the two-way mirror. He'd known what it was the minute he'd sat down. He wasn't stupid. He watched enough detective dramas to know behind it would be a bank of officers watching his every move, listening to his every word. Watching his every reaction. Just waiting for him to slip up.

He smiled to himself.

Peter Holloway didn't slip up.

He knew that one of the officers behind the mirror would be the new PC he'd spoken to first of all — he'd already forgotten the man's name, but he'd never forget those beady, bird-like eyes, and that narrow, bird-like nose. He'd asked him many of the same questions DCI Broadbent was asking now — but he'd detected something else in the young officer's voice. Something in his tone.

That beady-eyed PC suspected him; Peter Holloway knew that.

He'd have to watch him.

That man could be trouble one day.

* * *

Time: 6 p.m.
Date: Thursday 26 July 2012
Location: Acacia Avenue, Wimbledon, London

"It has to be him. He owns an ambulance." Carmichael approached the second patrol car and headed for the rear passenger door, taking one last look at the cordoned-off double garage awaiting forensic examination.

"I'm not sure that's enough. There's no law against owning an ambulance." Jack made his way to the front passenger side door.

"But it appears in all the CCTV footage — at every scene."

"Well, so do you, if I remember rightly."

A sheepish look entered Carmichael's eyes. "Yeah, well, that's different. Holloway's a killer. I know he is."

"I agree. It's him. Now we need to prove it." Jack's mobile beeped, the text message confirming DS Cooper and DC Cassidy were about to leave the café. He dashed off a quick reply while jumping into the passenger seat.

They would follow Patrick Mansfield back to the station, but even having apprehended the man didn't quieten the fear Jack still felt inside.

If anything, it made it worse.

Where was Isabel?

If Mansfield was their man, why wasn't she here?

CHAPTER FORTY-NINE

Time: 6 p.m.
Date: Thursday 26 July 2012
Location: Isabel's Café, King's Road, London

"What is it, Dom?" Sacha stood at Dominic's side, a flash of concern on her face. "What's the matter?"

Dominic continued stepping from one foot to the other — one-two-three, one-two-three, left then right. And he continued to grip his notebook firmly in his hands. He'd been like that for ten minutes.

"Dominic?" DS Cooper glanced outside, where Amanda was still waiting, somewhat impatiently now, by the patrol car. "Is there something you need to tell me? Because I really need to get going."

Dominic took in a deep breath. "I . . . I just wondered if you knew about the other house?"

"The *other* house? What other house?"

Dominic held out his notebook, the page already open to show several dated and timed entries. "There." He nodded at the open page. "His mother's house."

Cooper took the notebook.

12.51 p.m. Tuesday 3 July.
Patrick telephoned plumber to repair a broken shower.
12 Homefield Avenue, Fulham.

Cooper's mouth turned dry. "And this address — this is his mother's house?"

Dominic nodded. "I think so." He resumed his rhythmic sidestepping. "Patrick told me his mum used to live in Fulham — before she died. Did you know, Fulham is the oldest professional football team in London?"

"Shit." Cooper handed Dominic back his notebook and pulled out his phone. "We're at the wrong bloody house."

* * *

Time: 6.15 p.m.
Date: Thursday 26 July 2012
Location: Metropolitan Police HQ, London

Chief Superintendent Dougie King slid into the back seat of the unmarked Bentley and sighed. The day had gone from bad to worse. News of the arrest, and then the subsequent release, of Anthony Saunders, had hit every headline across the capital and beyond. No longer an exclusive with the *Daily Courier* — every tabloid and broadsheet was giving front-page space to the spectacular debacle.

The press and public relations department was being inundated with calls from reporters up and down the country, forcing them to switch all their telephone lines to answerphone until the furore died down.

And then there was the incident with Jack and DS Carmichael.

And the subsequent assault.

All witnessed by Commander Forsyth.

What a mess.

A hastily arranged press conference earlier that afternoon, which the chief superintendent expressly forbade Jack or Carmichael from attending, had done little to dampen down the disquiet. It'd been short and sweet, the chief superintendent addressing the media personally. After a concisely prepared statement, he'd refused to answer questions, exiting as quickly as his size nines would allow.

Sighing once again, he looked out of the window at the early evening sky. It wasn't like Jack to be so off the boil like this. He knew he'd recently resumed some long over-due psychotherapy — maybe that was affecting his usually pinpoint judgment. But if Jack didn't pull himself together voluntarily, he suspected they may have to go down the route of force-approved psychological assessment once again. It wasn't a road he was looking forward to travelling on — and especially not with Jack.

Dougie King pushed the thought from his mind.

Tonight he had bigger things to worry about.

The air conditioning in the car was a grateful release from the heat of the day, heat that wasn't just down to the weather, and he started to relax back in his seat.

"Heavy traffic out there tonight, sir." His driver, Charles Crosier, glanced in the rear-view mirror as he pulled out onto the main road. He caught the chief superintendent's eye. "There's a big dinner and speech at the Mansion House."

"Great." Dougie King settled further back into the soft leather upholstery. "Just what we need." He glanced at his watch. He was meant to be meeting the Right Honourable Bernard Saunders in approximately thirty-five minutes. It was already going to be an awkward drinks and dinner engagement, but if the chief superintendent showed up late as well, it'd be like adding further insult to an already painfully inflicted injury. "I don't suppose there's a quicker route?"

Crosier shook his head. "Sorry, sir. It's gridlocked everywhere tonight. The Mayor of London's delivering his pre-Olympics speech — followed by drinks and dinner. Should be a grand occasion judging by the looks of the traffic. I bet there'll be dignitaries coming in from all over. And the road traffic units will be out soon setting up diversions and road closures in readiness for the Opening Ceremony tomorrow."

Chief Superintendent King again looked out of his side window at the nose-to-tail traffic barely inching along. "All this for the Mayor of London?" he muttered, shaking his head. "Honestly, who do they think he is? The Prime Minister?"

Crosier indicated left and peeled away from the worst of the traffic, although the road he pulled onto seemed almost as bad. "You wait, sir. When he *is* Prime Minister, you won't be able to get anywhere."

The chief superintendent snorted in response. "Boris Johnson as Prime Minister? Pigs might fly."

* * *

Time: 6.30 p.m.
Date: Thursday 26 July 2012
Location: 12 Homefield Road, Fulham, London

The broad oak cellar door was opened without force — a wrought-iron key already in the lock. Armed officers, guns ready, flooded the darkness with the bright light from their head torches, quickly securing the shadowed space. Once it was ascertained there were no threats lurking in the cobwebbed corners, they trained their weapons on the motionless mound beneath the threadbare blanket.

"Clear." The command everyone was waiting to hear echoed back up the cellar steps to where DS Cooper and DC Cassidy were waiting behind another bank of armed officers. Once the all-clear had been raised, the wall of officers parted, allowing the detectives to run towards the steps, descending as quickly as they could.

Cooper reached the entrance to the cellar first, and motioned for Cassidy to stay back. His eyes were instantly drawn to the bundle on the mattress in the corner. Cautiously he stepped forward, his police baton outstretched in front of him. Crouching down next to the lifeless form, he felt the presence of four Glock 17 pistols trained over his shoulder.

Without touching the mattress, Cooper nudged the thin blanket with his baton. As it peeled away, he instantly recognised Isabel's pale face. Her eyes were closed, thick masking tape covering most of her nose and mouth, her face a deathly white.

Breaths were held.

Hearts pounded.

Eyes searched for any signs of life.

And then they saw it.

Isabel's chest rising and falling.

She was alive.

* * *

Time: 6.45 p.m.
Date: Thursday 24 July 2012
Location: Metropolitan Police HQ, London

"Peter Holloway — you are under arrest for the murders of Patricia Gordon, Georgina Dale, Hannah Fuller and Zoe Turner. In addition, you are under arrest for the kidnapping and false imprisonment of Isabel Faraday. You have already been cautioned, but I will remind you again — you do not have to say anything, but it may harm your defence if you do not mention when questioned something that you later rely on in court. Anything you do say may be given in evidence. Do you understand this caution?"

Holloway stood mutely at the custody desk, handcuffed at the wrists, and merely nodded.

"Is there anything you wish to say at this stage?" The custody sergeant tapped the details into the computer in front of him.

Holloway shook his head.

"Your detention has been authorised and you will now be taken to a holding cell, where preparations will be made to

interview you. You have the right to consult with a solicitor
— if you do not have your own, one will be appointed for
you. Do you wish to consult with a solicitor, Mr Holloway?"

Another silent shake of the head.

"If that should change, please make your request known
to the interviewing officers and arrangements will be made."
The custody sergeant nodded at Jack and DS Carmichael.
"Cell three."

* * *

Time: 7.15 p.m.
Date: Thursday 26 July 2012
Location: 12 Homefield Road, Fulham, London

DS Cooper watched as Isabel was helped into a waiting ambulance. She'd roused not long after the paramedics had arrived,
asking for water for her parched throat. Although Cooper wasn't
a doctor, it appeared to him that she was largely unharmed —
if a little dehydrated. Due to her drowsiness, the paramedics
suspected some form of sedation and immediately hooked her
up to some IV fluids, and dextrose for her low blood sugar.

DC Cassidy stood on the pavement, watching the door
to the ambulance closing. "I can't believe we found her.
Without that tip-off from Dominic, I don't think we ever
would have." The thought made her stomach churn.

The whole house was now sealed off as a potential crime
scene, the forensic team on their way. Before leaving the
cellar, both Cooper and Cassidy wondered just how many
women had been incarcerated in the dank space — and
where they'd met their deaths. It made them shiver, even
when outside beneath the warmth of the evening sun.

Despite her protests, Isabel had eventually agreed to go
to hospital for tests, and once the ambulance disappeared
around the corner, Cooper brought out his phone, dashing
off a quick message to Jack.

"Isabel safe. On way to hospital."

CHAPTER FIFTY

Time: 8.45 p.m.
Date: Thursday 26 July 2012
Location: Metropolitan Police HQ, London

"A full confession." Jack walked into the incident room where Cooper and Cassidy were waiting. "He wants to see a solicitor, and make a full confession."

"That's a turn-up," replied Cooper. "How come he's caving in so quickly? He's only been here a couple of hours — must be some kind of record."

"He must know the evidence against him is pretty compelling." Carmichael followed Jack into the room and closed the door behind him. "He'd be a fool to try and deny any of it."

"Even so," continued Cooper. "That doesn't usually stop them."

Jack sat down by the open window. "Whatever his motivation, it can only be good news for us. The ambulance has been recovered from his Wimbledon home — and forensics have already lifted various samples from inside. The Fulham address is currently cordoned off for a detailed forensics search, but even now reports are coming in about several mobile phones being found — they're being checked to see if they belong to any of our victims. A full paramedic's uniform was in one of the upstairs wardrobes. We'll know more tomorrow."

"Has he given any reason why yet?" Cassidy turned to the pinboard which was still in place — all four women's pictures still staring out at them. "Why he did what he did?"

"I guess his confession statement will tell us." Jack turned off the floor fan.

"You think he'll explain the relevance of the shoes?" Cooper nodded towards the photographs of the shoes that were also still pinned up on the board.

"Maybe. Maybe not." Jack shrugged. "My bet is they're a red herring. A way of playing with us, teasing us. Leaving us clues that weren't really clues. Dr Hunter was probably right — he wanted us to catch him, but he wanted to make us work for it. True psychopaths are like that — they get a kick out of being in control."

"You think there could be more?" Cooper asked the question that had been on everyone's lips since the discovery at the Fulham house. "More than the four we know about?"

Jack had to admit it was possible. "I hope not, but . . ." He left the question unanswered.

"Is it me or is the weather turning?" Cassidy got to her feet and went to close the open window. "It feels cooler somehow. I reckon there might be rain on the way." She peered out into the evening light.

Before anyone could reply, the door to the incident room opened and a PC popped his head in.

"DI MacIntosh? There's a message for you. From the forensics team at the Fulham house?"

Jack felt his stomach lurch. "What message?"

The PC shrugged. "Just that you need to call the crime scene manager. Something about bringing in machinery to lift the patio. Apparently, the dogs are going crazy — they think there's something buried under there."

CHAPTER FIFTY-ONE

Time: 4.30 p.m.
Date: Friday 27 July 2012
Location: The Duke of Wellington Public House

"Pint?" Carmichael glanced at Jack while raising a hand to attract the barman's attention.

Jack nodded. "Thanks. I'll have a lager." He scanned the rest of the pub, noticing a spare table in the far corner between the fireplace and a dartboard that was, thankfully, not in use. "I'll go and grab us a table."

Jack headed over to the spare table and waited until Carmichael brought over two pints of lager and a bag of salt and vinegar crisps.

"Cheers." Jack picked up his drink and took a sip. "Although it really should be me buying you a drink. You got us onto Mansfield, or whatever his real name is." He returned his glass to the table. "That was a good shout."

"It was that young lad from the café who put us onto the Fulham address, though. I'm not sure we'd have found it so quickly — or at all — if it wasn't for him."

"Dominic's a good lad." Jack paused and then nodded at DS Carmichael's face. "And I need to apologise for your lip. Again."

Carmichael smirked and took a sip of his lager, wincing as the drink hit the raw cut on his upper lip. "It's OK, boss. No real harm done." He opened the packet of crisps, offering Jack the packet. "And I probably did kind of ask for it."

Jack waved away the packet. "I'm not your boss in here. Call me Jack."

"I hear they think they've found human remains underneath Holloway's rear patio." Carmichael took a long sip from his lager.

Jack nodded. "I heard the same. At least two sets of remains. Too early to say for definite."

"There's no doubt in my mind. It's Carol and Jess. Has to be. Maybe even the mother, too."

"You're probably right. As soon as we get the IDs confirmed, we can charge him with those, too. In the light of his confession, he's been charged with all four murders, and the kidnapping. Jack took another mouthful of lager, wiping his top lip with the back of his hand. "And I've heard rumours that the cellar floor's about to be dug up. Apparently they've detected some unusual disturbance patterns underneath."

"Unusual disturbance patterns?"

Jack shrugged. "No idea, but do we really think he murdered his wife and daughter back in '98 and then waited fourteen years to do it again? I'm no psychologist, but . . ."

* * *

Time: 11.45 p.m.
Date: Sunday 14 June 1998
Location: 12 Homefield Road, Fulham, London

Peter Holloway pulled up outside number 12 and switched off the engine. Although it was late, he knew his mother would still be awake. She always was.

With a flicker of irritation, he exited the van and hurried up the short path to the front door. It was dark, which afforded him some privacy from nosy neighbours, but he didn't want to test his luck. He'd barely raised his hand to knock when the door was wrenched open.

A deep frown was etched into Doreen Holloway's brow. "What're you doing here at this time of night?"

"Hello, Mum." Holloway pushed past into the hallway. "Thought I'd pop by and see how you were."

Doreen followed her son through the house and into the kitchen at the rear. "You could've rung — I was about to go to bed."

Holloway saw the row of empty gin bottles standing side by side on the draining board. "Sure you were." He turned and plastered a wide smile onto his face. "I might stay here for a couple of days — you don't mind, do you?"

"Here?" Doreen frowned. "What's wrong with your own house?" She glanced back towards the front door. "Where are Carol and Jess? Are they coming, too?"

Holloway thought about the van parked outside — and the bodies rolled up in carpet in the back. "Not today. Maybe later."

"You haven't had another row with that poor girl, have you? You make her life a misery sometimes." Doreen turned away, muttering as she went. "Well, if you're staying here you can make yourself useful and finish laying that patio for me. I've been waiting for the builders to come back but I think they've gone out of business."

Holloway's eyes strayed to the kitchen window. The outside light illuminated an abandoned cement mixer and stack of patio slabs by its side.

"And first thing in the morning, you ring Carol and apologise for whatever it is you've done this time. You're just like your father — and a good-for-nothing waste of space he was. I don't know why I even bothered to have you sometimes."

Doreen shuffled across the kitchen, heading for the stairs. "I'm going to bed. Bring me up my slippers, won't you? Even you can manage that."

Holloway's blood began to simmer. As he followed his mother across the kitchen tiles, he noticed the door to the cellar was wide open and the light was on.

The decision was a simple one in the end. One firm shove to the back, between the shoulder blades, and Doreen Holloway tumbled headfirst into the depths below, her skull crunching against each concrete step on the way.

Holloway hovered over the top step. On impulse, he bent down to pick up his mother's slippers and hurled them into the cellar, watching them land next to her crumpled body. Slamming the cellar door, he headed back along the hallway.

Carol and Jess could come inside now.

He knew just where to put them.

* * *

Time: 4.45 p.m.
Date: Friday 27 July 2012
Location: The Duke of Wellington Public House

"More bodies, then?"

Jack gave a shrug. "Depends what they find beneath the cellar. If there's more remains, we'll go back through any unexplained disappearances from 1998 onwards and see what we find. Dr Hunter rang this morning — I filled her in on developments. She said it looked like a classic case of a power/control killer — and, with each new killing, Holloway was most likely trying to relive the original murders of his wife and daughter." Jack paused to take another sip of his drink. "He mentions in his confession that each victim reminded him in some way of Carol or Jess. It's a thing, apparently. Psychologically speaking."

Carmichael stuffed a handful of crisps into his mouth. "He must know they're about to dig up his cellar. If I was him, I'd be crapping myself right now."

"Maybe that's why he chose to make a confession early on. Dr Hunter mentioned that control killers like him sometimes fall apart when that control is suddenly taken away from them." Jack placed his empty glass back down on the table. "If he realises we're going to find more bodies under his cellar floor, maybe we'll get more confessions out of him."

"Carol Holloway was part of the forensics department at Sussex. I never met her but everyone was shocked by her sudden disappearance."

Jack cast his mind back to Dr Hunter's criminal profile. "At least that gives us the link to his knowledge of forensics and how he kept his crime scenes clean. You can't live with someone and not pick up on a few things."

Carmichael emptied the remains of the crisps into his mouth just as Jack got to his feet.

"Catch you later, Rob. Paperwork beckons — and I'd better see where we are on the other live cases we've got on the go. No rest for the wicked."

"See you, Jack." Carmichael raised a hand as Jack headed for the door, then turned his attention to the bar menu.

CHAPTER FIFTY-TWO

Time: 8.35 p.m.
Date: Friday 27 July 2012
Location: Metropolitan Police HQ, London

Jack pushed his cold cup of coffee to the side and yawned. He'd sent Cassidy and Cooper off home, via the pub, congratulating them on bringing the Holloway case to a conclusion. He'd briefly spoken to Stu; his brother confirmed that Isabel was recovering at home and he'd stick around to help as long as she needed.

Stifling another yawn, Jack tapped the keyboard and replayed the CCTV one more time. Once again, Joseph Geraghty darted out into Horseferry Road, Stu's motorbike colliding with the bollard a split-second later.

Joseph Geraghty.

Jack wanted to show Isabel the man's picture — find out if there was any reason why he seemed to be targeting her coffee shop; or, indeed, her.

But now wasn't the time.

Jack killed the images on the screen and switched off the monitor. Geraghty could wait. Someone who couldn't wait, however, was Dougie King. The summons to see the chief superintendent had come in over an hour ago — and Jack knew he couldn't put it off any longer. Grabbing his jacket and car keys, he left his office and headed for the stairs.

* * *

"Take a seat, Jack." Chief Superintendent Dougie King motioned towards the vacant seat opposite his desk, squeezing himself into his own leather swivel chair, sighing as he did so. "This won't take long. You're a difficult man to track down."

Jack did as he was told, watching as the chief superintendent reached for his desk drawer.

"Well earned, Jack, I think."

Jack didn't object as two glass tumblers, followed by a half-full bottle of single malt, landed in front of him.

Chief Superintendent King handed a good measure of Highland Park across the desk. "You came through for me, Jack. Well done. You took it to the wire, I might add — but you came through in the end."

Jack accepted the drink and took a sip. "It was a team effort, sir. They all did me proud."

"Even our friend, Carmichael?" A small smile teased the chief superintendent's lips as he swirled the contents of his glass tumbler before taking a large mouthful, savouring the warmth. "You two are best friends now, I take it?"

Jack hid his own smile behind his glass. "He proved his worth in the end, sir. I think we all underestimated him when he first arrived — maybe jumped to a few conclusions that we shouldn't have. I hold my hands up to being one of those."

"Indeed. And not just you, Jack." Chief Superintendent King refilled his glass, offering the bottle to Jack who placed a hand over the top of his. "I'll hold my own hands up and admit I wasn't sure about him myself."

"If we'd known the facts, sir . . ." Jack let the question hang in the air.

"Then we could've avoided a lot of misunderstandings and embarrassment. I know."

"Why was it such a secret?" Jack took another sip of the Highland Park, feeling the hot, fiery sensation slip comfortingly down his throat. "The team could've been trusted with the truth as to why he was really here — and who he really was. We've conducted undercover operations before."

"That was Commander Forsyth's decision." The chief superintendent barely hid the grimace behind his whisky. "Way above my head, Jack. The powers that be insisted on anonymity. Investigations into potential corruption — corruption by police officers, no less — is a hot topic, as you know. And as DS Carmichael was only investigating the *possibility* of police collusion in crimes against children, it seemed like a reasonable request in hindsight."

"Fair enough."

"So, what are your plans now?" Chief Superintendent King leaned forward, his elbows on his desk, resting his chin on steepled fingers.

"Plans?" Jack frowned at the conversation's subtle change of direction. "I'm not sure I have any plans, sir. The Hansen case is coming up in September — we'll be ready for that and make sure it's watertight." Jack lowered his gaze to his glass, seeing his reflection in the amber liquid. He knew now was the time to mention Joseph Geraghty — and the potential spanner he might throw into the works come the trial date. But for some reason only known to Jack, he decided to keep that little nugget of information to himself. Time would tell whether that decision would come back to bite him — and bite him hard.

Chief Superintendent King nodded, thoughtfully, fixing Jack with his dark brown eyes. "What would you say if I suggested a bit of time off?"

"Time off?"

"You need a break, Jack."

Jack wasn't surprised at the suggestion, and if he was being honest, he'd been expecting it for some time. "I know

405

I haven't been at my sharpest lately, sir." He drained the last of the single malt in his glass and nodded at the further top-up offered by his senior officer. He gazed down into the amber liquid once more, again seeing his reflection mirrored back up at him.

A distorted reflection.

A reflection that wasn't him.

A reflection that wasn't Jack MacIntosh.

"I took my eye off the ball a few times in this investigation, sir." Jack took another mouthful of whisky, distorting the reflection further. "I ignored my instincts. Let the facts get twisted. As a result, we went down too many blind alleys. If I'd been thinking more clearly . . ."

"We all make mistakes, Jack." The chief superintendent shook his head and replaced the bottle of Highland Park in his desk drawer. "It wasn't an easy investigation by any means, and with the time constraints I put you under . . ."

"That's no excuse, sir." Jack drained his glass. "I made too many mistakes. Mistakes I don't normally make. I mean, *Saunders*? I can't explain that."

Chief Superintendent King held up a hand. "No need to explain, Jack. I've smoothed things over with his father. I'm not sure we'll be invited to the next Bar Council dinner any time soon, but it'll all be forgotten in time." He paused and caught Jack's eye. "You're a great DI, Jack. In fact, you're my best DI. I need you."

It was Jack's turn to shake his head. "It's still no excuse, sir. And it wasn't just Saunders. I virtually arrested a fellow officer, accusing him of murder, and then physically assaulted him. That's not me."

"No, no, maybe not," replied Chief Superintendent King, nodding.

"So . . . maybe your suggestion of some time off might be a good idea." Jack reached into his pocket and drew out Dr Evelyn Riches' business card. "You gave this to me some time ago." He held the card up. "I've had one session. I think I'd like to have more."

Chief Superintendent King smiled, his eyes softening as they lowered to read the business card in Jack's hand. "I thought you'd thrown that away a long time ago."

"I nearly did," admitted Jack, nodding at his own memory of throwing the card into the back of the kitchen drawer. "As I say, I've only had one session, but . . . she's different."

"Different can be good, Jack." Chief Superintendent King inclined his head toward the card. "She does come highly recommended."

"So, if I were to take a period of leave — maybe a few months — after the Hansen trial, of course?"

"That'll be fine, Jack," confirmed the chief superintendent, smiling warmly. "I'll square it with whoever it needs to be squared with."

Jack nodded and made to get up out of his chair. He knew he needed a break. He knew he needed help. The nightmares wouldn't disappear on their own, that was becoming acutely obvious. He was permanently exhausted, sleep being no cure because sleep never came. And now it was affecting his work. In his eyes, he'd failed. And he'd failed because his head wasn't in the right place.

He had to deal with it.

He had to deal with it now.

"Sir." Jack turned towards the door, already feeling as though a weight was beginning to shift from his shoulders. He had a way to go, he knew that, but it was a start. They always said acknowledging the problem was the first step.

"Thank you once again, Jack." Chief Superintendent King had also risen from his chair and joined Jack at the doorway. "Getting the arrest in time for the Opening Ceremony."

"Just."

"Just," conceded the chief superintendent, his eyes twinkling. "As I said, you did cut it a little fine."

"The Opening Ceremony should be underway shortly."

"Indeed." Chief Superintendent King glanced at his watch. "James Bond and the Queen will be wowing the public any time now."

"Don't forget the corgis," smiled Jack, stepping out into the corridor.

"And the corgis," laughed the chief superintendent, raising a hand to Jack as he departed.

* * *

Time: 9.15 p.m.
Date: Friday 27 July 2012
Location: Metropolitan Police HQ, London

DS Carmichael was leaning against Jack's Mondeo as Jack crossed the car park towards him. As he approached, Carmichael stepped forwards and held out his hand.

"It's been good working with you, Jack. And the team. I hope the chief superintendent gave you the praise you deserve."

Jack took the proffered hand, sliding his car keys into Carmichael's open palm. "You're not getting away that easily, Carmichael. You're driving me home."

DS Carmichael frowned, taking the keys and watching as Jack headed towards the passenger side door.

"The chief superintendent was *very* thankful," explained Jack, indicating with his hand that he had had one or two drinks. "On an empty stomach. I think it's best that you drive."

* * *

Time: 9.45 p.m.
Date: Friday 27 July 2012
Location: Isabel's Café, Horseferry Road, London

"I'm not taking no for an answer." Mac virtually pushed Isabel up the stairs towards her flat, waving a tea towel in her wake. "You run yourself a hot bath. We'll finish up down here." Mac flashed a grateful look at Sacha and Dominic, who both disappeared towards the kitchen. "And then I'll order us a takeaway," he added.

408

"What would I do without you," came the reply, just as the door to the flat at the top of the stairs opened. "You really are the best."

Mac turned away, feeling his cheeks beginning to burn. He checked the rear patio doors were locked and then went through to the café. He could hear Sacha and Dominic finishing up in the kitchen — the dishwasher being loaded and turned on, the oven doors wiped down, ready for reopening the café in the morning. He straightened a few cushions, placed half-read paperbacks and magazines back onto the bookshelves, and tucked the bar stools neatly under the counter.

"Stop doubting yourself, and go and ask her."

Mac jumped at the sound of Sacha's voice, watching as she switched the kitchen lights off and swung her handbag up onto her shoulder.

"I don't know what you mean?"

"Stop right there, Stuart MacIntosh." Sacha strode out from behind the counter and wagged a finger in his direction. "You know damn well what I mean!" She suppressed the smile that was forming on her lips. "Just sit her down and ask her out. It's painful watching you two sometimes."

If Mac's cheeks had been tinged pink before, they were now in danger of flushing scarlet. "I . . . I . . . ." He shook his head and broke off. "She wouldn't be interested in someone like me. I'd be no good for her."

"Says who?" Sacha motioned for Dominic to follow her towards the door.

"We hardly know each other."

"Poppycock. Time means nothing when you're right for each other. She talks about you all the time — and you've been a godsend today, helping out when she really needed you. She notices things like that, does our Isabel."

"But my past . . ."

"Who cares about the past? Isabel certainly doesn't." Sacha opened the front door and turned round to face Mac, her voice softening. "Look, she likes you. I know she does.

And she can depend on you. You've shown that today."
Sacha reached forward, giving his arm a squeeze. "Be brave."

With that, she gave him a wink and both she and Dominic stepped out onto the pavement.

Mac locked the door behind them, the bell tinkling overhead.

Be brave, Mac.

Be brave.

But brave was very far away from how he felt.

* * *

Time: 10.35 p.m.
Date: Friday 27 July 2012
Location: Kettle's Yard Mews, London

The Opening Ceremony was indeed well underway. Jack had felt obliged to watch, but muted the sound after a while. There was only so much patriotism he could take today. With the images still flickering from the TV in the corner, he passed across another bottle of Budweiser and sank back onto the sofa.

"Cheers." Carmichael held his bottle up in the air before taking a sip.

Jack returned the gesture. "Here's to the Olympics."

The weather looked like it was finally on the turn, with a cooler, fresher breeze starting to blow across the capital from the north. Clouds had been bubbling up all day — dampening the exhibition by the Red Arrows once the Ceremony had been officially declared open. If he listened closely enough, Jack reckoned he would be able to hear a collective sigh of relief across the country as electric fans could finally be turned off, and air conditioning systems could grind to a grateful halt.

"So, what's next for the team?" Carmichael reached for a slice of the meat feast pizza that'd just been delivered. "I'm sure there must be plenty of other cases vying to fill the gap left by Peter Holloway, now he's finally off the streets."

Jack reached for some pizza himself. "We've still got masses of other cases to keep us busy. And there's still lots to do in building the case against Holloway — charging him is only the first step. We want a watertight case come the trial date."

"I can't see him wriggling out of this one. A signed confession within twenty-four hours of arrest? That's got to be some kind of record."

"I never count my chickens, Rob. Been in the job far too long for that. I've seen signed confessions thrown out of court one too many times. We need to make sure this one sticks fast."

And I don't need another Joseph Geraghty, mused Jack, stuffing his mouth with pizza. *One of those is enough for anybody.*

Carmichael murmured his agreement. "And once they formally identify the bodies found under the patio in Fulham as being Carol and Jess — which they *will* do, I'm sure of it — he'll have two more murder charges to answer to. And then whatever they find under the cellar."

* * *

Athletes were now parading through the Olympic Stadium — flags were being hoisted and waved, smiles directed towards the cameras. Jack watched as the Great Britain team entered the stadium to a huge roar — even with the sound turned down, Jack knew there would be a roar. He turned away from the screen. "So, is Carmichael your undercover name, or what?"

Carmichael reached for another slice of pizza. "It's my birth name. I went into care when I was five — my mother was an alcoholic and my father was serving life in prison for murder. I was sent from pillar to post for several years before I found my adoptive family."

"You came through the care system, too? I had no idea."

Carmichael shrugged and washed down a mouthful of pizza with the remains of his beer. "Why would you? You

411

know as well as I do, it's not something you shout about. But yes, in answer to your question, I use Carmichael for my undercover work. I guess I can't quite let go of the past."

"Not so undercover anymore, though." Jack passed over another bottle of Budweiser. "I think you've been rumbled."

Carmichael gave a grin behind his beer bottle. "Well, I won't tell if you won't. It can be our little secret."

"Any other little secrets I should know about?"

Carmichael smiled, ruefully. "Sorry about that. I know you all thought I was a right dick when I arrived — but that was how I was told to play it. I needed you not to like me — to not see me as part of your team. That way I could go off and do my own thing."

"So, it was all an act?"

Another grin broke out on Carmichael's face. "Well, maybe I can still be a dick on occasion — just ask my ex-wife. But yeah, it was an act."

"I'm glad to hear it." Jack glanced towards the TV, noting that the stadium was now nearly half full. He then turned his attention back to Carmichael. "I'll be taking a bit of time off now."

Carmichael raised his eyebrows. "Time off?"

Jack nodded. "It's a long story — but I've a few things I need to sort out. Something's not quite right, in here." He tapped a finger to the side of his temple. "A leave of absence is in order, and probably long overdue. I think if I didn't jump now of my own volition, I'd probably end up being pushed at some point."

"Well, when you're back on the job, give me a shout. I'll still be around for a while."

"Operation Evergreen?"

"The one and the same."

"The chief superintendent said it was likely to be the biggest investigation the Met have ever handled."

"And he's not wrong." Carmichael placed his beer bottle back down on the coffee table. "Operation Yewtree will blow your mind. We're tagging Operation Evergreen alongside it,

412

as there are some similarities that cross over between the two, but . . ." Carmichael paused and shook his head. "You won't believe some of the accusations that'll come out. And the evidence to go with it. It's shocking."

"He mentioned something to do with TV personalities?"

Carmichael nodded. "It's all under wraps at the moment. There's a TV documentary due to be shown in the next couple of months — that'll basically herald the start of Operation Yewtree. I can't say anything other than that. You need to watch it."

"I will."

"My investigation is more focused on local authority children's homes, foster homes, that kind of thing. But it ties in with Yewtree on some points."

"Children's homes?" Jack looked up from his pizza and caught Carmichael's gaze. "What kind of children's homes?"

Carmichael hesitated. "I didn't really want to do this, Jack, but — did your brother go to St Bartholomew's in Christchurch?"

Jack felt his insides turn to ice. "St Bartholomew's? Is that one of the homes you're looking into?"

Carmichael hesitated again, then gave a brief nod. "I won't lie, Jack. That home has come onto my radar."

"Are you saying . . . ?"

"I'm not saying anything. But I'll need to speak to your brother at some point." The statement hung silently in the air, suspended in the cool breeze that was wafting in through the open window.

Neither Jack nor Carmichael spoke for a while, both their gazes falling onto the muted television. More athletes were crowding into the stadium; some countries Jack had barely heard of, countries being represented by just one shot-putter or a swimmer, but feeling just as important as the likes of the USA and Great Britain. *And why shouldn't they*, thought Jack. *Why shouldn't they indeed.*

Interrupting the silence, Jack's mobile phone pinged with an incoming message. "Speak of the devil," he murmured, seeing his brother's name flash up on his screen. "My brother, Stuart," he explained to Carmichael's unspoken question. "I invited him round for a beer tonight — thought he could do with some company."

Jack opened the message and then began to chuckle.

"Good news?" enquired Carmichael. "Do we need to order more pizza?"

"Well, looks like he doesn't need any company from *me* tonight," replied Jack, typing out a swift reply. "Looks like he's got that covered, the dark horse."

Mac's message had been short and to the point.

Won't be over tonight. Staying over at Isabel's.

CHAPTER FIFTY-THREE

Time: 11.30 a.m.
Date: 30 November 2012
Location: Dr Evelyn Riches' office, St James's University, London

"Think back to your safe place, Jack." Dr Evelyn Riches spoke in her soft, measured tone. "Today we're going to step towards that door — and, if you feel like you want to, I'm going to ask you to open it."

Jack sank back into the familiar leather armchair, head down, with his chin resting lightly on his chest. His eyes were closed, his arms by his side.

"First of all, let's relax each and every muscle, each and every bone in your body. One at a time, from top to bottom." Dr Riches' voice floated through the air as if carried by an unseen force. "Starting from your head and neck, travelling down through your shoulders and arms, across your chest and abdomen. Down to your legs and feet. Feel those muscles relax, Jack. Feel how weightless you are."

Jack took in a deep breath.

He did feel weightless.

Truly weightless.

"Now, let's descend the stairs once again, Jack. One at a time."

Dr Evelyn Riches watched from her chair opposite, noting how the muscles in Jack's face and neck visibly seemed to smooth out and lose their tension. His shoulders sagged; his arms slumped on the armrests. This was now their eighth session and she'd been impressed with his progress. She admitted to being initially sceptical, having mentally made a wager with herself that DI Jack MacIntosh wouldn't show up for his second session, never mind the rest of the course. His problems were deep and complex — and very much ingrained. She didn't sense the necessary commitment or resolve at their initial session; didn't detect the underlying determination that would be required to face up to his fears, and then beat them.

But she'd been wrong.

For the first time in her professional life, she'd been *very* wrong.

Detective Inspector Jack MacIntosh had surprised her — booking a full ten-week intensive course, plus requesting additional resources for meditation and mindfulness.

"That's it, Jack," continued Dr Riches. "Take the first step now. Slowly does it. One step at a time."

Jack felt his body descending the staircase in his mind, floating weightlessly above each step. The air around him felt light and airy; he felt like he could breathe freely, each lungful he inhaled energised and refreshed him.

He took the first step.

"That's it, Jack. Ten steps to the bottom. Nice and slowly, a deep breath with each step you take towards your safe place."

Dr Riches knew that Jack's safe place was anything but. She knew the battle he'd had with the demons from his past; understood how the nightmares of his childhood now locked and imprisoned him in his adult world. And she also knew that the only way to beat these demons was to take Jack back to the place where the nightmares had started.

The door.

The door that led to the kitchen of his childhood home.

The door that led to the discovery of his mother's body.

"Another step down Jack. That's it. Feel your body growing lighter with each step you take."

Jack felt himself descending further. His footsteps felt so light, as if they were barely touching the floor. With every step he felt more relaxed, more toxins escaped from his muscles and more air filled his lungs.

He felt clean.

He felt pure.

He felt strong.

"Just a few more steps now, Jack. Your safe place is within reach." Dr Riches shifted slightly in her chair, pulling a notepad onto her knees. Jack had never reached further than this stage before. He had never managed to take that final step; never managed to step forwards towards the door; never managed to grip the handle and open the door into his past.

Dr Riches had attached a heart rate monitor to Jack before the session, and looking at the monitor beside her, his pulse was a steady sixty-five. Nice and relaxed. Nice and calm.

"You're almost at the bottom now, Jack." Dr Riches leaned forward to study Jack more closely, checking to see if he outwardly displayed any of the anxiety that she herself felt underneath. "Just one more step now, one more step and you're at the bottom." She held her breath and watched the heart rate monitor.

Sixty-five.

Sixty-four.

Sixty-three.

Jack's pulse rate was slowing.

"That's it, Jack. You've reached the bottom. Take a nice, deep breath and take a step forward towards the door."

They were now in uncharted territory.

"When you feel ready, Jack, reach out and touch the handle of the door."

Jack felt himself float towards the door. He felt as if his body no longer belonged to him; felt so light that movement was effortless. He felt his arm stretch out in front of him, gliding out into the blackness beyond him. He knew the door was in front of him, but he couldn't see it. Everything was black; there was no light, no illumination, no nothing.

One step forward and he was at the door; he could feel it; he could sense it.

Sixty-three.

Sixty-two.

Sixty-one.

The door.

The door to the past.

The door he needed to open one last time.

THE END

ACKNOWLEDEMENTS

There are a large number of people I need to thank for helping me get this far with the publication of *Seven Days* and all the books that come afterwards. Firstly, I must thank PS Rebecca McCarthy of Suffolk Police who has been on the end of my sometimes odd-sounding questions and queries on police procedure — if there are any remaining inaccuracies, then I can assure you that they are mine and mine alone! I must also thank Tracey Proctor for being my 'go-to' person for anything to do with forensics.

I also give huge thanks to all at Joffe Books for taking my books on, and giving me the opportunity to bring my stories to a much wider audience – and to Kate Lyall Grant in particular for helping shape *Seven Days* into the book it is today. I couldn't have got this far without any of you!

Then I have a whole host of people who have helped *Seven Days* become the book it is today. My heartfelt thanks go to Sarah Bezant, who has helped me to polish and shape it numerous times. I also have to thank my writer friends for giving me the encouragement and confidence to keep on writing — especially Jim Ody and Matt Rayner who have shown unwavering support from the beginning.

And of course my ever faithful advance readers — Agnieszka Andrzejak, Peter Woods and Ian White.

And finally it is you — the readers! Without you, none of these books would ever see the light of day. I thank each and every one of you.

Please keep in touch:

www.michellekiddauthor.com — sign up for my newsletter.

www.facebook.com/michellekiddauthor.

@AuthorKidd (Twitter)

@michellekiddauthor (Instagram)

Thank you for reading this book.

If you enjoyed it please leave feedback on Amazon or Goodreads, and if there is anything we missed or you have a question about, then please get in touch. We appreciate you choosing our book.

Founded in 2014 in Shoreditch, London, we at Joffe Books pride ourselves on our history of innovative publishing. We were thrilled to be shortlisted for Independent Publisher of the Year at the British Book Awards.

www.joffebooks.com

We're very grateful to eagle-eyed readers who take the time to contact us. Please send any errors you find to corrections@joffebooks.com. We'll get them fixed ASAP.